Philip Boast was born in 1952 — the year of the flood disaster in the Devon village of Lynmouth which appears in this novel. He lives in Devon with his wife Ros, young son Harry and daughter Zoe and is also the author of *London's Child* and *The Millionaire*.

Watersmeet

Philip Boast

HEADLINE

First published in 1990
by Random Century Group

First published in paperback in 1991
by HEADLINE BOOK PUBLISHING PLC

10 9 8 7 6 5 4 3 2

ISBN 0 7472 3446 9

Typeset by Medcalf Type Ltd, Bicester, Oxon
Printed and bound in Great Britain by
Collins, Glasgow

HEADLINE BOOK PUBLISHING PLC
Headline House
79 Great Titchfield Street
London W1P 7FN

For Rosalind

It was necessary for her to derive a sort of personal profit from things, she rejected as useless whatever did not minister to her heart's immediate fulfilment . . . in search of emotions, not of scenery.

Flaubert
Madame Bovary

PART ONE

Paradise

15 August 1939

'*Lauraaa* . . .'

Laura Benson glanced back, unbuttoning her blouse with flying fingers.

'Laura!' called Clara's whining voice again across the lawn.

Laura ducked back into the stable. She kicked off the nice black Victorian shoes under the manger, then wriggled out of her long black riding skirt and chucked it in the box with the neatsfoot oil. Outside everything was drowning in shadow already, the lawns, even the lower half of the tall deodar tree, but there was still no sign of life from the big house. Mother was resting with her headache, so Clara must have carried Laura's crippled father upstairs for his rest – a task, obviously, she had completed.

'Laura, are you in there?' Her half-sister's tall figure loped across the drive now.

Laura knotted the practical man's shirt around her midriff and pulled on the old beige jodhpurs, hissing when she caught her nail on a patch. She'd miss the glory of the sunset for sure, unless she rode like the wind.

'I knew I'd find you hiding here!' Clara exclaimed, peering in with squinting eyes. Laura ignored her, hopping into the stall while she struggled into her pride and joy, the riding boots Clara had smuggled back from White's of Boutport Street, in faraway Barum, that day she took tea with Rob's parents.

Blackbird was already saddled up – not the ladylike sidesaddle the old cripple insisted on but a proper man's saddle with stirrups Laura could stand up in.

'But you said you'd do my hair!' Clara leaned over the half door in her blowsy lilac housecoat. She sneezed, wafting her hand through the swirling motes of straw-dust, then looked at Laura accusingly. Laura ignored her; Clara was already in a terrible state, the nervous rash showing on her neck, her bosoms still heaving from her recent loyal exertions.

Laura swung lithely up into the saddle and backed Blackbird out of the stall, flicking the whip off the hook as she passed. 'Open the door, please, Clara.'

Clara hovered uncertainly. Her face was not dominated by her eyes, as Laura's was. She was formidably intelligent but lacked Laura's vivacious brilliance – solid and strong-boned, Clara was an attractive girl and quite pretty until she stood beside her young half-sister Laura. And then suddenly poor Clara was too tall, her hands a touch too big, her features too plain, and she was twelve years too old. All because of *her*.

'Clara! Open the door,' Laura ordered.

Clara actually hesitated. 'You're too late anyway.'

'Stop mothering me, don't be such an old woman!'

'You'll never make it in time.' Clara had lost already; she hadn't guessed that Laura was going to take the short cut.

'Laura,' she snivelled, 'why won't you stay with me just this one time?'

Laura was furious. She didn't say a word, or move her eyes.

'Promise me you'll do my hair later,' Clara begged.

She might cry. Things were that desperate between them.

Laura dragged open the door with her foot, but Clara hung clumsily on to the stirrup as far as the river. 'It's my day tomorrow. It's all mine. You promised.' Then suddenly she realized which way Laura must go, *the wrong way*, and her face changed. Her gentle blue eyes shone with a pale, jealous light.

Laura laughed and kicked on. Blackbird splashed into the shallow water, spraying across beside the stepping stones that stood out like giant Christmas puddings upstream from the stillness of Prideau's Pool, then took off straight up the grassy bank into the hanging woods on the far side.

'You can't go up there!' Clara was crying after her, 'Laura, Laura I care about you!'

Laura glanced back, then spurred on. Clara's puny voice dwindled away into the green density below her.

The wonderful peace of the forest engulfed Laura, where there was only the muffled thud of Blackbird's hooves scrambling in the moss as they climbed. Holding with her knees, she loosened her hair luxuriously, alone with herself at last.

When they came to the top path, Blackbird tried to go the way she knew.

Laura forced her on uphill. With a thrill she opened the spiked boundary gate that barred the steep, forbidden path, and climbed into the sunlight.

She stopped, and looked back.

Watersmeet.

The heat struck her left cheek, and when she took her hand from the rein and touched her long black hair, that silky weight was already hot too, as though the circles of her curls had trapped the heat within them.

She closed her eyes and rested her knuckles against her mouth.

She would never be sixteen years old again, ever.

Blackbird snorted, peacefully cropping the grasses of the forest floor, snuffling fastidiously around the prickly dashels with her soft muzzle. Laura leaned down impulsively and her hair cascaded forward as she laid her head against the hot, lovingly groomed neck.

She was hungry although she had eaten, thirsty although she had drunk a glass of water, still angry with her half-sister when she wanted to be happy for her. Laura sat back, confused by her feelings, staring down the valley.

Tomorrow Clara would be married.

Clara would be free.

Somewhere from a treetop a homescreech whistled a storm warning.

God, it's beautiful.

Watersmeet hung breathless in the brilliant glare. Heat trembled across the motionless treetops, a kit soared up on still wings above the slopes, then spilled and stooped from the blinding skyline into the shadows for invisible prey. Where Shelley and Wordsworth had written poetry a green shimmer of hanging woods tumbled sheer from the red rocks into a haze of wild flowers. Laura leaned out and pulled at a nittal branch to get the hazelnut, then gasped as it swung aside.

Beneath her the sudden drop was almost vertical, a hundred feet or more. She glimpsed white water, the pools and chutes of Hoaroak Water racing north between jagged black rocks to join the broader, ankle-deep East Lyn meandering from Paradise Woods on the right, where her parents' house was. The two streams met in front of Watersmeet Manor below, curving to make almost a separate island of the neat gardens hewn from the natural panorama.

What a wonderful place to spy from this was! From her eyrie she observed one of Sir George Pervane's estate workers rollering the civilized green lawns between the gnarled old Monterey pine and the imported rhododendron bushes. Faintly she heard someone, probably Silas the family's handyman, tapping pins around the new pane in the ornate Victorian orangery. Drumbledranes buzzed drowsily between the honey hives that would one day be hers, the whole wonderful house that would be Laura's one day: everyone knew that Francis would marry her, and all this would be her own.

Laura stared out. Mingling, the streams ran north, gliding like an aquamarine serpent along the curve of the valley, dwarfed by the sweeping slopes of the great cleave cut over millions of years.

Everywhere, Laura knew, secret paths wound hither and thither along the valley like veins and arteries beneath the ancient, concealing canopy of durmast oak. This cloak of furry, tangling branches, green with oak-moss lichen, hid the many ways even in winter – Arnold's Linhay path climbing to the great iron-age promontory fort, the steep Chiselcombe path between the scree-slopes, Winston's path, and the winding track from Paradise Woods up to Countisbury – all known only to locals, and below the treeline even Laura could not pick out their thousand-foot rise from the valley floor.

She clicked her tongue, rising smoothly to the trot as Blackbird carried her to the top of the bluff. The Hellebore Woods were named after the plant that once grew here, but there was no sign of the ruined house. All this land had been owned by the Barronet family for a thousand years before they fell from grace. Pride had been their downfall. Broken by their immemorial feud with the Pervane family – who had once been their servants – from having everything they lost everything. So Clara said, who knew such things.

Laura stopped. Had Clara ever been up here? Then she laughed in the silence – Clara would never have had the nerve.

The path split into two – straight on along the side of the Hoaroak Combe to the open moor, or turning between the crumbling stones of the old gate into the woods. The sandstone pillars stared out, like Ozymandias, over the abyss they had once ruled. The hidden stream hissed far below. On the other side of the cleave, only the track from Lynmouth made its mark along the vivid wall of trees, and on it a tiny motor car trailing a cloud of red dust.

Laura stared at the fallen gates. A strange, short plant swarming with ants made a cup of its leaves through the iron bars. She was sure it was a hellebore, the medicinal plant prized by medieval doctors. This family once thought nothing of building the massive kilns by the river just to burn lime and sweeten the acid soil so that their precious, deadly hellebore could thrive. The purgative killed as often as it cured, but sometimes the cures seemed miraculous.

The kilns were long derelict and the soil was

reverting, so she saw no more of the little plants. Laura turned away from the ruined gates, bored already, then clapped her heels decisively against the horse's flanks, and cantered Blackbird along the twisting Hoaroak path. The stream rose to meet her. From Hillsford Bridge she climbed the dusty lane towards Cheriton, taking to the open moor short of the church where Clara would be wed tomorrow. As Laura leaned forward, Blackbird raced due south across the rich purple heather, along the wide spine of the ridge, up into the emptiness with the wind in their faces until it seemed they were flying.

Finally she dismounted and stood in the chilly silence of the wild moorland. Suddenly a fuzzchat sang around her like a ventriloquist, she could not tell from where. Clara swore this heather hid a web of bronze-age farmsteads, from the days when the weather here had been as warm as ancient Greece. But nothing lasts for ever. The smooth Exmoor wind blew steadily from nowhere, pulling Laura's hair out behind her. She felt very small, and she could see for miles and miles.

Beyond the dense green cleft of Watersmeet curving down towards the jagged hogsback coastline, the Severn Sea stretched far out to the white cliffs of Wales. Clara said a million ships a year risked these turbulent waters, where the tides were the highest in the world and flowed on to the Devon cliffs faster than a man could run. 'But once it was a desert,' Clara had whispered. 'Instead of the sea a huge desert of red sand, a mighty continent, rose away to the north, and when it began to rain four hundred million years ago, the floods washed the sand down. That's where our red Devon rock comes from.'

Rocks. Clara was the romantic one, you'd think a woman in love would show more feelings.

'Clara,' Laura asked her when Rob was hooked at last, 'what is it *really* like to be in love?'

'It's marvellous, of course,' Clara said, looking away.

'Have you swooned?' Laura dared ask: 'Have you made *him* swoon?'

'Men don't,' Clara said. Rob was a good catch and she knew how lucky she was. She had almost given up hope.

'Do you scream for love?' Laura wanted passion.

Clara looked down. 'Oh, Laura, you're so young!'

Now Laura stared at the cloud blowing in on the wind from the sea as the breeze turned cold in her face. Life would be unbearable when Clara escaped from Watersmeet. The girls had grown apart, but they still loved to feud. Laura needed someone to provoke, and in a way Clara needed to be provoked, it gave her life. Though she was happy that Clara had fallen in love, Laura knew she would miss her terribly, and not just because the whole burden of looking after Laura's father, the task Clara had faithfully borne, would henceforth fall on Laura's shoulders alone.

The shadow of darkness swept over her, and the watery sunlight died. Moorland weather always changed quickly, but now it grew black so rapidly that Laura knew she would be caught in the approaching storm. The heather had lost its colour and the moor was dull and flat.

There would be no sunset on the last day before her seventeenth birthday after all.

As she swung into the saddle Laura tasted the cold

shock of the first drops of rain on her lips. Then it came pelting.

She knew what to do. Keeping the Hoaroak Combe on her left so that she could not get lost, she decided to canter Blackbird a little below the Cheriton ridgeline, out of the increasing wind. Soon she was soaked, her hair grew heavy, and she started to worry about what her mother would say. Over Hillsford Bridge she took the wrong way to save time, dropping gratefully into the shelter of the trees.

The treetops roared in the gale above, but Laura knew she was safe here down by the stream. Thunder rolled. She held Blackbird back, making herself calm for the sake of the animal. She had always been the practical one. Clara would have been terrified of lightning, or a tree falling on her head. Then Laura saw him.

The stream had fallen away from her left, and the ground was sloping where the path wound between the tree trunks. The leaves were dropping drenching showers all around her as the wind eddied in the glade ahead. Blackbird had stopped, frightened by the shape of the white shirt moving amongst the shadows.

Laura stared, thrilled.

He had his back to her.

Soaked through, the shirt clung to his broad shoulders and the curve of his spine. At his hips the material was tucked carelessly into the heavy rope holding his trousers. His hair was wet, and Laura thought he wore it much too long. She watched as he worked over the hornbeam tree stub he was using as a block.

He didn't see the girl on horseback behind him.

Laura made him jump out of his skin. 'Hallo!' she said.

The man whirled with a shout. His shirt was rolled up his arms, and he was covered to the elbows in blood.

Blackbird reared and Laura leaned forward to keep her balance. The man didn't move, but he didn't take his eyes off her.

Laura stared, fascinated. What compelled her was his extraordinary face, and the appalled light in his eyes. He was a lost man. It was not she who was in danger; it was he.

The horse galloped away down the path with Laura clinging on, still staring back over her shoulder.

So who was he?

Laura swung her head so that the water flew out of her hair, then tossed it back, excited, holding her lower lip in her teeth through her smile. At last she had news to put Clara in her place. Because she'd dared go *the wrong way*, she'd been rewarded with a real adventure. Clara, who had dreamed but never dared, would be *green*.

Still elated, Laura crossed into Paradise Woods, and closed the boundary gate behind her.

As Blackbird splashed home across the river, Laura heard the stable clock striking eight. Now she was for it, because Daddy was bound to be worried about her getting caught in the rain. Letting her go riding at all, he regarded as a loving indulgence on his part. The world was full of perils, and he wished he could make Laura safe from them all.

Watersmeet was beautiful, wrapped in a green intensity of nature, a treasure house of wild flowers, herbs and mosses. The rivers had their moods, sometimes splashing merrily, trout streams clear as glass, sometimes on heavy summer days barely trickling between the mossy boulders, sometimes swirling and roaring in flood with great foamy surges of energy. And the valley, too, constantly changed its shape, texture, and colour according to the season. Laura lived with her parents who loved her, and she loved them. This was happiness.

She kept off the drive, riding silently along the verge. If Daddy saw her in these dirty jodhpurs he'd be furious, he disapproved of women riding astride. He would punish her because he loved her and if he ever found out that she had gone *the wrong way* through Hellebore he'd probably explode, because he didn't want to fall out with Pervane.

Suddenly the lights came on downstairs in Paradise House, and Laura hoped her return was lost against the dark background of trees. With any luck she could sneak quietly into the stable. But the lower half of the stable door had been closed in spite.

'They'll catch you,' Clara said. 'They'll know.' She was sitting on the stool, wearing her dress now, so she had been back to the house. Perhaps she'd spoken to them. Her hair hung down in straight brown lanks, because of Laura.

'Not unless you told them.' Laura outdid her by opening the bolt with a skilful flick of her fingers and ducked inside without dismounting. The rain took on a deeper note to her ears, drumming on the roof. Blackbird's hooves thumped on the straw bedding of the stall.

Laura slipped down and wiped her hands on her jods like a tomboy, still staring at the reproachful shape almost lost in the shadows.

'I told them you were riding to Watersmeet Manor,' came Clara's voice. Nothing about Hellebore Woods then, good old Clara, loyal Clara. She turned with a rustle of clothes, her usually smooth features disturbed. 'What will you do without me?' she demanded earnestly.

Laura turned on the light and Clara flinched. She was crying, or had been. This was because of the wedding tomorrow. They were all exhausted. It was really going to happen: the first boy Clara walked out with would be her husband.

'You'll be fine!' Laura said, unbuckling the girth and heaving the saddle on to the rack, hanging up the harness ready for sponging. She was no dreamy ingénue, she did all the cleaning and mucking out herself. 'You'll be fine!' Laura repeated decisively, trying to be kind. Clara had obviously got the collywobbles about tomorrow.

Then, as always, Clara spoiled it. 'You didn't really go up there.' *The wrong way.* She wouldn't say the words. ' . . . Did you?'

Laura, hiding her irritation, poured a bucket of water into Blackbird's trough, then put it back under the spigot. She held her booted leg out over Clara's lap.

'What happened?' nagged Clara, then tugged obediently at the boot. Laura unknotted her soaking shirt and unpeeled the jodhpurs, which had tightened in the wet, from her long graceful legs.

'Well?' demanded Clara, looking coldly at Laura's face with its lovely radiant glow of perspiration, the rainwater squeezing from Laura's hair as she tied it back.

'Nothing,' Laura taunted her.

She pulled her ladylike blouse, white silk cravat and long black riding skirt from the box, dropped them in the bucket of rainwater and dunked them with her foot. Then she heaved them out and matter-of-factly buttoned on the freezing, sodden clothes over her bare goosepimply flesh, while Clara watched, both admiring and appalled. Laura would not be caught.

'They'll never know anything unless you tell them,' Laura said, turning off the light and walking into the rain. She heard the sound of an umbrella opening.

Clara ran up beside her. 'Tell me!' she insisted. 'I know you, little Laura. I know something happened,' she begged.

'Yes,' snapped Laura, 'I got wet!'

Their feet crunched on the gravel.

'I used to whisper the Gondwana stories to you,' Clara murmured. 'Once we were so close. Now we'll hardly see one another ever again and we won't be friends.'

Laura ignored Clara's olive branch. *Friends.* It was a bad word. She had lost touch with her friends when her father took her out of the Bristol nonconformist school. Everyone said they'd keep in touch. Even Penny Haberstam hadn't. Laura had been happier there than ever in her life. For a moment she closed her eyes, remembering the warmth of friends of her own age.

'Please,' whispered Clara.

Paradise House loomed over them.

'If only you knew!' Laura goaded her.

Clara stopped by the solarium whose long windows multiplied her into a dozen Claras, all equally accusing, and made their voices echo.

'Lauraaa . . . ' Clara hissed. But Laura shook her head, staring up at the old house, her home. Prideau's House: its name shortened to Paradise by time and the broad local dialect. Built as a fishing lodge in the 1780s by John Prideau, gentleman, speculator, and above all fisherman – the overfall from Prideau's Pool was a fly-fisherman's paradise when the salmon were running – and the deep waters of the pool still raced with the shadows of brown trout as cunning, no doubt, as he. When he was bilked of his money on the Exchange and had to sell up, this land was the last he let go, and it broke his heart. When he died they said he had loved his fishing more than his sons.

During the Napoleonic Wars when Lynmouth was a fashionable holiday resort with the gentry, Prideau's House had a succession of owners until the Bensons stuck. This side of the family had lived here for over a century now, Colonel Ernest Benson for more than half that time. Laura could see him now in his lighted study, head bent over his desk. Papers; weighty matters that only her father could understand.

The soft sandstone walls dug from the old quarry up the hill were by now weathered almost black – the house was not as solid as its foursquare appearance suggested – but the flaking surface was hidden beneath thick ivy, cut back by the girls from around the high windows every year. The glassy, jutting solarium that Sybil had always dreamed of was still new enough to look odd. Laura always felt that it was an ugly, kindly house; made of the stones that formed the hills around its lovely setting, the cleft cut by the sparkling goyle rushing down to join

16

the river. Facing south, the cleft held the sun in the middle of the day, so that even lemon trees grew outside, though they had to be protected with tarpaulins during hard winters.

Laura turned on the steps, still leading Clara on. 'After all, I set the tea for you,' Clara bargained, then sounded like her mother: 'I had a thousand other things to do.' She always made it so difficult for Laura to want to be nice to her. But now Laura could afford to take mercy on her half-sister from a position of strength, as the possessor of a revelation

'Yes, I'll do your hair after supper,' she promised, because Clara would beg her to whisper her secret, and they would be close. Clara ran up and kissed her, then laughed. 'Yuk, you're wet!' she trilled joyously. Laura lifted the hem of her sodden skirt and followed Clara inside.

Mother stopped dead when she saw them in the polished parquet hall. 'Oh, Laura, what are we to do with you.' Laura tried to melt past, but Sybil put out her hand. Clara paused too, but from Mother's averted face it seemed she had already ceased to exist, and she escaped upstairs.

'It rained!' Laura laughed, telling her mother the truth with a charming smile. She could wind her father around her little finger, but Mother was different.

Sybil looked at her wilful daughter fondly. 'We've been worried,' she sighed, knocking on the study door. 'He'll be so relieved you're safe. Laura, it's really not fair of you.' She knocked again; the wireless was on of course, the source of the mumbling voices and half-heard scraps of music which permeated the house.

17

Laura daydreamed about the stranger in the woods.

'Ernest, she's back,' Sybil called into the study. Over her shoulder Laura saw the row of photographs in their ebony-black frames. How poor Mother's looks had changed from those days: the young wife smiling out of the posed studio photographs was pretty, with something of the gentle, smooth features she had later passed on to Clara, but given point and force by the beestung alluring lips that must have made her deeply attractive to men. Looking so bright and carefree, with dreamy eyes, she seemed younger than Clara did now. Laura had cleaned them a thousand times, those black-bordered mourning photographs of almost another woman. If only they could come back to life, she would give her mother back her youth as a gift.

Even now Sybil stood like a woman still very aware of her body – tall, gracefully balanced, one knee forward, her breasts full and curved above the clamp of her bodice, showing her cleavage . . . it was all terribly old-fashioned, motionless and intensely passionate, withholding, almost religious in its heat and cold: the ecstasy of renunciation, the hands pressed demurely together like a nun, those bruised, loving eyes. *All I have given up for you*. How lucky Laura was.

Years of sacrifice had worn Sybil down, leaving her white face now cleft with strong, bitter lines from nose to pinched mouth. Her swollen eyelids were dark, almost sultry. Her gentle, selfless blue eyes were tired, her brown hair dragged back into a simple bun. She had given up her life to caring for the Colonel. She made Laura feel guilty about being free for an hour.

Laura's heart went out to Sybil, who had lost so much.

Sybil's first husband, Alex Summers, had died tragically, leaving her with Clara.

Of course her subsequent marriage to Colonel Ernest Benson was for many years childless, as she must have expected, having married a man who had suffered such dreadful injuries. Then when Clara was almost thirteen, Laura was born. Laura, who inherited her father's intensely dark blue eyes, slim athletic body, raven-black hair, and the heat he had long ago lost. A most handsome man before the field amputation of his legs and the trauma, he found himself doomed to his half life in a wheelchair, but he had passed on to his only daughter the gift of spirit and fire that had been crushed out of his own body.

He never had a son.

'Mummy, I love you,' Laura whispered.

Tomorrow Clara would be married: because of this betrayal, Sybil was losing Alex's daughter. She still wore the old youthful pale dress with faded blue bands below the knee, once azure. Characteristically, she kept Laura still standing, still dripping.

Laura heard her father's wheelchair. God knows how they would manage him without Clara.

'She's safe!' Sybil said.

Through the doorway swung a smiling, seated figure in the usual grey shooting jacket with neatly folded and pinned-back trouser legs, turning to face his daughter with a powerful flick of his wrists. Ernest was a strong man, sixty years old, silver-haired now. He lived on a constant see-saw of pain that he fought to conceal, so that its lines showed on Sybil's face more than his – except in his haunted eyes, the enlarged pupils like a dark vacuum. The electric rapidity of his features, his smiles, frowns, the quick interrogation of his cocked eyebrows, contrasted so oddly with the immobility of his body. He could be very difficult and demanding, but no one blamed him for that. His long career with the North Devon Regiment of the Royal Devon Yeomanry had ended before the first Christmas of the Great War, when a field gun simply broke free of its ramp and rolled back over his life like a juggernaut. Because of the soft mud he had retained his crushed left leg to just below the knee, but it was nerveless and flopped uselessly. The neatly severed stump of his right leg retained all its nerves, every single one.

Now he held his daughter's hand, smiling.

'Anyone can go out riding and get caught in the rain!' he reproved Sybil over his shoulder. He could not.

Laura said nothing. Had he seen her riding like a man? Suddenly she was quite certain that he had, and felt awful.

'Laura, little Laura, I have always loved you the best,' Ernest said softly. Laura's heart thrilled at his flattery. He must have said the same thing to Clara, who deserved it so much more, and she felt worse than ever. She must work to improve herself. She really had let him down – suppose she *had* fallen off her horse somewhere in the woods . . .

'I have not forgotten your birthday tomorrow,' Ernest promised, and made Laura ashamed of her jealousy. Tomorrow had been Clara's day for so long that she had felt ignored, but in fact the opposite was true: he would prove his love with a special birthday present. Laura's mind worked hungrily. Perhaps a dress, something fashionable shaped to the hips and bust, or even jewellery – something from Pervane's of Barum that she could wear at the wedding . . . She could not help an eager smile breaking out over her face, she would love it whatever it was, because it was from him.

'You should punish her,' Sybil dared say.

Ernest laughed. He was much more clever than that. 'Run along and change into your dry clothes, Laura.' He held her back by her hand. 'I shall give you your present at tea,' he whispered.

Laura ran up to her bedroom. The rainwater was rippling loudly along the gutter outside the open window and she could already hear the tanks overflowing, so there would be plenty of water for baths tomorrow. She undressed in front of the mirror, then stopped. Her wet blouse dropped from her hand. She smiled at her image, then frowned and raised one haughty eyebrow. She threw her hair forward, then with her forearm swept it back. She could hear the rain in the treetops, the river's sullen roar.

Laura stared at herself. *What had he seen?* Laughing, she slipped into the blue woollen dress, tied back her hair with her brightest blue ribbon, and skipped downstairs to the dining room. With a high ceiling, like all the rooms in the oldest part of the house, it was small but neat with tall cream-painted walls lit by one-hundred-cycle electric light, and heavy furniture in dark, angular wood on the polished parquet floor. Despite the backgammon

21

table in the corner the effect was severe, even puritan. The curtain had not been pulled and the window was a black mirror on the forest of Watersmeet beyond her mother's reflection. Her father was sitting in his wheelchair at the head of the table. 'Ah, here's my happy smiling girl,' he said, touching his napkin.

'I'm sorry I'm late, Father.' There was no sign of a gift on the long white tablecloth. Laura kissed his cheek and sat in her place opposite Clara.

It was their last meal together as the family they had been. Laura tried to look solemn. Clara sat staring at her plate, her fingers fiddling in her lap. Sybil bowed her head over her clenched hands and said a long grace. From under long lashes Laura eyed the biggest wedge of home-made cheese and planned her attack on the biscuits. Jewellery would fit in his jacket pocket, of course. Sybil went on and on asking the Lord to care for Clara and praying that she would be happy in the world away from Watersmeet. Clara's fingers twined as if she were mentally doing her hair, as if it were her funeral tomorrow rather than her wedding. She had failed her mother, she must be sorry. But Laura was amazed to see Clara staring straight ahead, defiant and unrepentant.

Ernest glanced at his daughters almost mockingly – *you and I, my girls*, he seemed to be saying, *we know what it's all about really, don't we – we know what keeps the world ticking*. Laura closed her eyes, listening to the fall of her mother's lovely, liquid voice. This was still home. But she had thought it would last for ever.

Ernest waited until Sybil was finished then cleared his throat. 'Thank you, dear.' He clicked his fingers for the cheese. 'I'm afraid I must tell you all that the storm clouds of war are gathering.' His wireless made him their oracle, enabling him to select what they heard of the outside world, confirming his position as head of the family. With this power he could preside tolerantly over Sybil, Clara and Laura's local conversation; women's talk. They almost never ventured further than Lynmouth, Watersmeet was all they knew. 'The tension is mounting in Poland.' He broke off, looking impatiently from his empty plate to Clara.

'I'm sure there's no need for it to worry us here,' said Sybil, catching Clara's eye with a smile. Clara dutifully reached out to offer the cheese platter to her father. Sybil had long ago been crushed into obedience and naturally been ruthless in passing on that creed to Clara.

But now Clara had fallen in love, at the age of twenty-nine, and instead of holding the platter politely under her father's nose like a waitress at the Watersmeet Falls Hotel, she just pushed it over the table and crossed her arms. Smoothly Sybil ignored this staff problem and helped him to potato salad.

Laura watched her father on tenterhooks. She moved her feet under the table but they encountered nothing. No dress box there. It must be jewellery, and in his pocket. That hearty tweed shooting jacket had big pockets. Perhaps something wonderful, a real gold bracelet with her name on it.

'Laura,' Ernest said, ignoring Clara, 'I want you to promise me something.' He pulled the wire carefully through a piece of cheese. Laura nearly died of suspense.

'Anything, Father,' she agreed at last.

He looked satisfied. 'Laura, you must promise me that you will always wear a proper hard riding hat in future. No, listen to me, you could fall off that horse and crack your head on a tree root – or an overhanging branch . . .'

'Blackbird would never throw me!' Laura protested, defending her only friend.

He passed the cheese platter to Sybil.

'You see, darling,' Sybil explained, 'we could never forgive ourselves if you were hurt.'

'Blackbird never would!' Laura said again, but she knew she had been outmanoeuvred.

'Why not let her go out riding if she wants to, it's her life,' Clara said. Everyone looked at her, astonished. Clara exhaled slowly.

'I beg your pardon?' Sybil said.

'You heard what I said. It's her own life.'

'Clara is going to stand on her own two feet now,' Ernest said in a pleasant aside to Laura, 'she doesn't need us now, you see.'

In the silence they all listened to the background murmur of the rain. But when Laura cut the bread she had baked that morning the crust sounded very loud.

'Clara has made her bed,' said Ernest suddenly, with that hoarse edge of rage in his voice, 'and now she must lie upon it.' Sybil laid her hand tenderly over his. The two girls looked down at the food on their plates and ate quietly.

Then Clara got up and threw down her napkin. 'You're both hateful! You've ruined my life.' They waited for her to sit down. 'Now you won't be able to put me down any more,' Clara said, trembling.

'Don't upset your father,' Sybil begged. Clara hesitated, then sat. 'She's nervous about tomorrow,' Sybil explained fondly, 'she's a young woman in love.' Ernest drank his wine. Clara sat twining her fingers, her plate empty, and he did not even look at her. He was waiting for Laura.

'Yes, Father, I promise,' Laura said. Clara made an anguished little sound.

'You must eat, dear,' Sybil urged. 'Here's a lovely piece of ham.'

Clara said, 'Can I get down from the table, please?'

'Yes,' Ernest said, 'go!' Clara ran out.

'Nerves,' Sybil said. They sat looking contentedly at Laura.

Ernest reached into his pocket and pulled out a gift in gilt wrapping. He laid it gently on the table, then pushed it across to her.

'With all our love,' he promised smoothly. 'Happy birthday, Laura.'

Laura opened it, and gasped. He had given her an Ingersoll ladies' wristwatch, just like the men's but smaller, with a pretty gold-plated chasing around the face that caught the light. She held out her arm and her father buckled it on her wrist.

'It's beautiful,' she whispered, looking at him with shining eyes.

'What's the time?' he asked her, laughing. He feared losing her more than anything. 'Now I shall always be able to ask you!' Even Sybil smiled. 'What's the time, Laura?'

Laura stared into the window, seeing past her reflection into the rain-lashed darkness and treetops down the river towards Watersmeet Manor, and above the manor, the high bluff.

'What's the matter with Laura?' she heard her father ask.

'She's dreaming of being married,' said Sybil indulgently: to Francis Pervane, of course. But Laura remembered the man with blood-spattered arms, and she shook her head.

'Daddy, may I show my watch to Clara? And I said I'd do her hair.'

He pointed to his glass for more wine, then allowed her to go.

'She can't lie to her mother,' Sybil said proudly, amused.

Ernest shrugged. Now they were alone he began to writhe slowly from side to side on his buttocks in the agony no doctor could assuage. He longed for release, but Sybil sat with her cold hands flat on the tablecloth, looking at him sympathetically. She was a woman of supreme ruthlessness, and she knew what she could do and what she could not. At first that had attracted him, that cold exterior of hers and beneath it the heat of the passion he had been able to arouse in her, to her shame: only in that, in the dark, had he conquered her. Whose face did she see in that darkness? Ernest did not care if it was love between them. For the moments he possessed her, he was whole.

Clara's bedroom lay along the second corridor at the top of the stairs. Laura knocked, expecting to hear her crying, but there was only the drumming of raindrops. She knocked again and breezed in. Under a single brilliant light in a room full of the sound of water, Clara was sitting on the end of her bed flipping through one of the morocco-bound volumes densely written in her own hand. Then she tossed it back in the wardrobe. For a moment they stared at one another, searching for words with dry eyes.

Laura closed the door. 'Why did you never stand up for me before?' she asked, direct as always.

'But I always have,' said Clara gently. She came over and did something she never did, taking Laura's spirited, upturned face tenderly in her big hands; it was Clara's last night. 'Didn't you know?'

'You never did!' Laura turned away defensively.

'There's so much you don't know,' Clara said.

Laura looked assertively around the bedroom that would soon be empty, aware of Clara's eyes following her.

Being exactly on the other side of the house, Clara's room was the mirror image of her own. But the smell of Clara was – had been – of carbolic soap, old books, camphor mothballs, and still on the dresser stood a pathetic few dusty bottles of inexpensive perfume nine-tenths empty. Laura's room was rich with the smell of oiled leather harness and brass cleaner, stray cats, occasionally the cigarettes she secretly smoked, and the breeze from her open window would have sent these old bits of paper flying, and that bridal dress hung on the back of the door would have been stirring and fluttering in its tissue paper. Laura couldn't resist another peep – the white dress that had cost more than all the rest of the wedding put together.

'You're so excited,' Clara sighed.

'Aren't you?'

'I'm glad you're happy for me, it does mean more than anything. It's you I'm going to miss, Laura.' Clara made an astonishing confession. 'It's not my mama or my stepfather I'm sad about leaving, it is you.'

Laura shook her head. 'Why?'

Clara stared at her, then turned away as though it was obvious.

Laura hoped she would get ready in time – Clara should have been busy packing up the remnants of her old life instead of mooning over them – the trunk room at the end of the corridor was already full of her odds and ends to be sent on after the honeymoon, the mysterious, magical honeymoon. Laura was dying to ask where they were going. Clara must be terrifically excited, really. In Gondwana when they fell in love the action always stopped romantically at the bedroom door, but tomorrow it wouldn't. Real life didn't. Laura turned – then saw Clara's face and kept her mouth shut, pretending to examine the wardrobe.

'You can have the wardrobe and anything I leave in it,' Clara said suddenly. 'The stories. Other rubbish.' She held out her hand, but Laura was looking away.

They had not always been so far apart. Laura grew up adoring Clara, copying her in everything, wanting to dream the same dreams, as close to her as if they had been real sisters, closer. But when young Laura was twelve and wanted her own room – was that really it? – everything abruptly changed. Almost overnight the differences that had seemed so vivid and interesting – Clara's imagination, her maturity, her sense of duty – suddenly separated them, and made Clara stiff and stodgy, her mother's nagging servant. Yet Laura was the practical one, the girl-girl with life, energy, vivacity, selfishness, who could get things arranged in a twinkling, if only she cared. Laura, unrepentant Laura, with her mother's stubbornness. And poor lonely Clara had nothing but dreams. But what dreams they once had been.

'I'll start your hair,' Laura offered. 'Have you got the pipe-cleaners ready?'

Clara drew the curtain over her bedroom window and sat down at the dressing table with a visible shiver of pleasure. She was wearing her old pink cotton shift but Laura could see the famous shop-bought white filigree nightdress that Clara would wear tomorrow night laid out on the bed.

'You can try it on,' Clara said.

'I couldn't!' Nothing would have persuaded Laura to let another girl try on *her* nightdress, if she had one, in which she would lie in the arms of the man she loved on her honeymoon. Clara was less possessive, or indifferent.

But Laura held it against her and twirled with a flash of ankles to please Clara. 'You look spectacular,' Clara said, and Laura showed her Daddy's watch. 'It's nice,' Clara said in the same stilted voice. Laura put her hands in Clara's hair and lifted them in the mirror.

'Yes, I look a sight,' said Clara.

'I'll make you ever so pretty for Rob, you'll see.' Laura bent the end of the pipe-cleaner, fitted it over a length of Clara's dead-straight hair and started to roll it up tight. Clara had always dreamed of being married in a mass of curls.

'Ouch!' Laura did nothing by halves. 'Not quite so tight, darling.' Then Clara closed her eyes again.

'You'll be terrific,' Laura said enthusiastically. Rob was an English teacher at the grammar school in

Barum. He wore a straggly black beard and Harris
jackets with leather patches on the elbows, chalk-
dust engrained under the lapels. It was a good job,
paying more than four hundred pounds a year, and
he was buying a semi-detached house on the new
estate. It was very far from Watersmeet. Clara would
see people any time she liked. She could go around
the busy shops, walk down Barum's Strand and take
tea in Bromley's Restaurant overlooking the river,
or go into the Regal and see Clark Gable . . . there
was no limit to the wonderful variety of Clara's new
life. She would not have to churn butter any more
. . . oh, the luxury of crossing metalled roads, of
simply buying a proper packet of butter from a shop.

'Yes, it will be marvellous,' said Clara. There really
was something in her voice.

Laura folded the pipe-cleaner tightly around the
roll of hair to hold it up. She kept glancing at Clara's
reposed face as she worked. Then she whispered: '*Do
you really love him?*'

Clara opened her eyes. 'What a question! Carry on
with your work, please, miss.'

Laura rolled another curl in silence.

'Of course I do.'

Laura squeezed the last pipe-cleaner closed. This
talking like strangers was so sad. Clara was trying
to say something she was frightened to say, and
Laura was frightened to hear. *Do* you really love
him?

'Do you remember Gondwana?' Clara asked gaily,
and Laura's eyes sparkled.

Perhaps everyone dreamed of such places; but Clara
actually wrote down her romances about her imaginary island of palaces and broken hearts. She had

whispered its secrets to her little half-sister beneath the sheets back when they shared this very room. Gondwana was a real place to them both, they'd shivered in the snowstorms that swept off the central mountains, sweltered in the Great Red Desert, gasped with the princess in the tower when the dragon-master's thunderous summons came on the door, and gulped with horrendous vertigo when the prince swam to safety in the Sea of Air. Practical Laura had even added the list of Gondwana's market towns and city states to the index of her geography textbook.

Then the love stories suddenly ceased. Clara stopped them overnight – *that* was it – and they'd been in their own rooms for three or four years now. Laura finished and leaned down.

'Tomorrow,' she whispered, 'you'll know what it feels like to be married.'

'I'm an adult now, and I'm not sure quite what I feel,' said Clara, looking at her in the mirror. 'Laura – I wish we'd been kinder to one another. I wish we'd been able to be.'

Laura touched her shoulder. 'See you tomorrow then.'

'Yes,' Clara said at last.

'Goodnight.' Laura closed the door behind her and stood alone in the corridor, listening to the rain.

She doesn't love him.

Laura's eyes shone. Maybe at the last minute, instead of saying *I will*, Clara would shout *I won't!*: would fling down her bouquet and run alone from the church.

Sybil's voice called up the staircase. 'He's ready for you to carry him up, darling.' Ernest always slept upstairs, refusing to allow his disability to compromise his will. He would not sleep parted from Sybil. Laura looked round, but Clara's door remained obstinately closed. 'Coming,' she called, and realized how hard Clara's life had been, how privileged her own away from home.

Normally this lifting was Clara's job, who was much stronger, but Laura knew everything must change now. She would have to perform this exhausting ritual every single night.

'We'll have to feed you up!' Ernest grinned up at her as Laura struggled to lift him from his wheelchair, then he heaved obligingly on the newel post with his enormously strong arms, and locked his left arm around her neck. The unscented masculine tweed-and-tobacco smell of him, the hardness of his muscles and the way his left thigh flopped against her as she lifted, she knew would soon be as familiar to her as the feel of her own limbs.

Sybil slipped under his other arm with the matter-of-fact competence of long practice, no movement wasted, and together they climbed slowly upstairs holding his torso braced between them – even so he must weigh a hundred and forty pounds. Laura was gasping as they lowered him into the upstairs wheelchair. He pulled her against him affectionately. 'What's the time, Laura?'

He touched the gift ticking on her wrist, then kissed her cheek with a smile, and hugged her to him again.

Laura lay awake on her back with her hands behind her head on the pillow, staring up into the dark. Now that she had woken she was too excited to sleep. The house was silent but for the murmur of the falling rain beyond the open window, the friendly sound of water sliding in the gutters, and of the rising river foaming invisibly on its course past the old abandoned lime kilns towards Watersmeet.

She swung her legs out of bed and felt her way to the door. The solid blackness of the corridor echoed softly with the rain, and then she realized she could see a faint flickering glow on the walls. Candlelight memories; Clara was saying goodbye to the house where she had lived all her life.

Laura crept to the head of the stairs and looked down. Clara was sitting on the seventh step – above the one that squeaked – and Laura smiled, remembering creeping down one Christmas morning to hear plain Clara whisper the latest news from Gondwana. Laura chuckled, now almost an adult, then twitched her nightdress above her ankles and slipped down, missing out the sixth riser, and sat on the step below. It still felt comfortable, still familiar. Drawing her legs up she wrapped her arms around her knees and looked up at Clara with an eager, excited smile. But such an easy return to childhood, to Christmas, was not to be.

'They don't come true,' Clara whispered, and Laura was frightened that she would cry.

'Don't.' Laura hated tears, except her own. 'Come on, be happy, you're getting married today! Everything you ever dreamed of.' She made a small sacrifice. 'I'm envious.'

'Not everything I dreamed,' Clara said. The candle cast its light down only the far side of her face. 'I feel like a traitor.'

Laura reached up and took her hand, entwining

their fingers. Clara's were cold, she must have been sitting here for hours.

'I feel so guilty about leaving – ' she half smiled down at Laura, 'leaving Watersmeet. And yet I must go.'

'You can always come back! We won't fight, because we won't have seen each other much. We'll be happy.'

Clara shook her head.

'You will love him,' Laura said desperately. It was after midnight. She was seventeen.

'Stop it.'

'I never meant to hurt you.' Laura must have been unbearable – she had never meant to be. Oh, of course she had! Taking her frustration out on Clara because Clara just sat there indifferent to pain and took it, she was such a lump. Laura wanted to scream, she wanted to live. She wanted the world. Everyone did. Clara had such dreams of her own life once . . . If she had given up, that was a horrifying prospect. Laura clenched her fingers as tight as she could until Clara's fingers went white between them, and wished with all her heart that Clara could be happy. 'Let's be friends, elder sister.'

Sister . . . that lie got her, and Clara reached down with her other hand and stroked Laura's hair with that mixture of fondness and envy, and Laura thought she had won, thinking it was love. And it was, partly, but the candlelight flickered and hid half the feelings on Clara's face.

'I wish I was you,' Clara said tenderly, letting go.

They sat with their knees drawn up comfortably inside their nightdresses just like the old days, sharing confidences that were the more piquant because both of them knew it was for the last time.

'We'll write, won't we?' Laura said. 'I'll write to you every week.'

Clara shook her head slowly. She knew Laura wouldn't.

'You aren't leaving us for ever,' Laura said.

'I won't ever come back to Watersmeet.'

'Not even to see me?'

There was a pause. 'You really don't know,' Clara said. 'One day you'll be the lady of the manor, you will marry Francis. You'll be Mistress of Watersmeet. And I should come back to envy you in your happiness.'

Laura didn't have the words to ameliorate such despair. She reached up. 'It's only natural to feel sorry to leave the parents you love.' Her touch worked where her words failed. Clara took Laura's slim, graceful hands, lifted them, pressed them between her own.

'Laura, I don't love them,' she murmured, 'any more than they love you.'

Laura was so astonished that for a moment she was angry, then she felt sick. She tugged back her hands, but Clara wouldn't let go. They rocked back and forth, then sat with their faces close together, like conspirators.

Clara said sadly, 'He's nothing like my father. It was Alex she really loved, *my* father. Look at me, my life for my mother's . . . guilt. And her own. She was driving, you know, when he was killed.'

'They do love me!'

'They need you. I tried to warn you. They're as selfish as you are, you're getting what you deserve.'

Clara said dully: 'Now I'm free of them, free of you, and free of Watersmeet.'

They sat listening to the whispering rain in the night.

All Laura wanted to talk about was broad daylight, what being married was like, how wonderful love was, what Clara really felt about *the best bit*.

'Let me in on the big secret . . .'

'Torquay,' whispered Clara, recovering her smile, 'the Imperial.'

'I guessed!'

'Sir George Pervane,' confided Clara, 'is letting us have the Bridal Suite at the Watersmeet Falls Hotel in Lynmouth for the first night.'

'Your first night together,' Laura said eagerly.

'Oh, that. The next morning we'll take the bus to Barum. Then the train . . . ' Laura listened entranced by the whole, wide outside world in Clara's voice.

'Oh, that,' she scoffed. What would it feel like? A full moon would be showing if the sky was clear, the Watersmeet Falls Hotel had a Palm Court and the orchestra would play . . . 'Don't pretend you aren't excited. You know . . .'

'You just give in.' Clara looked down. 'That's all you have to do.'

Laura was intensely disappointed. 'Is that enough?'

'Laura, it's all there is.'

Laura wondered what would *really* happen when Clara gave in, and her elbows squeaked the sixth step. Both girls looked round fearfully. They heard nothing, only rain and silence, but it had been a fright.

'Do you want to know a secret?'

Clara almost clapped her hands. 'What is it?'

'Do you want to know what happened this afternoon?'

'Yes, tell me,' Clara said flatly.

Laura whispered: 'I think I saw a murder.'

'How *wonderful!*' For a moment the old, secret Clara, the one whose spirit was unbroken and youth not lost, shone out of her eyes. 'I just knew something happened!'

'I did go *the wrong way* . . .'

Clara's face didn't change. She knew that. If Laura had seen Bart up there, she'd never forgive her, never.

'When I came back it was pouring with rain,' Laura said. 'It was terrible. Clara, I saw a man, and he saw me.'

'It was probably just a poacher.'

'I don't think it was. He had blood all over his arms, and I could smell it.'

'You must have been terrified! Did you run away?'

'I think it was Bart.'

The shine went out of Clara's eyes. 'You are an idiot. He might have murdered *you*. You didn't speak to him, did you?'

'No, I kept looking back, but he didn't follow.'

'He wouldn't, he hates women.' Clara changed her mind. 'He doesn't care about women.'

'How do you know?'

Clara shrugged. 'Men don't care, not like we do. They don't have the same feelings. They don't have friends.'

'Do you believe really everything you hear about him?'

'Yes!' Clara said.

Laura murmured, 'I know what the Pervanes say
. . . but he can't be as bad as they say.'

'He's just a poacher,' Clara said viciously. Her voice
rose: 'He kills rabbits and eats birds, he breaks their
necks in his hands and they're dead in a flash. Sir
George swore he'd set mantraps if there was any
more poaching. He would, too. It's been quiet for
years since the Master died, but now the old business
has flared up again. I hope they do catch him, and
teach him the lesson he deserves.'

The Pervanes' centuries-long feud with their other
neighbours, the once magnificent family of the
Barronets, would end only when one dynasty or the
other was extinct. Their hatred, Clara whispered,
was as true and real a passion as love. Blood had been
spilt. Laura listened entranced. Any reason, if reason
there was, lay buried deep. For Pervane and
Barronet alike, the virus was in the blood, bred from
father to son, an affair of honour which none dared
fail.

Exmoor was a land apart, an island within an
island. Long ago the peaceful hill farmers with their
bronze tools fled into its deep valley to escape the
iron-tipped weapons of the Celts, and were enslaved
but never assimilated. Afterwards the Celtic tribes
were left alone and apart on Exmoor by their Roman
masters, just as a thousand years later their
conquerors, the Anglo-Saxon farmers of the combes,
were subjugated as a separate class by the new
Norman masters of the hilltops and towns. Exmoor
had never been a melting pot, there were too many
wild places to hide. Bloodlines ran through history
in separate strands.

Everyone knew Devon was a country of thick blood

and long memories: in any isolated pub or livestock market, a man greeted another man with a smile but ignored his neighbour, who was shaken by the hand by another set. Eyes that knew the signs discerned a vast interconnection of human friendships and enmities that were as real, solid and intricate as the hills and rivers of the Exmoor Forest. Unmapped, but that was what local knowledge was all about.

So it was between the Pervanes and the Barronets. No Benson knew or cared what the ghastly reason for such stupidity was. Laura was quite certain that it was something about nothing, just an excuse for men to have fun and show off with Saturday night fighting. A sensible woman would knock their silly heads together and make them see sense. 'You don't believe everything the Pervanes tell you, do you?'

'Bart has no family,' Clara said wretchedly. Something in her voice stopped Laura. 'He is the last of his line, fallen from grace, humiliated and impoverished.'

Laura whispered: 'Is it true that the Barronets once owned all of Exmoor?'

'They say they come from the de Barreneau family who came over with William the Conqueror, and stole the Combe Martin silver mines a thousand years ago.'

Laura said: 'He looked so sad.' She didn't mention the sense of him being in danger – did he really believe she would betray him to Sir George Pervane? No, Laura dreamed that Bart Barronet was his own man, fearing no one.

'He is the last survivor.' Clara shivered. She asked, very quietly: 'Did he really look so very sad?'

'Much more than sad!' Laura said enthusiastically.

She struggled to put it into words. 'At first I think he was smiling, as if he was amused.'

'Amazed, more likely, seeing you out in that weather!'

'No, not startled.' Laura wanted to be clear in her own mind. 'Amused, almost as if he was toying with an idea – as if a girl on horseback was an amusing diversion. Almost contemptuous. And then he saw something else.' Words escaped her. 'Something else, Clara.'

'Stop it,' Clara said.

'I wasn't frightened – the rain was pouring, my face must have been a sight I suppose.' She shrugged and smiled, proud that she had not been afraid.

'It's not funny!' Clara hissed, watching her. 'Stay clear of him. You must!'

'Why?'

'Because it isn't a game, Laura.'

'I never said it was.'

'You're safe, he'll never come here. But you must never go back there.'

Laura turned her head slightly away. 'Why not?'

'Because I know.'

'What do you know?' Laura blazed up suddenly, facing her half-sister head on. *'Give in, that's all you have to do*, is that all there is?' she cried impetuously. 'It's not enough!' She flung her arms around Clara's neck. 'I'm sorry. I'm not you, that's all.'

Clara sat like a stone. 'You always hurt me better than anyone.'

'You always ask for it! Just leave me alone.' Laura pulled back. She propped her chin on her hands. Then she swept back her hair.

Clara spoke very quietly. 'It's different for you.'

'What do you mean?'

'You *must* know.' Poor Clara looked at her half-sister smugly, almost victoriously, at her long black hair flowing in its gorgeous waves and curls, the pools of her dark vivid eyes, then Clara's smugness dissolved into something Laura had never seen before, an expression of the most terrifying jealousy.

Clara said: 'Because you are beautiful, Laura.'

They stared at one another. The rain had stopped and suddenly they were both aware of the change, and of the silence between them.

Clara touched Laura's shoulder sadly: goodbye.

Laura sat alone in the candlelight. She pressed her fingertips lightly to her lips, then her nose, her eyelids. She ran the palms of her hands slowly back through her hair. She could hear her heart beating. 'So what, anyway!' she said defiantly. 'So what if I am?'

Laura never needed much sleep, and she woke in a flash. Her blue boarding school uniform still hung in the wardrobe, and for a moment her hand reached out to take it as if the second bell had rung and the dormitory would explode with frantic life around her, bedclothes thrown back, the girls slipping half-buttoned blouses over their heads, except Penny Haberstam who was oversleeping as usual, and Miss Elliot's footsteps already approaching down the tiled corridor . . . Laura sat up. She was in her own bedroom, alone.

The tiny, warning hands of her new watch almost touched six o'clock – and she was late! Clara would not get the breakfast today. Laura groaned then swept her nightdress over her head and threw it on the floor, walking over it to the bowl of water on the window sill. The homescreech was still whistling his clear storm warning but there was no more rain. She splashed her face and reddened her clear complexion, gasping, on the rough towel. Though the wind was not too bad down here, higher up the valley walls the treetops rocked, and the tall flexible tip of the deodar was whipped from side to side like a hairy green tail.

Pulling on her woollen dress she fled downstairs. Outside the scullery door she fetched the splintered beechwood from the lean-to and ran back to the kitchen, shivering, feeding it into the simmering Aga for a flare, then fetched more substantial logs to boost the fire – everyone would want a hot bath today. Turning on the spigot over the big square sink for rainwater, she filled the two big coppers, swayed them stiff-legged on to the hotplates, then fetched the two white pitchers for drinking water and went outside.

Her ankles were soaked immediately in the long wet grass as instead of following the looping path she cut straight across to the goyle, and held each pitcher under the leaping silver waters in turn. It was dangerous to drink rainwater without putting an eel in the house-tank to keep the water fresh, but impossible to pipe this drinking water, purified by the soil, from the goyle to the house because of its acidity – the same acidity which turned bathwater blue as soon as soap was used, left the bath sides stained bright blue, and ate through copper pipes and hot-water tanks in no time at all; and Father refused to pay out for the expensive stainless steel pipes which alone resisted it. To fetch drinking water by hand made hark work for Laura, but he was not rich. He would have given anything to walk through the grass as she did.

The house was waking up. Clara's sash window shot open. 'My ribbons! I've lost my ribbons!' she shrieked across the tossing tops of the vegetable garden.

'They were in the bottom drawer last night,' Laura yelled.

Clara's head, still covered with the white squiggles of the pipe-cleaners, snatched back inside. Down in the village the pageboys and bridesmaids would also be getting ready, and they would all join up at the church.

Laura hefted the pitchers back through the stone-flagged scullery. It was the largest room in the house with an enormous central oak-barrelled butter churn standing on iron A-frames, the rainwater tanks mounted over the row of fireclay sinks, scrubbed washboards, and an ornate cream wrought-iron mangle in the corner. The ironing board folded down out of the alcove. The curve-topped door to her left, showing the gap beneath it where before the Great War, when labour was affordable, generations of serving girls' feet fetching to and fro had worn a scoop in the stone, opened on the first cool room with its thick slate shelves piled with home-made yoghurt, Paradise cheese, cream, soft pungent cheese from the goat, rich yellow butter ready for scooping and patting. In the second room that lay beyond, the floor was stacked with what was left of last year's jams and the cleansed jars ready for the coming season, pickles, a few strings of onions, salted and cured meats, a row of smoked hams hanging on the bone, some flitches of back bacon. In the third room the salted or dried fish was stored, flitches of halibut or haddock wrapped in muslin, and their home-smoked and tiny delicious trout. In all except the ham, bacon and salt-water fish, delivered from his own farms and fishery interests by the neighbourly generosity of Sir George Pervane, the Benson family ate their own produce. In the pea season they ate nothing but peas, and once the carrots started it was nothing but carrots. Laura loathed peas.

The other doorway led to the storeroom for flour and rice, the dried sugared fruit her father adored – apart from the love of gambling his only weakness was his sweet tooth – loaves of home-baked bread, and bright tins of biscuits.

Clara had coped with it for years; all these duties were Laura's now, drone in the hive of which Sybil was the queen. Laura paused, catching sight of her sulking face in a bright reflection.

You are beautiful, Laura.

That was hardly true now. Puffing and blowing, Laura put down the pitchers on the oak table and filled the iron kettle for tea, then put the yeast on the side of the Aga to warm. Only rolls today; Sir George had very kindly offered the use of Watersmeet Manor for the wedding reception, tactfully saving the newlyweds the long dogleg back here out of their way. Laura left the dough to stand, made the tea and left her parents' tray outside their bedroom door after knocking respectfully, then took a cup and saucer with two biscuits slanted in it along to Clara's room, knocked and breezed in. Clara was still in a terrific panic, scattering ribbons and bobs and bows everywhere.

Laura picked up the one she was looking for and held it out.

'I can't drink, I think I'm going to be sick,' Clara said. 'I must be mad.'

She ate the biscuits and Laura returned to the kitchen, put the rolls in the oven and snatched a mouthful of tea on her way outside. Gladys the cow was pleased to see her, the storm had blown away most of the flies and she stood contentedly chewing, twitching her ears while Laura milked her. Having milked the goat Laura carried the separate buckets back to the scullery. The rolls were burning, and there was the kedgeree to prepare – her father's favourite, smoked haddock and hard-boiled eggs flaked into boiled rice, with Laura's special touch, the authentic slices of green ginger. Sybil came down in her dressing gown and stood looking around the kitchen at the mixing bowls that had not been rinsed and the hot water that had not been carried up, and her disappointment in Laura showed in her gentle, bruised eyes. There was so much to do, and she went to help Laura out by laying the dining room table for breakfast. It was seven o'clock already; Laura had hardly noticed the time flying until she looked at her watch.

After they had pecked at their breakfast Laura cleared the table and washed up alone. Coming out into the hall, she could hear the wireless mumbling in her father's study. Drying her hands she climbed upstairs to find that Clara hadn't left the last empty copper outside the bathroom door. She entered the high-ceilinged, white-tiled room with its enormous freestanding Victorian bath, the single cold rainwater faucet glittering with drops of condensation. Clara was sitting amidst clouds of steam like a French Impressionist painting of a woman bathing, elbows up, soaping herself.

'I haven't got my hair wet, have I?' She squinted at Laura anxiously.

'No.'

'I've finished with it,' Clara dismissed her, and Laura picked up the empty copper and stood watching those big flat hands, the nails not yet lacquered, sliding soap over pale skin. She tried to look at Clara as Rob would, the knobbly curve of the spine, the substantial brown-tipped breasts, the broad hips rolling in the suds, then for a moment the black cleave revealed as Clara rinsed with a gasp of cold, clear water. There must be more than this to love.

Clara stood up, reaching for the towel. Her powerful female form was nearly tall enough to be attractively statuesque, but her hands and elbows were too red, she did not care about herself enough, and there was too much calculation in her eyes. She was not a starry-eyed girl, she was a defeated woman, and she was getting married. 'Do you want my water?' Clara asked.

'I've got my bath ready downstairs,' Laura lied, and fled.

She refilled the second copper and set it on the Aga to warm. The flames were roaring merrily now. In the small room off the kitchen she set out her things around the antique, exquisite china bath that she loved to use. Its high back was decorated with Georgian-blue flowers and stems intertwined, the low sides sprouting gilded handles in the form of nymphs, and she imagined John Prideau falling in love with it to put in his new house. Really it should be used for bathing beside a blazing parlour fire, not on this coconut matting over the cold stone floor, but it was wonderful anywhere. She poured in the water and slipped out of her clothes, testing the heat with her toe, then caught sight of herself in the flyblown mirror, stark, slim, vulnerable. She lowered herself slowly into the warm caress of the water, and leaned back with a sigh of luxury.

She pulled out the stopper and towelled herself dry, then as the water sluiced away through the central drain in the floor, wrapped the towel around her hair and slipped into her dressing gown. She scampered upstairs and opened her wardrobe door with a thrill. Today she would be a real lady!

Humming the popular song that had been all the rage, she let the dressing gown slip to the floor and kicked it away, then began the ritual she had planned to the last detail.

First she put on the ultimate luxury, the oatmeal-coloured Jaeger underwear and petticoat, slipped her hands over her hips and did a twirl. *Keep young and beautiful . . .* She had begged Mama for the Joan Crawford dress with the built-up sleeves and collar but had to make do with this elegant emerald-green mail-order Marley Gown, the first sized dress she'd ever had bought for her, the perfect fashionable length just below the knee, pulled in to show off her waist, and a sharply cut caracul collar just like Ginger Rogers wore . . . *if you want to be loved.* She cocked her knee and ran her palms down her smooth stomach, showing her white teeth in a model's smile, then shook out her raven-black hair into its natural waves – Mama wanted her to wear it piled up like an Edwardian, which had been the cause of another family row, because then she wouldn't be able to wear the shallow-crown hat – now Laura gently lowered the precious green colour-coordinated hat on to her head, tipping the wide flat brim forward in the mirror until she looked ultra sophisticated, her eyes gleaming in the glamorous emerald shadow. She pinned it lightly, and still humming ran a touch of lipstick across her mouth, then flicked her fingertips up the dark arches of her eyebrows, and wished there was something more she could do. She was ready.

She found Clara standing in the wedding dress on the landing, having something around the back dealt with by Sybil. Clara's face showed panic and resignation. She stood with her head down, holding the hem off the floor, the puffed sleeve heads making her look top-heavy and imposing. She looked round at Laura and gasped.

'Do you like it?' Laura twirled eagerly. 'You look *marvellous.*'

'Laura, go and sit downstairs somewhere quietly out of the way.' Sybil instructed. She wore her hair up and her dark brown coat with the fox fur accessory clipped head-to-tail in a lasso around her shoulders.

Swinging her handbag, Laura went into the solarium. She watched the grey, turgid sky flying silently overhead beyond the glass. Then she sat neatly and demurely looking at her hands on her knees, and her eyes began to close. Occasionally an eddy in the wind rattled the glass. She felt quite apart from the wedding-morning panic continuing in the body of the house, slamming doors, misplaced pins, Clara shrieking about her grandmother's lost lace collar. 'Laura!' called Sybil's voice, her hat wouldn't stay on at the proper angle. Then she must have got it right, because she didn't call again. Laura sat pensively on a window seat overlooking the drive, staring at her shadow in the glass. *The wrong way* . . . She felt the same after yesterday's event. *She* was the same, but everything else had changed, and the girl in beautiful clothes who gazed mockingly back seemed to know so much more than she did . . . something moved in her face, startling her, and she saw it was him.

Then her eyes opened wide. It really was.

It was the figure of the man walking up their drive. Laura didn't move.

He walked as carelessly and confidently as though *he* owned this place that had belonged to the Bensons all their lives.

Washed and combed, that long wavy hair looked almost blond, his tawny eyes gleaming in the sun-darkened planes of his face. He wore an old-fashioned scuffed maroon jacket, unbuttoned and swinging open down the front, which reached halfway down his thighs. Yet it was carefully brushed. His hefty black nail-boots were so old that despite the obvious long hours of buffing, cracks crazed the polish. His trousers, flaunting unusual seams, were heavyweight black Bedford cord with worn knees, secured by a thick shiny belt of very dark brown leather with a flat silver buckle, where she could see his open-necked white shirt tucked in tight. His ankles were supported by stiff buckskins of the same dark brown leather, tightly held by flat silver buckles, obviously part of a set that to Laura's

49

eyes must once have been completed by matching brown boots and buckles. That was long ago. Now even those non-matching replacement boots were almost worn out. He was poor.

Laura turned slowly as he walked. He was so solid that she could feel his weight. He stepped between the twigs the wind had brought down, moving with a distinctive firm grace, passing soundlessly by her beyond the glass, but he knew she was there.

Behind his back, she saw he gripped a bouquet of wild flowers in his hand.

Still he did not look at her. Yet he was so aware of her, Laura felt it in every move he made, each step he took. The smooth shine on his jaw betrayed the care he had taken shaving. All because she might see him.

Laura smiled to herself, keen and anxious, holding herself to let no hint of what she felt show on her face, waiting for him to acknowledge her.

He paused, and glanced over. He looked straight through her. Then he took the steps two at a time with casualness, going out of her view on to the porch.

She waited, but his summons did not come on the front door. Laura hesitated, but still she did not call her father from his study. She went through into the hall and sensed him on the other side of the door. Smiling slightly to herself, she laid her fingers lightly on the door handle, then swung the heavy door open.

The porch was empty. The wedding bouquet, propped against the panels, fell into her hands as she stooped. She dropped it as though she had been stung. On a piece of card was written a single word in elegant goosequill script, quite unlike what she would have expected from such a man. The word was CLARA.

'Did you speak to him?'

Laura stared from the steps. He might be watching her from the trees.

'Laura!'

She turned to her father in his wheelchair. She shook her head.

'I am a *patient* man . . .'

'He did not say a word,' Laura said. But he had looked at her.

'He has the gall to come here!' Ernest was outraged. 'He knows we are friends of the Pervanes. You will tell me if he reappears.'

'Yes, Father.'

'Promise me.'

Laura dared say: 'Father, must I promise you everything?' Her fingers played at the buckle of her watch with a life of their own. She forced them to be still, looking down, then met his eyes.

Ernest was wearing a formal grey jacket with the row of medals over his left breast, the grey top hat placed on the seat in front of him where his right thigh should have been. He held out his hand tolerantly for the card, and when Laura gave it to him, he tore it in half, then into quarters, then tiny pieces with his strong fingers, and scattered them.

'You will tell me, do you understand?'

'What would you do?'

'I do not keep a shotgun for nothing.'

His rage was ridiculous, and she could almost have laughed at him for being so silly. Yet she sensed that his threat was deadly serious. She saw her father's fading eyes, his drying skin. But at the same moment

that she turned away from him inside, she felt
adult pity for him, understanding how vulnerable he
was.

She knelt obediently to pick up the pieces of card
from the parquet.

But she asked in a low voice: 'Shall we see Bart
Barronet in the church?'

Ernest was silent. She looked up, demanding an
answer.

For a moment he spoke in his enraged voice. 'No,
that man isn't allowed in church, any more than a
dog is! My darling daughter,' Ernest said
affectionately, 'there is so much you must never
know about life.'

'But surely –'

'None of the Barronets has any more soul than a
dog does. Once they owned the churches and all
these lands,' he explained. 'Now he is excluded,
excommunicated. That murderous family ends with
him, Laura. Exmoor justice will be done. He is
unbaptized.'

Laura lowered her head. She could bring herself
to say nothing.

'Sir George Pervane has won,' Ernest said. 'The
Pervanes have put all that business behind them
now.'

Still Laura could not let go. 'Unbaptized?'

'You know what that means.'

Laura murmured: 'When Bart dies, he will go to
hell.'

Laura sat alone, sadly staring out of the window at
the empty drive, seeing him in every detail,
imagining what such a life must be like. What did he

feel, with such a prospect in front of him? She had never seen anyone so solidly alive.

He dared himself to come here! After yesterday, he couldn't get her out of his mind, couldn't sleep, had to see her. Laura jumped up, excited. That was it: because she was beautiful. She looked for her image in the glass to admire herself in her dress, pushing her fingertip into a curl of her hair, then stopped. She was building castles in the air.

He had looked at her, that was all, and walked on. Laura slumped back on the bench, ashamed of herself.

But she couldn't help remembering everything about him.

She was sure he had noticed the exact shade of green she wore, indifferent to the cost of her forty-shilling platform shoes which she didn't like much herself, but filling himself with every detail of her that mattered, her long fingernails, her dark eyelashes, her transparent complexion with the rush of colour to the cheeks, and as aware as she of the curve of her breasts, her interested gaze.

He had behaved with defiance, then slipped away. Didn't he have the guts to say hallo? Who did he think he was? If she saw him again she'd teach him a lesson, she wouldn't speak to him.

The air in the solarium smelt warm and moist, carrying the scent of oranges that Sybil grew in pale imitation of the ones at Watersmeet Manor.

Laura gasped. She had forgotten all about the posy she had promised to pick for Clara! She flew into the hall, but it was too late. Clara was descending the staircase in all her bridal glory. Her hair was up so that she looked taller than ever, the veils tied back over her head, scarlet lipstick making a Cupid's bow of her mouth. She stopped on the bottom step, waiting for Laura's opinion.

Laura hugged her. 'You look lovely!'

Clara's eyes fell on the bouquet by Laura's foot. Laura made the best of it, curtseying smoothly, and presented the flowers with a smile. But almost at once Clara fingered a helleborine orchid, and knew. Her damp eyes met Laura's.

'Did he come here?'

Laura shrugged.

'I was so sure he wouldn't,' Clara said.

'It was only a neighbourly gesture.'

'He came here to see you.'

Laura didn't say anything.

Then Clara burst out: 'Wasn't there even a message?'

They heard footsteps on the landing. 'Clara,' Laura said. 'Just your name.'

Clara's face twisted bitterly.

'Something old, something new, something borrowed, something blue.' Sybil, wearing her 'where there's a will there's a waist' dress and her hair rolled up inside a snood, came tripping downstairs swinging from her finger the blue garter she wore for her own wedding. Not to Ernest, to Alex. She knelt and tied it high around Clara's dimpled thigh.

'Come on,' called Ernest's voice from the drive, 'we haven't got all day!' He was waiting in the trap, staring straight ahead with the whip vertical in his hand, hating being late.

Laura fetched the cloak to protect the precious dress. Sybil snatched it out of her hands and put it

tenderly round Clara's shoulders, then hugged her
and kissed her cheek sentimentally. 'My little girl will
come back and see her mama.' Now that Clara was
almost gone, she was all over her.

But Clara had decided. She would not turn or look
back at her home once. Sybil draped a tarpaulin over
the wheel to stop it marking Clara's train or the
trailing accoutrements and helped her on to the hard
front seat beside Laura's father. Laura dashed back
inside the house and brushed the last imaginary flick
off her green lambswool outdoor coat with the sharp
lapels that so suited her, corrected the smashing hat's
rakish angle, then hastily decided to double up on
the hatpins, as it was bound to be windy up on
Cheriton Ridge.

Fed up with waiting between the shafts, Blackbird
whinnied with pleasure and clouted the gravel with
her forehoof when Laura ran down the steps. Ernest,
forgetting the horse was not the obedient pony
they'd had to sell, dragged back too hard on the reins
and Blackbird gave an impatient thoroughbred jump
that made the mudguards rattle. 'Steady there,
steady!' Ernest yelled.

Laura giggled: Steady was her father's nickname
in the army, from – she thought – the officer's
steadying command given to gunners anxious to fire
too early. Ernest didn't see what made her laugh;
for all his smiles, he never did.

In fact Steady had been one of those ironical
nicknames given to people who display the opposite
characteristic: Steady had been quite a rakehell as
a young Regular, rarely sober or out of debt, and it
was not his injury that embittered him. The cause
of the Benson family's decline lay further back, with

old Montague Benson of Simonsbath, childless but still family, who on returning from missionary duty in Latin America to end his life a religious recluse, had naturally been expected to leave his fortune, art collection and a mighty acreage of the prime stag-hunting yeth between Simonsbath and Minehead to his young relative. Instead he willed the money and property to a distant London cousin on the distaff side, Ozwald Benton-Benson. Montague's disapproval of young Ernest's gambling was said to be the reason; but Ernest had persuaded himself the old pope-lover just wanted to leave the money to a Catholic. He never blamed himself. And so the family's fate was already sealed before the accident.

Laura scrambled up behind her father, pouting that he wouldn't trust her to drive, then wished she hadn't laughed at him. His single thigh was clamped to the seat-boards with the cruel metal braces at knee and hip that enabled him to balance, the agonized roll of knuckle on his other side being quite useless for that purpose.

'Giddyup! Trot on!' he called, cracking the whip.

To be fair, Sybil would not have trusted Laura to drive either, perhaps because of her own experience. Ernest was *safe*. He planned for every danger. They both knew how easily, a wasp-sting, an overhanging branch, a life could go wrong. That was why they lived in Watersmeet.

'Steady, girl, steady there.' But Blackbird loved to accelerate. Ernest dragged back and Laura saw the metal brace almost disappear in his thigh, so deeply did it bite into the flesh as his body twisted, though he betrayed no sign of pain.

All this for a malt dram and the chance of a

reminiscence with Sir George Pervane at the Manor; they were both old Royal Devon's, but Sir George got an OBE as well as an MC before retiring to Watersmeet Manor; of which house, curtilage and purlieu he was lord through the Royal Prerogative of King Charles. Nowadays Sir George was recognized by no official title outside Exmoor, but known as the Master by the only people who mattered – the followers of the North Devon Staghounds. No one looked down on the Pervanes as merchants now.

The trap took the path winding up out of the glen into the trees. Soon they passed across the top of the cliff and saw the old lime kilns on the other side of the river below them, where the Barton Woods rose up like a green fountain towards Hellebore and the grey sky. Then the track wound down in hairpin turns and the formal oasis of Watersmeet Manor appeared deep below them between the hills, the long house with its odd turret or two rambling along the curving riverbank at the meeting of the waters. Even over the peaceful clopping of Blackbird's hooves and the trap's squeaky axles they heard the sullen roar of the East Lyn, its broad loop around the house running red with sediment deposited in the long summer dry spell. The waterfalls of the Hoaroak hissing down from the high moor looked leaden grey and double yesterday's size from the rains.

Passing the white manor gate they turned downstream to Watersmeet Steps, crossing the mingled stream on the massive stone slabs of prehistoric clapper bridge, the wheels fitting easily between the modern iron handrails added by Sir George after his wife was drowned, then climbing up to the county road and turning left along the rising west side of the valley.

This was the right way, the safe way. But Laura's gaze rested in the steep trees on the forbidden east side, where she rode yesterday. For a moment she glimpsed the rock face dropping almost sheer to Lucy's Pool, the swirling surface of the water down there, both fed and drained by waterfalls as the Hoaroak leapt on towards Watersmeet. An ancient oak tree, called by tradition the Druid's Oak, grew half-uprooted from a ledge near the top of the bluff, and Laura marvelled that yesterday she had been unaware of that broad, dying treetop struggling to reach the sun just beneath her. But now she saw its withered leaves already yellow and flaking in the wind, lying scattered like gold coins down on the wet rocks far below. She looked up and above the oak discerned yesterday's gateposts just visible in the trees, and suddenly a gleam of light beyond them – the sky in a window.

So that was where it was.

Laura was disappointed. Now that she knew exactly where the house was it lost some of its mystery. Then the curve of the valley swung round, and it was gone.

Blackbird slowed on the stiff climb up to Cheriton, so Laura volunteered to get out and walk. The rain had settled the red dust, and it was pleasantly cool between the tall hedgerows. She picked a stalk of sheep's sorrel and swished it casually over her head as she walked, but as she came to the exposed top the wind blew away the flies. To avoid arriving early her father had parked in the shelter of the hedge on the Lyncombe path, and Laura saw them from behind, their silhouettes waiting motionless and without conversation as the sky raced above their heads. What was Clara feeling?

She walked on, watching Sybil join the wedding guests standing around in the churchyard with fluttering hats and dresses, small temporary creatures clinging on the bald face of the earth in the mouth of the gale. How desolate and eternal it looked, Laura thought, this joining of two souls, the grey moor, grey sky, the weathered church bracing its square tower against the wind as it had for a thousand years. No clouds of yellow flowers or beaming sunlight for Clara's wedding. The Saxons were the first to build their wooden, aisle-less chapel here on this windy ridgeway pointing towards the heart of the moor. That structure was long lost beneath Norman stonework, but people did not change. Their lives were so brief.

Instead of joining the others Laura came round through the back gate and lingered amongst the headstones, watching the grass thrashing in the wind between all those mossy, crumbling *Hic Iacets: here lies* . . . She held down her hat-brim as she came around the side of the church. She recognized Rob Stall by his beard, standing with older folks who must be his parents, in the shelter of the lych-gate. His arms uncomfortably crossed, he glanced at her in an assertive, almost bullying way, slightly drunk, out of his element and thoroughly intimidated by all these country folk. She thought he had noticed her legs, but he looked away. She hoped he wouldn't come over. She looked about for Francis to cheer her up, but he was nowhere to be seen.

A hand fell on her shoulder. She jumped, then

heard his chuckle. He had been waiting behind her. Francis Pervane, two years older than Laura, stood frowning down on her with pleasure. Then he smiled. *Gotcha*.

Francis had sleepy dark eyes, with a charming elegant manner and black hair brushed smoothly back from his temples. Laura was sure he would go a very sophisticated grey one day.

They did not need to say a word.

With his long, sensitive fingers Francis stroked her smart green shoulder, obviously mocking Laura's new feminine airs and graces, knowing the practical working clothes she usually wore. Francis and Laura; they had always taken one another for granted, but now Laura regarded him seriously. Did he really like her in green? He'd like it because *she* wore it, put his hand over his heart and turn up his eyes in front of everyone. She hated that sort of joke on their friendship, but he was bound to do it if Sir George was watching. Laura had seen Francis weep as though his heart was broken in two after his mother died, and knew what feelings he hid inside himself – as, like her, he had been educated to do. Earlier he must have been putting flowers on his mother's grave, she could see the damp patches on the knees of his trousers where he had knelt down. If only he wouldn't make a joke of everything now. Intuitively Laura sensed that Francis buried nearly everything that meant anything to him inside. He started to say something to make her laugh, then saw her eyes and stopped.

Instead, Francis took both Laura Benson's hands in his and drew her after him into the shelter of the porch. His fingers were cold – really cold – from

his long wait for her, and *that* was what she liked.
Alone, his gaze became troubled as he searched her
eyes. He said awkwardly: 'My Laura – you look
divine.' From him, who was good with words, that
sounded clumsy and trite, which pleased her: it must
be true. *My* Laura? Anyway, he was obviously
unsure of her, and that pleased her even more.

She looked at him in a different way. He was older,
his natural slimness almost thin nowadays, draining
the youthful softness from his features to reveal a
maturity with much more character, but he still
looked kind. He wore a tailored pinstripe suit – he
wore dark suits, his father always wore tweeds –
and Laura admired the way Francis had the *savoir-
faire* to get the fashionable broad cut, which didn't
flatter his slim tall figure, subtly waisted. No mail-
order or five bob Marks and Spencer's clothes for
him; the Pervanes had always had money. Francis
looked businesslike and in control. But not of Laura.
He was still holding her hands.

He drew her lightly towards him with his fingers
and she really thought he would kiss her on the
mouth, but at the last moment he pecked her cheek,
then held her at arm's length again. He whispered:
'My Laura, you are the prettiest girl at the wedding.'

Only the prettiest! Laura wanted at least Clara's
word from him.

He mistook her dismay for sophistication and
looked at her admiringly. 'You're beautiful, Laura.'

It was different coming from a man. She resisted
the impulse to smile or to run the palms of her hands
up her lapels to check the wind hadn't bent them
out stupidly, or blown her hair round.

He straightened a bob of hair on her shoulder,

possessively, and she let him. Francis and she had
long been sweethearts, that was as old as the hills,
he had always carried her satchel home from
Lynmouth school, a serious boy scratching his heart
earnestly on the bottom of her pencil-case before he
was sent to board at Bampfylde. The contemptuous
shyness he learned from the other lads had come
between them like a wall, suddenly he and Laura
were different; to Laura no boy could compete with
Blackbird, and she couldn't care less about his soccer
cards or butterfly collection with its horrid
chloroform and the killing-jars. Then his asthma
attacks took him out of school and she came to like
his awkward loneliness, because he followed where
she led – and knowing he was there gave her the
confidence to lead him further than she would
otherwise have gone, like the time she broke the ice
to swim in Prideau's Pool and dived in, daring him
to jump after her, feeling the bobbing ice knocking
terrifyingly against her ribs as she taunted him. And
so Francis jumped, for her, and learned to act for her
as though he were not afraid, because he adored her.

Laura had always known he was her friend, but
now in the church porch that was not quite what
they were. Francis held on to the lock of Laura's hair
for several seconds too long, and only then
relinquished it from his fingertips. His eyes met hers
for a moment. Then he winked, embarrassed.

The charabanc of scowling pageboys and
enchanted bridesmaids from Lynmouth Primary
School had arrived at last, and it was time for them
all to go inside. Francis placed Laura's hand in the
crook of his arm. 'One day this will be us,' he said,
leading her into the vaulted stillness, matter-of-factly

looking up the aisle. He opened the panelled door to one of the tall eighteenth-century box pews on the left and sat beside her. Everyone was coming now. Sir George, Francis' father and present lord of the manor of Watersmeet, put his hands on his knees and plumped down into the pew in front, thank God, so he would not be watching the backs of their necks all the time. Just once the bluff squire twisted in his seat and smiled at Laura in silent greeting.

Francis jealously watched her smile back. Everyone responded to Sir George's geniality, and it was obvious that Laura genuinely liked the tyrant. And Sir George liked her. Laura had plenty of personality, she could hold her own.

He glanced at Francis, then turned his back. The church echoed with the hollow clonks of the pew doors opening and closing, shuffling feet, whispers. Now he had got her to himself Francis covertly studied Laura's profile beneath her broad hat-brim, the delicate moist corners of her eyes, lips, the dark arch of her eyebrow – then the sudden shock of her gleaming blue-black gaze meeting his.

'I'm sorry,' he apologized, 'I was . . . miles away.'

She shook her head, not minding, studying the order of service in her lap.

Beneath the hem of her dress he could see her smoothly crossed calves, the seams up the back of her stockings, and imagined pressing his fingers against them. He could have got her better shoes than those. He felt passionately in love with her and longed to jog her shoulder to make her giggle.

Laura looked round as the thin violin music started – St Brendan's had no organ and the back of the nave where the musicians were rose like a theatre.

Clara would come in any moment now. By the three-decker pulpit the minister waited with his white surplice gleaming, his hands clasped in front of his groin. Near him Laura saw the tomb of Ranulph de Barreneau, the first lord of Exmoor, and his wife, the stone faces of their effigies lying side by side gouged by some act of medieval vandalism. The angle of the sarcophagus looked wrong against the bench-pews added at the front in the sixteenth century – when the Norman was laid to rest the serfs worshipped without seats, excepting the stone slab along the wall for the old and sick; the walls were painted dark red, the altar protected by a wooden screen to stop dogs cocking their legs on the holy vestments, and Laura realized how little she really knew about life. The weight pressed down on her and it seemed terribly wrong that Clara was getting married if she wasn't sure what she was doing.

'Weddings always make girls feel funny,' remarked Francis, looking down with a sly wink. Laura realized that everyone was standing and jumped to her feet. She could see those poor smashed faces clearly.

'Who was the woman?' she whispered.

Francis followed her eyes to the sarcophagus. 'Does it matter?' He didn't answer.

'Francis,' she insisted.

He shrugged and gave in as if it didn't matter to him. 'The Fox, she was called. Everyone knew them as the Wolf and the Fox. You know what the Barronets did to Exmoor.'

'But she – why was her face broken too?'

'Because she was beautiful.' Francis explained: 'He loved her.'

'But how could that be wrong?'

Francis explained as if to a child. 'By marrying him she betrayed her race. She was Anglo-Saxon. The princes and thanes of her own people lost all they had to the Normans, often their lives. But *her* parents were allowed to end their days in peace in Radworthy, and the traitress received Watersmeet entire in all its beauty as her wedding gift.'

Laura gazed at the battered outline of the wife still lying beside her stone husband after so many years, and her heart went out to them.

The church door slammed closed.

Laura whispered: 'What was her name?'

'Resda,' he murmured with a shrug. 'Just a farmer's daughter, the Torrs family. She was the first Mistress of Watersmeet.' He glanced lightly at Laura.

It was almost time for the ceremony to begin.

'Here comes Clara!' Laura whispered excitedly, and turned to watch.

Clara wheeled her stepfather ahead of her along the aisle. He was hunched in the wheelchair and holding his hands bent in his lap, all knuckles. What had passed between them while they waited? Laura knew his indomitable, introverted will, and for a moment saw Clara's guilt written on her face, the weight of her betrayal stamped on her rounded shoulders as she pushed him forward. Then the wheelchair seemed to pick up speed and she walked forward easily, in serene command of herself, not meekly as if it were he giving her away, more as if she were offering him up as a sacrifice. She really didn't like him. All those years of care, and poor Clara had failed to become a perfect woman through suffering. Now she was almost free of him and her mother at last. Hardly a trace of disappointment showed in her face as she took her place beside Rob.

Good luck, Clara, good luck! prayed Laura silently.

This was Clara's great day, but she would not play up to it, avoiding everyone's eyes. Laura became angry. This was not Clara's victory but her defeat.

Ernest turned his head up to kiss her and Clara bent from the hips to receive it on her veiled cheek. Then Sybil took him and retreated to the front row. The bass viol moaned and the service began. Clara stood with Rob's hand clenched in hers as if he were already her property.

So this was what it was to be a woman, Laura realized. There was no last-minute shout of *I won't!* – Clara did not fling down her bouquet and run alone from the church. Laura watched Rob slip the gold ring slowly on Clara's finger. The minister pronounced them husband and wife, and suddenly it was all over.

Clara had given up and given in. Mr and Mrs Rob Stall went to sign the register.

Laura pushed past Francis and ran outside. Watersmeet looked like an emerald cleft cut between the hills below her by a knife, the unshining sea rising beyond.

The wind had veered and this side of the church was quiet, the clouds seemed to sail out of the roof. Suddenly the sun burst out overhead, making the green graveyard, her green coat, brilliant. Laura pressed the back of her hand to her mouth. Francis put a concerned arm around her shoulder.

'I'm fine.' She leaned into him gratefully.

'Told you weddings make girls feel funny. Sure, now?' He didn't take his arm away until she nodded.

The other guests came out and milled around. Francis found her again. 'Have you got your confetti? Any moment . . . ' Ernest was smiling to see them together, and Laura blushed. For a moment she almost hated Francis for being so . . . *there*, so reliable, so possessive.

At last the happy couple appeared in the doorway. Standing apart from the crowd while the photographer did his job, Rob was bored and uncomfortable in his hired suit, but Clara, her veil thrown back, looked tall and pretty beside him. They started down the path towards Sir George's Humber motor car that would take them for their brief hour to the reception at Watersmeet Manor. Laura cheered and flung her confetti along with everybody else, which the wind swept away before it struck the happy couple. Clara looked back from the car door. Who would she throw her bouquet to? Who would be next to be married? She smiled at Laura smugly, almost victoriously, and threw the bouquet unerringly.

'She did it deliberately.' Laura couldn't bring herself to enjoy the taxi ride back to Watersmeet Manor; the walls of the valley rose around them and she felt stifled and depressed and wished she wasn't with Francis. He sat with his legs crossed looking out of the window as though she were not there.

'Why does everyone hate me?' Laura demanded.

Francis laughed. He was very clever and he thought he knew Laura well. 'You did catch it deliberately,' he pointed out. The arcane ways of the fair sex obviously amused him.

Laura's cheeks were still bright red and she could

have killed him. It had been Bart's gift to Clara, she couldn't explain.

'She meant well, didn't she?' Francis turned from the window and again she wondered if he would kiss her on the lips, but apparently no such thought had crossed his mind. She wished he would. She was much too young. It would have been fun. The taxi stopped at the turning down to the bridge and Francis got out. She watched him pay off the driver from a handful of loose cash, carefully selecting the coins for the exact fare plus an exact tip, then he opened Laura's door and helped her down. He made her into a lady. He walked a little ahead of her going down to the clapper bridge, then a little behind her crossing it, but he didn't hold her hand again although she gave him the chance. Touched by his attentiveness, she let him open the white gate and together they entered the grounds of Watersmeet Manor. So many people there transformed it.

By the rosewood Bechstein grand piano Sir George was holding court in the Long Room, the lounge designed by Frank Lloyd Wright, not Lutyens, forming the modern wing of the house with its huge windows. Sir George was drinking port, the gentleman's drink, leaning into his stick and grunting while the mayor of Lynmouth prattled. Then his watery oyster-blue eyes saw Laura and Sir George came to life, put his arm around her shoulder, claiming her from Francis. 'Happy birthday!' He raised his stick, and she felt him draw a deep breath. 'It's Laura's birthday, everyone!' All heads turned and Laura's eyes shone to be the centre of attention. 'Sweet seventeen today. Got the key of the door, never been kissed before.' He kissed her roundly and

Laura tasted port on her lips. 'I kissed the bride too, that's both girls in one day. Have a drink.' Champagne. Laura was swept through introductions to no one she knew. Francis was watching from the fireplace. Laura sipped and her head swam. Sir George dragged her over to Ernest. 'Did he give you the watch?' he stage-whispered to Laura on the way over. 'Hope it was all right, chose it myself.'

'It's lovely.'

'Guaranteed for twelve months.' He drew another breath. 'Ernest,' he boomed, 'stop drinking all my malt, I've appropriated your smashing daughter.'

Ernest looked up, impressed by Sir George Pervane's show, the confident wealth that could afford such generosity, and worried how he could possibly repay him. Most of the people here he had never met, their faces overwhelmed him, half the gentry of North Devon was here amongst the square arty lampshades and easy chairs: the Fulfords who like the Pervanes could claim a thousand years of uninterrupted descent through the male line, the Luttrells who could only claim six hundred, the Aclands, even the Baroness Le Clement de Taintegnies, once a famous beauty, now so old she was almost transparent. Sir George *wanted* him to be impressed. Ernest was baffled. Sir George had never been promoted higher than captain in the Regular Army, of course.

'But I need her,' Ernest said without thinking.

The Regular Army was always a special bond. Sir George had been wounded on the Somme, his fierce red face with its network of ruptured blood vessels not the symptom of high blood pressure it appeared to be, but rather a lingering effect of chlorine gas.

Now he called his business activities his retirement, as if they were easy or not important, but he drove his shining black Humber into Lynmouth or Barum nearly every day, and the Manor estate didn't run itself. He often said that nothing meant more to him than being elected Master of the North Devon Staghounds – a position hereditary until recently – which put him next to God in the eyes of most local people.

'I proposed to her but she turned me down.' He tickled Laura's ribs slyly. 'Said I was too old.'

Laura knew him much better than her father did. Uncle George was first and foremost a businessman. A private man since his wife passed away, a gentle man driven half to distraction by his son's asthma attacks that nothing seemed to help. He had been very kind to young Laura when her parents' marriage went through the sticky patch, which was why this room and the new part of the house were still so familiar to her. He meant no harm and she could handle him – she genuinely liked him, and knew he liked her. She had faith in Sir George; but she didn't trust him.

Ernest was desperate to talk shop. 'Well, Master, there's not much doubt Adolf's done it this time.'

Laura made a face and drifted away, bored. The wedding cake had three sparkling-white tiers topped with a toy man and woman holding hands. Clara and Rob were the centre of attraction in the middle of the room. Laura turned the other way. The Watersmeet Falls Hotel had done the catering of course: Lynmouth smoked salmon and roast Devon beef, pasties and pastries, sweet sugary confections and André the chef's own chocolate-coated Swiss cherries, far more than they could possibly get through but a fitting feast for the eyes in the Switzerland of England. Along the table rows of glasses sparkled in the sun pouring through the picture windows that slid open for guests to amble through on to the immaculate lawns to admire the valley views. Laura went outside past the two-hundred-years-old camellia known as the Spanish Camellia because it was reputedly a cutting brought back by some long-forgotten member of the family during the Spanish war. She crossed the formal garden and stood on the riverbank by the swirling junction of the waters.

It was said that there had been a summerhouse here once; now the sequoia planted in its place by Roderick, Sir George's father, rustled its leaves softly above her in the breeze. Laura noticed that already the Lyn river was running clear again after the rains, but the waterfalls roaring down the Hoaroak from the high moor would not start dwindling for some time yet. Francis fetched her more champagne from one of the little black-frocked waitresses. He didn't drink himself.

She tried to strike a spark from him. 'Francis, you are trying to get me tipsy!' She span the glass by its stem.

'Don't be silly.' He sipped his tumbler of lemonade.

'Don't be so serious,' she taunted him, wanting him to play up to her. The champagne made her head buzz pleasantly.

He rose to the bait in the wrong way, with words. 'I do take you seriously, Laura,' he said earnestly. Did he? How could she tell? He was still looking into his lemonade. 'We are still friends, aren't we?'

She sighed impatiently.

'It's not me, it's you,' he said. 'I can't get you out of my mind.' That was better. 'At the church you looked so lovely standing there.' He twisted his toecap in the turf. 'You make my heart beat faster.' Laura could not hide her smile.

'Thank you, Francis, that's such a sweet thing to say.'

'Is it? As soon as we got here you left me alone! You just left me, Laura.'

They walked towards the orangery built by his grandfather over the old cellars that by legend lay beneath.

'What did you want me to do?' She waited until Francis shrugged, and when he did, she felt her power. She could manipulate him. 'Your father—'

But then her interrupted her. 'You shouldn't have let him take you in,' he burst out. 'You played up to him.'

Laura flushed.

'He was almost too drunk to stand.' Now she understood what was in his voice: disgust. And perhaps a trace of fear. Laura laughed. 'And you were laughing and chirping away,' he accused her. 'Encouraging him,' he added jealously, going too far.

Laura searched for something to say that would hurt Francis Pervane.

She held out her glass by the stem. 'Have a drink.' She didn't lower the glass. She meant it. Suddenly he laughed, took it and tossed the liquid down in one, and she realized how desirable jealousy could be. He glanced at her with something angry in his eyes, really very attractive now. She honestly thought he would reach out and grab her arms, and a hot shiver ran up her spine.

But he didn't. He turned away with the back of his hand to his mouth.

'I'm sorry,' he said, waiting.

She was damned if she was sorry. She stood with her body rigid, wanting him to feel how furious she was. Still he didn't take her in his arms like a real man – they were behind the orangery, no one would see, or care if they did. It was none of their business anyway.

'What's the matter? Francis said at last.

'Nothing.' Laura wanted to cry. He didn't know her at all.

Francis pointed at the house. 'You will not be Mistress of Watersmeet,' he explained, 'while *he* is still Master.' He took her completely for granted.

'I never will be at all – I don't care about . . . you!' Laura flamed, and stormed back towards the house. He didn't run after her. Laura stopped. She didn't want to go back home yet.

Francis looked after her without heat, sure of his victory. 'Lauraaa . . . ' he called, 'come on, what's the matter?' He laughed, shaking his head.

The lights were coming on in the house. She ran inside.

Uncle George was now holding court from an armchair. Smiling, he waved the people around him aside and Laura saw her father.

'Clara is departing shortly.' Ernest told her, 'and then we'll go home.' He looked tired from his unaccustomed socializing and was probably afraid of outstaying his welcome.

Laura went back into the garden to have a go at

Francis again but he was nowhere to be seen. She walked past the tree, then down the river, then back again. She didn't feel anything for him. He was so insipid.

'I couldn't find you,' Francis said smoothly behind her. 'They're just going, you know.'

'I'm surprised you could be bothered to look for me!'

'I'm sorry,' he repeated. 'Peace?'

She looked at him with contempt, knowing he had given in.

'Love you!' he laughed.

They joined the group by the drive. The black Humber was almost lost in the dusk. They watched the vee of white ribbons over the bonnet rise through the dark trees to the county road, then turn down towards Lynmouth and a new life.

'We must get home before it's too dark,' came Ernest's voice.

Francis hadn't taken his eyes off Laura all the time. When he kissed her cheek goodnight, Laura turned her head so that his lips met hers.

Paradise House was absolutely quiet and dark. Laura stood on the stairs. She was frightened. No sounding raindrops like last night, no wind to cover the whispering voices of two girls excitedly exchanging secrets on the stairs. Silence, absolutely black: and she felt how lonely she was going to be now that Clara was gone.

She could see nothing ahead of her. She was on the chain gang, her life mapped out for her. She moved, and the stair squeaked under her foot. She backed a step and sat down suddenly. Clara's place.

Laura sat there on the stairs alone.

She could see herself sitting in the dark, feet drawn up inside her green dress, propping up her elbows on her knees with her chin in her hands and her fingers bunched like fists over her high cheekbones, so that their tips rested in the corners of her eyes.

When she had carried her father upstairs without her mother's help – Sybil had one of her migraines, exhausted by Sir George's bonhomie – Laura had not found Ernest's weight quite such a strain as yesterday. She'd got the knack of keeping her back straight as she lifted, climbing the stairs with a steady rhythm, his hip bumping against her tummy-button, getting her balance just right to let him down into his wheelchair.

'Have you locked the front door?' he demanded.

'I won't forget,' she promised, wheeling him down to his room, a thing he could have done himself, and kissed him goodnight. But she did forget.

She said goodnight again, and closed their door behind her: her parents' bedroom, where she had been conceived, presumably. Laura roamed the house unhappily. The nursery seemed so small now, dry of magic: all her imaginary friends had gone. It was a room made to contain another person, not her. But of course she had been just a baby.

Clara's silent square room: in the middle of the floor was piled *all that rubbish*, the stories, camphor mothballs, a pencil-case, discarded underwear thoughtfully left to be made into rags, the precious copy of *Vogue*, a few wires dangling from the earplug of the cat's-whisker radio that never worked because of the hills. And that was that, a room without Clara: the dry shucked-off skin of a departed life.

Still she hadn't locked the front door. All she had to do was turn the key, locking herself in, and go to bed, go to sleep. Yet her sweetness to Francis cloyed in her own mouth. And in the garden she had behaved awfully to him. If only Francis had been ten years older it would have been him standing beside Clara at the altar today. To be Lady Pervane, Mistress of Watersmeet by long tradition, with a fine manor house in a setting, as Wordsworth described it *Made by nature for herself*, would have been Clara's every dream come true. Instead she was Mrs Rob Stall of the Park Estate, Barum, with a wicker shopping trolley and a nice house with a print of *The Hay Wain* over the mantleshelf.

But for Laura, one day, the dream would come true. She must be mad to be unhappy. Then Laura realized the truth. Her hands dropped limply into her lap. She was in love.

It was so obvious. The way she'd deliberately picked that row with Francis, forcing him to react to her. And he had! He had even said the words. *Love you!*

Probably she was the last to know. Laura felt her cheeks burn. Even Clara had known – she had thrown the bouquet directly at Laura – *everyone* knew! And certainly Francis loved her, she remembered how cold his poor fingers were from waiting for her outside the church. His solicitousness, his jealousy of his father – wanting to keep her all for himself!

Laura felt her eyes dampen. '*Oh, Francis,*' she whispered.

Uncle George approved for three reasons. First, he liked Laura, not only for herself but because, in his arrogance, he thought she would be good for Francis.

The second reason was the alliance: if the old trouble flared up again he wanted the Bensons on his side – though they had lost so much of their influence when Montague Benson died, they still owned Paradise Woods, part of which abutted Hellebore property. The Colonel could still be useful; worth half a bottle of malt whisky, a few plates of beluga and admission to Watersmeet Manor for the sly ghost of the wedding reception yet to be.

Finally, and most important, when Francis married Laura it meant the Benson land would eventually fall secure in Pervane hands. Now Laura understood Francis' angry oath: *You will not be Mistress of Watersmeet while* he *is still Master*.

The parlour clock gently gonged midnight. She *could* hear the river, its soft chuckle running down to Watersmeet, and by looking slightly askance from the front door could just make out the dark blue outline of the glass fanlight above it.

She stretched her feet over the stair below her and stood, walked slowly down the hall. The musty air whispered past her. Her footsteps quickened and she approached the door, already reaching out her hand. She tugged the heavy brass knob, the door yawned open on the night. Here in the open the river's roar washed around her, hissing off the building behind her, and she could see the silent starry sky winding above the valley, a pale sky-river beginning to glow with the unrisen moon. Her feet pattered down the steps; by the time she reached the stable, she was running.

Blackbird munched her hay tolerantly as Laura heaved the saddle on to her back and only held her teeth shut in protest against the bit for a moment, then resumed her chewing. Her black coat gleamed under the overhead bulb – the Lyn river's hydro-electric turbine never shut down. Laura pulled her dress over her head and donned the jodhpurs off the rail. She shrugged a riding jacket on over her shirt this time, then swung smoothly up into the saddle. Flicking the whip off its nail, she ducked through the doorway and kicked on down the grass path towards Watersmeet. Blackbird sensed her mood, as always. The dark tree trunks whipped by, the deepening valley rose around her, and suddenly the moon broke through down the Hoaroak Cleave, dousing her with stark pale light. She reined in. The two valleys joined below, the windows of Watersmeet Manor glittered cold and blue where Francis slept. Did he imagine her in his dreams? Laura was quite certain of that. Did he toss and turn uneasily at this very moment, sensing her looking down from the path? She rode on. The joined river rushed black and silver on her left as the Manor fell behind her, then Myrtleberry Cleave soared above her like a huge serving of blue ice cream. The river foamed amongst giant boulders, the path wound back and forth, sometimes down to the torrent, sometimes high above, screened by the ultramarine hanging woods. Then at last she rounded a corner and saw the sea shimmering below her as the valley fell away.

She let Blackbird pick her way down towards the little yellow lights of the village. The view of the harbour at low tide looked spectacular in the moonlight below the row of gloomy houses. It was easy to pick out the steep roof of the Watersmeet Falls Hotel, the biggest building in Lynmouth, placed right at its heart next to the little church. The lights on the patio were going out. She stopped on the dusty trail of the Tors Road, staring across the water. She might have heard a few bars of the Palm Court orchestra's last melody, but the river's rush drowned it, and then the lights were going out there too. No one else was about. The fishing boats would be out early. Laura watched, shivering. She knew which room was Clara's. The Bridal Suite was on the third floor. The light came on, then a figure crossed the room – just a glimpse. Clara. she was wearing something pale, and Laura thought: *The nightdress, the famous shop-bought filigree nightdress.*

Laura was spellbound. She could not break away even though she knew she was doing wrong. It wasn't Rob and Clara up there. It was she and Francis in the light, his embrace enclosing Laura, his lips pressed to hers. She would have thrown the window open to hear the roar of the river . . .

Clara reappeared. She reached up her arms and drew the curtains closed, and the light went out, hiding a secret in the dark.

Laura could hear Clara's voice as clearly as though she was speaking now.

You just give in. Give up, that's all you have to do.

I won't! Laura thought. And it wasn't Francis' face she imagined in the dark. It was Bart Barronet's.

PART TWO

Temptation

In January Laura dug over the kitchen garden, planted rhubarb under glass, and sprayed the fruit trees with her hair tied up under a cloth to keep out the tar-oil wash. Life went on as before; it always did in Watersmeet. The weather wasn't on Laura's side, one night the temperature fell to forty below zero above the valley and on the twenty-sixth 'ice-ships' rolled and bumped down the tossing meltwater river, carrying away part of the nineteenth-century approach road to the prehistoric clapper bridge. Though the massive central slabs of the bridge itself stood firm as they had for the last two or four thousand years, the middle section of the Tarr Steps, the equally ancient crossing near Dulverton, had been torn away. Not until the very end of the month did the ground thaw enough for her to get a spade into it, and the onions sown in the greenhouse. The damson trees would survive anything, but she hardly dared peep under the tarpaulins to see if the lemon trees had made it through.

In February she sowed broad beans and parsnips whether she liked them or not, and defiantly planted roses. Then in March, suddenly as warm as summer, Laura planted potatoes, the early Ulster Sceptres, got the herbs going, mint, thyme, and sowed the peas as soon as she dared. She sowed them in April, May and June as well, but they'd all arrive at the same time. They were going to eat nothing but peas again, she could see it coming. Suppose children were evacuated to them from London? On the first day of the war the villages had been inundated with dirty-faced Cockney brats crawling with vermin, but they hated the country and couldn't wait to get home. To Laura's disappointment and Sybil's relief none got as far as Watersmeet, but Sybil did her bit for the war by ordering velvet swish curtains from Barum for the blackout, and in the evening they knitted mufflers for the Navy.

There was talk of organizing the local women into a Wild Herbs Committee to collect natural herbs and plants in the season to help the war effort, sphagnum moss for wound dressings, foxglove for digitalis heart medicine, horse chestnuts for animal feedstuffs and fire extinguishers; dandelion, hellebore, deadly nightshade, nettle leaves, rosehips, all would have their uses.

Someone bright-eyed from the Ministry found Paradise House and counted their chickens, checked they hadn't hidden any, made a note of Gladys the cow, the nanny-goat, how many wheelbarrows they had available to carry emergency casualties, the number of buckets of sand for firefighting, told Ernest he would have to obtain a vehicle licence for his trap, and why was Laura not carrying her gas mask with her as required by law? He gave the impression that if her father hadn't been crippled Laura would have been drafted into the Land Army.

When he went away Watersmeet felt more remote than ever – according to the postman there were barbed wire and tank traps on Lynmouth beach.

Petty regulations fenced them in, and the war was just the radio overheard across the hall while Laura Ewbanked the parlour carpet. Denmark, Norway, Holland, Belgium, even France. She beeswaxed the parquet flooring, she dusted furiously at the tables and shelves – the open wood fires created a ferocious amount of dust, and when the beechwood was exhausted they had to rely on fallen sessile oak cut up by estate workers loaned by Uncle George now that Watersmeet Manor was officially a farm, owning the grazing and arable land over towards Higher Lyn. But the tough oakwood burned like a brick, casting no cheerful flame even when she could get it to light.

She thought of him constantly.

In the evenings Sybil read Rupert Brooke's poems aloud. Clara had adored his work. Apart from a Christmas card and a copy of the *Park School News* they heard nothing from Clara, no cheerful visit back to see how they were doing, not even a letter, but Laura wondered if some corner of her heart would be forever Watersmeet. Could that actually be the reason Clara stayed away? Laura could understand that decision. Sybil went and saw her house in Barum when she bought the curtains, but Clara was out.

That same day Laura rode across the river again and climbed into the hanging woods on the far side. The tall iron-spike boundary gate was closed. She stared through the bars. She hadn't seen him again, not once. She was sure he wouldn't go away. He loved this place. He wouldn't leave.

Watersmeet budded, bloomed and blossomed as usual. The tangled winter-dark slopes, rimmed with the black bars of tree trunks showing the sky behind them, showed first a pale green haze. Then the heavy leaves unfolded luxuriantly, coming forward, closing in on the valley, trapping the summery heat. The lemon trees showed tiny lemons.

And she found a trammel-net lying on a rock by the pool where she had gone to bathe. The footprint beside it was still wet. Next morning, the net was gone.

A man she had never even met . . . she hoed the fine earth between the lettuces with the flies buzzing around her head. The flies she didn't mind; the horseflies that jabbed at her unmercifully she flicked with finger and thumb so that her nail broke their hard bodies. The dust settled in the corners of her eyes and made her look as if she had been weeping. Everyone thought she was in love with Francis. She was. If only that was all. She imagined Bart Barronet, the wild countryman fallen from grace, last descendant of the Wolf and the Fox. She couldn't get him out of her mind. It was just daydreams. When she turned out her light, last thing, she whispered goodnight to him, knowing he was somewhere out there.

The glorious spring turned into a glorious summer, though the Western National holiday coach tours across Exmoor had been cancelled since Whitsun because of the French situation and Lynmouth was said to be quieter than for a hundred and fifty years, with only evacuated families and a few officers and their wives staying in the Watersmeet Falls Hotel. Laura saw no one on her weekly rides along the deserted paths, riding alone in the dappled sunlight, wearing proper riding clothes and a hard black hat as she had promised. At first she slipped the hat in the saddlebag and shook out her hair as soon as she was away from the house but now she no longer minded. Francis confessed he liked her much better properly turned out.

'It's the way I always imagined you,' he told her admiringly.

He had stepped out from behind a tree, making Blackbird shy back.

She snapped: 'Francis – for God's sake! You nearly had me off!'

He could never predict her moods. 'Come in for tea.' He held out his arm, and she couldn't resist his invitation.

Francis, dressed in dark grey flannels and a blazer, had matured. The nervous laugh had gone and he had acquired the stillness of confidence. He helped her down with a steady grip, and met her eyes as she stood in front of him. She trusted him – it was very simple between them now, almost a routine. And he had lost none of the possessiveness that had always made him so attractive.

He took her hand and they walked together across the smooth shaved grass of the formal gardens that Sir George refused to dig up to potatoes.

'How is he now?' she asked, taking off the hat, shaking out her hair for Francis to notice, but he didn't. He wanted her to cut it short. Laura deliberately let it grow.

'Papa? Up and about again.' Sir George had taken a nasty fall off horseback in the Molland coverts while hunting – the North Devon Staghounds had been disbanded during the first war and he didn't intend to let that level of crop damage recur, or the trapping, poisoning and poaching of such fine animals as his wild red Exmoor deer. 'He's mustering the Local Defence Volunteers parade at the church hall. As vigorous as ever, but of course I handle the farm management now he's got his hands full knocking the Home Guard into shape. Everyone comes in after work, he's even got some uniforms for them. You know how he enjoys that sort of thing, they call him Major and salute. Sit down, I'll be back with the tea.'

She ignored the white wrought-iron chairs and sat in the long grass at the water's edge. Blackbird drank, then grazed nearby. Laura almost dozed, peeled off the tight black riding shoes and white socks, dabbled her toes in the water. The broad, shallow Lyn was surprisingly warm in the sun. She lay back and turned up her face. A peacock uttered its grating cry.

Francis returned. His heart softened, how lovely she was: her pale face, white blouse secured by a silver clasp at her throat, tight black jacket, flowing black skirt, her pale feet speckled with shining drops of water. Her eyes opened slowly. She might look like this after they had just made love.

'Francis?' she said, shading her eyes against the sun. 'How I hate those birds.'

'Peacocks are traditional at Watersmeet Manor,' he said comfortably. He went to the table and put down the tray with its silver pot and fine white cups and saucers. 'Sorry it took so long, the daily's gone, I had to make it myself.'

'How terrible for you.' He missed her joke. She joined him and poured the tea, handed him his cup with her work-reddened fingers.

'Oh, I see!' he laughed.

Instead of sitting opposite him at the table as usual she crouched by the flowing water and swished her hands in its surface, then pressed her cool palms to her cheeks.

'What is it?' he called at last.

'Do you talk to me, Francis? Do you really tell me everything?'

He didn't hesitate. 'Everything there is.'

She looked over her shoulder. 'Yes, I know,' she sighed.

'Come to me. What is it?' he asked gently.

'Sometimes – sometimes I think I'm going to suffocate.' The trouble was, she didn't, not now he was holding her in his arms. She felt content with Francis. She could speak to him lightly and openly about this and that but she couldn't explain her feelings to him. 'Sometimes it feels as though the valley is closing in around me. Don't you ever feel that, Francis?' His expression didn't change. 'Am I talking too much?'

He didn't understand her appeal. 'I love it when you talk to me.'

She pressed her lips together at his obtuseness, then had to laugh.

Francis wanted to clasp her tight against him, stopping her talk. When they talked he could feel his hold on her slipping. So he kissed her.

'Nothing else matters to me, except you and me,' Francis murmured seriously. 'Your happiness, Laura, simply your happiness.'

Francis was almost perfect. She liked him a lot. But how could she explain to a man that she didn't want to be *contented* – which was what he was talking about. Francis was much too nice. Yet what more could she ask for? When he kissed her, she believed him.

Laura was waiting for something to happen.

She deliberately avoided going near Hellebore Cleave. But what a summer it was. August was so dry that the rainwater tanks were almost empty, only Ernest bathed in the house. Sybil and Laura strip-washed in the kitchen, at different times, or used the makeshift shower set up in the steepest part of the goyle, but the tip-cistern contained only a couple of gallons in a single icy douche. Laura had continued to grow her hair and when she wanted to wash it properly she wore a bathing costume under her clothes, took Blackbird, and went to swim in one of her secret pools in the steep Dumbledon section downstream from Prideau's, near the lime kilns.

Sybil did not see her go. She thought Laura was in the muniment room by the old nursery in the roof, totalling the household accounts, another job which Sybil preferred to inspect rather than do herself. Laura saw her father sitting out on the front lawn, his fly-fishing rod whipping in his expert hands, practising casting at his beret lying on the grass thirty paces away. The old devil hit it every time.

Laura took Blackbird round behind the stables, rode up the path a short way, then slid down between the tangled oaks to the river. She took off her hat, unpinning her hair as Blackbird splashed between the boulders. She tethered the horse to a tree by a rocky pool with a waterfall pattering into it, looked around her, then took off her riding clothes. Beneath them she wore her mother's very chaste Edwardian swimming costume with the plum stripes redeemed by lacy frills around the elbows and knees. She left her shampoo bottle on the usual flat rock and dived beneath the waterfall, where the water was deepest. Sometimes as children she and Francis were taken to the tidal swimming pool on Lynmouth beach. Here in the gorge with its boulders and overhanging trees she could scarcely see the sky. She shampooed her hair sitting on a rock in the leafy shade, slipped back into the water and swam under the waterfall, letting the tumbling drops clout down on top of her head, then kicked out underwater into the middle of the pool again, and surfaced in the sunlight.

He was standing on the flat rock, his shadow rippling across the water.

'I knew you were there!' she laughed, swinging her hair out of her eyes, then saw there was no one there now, only Blackbird peacefully cropping the grass by the pebble beach, head down.

Yet Laura knew she was witnessed from the trees. She felt it. She could *feel* his examination, her intuition was like a weight pressing lightly on her eyes. But Blackbird would have warned her of any sudden danger. Yet Laura was in some kind of danger; she could feel it. She wasn't afraid. She was excited. It was Bart.

She remembered how silently the woodsman had come up the drive, without stepping on any twigs or fallen leaves. She shaded her eyes against the flickering ribbon of the sky. She couldn't see him, but she sensed him. 'What are you frightened of?' she shouted.

Then she knew. Her. *Because you are beautiful, Laura.* She remembered the envy and spite in Clara's warning, and smiled to herself as she circled flirtatiously in the water, gazing up. The echoes of her challenge died away between the cliffs, but no voice responded and she felt his presence depart.

She got out and squeezed the water petulantly from her hair. He had ignored her, rejected her. Francis never did, he was pleasant, she had only to snap her fingers and he was there. Laura dressed behind a rock and swung on to Blackbird. It was time Bart Barronet was faced. She would provoke him, force him to pay attention to her. She would go to Hellebore House.

Her heart was in her mouth as Blackbird splashed across the river and she rode up amongst the trees, but she didn't see him. Then she reached the path and rode much faster than a man could run, panting with excitement as she opened the spiked boundary gate, but there was no sign of him. She pressed her hands against her ribs, sliding them down the black riding jacket to control her breathing, then cantered Blackbird forward up the steep track high above Watersmeet. The sun struck hot across her face and drying hair as she came to the top of the bluff, and she paused between the crumbling gateposts with the echoing drop to Lucy's Pool safely behind her.

In the year that had passed since Laura came by here, the fallen gates had almost disappeared beneath the tangle of dashels and weeds, the iron rusting into the soil, and Blackbird's hoof rang on metal only once as she entered the domain.

Laura rode slowly over the red, overgrown dust

of the drive. The angle steepened deceptively beneath the canopy of leaves so that she could not see what lay ahead, but almost at once she heard the clip-clop sound of horse hooves coming back at her. She reined in and they stopped.

Laura slipped down from the saddle and led Blackbird forward on the rein. She glimpsed a wall ahead of her now, local red sandstone, and the echoes clipped and clopped all around her. She was nearing the house. So at least some of the stories about the Barronets were true. Laura stood on the overgrown grass and stared. Then she clapped her hands.

A flight of steps climbed without railings to an entrance on the first storey, like a ziggurat. The ground floor must be servants' quarters, kitchens, sculleries. Perhaps the dwelling had once been part of a monastery – she saw the pillars of a dwarf gallery that might once have been a cloister. But the rest of it baffled her with its shabby Englishness, its mixture of natural styles growing out of one another, on top of one another in the course of time, as though stone were organic. At first it seemed that nothing had been knocked down, nothing taken away, only added to – enormous mullioned windows with leaded lights the Tudors loved, ivy-covered walls, striped Jacobean redbrick chimneys without smoke, the ornamentation almost weathered away. At the north corner of the house she saw a grey turret in the Gothic style like a romantic Victorian folly, but beneath it a section of wall obviously much older that seemed to have been preserved for the window cut in it. Laura remembered the same style from St Brendan's church: it was called plate tracery, and it dated from the twelfth century.

The sunlight penetrating the drive streamed around Laura and bathed the house in warm, friendly light. The latticed windows shone pale yellow in reflection of the western sky behind her, but broken glass glittered and flashed from the transoms, and many openings were dark. Parts of the roof were missing, weaving ragged lines of joists against the sky behind them. It was delightful, and mysterious.

Laura fell in love with Hellebore House, but did not always think of it by that frightening name. She often thought of it as the House of Ruins.

To her it looked more like a talisman than a house, nothing thrown away, only added to. The bartizan turret projecting from the south-western corner seemed to have been imitated by the Pervanes on the old part of Watersmeet Manor, just as Sybil's solarium was in imitation of Sir George's orangery. There was no such modern addition here. This house had been in decline for a very long time.

Blackbird grazed over towards the stables, built and rebuilt in the style of a Devon longhouse. Laura stood in the centre of the carriage circle. Her hair was dry and she ought to comb it out. She had travelled far faster than a man on foot could hope to do, and she told herself she had plenty of time to have a nose round. She pretended that she would get away long before Bart could arrive, but part of her wanted to be caught.

Confidently combing out her hair, kicking the hem of her long riding skirt before her, she strode up the steps. The door was not locked and she slipped inside.

The big entrance hall was uncared for and dark, illuminated by only the harsh rectangle of light from the door. No vases of flowers or a place for people to put their boots, not even a few rugs scattered over the bare boards. She longed for a broom and bucket brimming with suds to set it to rights. The panelling was black with grime, the imposing wooden staircase dulled and dusty. Above the panelling the walls were mouldy, the bas-relief flaking. The ceiling frescoes were receding indecipherably into the soggy plaster from which their classical themes once shone, cherubs melting into clouds of mould, proud prancing horses showing the bare lath behind their eyes.

How sad, how pointless, how masculine all this was – she sensed his terrible loneliness, the weight of time. The House of Ruins had lost its battle, like the Barronet family. But somehow it couldn't quite give up.

The sunlight extending now across the floor and partly up one wall caught the cracked glaze of a painting. Laura went over. She saw a girl a little older than herself, with valley flowers wound in her hair in the Pre-Raphaelite style, wearing a shiny blue dress, very long, with puffed-out shoulders and three flounces. She was beautiful, with laughing modern blue eyes that looked straight into your own, and she was offering flowers like a supplication from her arms. The detail was absolutely phenomenal: every green stalk perfectly twined, life in each tiny translucent petal. There was no signature but the work showed such an intensity of feeling – one look at those eyes and you *knew* she was in love – and you sensed her

personality in the strong, determined line of her
eyebrows. Behind her was a cloudscape, then rich
purple moorland and the distinctive Y outline of the
Watersmeet valley falling away behind her – and
not one thing in that natural landscape so familiar
to Laura had changed.

She felt that she was witnessing someone still
alive. But the picture was too tall, too narrow. It
seemed odd that such a skilled artist had got the
proportions so wrong. The strangest detail of all was
in the lower corner, a little dog standing faithfully
by the girl's foot in the convention of the time. The
dog was headless. Only its painted hindquarters
stuck into the picture, complete with an obviously
wagging tail. Perhaps its head was hidden beneath
the gilt frame?

Laura recoiled. Now she saw that it was really a
sad picture, emanating an unspoken tragedy: Laura
stared at the enigmatic smile of those delicate lips,
and wondered what a story they might have told.
She was desperate to know who the girl was.

Beneath the varnish at the bottom of the picture
the artist had cunningly woven the girl's name in
flowers. Laura peered, sweeping off the patina of
dust with her fingertips. Simply a first name: LUCY.

Laura looked round. She knew she must go; but
that doorway was too tempting. She opened the
solid mahogany door, and gasped with wonder. This
high, bright room was a treasure trove. The panelled
walls were simply covered with paintings, more
were stored higgledy-piggledy over the tables, a tall
wooden statue of a Spanish grandee complete with
a pointy beard stood by the fireplace. She saw bits
of armour, a steel glove, a complete chaos of odds

and ends from farm implements through children's toys to duelling pistols, books, books everywhere, and through the half-open door on the far side yet another room where silver salvers, punchbowls, chalices, piled high, glinted through cobwebs.

Laura wandered to the window entranced. The huge Elizabethan windows held an astonishing view over the treetops down to Watersmeet, now filling with shadow; she saw Bart Barronet crossing the carriage circle. The outer door was slammed with finality. Had it been real blood she saw on his arms that day? She didn't try to run. She was sure of it. There was nothing fake here, not one single thing.

He stood in the doorway and they stared at one another. Then he said one word: her name. He knew her name.

Laura lost her nerve, turned weakly away from him. She was letting herself down and she knew it. She wanted to tell him that she'd found the door open, that she was sorry, that she wanted to go, but none of it was true and she couldn't lie to him. God, she could even see part of Watersmeet Manor from up here, like a toy house, the lights shining like tiny yellow glow-worms by the gates. Five hundred feet above the purple shadows of the valley that curved round it on three sides, the site of the iron-age fort over the Myrtleberry Hangings stuck up like a shaved head into the last of the sunlight. But for that enormous obstacle she saw to Lynmouth and the sea.

He spoke softly.

'It is a truth universally acknowledged, that a single man in possession of a good fortune, must be in want of a wife.' Jane Austen's words, but not her witty observation, he turned them on their head with contempt. Laura's face burned, she knew the truth when it bit her. He knew she had Francis in her sights.

She fiddled with the whip that hung on its thong from her wrist. 'I love him.'

She turned on him furiously when he laughed.

What was it she saw in Bart Barronet's face?

He stood watching her, motionless as a tree, a little over six foot tall, but broad in proportion. Such solidity. She could have pressed her hands against his chest, knowing how he would feel against her palms, like a warm stone, out in the sun all day. In repose his face was powerful, strong-featured, his complexion dark from the sun, or perhaps that was his Spanish blood – she was sure he had foreign blood. There was so much passion about him . . . if he had moved his little finger she would have jumped. His eyes really were as tawny as a cat's, he would see through the dark. She saw herself in them.

'You don't know me at all,' she said.

He looked at her with a smile, and she could have bitten her lips. He crossed to the fireplace, laid his hand on the back of the armchair and poked sparks from the embers. He burned a fire to keep out the damp. For her the tension of not saying anything became unbearable, and Laura started a dozen conversations in her head. He prowled to the window and stared out.

'As you see, I am already possessed,' Bart said gently, 'Laura.' But not by her. He looked out over the valley. Behind him Laura turned like a weathercock between the fire and the door: to stay, or go. She felt overwhelmed and scared; she wanted to think him out. Who was there in his life? She wanted to know everything about him. The woman who lived eternally young in the painting, Lucy – she would have been too old to be his mother, but she could have been his grandmother perhaps, and sometimes the very young and the very old were closest. Men never escaped women.

Laura came and stood beside Bart, staring over the panorama with him, and began to understand. His life, his love, was *his* valley, *his* house, his masculine conceit that *he* held his destiny in his own hands. His determination to be the last.

He ignored her. Laura's beauty, her femininity were nothing to him. She could have worn the most expensive perfumes, the most costly jewellery and still not touched him. Only the beauty of the natural world out there mattered to him: Watersmeet.

'Once everything was ours,' he said. 'Ours as far as the eye could see.'

The rage in his voice was like a slap in the face for her. He looked at her, through her. Laura had seen that look before, through the solarium glass, when he delivered Clara's bouquet but had really come to see Laura. She was getting his measure now. She knew that he was as aware of her standing beside him as she was of him; the attractive earthy scent of his sweat, the dampness of it still in his hair, darkening the Viking blond to brown, streaked with paler gleams where he had swept it back. The straight black eyebrows. Like Lucy's.

Laura was almost in agony. If only he would touch her, then she would know where she was. She turned her face up to him.

He was too honest. He didn't patronize her, compliment her, treat her ladylike, and he should have done all those things, if he really wanted to drive her away. He took her as his equal, and that was his mistake. He tried to ignore the fact that she wore skirts, the long black riding skirt tight at the waist that flowed almost to the floor, the material whispering as she moved, her waisted velvet jacket that showed the curve of her breasts, the clasp that glittered at her pale throat just below the pulse. She saw him looking at her and drew in her breath slightly. But he made himself look away. She, too, turned deliberately away from him and wiped her hand across a filthy tabletop. 'Don't you believe in dusting all this rubbish?' The place was ineffably male, needed a woman's touch.

'A woman alone stands no chance,' Bart said simply. As she stared at him doubtfully he said: 'You'll marry Francis Pervane.'

'Oh!' she laughed, 'so that's why you treat me as though I'm red-hot!' The feud – she was an enemy agent! Because one day she would be Laura Pervane! She laughed in his face, then stopped. She remembered the tidal swimming pool on Lynmouth's western beach where the children played. In the centre you could stand up on a boulder out of the water to your chest, all the other kids trying to push you off, waving your arms with the seagulls wheeling above you in the free arch of the sky, and then one little step further forward, you plunged out of your depth into deep salt water. She had the same feeling now. She'd stepped over the edge.

She whispered: 'Why do you hate the Pervanes?'

'Merchants,' he sneered. 'They total. They

succeed. But they don't feel what's inside them.'
He threw out his arm at the window. The valley.

She lied: 'I love Francis Pervane.' And this time
he knew she lied.

He reached out and swung her round. She looked
coolly at his hand, then stared up at him with a
smile: at last she had got him to touch her.

He said: 'You don't know what you're doing.'

'On the contrary,' she whispered, 'I know
exactly.'

He shook his head.

She smiled quietly to herself, and did not attempt
to remove his hand from her shoulder. There was
an engraving on the table and she pointed to it: neat
stylized trees, geometrical gardens and ranked
terraces in front of a large E-shaped house. 'That's
pretty. Is it this house?'

He looked down. *'Pretty?* That's the trouble with
you, Laura.' He obviously thought he knew her so
well already. He picked up the engraving, then held
out his hand to her. 'Come with me. I'll show you
what I mean. The most precious thing here. You
won't like it.'

'I ought to be getting home . . .'

He merely glanced back from the door.

She forced herself not to hurry after him. *The most
precious thing* – what could it be? Jewellery? Laura
hungered for jewellery, but she'd been disappointed
before, all she had was the gold-plated watch that
was supposed to keep her in her father's pocket,
until she found out he hadn't bothered to select it
himself. A Gainsborough painting? But there were
paintings all over the place, and the room she

followed him into was the one with the silver laid out as if for cleaning, blue-grey with tarnish and rigged with cobwebs. Silver services weren't fashionable enough to be very valuable, they were precious only because handed down through families for so many generations: she loved the enormous bowl held up by silver horses, exquisitely worked, each braided hair of mane and tail picked out. She saw a galleon as long as her arm crafted from a single bone, once white, now dark yellow like a skeleton's tooth. And hunting memorabilia of course – once the Master of the North Devon Staghounds was by right immemorial a Barronet – stacked by the wall Laura saw a silver hoof, a long silver mort-horn, the silver cup which would be tied in a killed stag's mouth for the huntsmen and whippers-in to drink their pagan toast to the dead animal. Some of the pieces were so old that they looked almost foreign in style, sometimes quite dented, probably having survived burial during the Civil War. 'Bart,' she called, 'this must be worth a fortune.'

'Now you are even starting to *sound* like them.' *Them*. The name of the Pervanes was not called up lightly in this house.

Damp streaked the walls of the next room he led her through and the ornate plaster ceiling visibly bulged. Their feet crunched on glass from the line of broken windows. Laura imagined Elizabethan gentlewomen parading up and down here in their enormous dresses on rainy days. Clara would have been over the moon but Laura found it stuffy.

'You don't actually live in this place?' She ran to catch him up.

'It's my home.' He touched the engraving he carried under his arm.

She followed him down the circular stone steps at the end into a much older part of the house. The Barronets were quite ordinary really, Laura decided. Like most families, they didn't like throwing things away, so over the years they got put in the attic, then when the roof started leaking they stored them temporarily in little-used rooms, where they stayed. There'd been a lot of rooms once, but now the damp was closing in. Laura sensed the burden of history on Bart's shoulders. He was the survivor.

Ironically, this oldest part of the house was driest. The low, vaulted ceilings and pillared walls were free of damp. In the tiny storerooms rolls of carpet were stacked up, one or two faded tapestries were still hanging. He told her about his family's blood through the centuries, the dynasty of the de Barreneaus, the robber barons, the Armada shipwreck and the Civil War, their rise and fall until only these relics were left: and Watersmeet.

She called: 'What were you doing covered in blood, that day?'

He stopped, and turned.

He stared at his hands. 'I killed my house-pig. Ham, bacon, salt pork to see me through the winter. I don't have money.'

'You could sell some of that silver.' He didn't bother to reply. Again she had to run after him.

He said: 'Where you saw me was the old terrace gardens, worn away and overgrown now. The arrogance of our family, we were always builders. Once even Arnold's Linhay was terraced, we would have made a formal, pretty garden of the whole valley if we could. But it all goes back to nature in the end . . . ' He showed her the engraving. 'This is what the house looked like during John Leland's visit in 1540, the peak of our pride. Henry VIII had commissioned Leland to travel the length and breadth of England to record antiquities. Hellebore House was at that time called Watersmeet Manor. Those rights and privileges were taken away from us by King Charles II after the Civil War – Sir Lionel Barronet judged the Parliamentarians would win. We have always been interested in winning. He lost.'

'So the Pervanes' house down there wasn't always Watersmeet Manor?'

His voice deepened. 'A hovel. Cob walls, no floor, no chimney. The Pervanes were nobody, dirt farmers, a few sheep.'

Laura was greatly daring. 'Francis claimed that once they were princes.'

Bart surprised her. 'That's true. But you have to go back more than a thousand years to find it.' He turned back to the Leland engraving. 'By Leland's day the place was no longer a monastery, of course. Originally Ranulph de Barreneau – the Norman name wasn't anglicized until his grandson's time – built the place as an out-fort. But probably he lived at Exmoor Manor, near Simonsbath, where his son was baptized in the river – the Saxon roads met there, he could move fast, cut out trouble before it occurred, collect taxes – herbage, tollage, chief and rack rents, whatever he could impound or extort as Warden of the Forest. Only the rabbit warrens remain today. He got his genocidal reputation because of his treatment of the Saxon serfs. He burned the Royal Manor of

Molland and killed everyone there for their loyalty to Harold, the Saxon King. He roamed Exmoor like a wild animal, that's why they called him the Wolf. No one could control him.'

'Didn't he fall in love with a Saxon woman?' Laura's expression betrayed no clue who had told her this: Francis.

'Resda Torr, so beautiful she broke his heart.'

The corridor ended. Bart unlocked a heavy lancet-arched door, its stone architrave carved with a dogtooth pattern soft with age, but it led only to a small room, almost a cell. Standing incongruously opposite the plate-tracery window was a fine inlaid cabinet, which he opened to reveal dozens of drawers of the sort a naturalist might use. Bart touched a tiny brass handle with his fingertips and pulled out a single flat drawer. At first Laura thought it was empty except for a backing-sheet, a piece of canvas with a faint pattern worn into it.

'The original. I told you it was precious.'

The ancient fragment of wool needlework was little larger than his hand: a woman's face. 'It's her,' Laura said. Stylized though it was, she recognized the straight dark eyebrows in the oval face, the wide eyes. This was the woman whose face was vandalized by hammer-blows in the church.

He spoke softly. 'This is a rare work of art firstly because she is a woman, and doubly rare because she's depicted full face. Resda Torr. I like to think the nuns who sewed this knew her. It really is her.'

'The Greta Garbo of her age.' Laura was determined not to be impressed.

'It's time for you to go home.' He replaced the

drawer carefully, shutting her out. Laura quickly accepted the rebuke.

'I'm sorry, Bart. Please tell me everything.'

He ran his hands through his hair. 'The Wolf met his match in her. She bewitched him, they said later. But he simply loved her. He was a strong man and she was his one weakness. And she was clever – she was called the Fox, remember. She made him pay a high price. She saved her family, who farmed Radworthy. She persuaded him – perhaps forced him – to spare other of her kinsmen, even the thane, Harold's man, who once ruled them. And Ranulph agreed – on condition they became slaves. Perhaps she expected their gratitude for saving their lives . . .'

'Why shouldn't she?'

'Because they never forgot what they had been, and they never forgave her.'

'But they kept their skins.'

'But,' he explained, 'they had once been princes.'

Now she understood. 'The Pervanes? How *wonderful!*'

'No,' he said, 'how dreadful. Laura, these are real lives, Ranulph and Resda, Alder and Edith, who fell so low. They felt the same as us. We never forget our beginnings.'

'So this feud really does exist between you and the Pervanes.'

'It ends with me.'

She cleared her throat. 'Sir George hates your poaching.'

'Laura. Watersmeet is for everyone. The Pervanes can't own the water, the sky, the rocks, the trees, every fish and bird. Or me. They won't keep me out.'

Laura turned back to the tapestry.

'Could such a beautiful woman really love such a man?'

'No,' he said. 'She loved Watersmeet.'

Laura murmured: 'As you do.'

'As I do, Laura. She didn't marry him for love. She gave him Simon, his son. Then Resda got her husband to endow the monastery at Watersmeet, and she retired here with her retinue of servants. You can still see traces of the old fort walls. Look through this window – she did. This was her view, it hasn't changed. Watersmeet.'

Laura had heard enough of the valley. Bart stood with his arms braced across the window, his profile black against the evening sky, seeming to grow out of the dark woodlands below, but she wanted to touch *him*.

'I must go home, Bart,' she said.

He swung round at once. 'Will you be all right? I'll come with you.'

She made him work for it. 'I can look after myself, you know.'

'Yes, I know.' He turned back to the window.

Never a word from him that they would meet again. But they would. She was determined.

'You're wrong,' she called back. 'I did like her.'

Laura rode back home on Blackbird but she wanted to jump down and run, run with all her energy like the wind. She wanted to kick pebbles in her elation. The valley was full of shadow to the brim. A brilliant star winked in the cerulean sky where the sun had set. Somewhere in the pale expanse a kit cried *peeoo* – they always did this time of year, teaching their young. The woods were very dark as she came back to Paradise House, the house martins had disappeared under the eaves and the tiny hand-winged flittermice were just coming out, flickering and whizzing half-seen but unerring over her head, finishing off the insects the birds had missed.

'What time do you call this?' Ernest demanded angrily from his wheelchair. 'Where have you been?'

Laura dropped her eyes demurely. 'Father, I've been with Francis,' she said.

During the night it poured. At six Laura got up and stared from the kitchen windows at the pelting grey rain. The atmosphere was so muggy that her clothes clung to her body, and with squeaking fingers she kept wiping off the mist her face made on the glass. She fed the Aga, warmed the yeast and dashed through the rain holding a coat over her head to fetch drinking water, then did the milking in the outhouse with the rain clattering on the tin roof. Her fingers performed her task automatically while she imagined the beautiful Resda Torr and her extraordinary rise from farm-girl to great lady, married to the most powerful man in the province. Her reasons for that marriage were obvious. She didn't have to love him, and Laura understood that very well. Bart didn't know women – *she loved Watersmeet!* – he didn't feel the way Resda's mind really worked. He was a man. To Laura, Resda obviously saved Alder and made the prince her servant because she was in love with him. Only love made sense. Bart, a man, couldn't see it; neither had de Barreneau of course.

Here at Watersmeet, Resda de Barreneau had

welcomed Alder Pervane to her bed. Right from the start, the two families, Barronet and Pervane, were fated and bound. Perhaps she used him as a gardener – there would be plenty of opportunities to meet, secret stairways, dark nights, leafy bowers, but sooner or later, everyone would know. Including his wife, Edith, once a great lady sharing the name of the dead Queen – perhaps even named after her. How Edith must have hated Lady Resda! There, there was the root of the enmity passed down to the children. Laura knew more about Bart Barronet than he knew himself! She could picture that first Pervane, Alder, cast down and humiliated, slipping from his wife's bed of straw to enjoy his secret victory in his mistress' goose-down bedchamber, her arms rising to receive him, the moon hanging in the open plate-tracery window, and the wild sighing passion of their true love. Laura dreamed.

In his old age de Barreneau still loved Resda, they were interred together at St Brendan's. But Laura knew Resda wanted to be buried in Watersmeet, where she had been so happy. For appearances' sake she had to settle for that wild place between Watersmeet and the Moor.

Laura churned the butter round and round and round, then set out the bread and cheeses for lunch. Once or twice she caught her father's eye on her. He had noticed the change in her, and was smiling to himself. He pointed at the piece of cheese he wanted cut for his plate.

'Will you be riding down to the Manor this afternoon?'

She said casually: 'I thought I might.'

'But it's raining,' Sybil protested.

'Dear,' laughed Ernest, 'she isn't made of sugar, she won't melt.' Laura put the wedge on his plate. The mention of Francis last night had worked on her father like magic.

'She'll be no good to him if she gives him a cold!' Her mother's hostility, as always, was exactly because of her father's generosity: the jobs which Laura was let off would fall to Sybil. But Laura knew that he would let her go and see Francis.

That she did, in fact, ride pell-mell up through the dripping trees to Hellebore House would have been inconceivable to them; and the name she shouted.

'Bart!'

The echoes died away and water tip-tapped on the boards, then her footsteps sounded very loud as she crossed beneath the painting of Lucy, the girl in love, with flowers twined in her hair. Laura forgot to knock and the door seemed to open as though he pulled it even as she pushed it.

His scuffed maroon coat, close enough to touch. She stood tensely in the doorway, looking down.

'I was passing,' she murmured, then looked him coolly in the eye.

Bart gripped her elbow and led her to the fire. There was a buff envelope marked OHMS on the table and a letter he had written in reply. He hung her cape over the back of a simple hoop-backed chair to dry. 'Your skirt is soaking.' He didn't sound as if he cared.

'It doesn't matter. Only below the knee, and I'm wearing riding boots.'

He ignored her. 'You shouldn't come here. Laura.'

She closed her eyes, then rubbed her hands in

front of the flames to warm them. 'Oh? Why shouldn't I?'

He turned an armchair round for her. 'I was going out . . .'

'In the rain.' They would go together. But he made her sit.

'I love the rain.' He held up something tiny between his fingers, and no longer tried to hide the enthusiasm in his voice. 'Fishing in the rain. The river's in spate, the salmon will run. This fly is Thunder and Lightning, fish love it, jump on the hook.' Laura shivered. He held up another fishing fly that shimmered like a rainbow. 'Walton learned to tie this one here, and he immortalized it in *The Compleat Angler*. He'd been invited to fish the Lyn river in 1652 with his clergymen friends, Sir Lionel Barronet was mad for God. I make my own, it's a wonderful art. You see this feather?' He looked boyish, mischievous, and now she listened entranced. 'Stolen from the tail of Sir George Pervane's peacock!'

The Pervanes again.

Laura snatched her opportunity. 'You men are such children,' she said provocatively, leaning into the backrest with a laugh. 'It's so silly, you know, this bad feeling with the Pervanes. Someone ought to make you see sense.' It was obvious who. She lay her elbows on the padded arms on each side of her, her fingers steepled below her mocking smile, challenging him. Now Bart would have to take her seriously. But he laughed at her, and her colour rose. She struggled to sit up. He held out his hand and touched hers.

'Laura.'

111

She knew she'd let herself down. She had been play-acting, and she could have kicked herself. Their faces were almost close enough to meet. He held her hand. She trembled with relief. So he did care about her. Then he stood and gradually her hand slipped out of his. He crossed to the window. She thought of going after him but when he spoke, he excluded her.

'Laura, the Pervanes were *good* servants. They never forgot who they had been. Serving as they were once served maintained their belief in the order of things.' He shrugged, then murmured: 'Pride has its uses. But they were well rewarded, too well, appointed to powerful positions in our family house, chamberlains, stewards. In time they came to think of themselves, again, as great. The sons of the two families played knockabout together.

'The Leland engraving shows how much grander this house once was. Simon had followed his mother to Watersmeet. Over the next four hundred years the windows were enlarged by successive Masters, chimneys put in, wings added. It was magnificent. But only ten years after Leland's visit, when Sir Casper Barronet was Master of Watersmeet, a terrible thing happened.'

Laura came and stood behind him, but Bart did not turn, and she could not reach out. He spoke with his back to her, to the window.

'The two little boys were about nine years old, Jack Barronet and Oliver Pervane, young rascals, great pals. There's a miniature of Jack painted years later by Hilliard, *Portrait of an Unknown Man*, a handsome dark-haired fellow with haunted eyes standing against a background of flames. Hilliard was a poetic painter and experts suppose they're the amorous flames of love in Elizabethan poetry. Haunted by love. But they're real flames.'

Laura murmured: 'Jack burned the place down? The children were playing? There was some sort of terrible accident and Oliver died in the fire?'

'Mothers always tell their children *never* to play with fire, don't they? But Mary had died in childbirth with her second son and Sir Casper was too busy fighting the Scots or the French for his country. He had the temper of the devil, more cunning than bright. Jack was bright, both those wild boys were as bright as two shiny new buttons. They found a magnifying glass by the window on the stairs – they probably played peering at insects or fingernail-parings, you know what boys are like. When the sun came out they burned holes in bits of linen-paper. Then somehow one of the hanging tapestries caught fire and by the time Sir Casper dashed up the walls were a mass of flame, and young Oliver Pervane, crying his eyes out, was caught holding the glass in his hand. Imagine that moment. In his rage Sir Casper, unarmed, tore down the blazing tapestry rail and struck the boy through the ribs with the blunt end clear to the other side. It could not be withdrawn, and it seemed impossible that the child could survive. Sir Casper was stricken with remorse.'

Laura whispered: 'And Jack had put the glass into poor Oliver's hand? He was the one to blame?'

Bart said: 'Half the house was lost. The servants and the local people – and more than fifty arrived to man the bucket-chain – believed the story that

Jack started the fire, then panicked when he heard his father coming. The mood of the crowd turned ugly. Casper stood by his son, locked himself in, awaiting reinforcements. In the two days and nights while little Oliver Pervane lay dying in the shepherd's hut where Watersmeet Manor is now, a vigil of common people began to gather. On the third morning John Pervane came out carrying his dead son in his arms. The crowd parted to let him through, then followed him up the winding path that leads here.

'Under the midday sun the militia arrived galloping from Barum and formed a cordon below the steps of Hellebore House. The crowd gathered silently outside the smoking walls they had saved from total destruction, held back by the thin line of glittering armour and levelled pikes.

'John Pervane stood in front of the crowd, his child's body in his arms, waiting.

'At last Sir Casper came down the steps and said to John Pervane that they had both suffered enough, John Pervane by the loss of his son, he by the loss of so much property.

'Later Sir Casper, who knew for certain of his son Jack's guilt, came out again, and demanded of John Pervane why he still stood there.

'John Pervane knew the law would never touch Sir Casper Barronet, Lord of the Manor, Warden of Exmoor. But they were both men of honour. John Pervane said: "You know who you are, and you know who I am. You know what is fair and right according to ancient law. Your son's life for my son's life."

'Sir Casper returned into this house, and after an

hour, sword in hand, he reappeared pulling his son behind him down the steps. Jack was so pale he looked already dead, shuffling but obedient, in a state of shock. Sir Casper forced him to his knees and raised his sword to kill him. Then he turned with an oath and slammed the blade through John Pervane's heart to the fist.

'And so John Pervane was buried beside his son. But he had other sons . . .'

Laura listened horrified and enthralled. Now she understood Bart Barronet.

'John Pervane's sons pursued Sir Casper through courts, but of course he was never brought to book. They had to take their revenge in other ways, defacing and ransacking the tomb of Resda and her husband, scattering the Barronet bones. Violence is the son of violence, sheep were found with their throats cut, hayricks burned, boundaries disputed. The Pervane family stuck it out in their turf hut where the waters meet, and when it was trampled by horsemen they rebuilt it in cob, with a thatched roof. When the thatch was burned they replaced it with a slate roof, they never gave up: standing in their shabby doorway they could look up above the treetops, above the bare terraces, and see Barronet's great house being slowly restored. When local people could not be found to work on it, Sir Casper imported workers from Barum. When he could no longer bear the sight of the little house below him in the valley, he knocked down the terraces and let the formal gardens run wild, and the trees grow, and lived like a hermit in the turret he built, and died there. Jack's son Christopher was ambushed in the woods and beaten to death. It was

Jack, out of his mind with grief over the death of his only son, who began the Barronet's legendary study of chemistry, alchemy, necromancy, and built the lime kilns to feed his medicinal plants, black hellebore, Christmas rose, the spurges, foxglove, lilies and orchids. In the 1580s he took a new young wife, but then visited Bohemia with Dr Dee to study the black arts, returning the year after the Armada. His wizardry called up the winds that swept the galleon *Nuestra Señora de Ulua*, struggling back home to Spain around Ireland, on to the jagged hogsback cliffs of Foreland point and made Don Juan Delgadillo de Spes his prisoner.'

'That's him?' Laura went over to the handsome wooden grandee standing by the fireplace.

'That's him,' agreed Bart, patting the head affectionately. 'Carved from the main spar of the *Ulua*, washed up on Lynmouth beach. My ancestor.'

'But all the time, the stupid feud with the Pervanes went on?'

'It got worse. Then better, then worse. Then much worse, you know how these things go once they've got started. They live a life of their own.'

'And nobody tried to kill this thing?'

He didn't answer her at first. Then: 'Yes. They tried. But hatred, they say, like love, lives a life of its own. We cannot deny our fate.' He looked at her distantly. 'It's time for you to go. The salmon are running and I love to see them.'

She pouted. 'You're going to throw me out in the rain?'

He used exactly the same words her father had. 'You aren't made of sugar, you won't melt.'

She followed him into the hall, then called him

back and pointed at the painting. 'Who is she?'

He didn't want to talk about that, but the picture obviously meant much to him – he hardly glanced at it, so it was very familiar.

'Lucy,' he said.

'Another of your ancestors?'

Slowly he came back and looked up at Lucy's picture, the gathered flowers, Watersmeet, the headless dog.

'Lucy was born a Barronet and I like to think she died one. Yes, that Lucy was a Barronet again in the end.' He brushed the grime off a plaque that Laura had not noticed below the frame and Laura saw her married name, shocking in this place, picked out in the neat copperplate beloved by the Victorians: LUCY PERVANE.

Laura turned with an exclamation. Pervane! But Bart was holding his finger to his lips: he would not permit her to say it aloud. His face was all angles and planes of reflected light.

Laura whispered, 'Of what did she die?'

Bart said: 'Of love.'

What would Bart Barronet be like in love?

She *had* to see him again. Her life at Paradise House was so depressing; worse, it was *boring*. Sybil got her revenge in a dozen subtle ways, keeping Laura in, or saying she could go out then at the last minute remembering something that *must* be done before she left, and then there was always something else – had she laid the bedroom fires yet? – and then just *one last thing*, and by that time the light was fading and it was too late for Laura to saddle up. 'I'm very sorry,' Sybil would smile, 'but you know how it is, a woman's work is never done, is it? I promise we'll make it up to you tomorrow.' But there was bound to be *just one last thing*. And it became easier for Sybil as the evenings drew in, two minutes earlier every day – drawing the heavy blackout curtains after supper and shutting out the roar of the river in spate, the wind surfing in the treetops, the natural night sounds of Watersmeet, with those heavy muffling drapes, sitting around like prisoners in their own living room. Soon Laura had to draw the blackouts before supper; then before she even prepared the meal, and the black evenings that followed seemed endless. For hours the two women – by now Laura almost hated her mother – sat clicking knitting needles, Ernest sucking his pipe, while the slow hours ticked by until nine o'clock, when he wheeled himself amiably into his study and as the valves warmed up they heard '. . . *the news, and this is Alvar Liddell reading it . . .*' and then the study door clunked closed, and that was that. Laura got up and made the Horlicks. They commenced the long, polite process of going to bed, her parents never finally calling out goodnight before eleven, and often it was nearly midnight before Laura finished up and turned the key in the front door. She started to feel sorry for herself.

Even poor Clara had Rob; Laura had nobody. Except one person. In the darkness she wrapped herself in her eiderdown in front of her bedroom fire and sat staring into the flames. Was it really possible to die of love? She didn't know about that. It was certainly possible to feel trapped by life in the valley she loved.

She crossed to the window and lifted the sash open, stared out into the freezing night. There was no moon and the sky was a glory; the Milky Way trailed directly along the line of the valley in a shimmering arch. Stars gleamed up from the puddles along the drive, picking out in darkness the menacing shape of the deodar tree. He was out there, somewhere. She knew what she wanted to do. She wanted to touch him.

That he had never kissed her seemed unbearable. She remembered her hand slipping gradually out of his grasp. She remembered their faces almost close enough to meet.

He'd *wanted* to – hadn't he? He did care about her.

One day Laura escaped – that was how she thought of it – and stood looking at Hellebore House, her enemy, with the wind swirling big yellow oak leaves around her, snatching at her dress, fluttering her hat-brim – the big soft hat with the red band around the crown, held by a red cord under her chin. She just stood staring up at the rock-solid house with the leaves piling up against the steps, and knew he wasn't there. *Didn't* he care?

In a way she was glad she was kept in, she dreaded going there again to find him out. On the way home, she had cried. Without Clara to have a go at she was in a miserable bad temper for days and raked Francis when he rode over proudly to show her the roan horse he had purchased at Barum's Friday market, but he kept smiling.

'Now we can go riding together,' he grinned.

'If you can keep up.'

She couldn't be angry with him for long, and they

119

did go riding. Everyone said how beautiful Watersmeet was in the autumn, orange and red, like a valley of fire. She enjoyed riding along the forest paths with him. The trouble was, she was so contented with Francis. He *showed* he cared about her, he tolerated her moods, he had a good sense of humour. He wasn't a good horseman, but a steady reliable rider. And it was lovely when he chased her through the flame-coloured trees, because sometimes she held Blackbird back and let him catch her, and kiss her. So why wasn't it Francis she thought of now, standing wrapped in her eiderdown looking out through the open window at the wintry stars?

When Laura went down in the morning to start her chores she got a shock to see her mother already in the kitchen, the teapot steaming on the Aga beside the big ochre bowl where the kneaded dough had been left to rise. Laura looked guiltily at her watch.

'I couldn't sleep, darling,' Sybil glanced up. 'Pour yourself a cup of tea. Do sit down, I want a little talk.' Did she know about Bart? Laura lowered her eyes so that her mother could not read anything of what she felt, poured her tea and took it to the table.

'Now, Laura, we both know your father wants to see you living at Watersmeet Manor. You are his dream come true in any event. For you to wed Francis . . . well, that would truly put the icing on his cake.' She slammed the dough back and forth with her strong, lined hands, parted it, floured it, put it on the baking tray. Her eyes met Laura's. 'I do not think Francis is good for you.'

Laura could not hide her surprise. 'But – I thought . . .'

'I may be wrong–'

'You certainly are wrong about Francis!'

Sybil dusted the flour off her hands, slipped the tray in the oven. She took off her apron and sat down. 'I'll ask you a serious question. Do you really love him?'

Laura was embarrassed. 'Of course I do.'

'Look at me. With all your heart?'

'I suppose so.'

'Then that's all that needs to be said.' Sybil pushed away her tea, braced her hands on the table and stood up. 'I believe in love, darling. I was happy once.'

'Mummy, I wish I could give it back to you.'

She put her hand on Laura's shoulder. 'I hope he'll be as good for you as . . .' she admitted it: '. . . as Alex was for me. Don't bother about your jobs today, I'll cover them.'

Laura ran out to the stable. Her mother had just looked at her face, and *believed* her. She flung the saddle on Blackbird, and rode galloping through the woods between soft trunks hairy with oak-moss, the bare branches tangled like a black net above her. She took the Watersmeet path for appearances' sake, then crossed the river through the Barton Woods from which Bart took his name, and came to Hellebore. A strand of smoke rose from a single chimney.

I was just passing wouldn't work again, and she didn't want it to. She wanted to tell him the truth. 'I had to see you!'

He never showed surprise. Bart was standing with

a spoon halfway to his mouth, a bowl of oatmeal porridge in his left hand, looking domesticated. He wore a white open-necked shirt with black buttons.

'Bart!' she said.

He looked from his spoon to her. He seemed mildly amused at her ferocity of manner. 'Well, come in. Make yourself at home.'

'I *hate* this place!' she said. Still she didn't move from the door.

He put down his spoon. 'Then why have you come here?' he demanded softly.

It was obvious. She said: 'You.'

She saw that look on his face, the flash of light in his eyes. He couldn't look through her now; he acknowledged her.

'Let me finish my breakfast in peace.' But he didn't dare say her name. That would have let him down.

'Damn you, you *know*,' she almost wept. 'Don't pretend to me, Bart.' She dropped her hands to her sides but he didn't move. His presence was so formidable she felt weightless. She'd made a fool of herself.

'No, it's my fault.' He dropped the bowl on the table, then tossed the spoon clattering after it. 'I thought you'd never come back, I thought there was no need for it any more.'

She tried not to cry. 'I've just had the most bloody awful conversation of my life with my mother.' She was dabbing the backs of her hands to her cheeks and they came away shining. She was crying after all.

He moved forward. 'Laura.'

She stopped, staring at him.

122

Then she whispered: 'I love you.'

But he had covered her mouth with his mouth. Laura tilted her head and her unbound hair fell over his hand in the small of her back, holding her. His fingertips slipped down the line of her jaw to her neck, on to the exposed curve of her throat. She pushed away from him with her palms flat against his chest, her long fingernails bending back with the pressure, forcing him to hold her. She could feel his knee between her knees, taking her weight as she leaned back, her dress tightening over her thighs, then his mouth came down again over hers and she clasped her hands around the back of his head.

When he pulled away she clung on to his arms. 'I'm not ashamed,' she whispered, electrified. She would have let him do anything.

He set her gently on her feet and looked at her. He'd tangled her hair and it was everywhere over her shoulders. The mystery in those deep blue eyes, the darkest blue he had ever seen. She wore no makeup whatsoever, her breasts lifted and fell with each breath. She was wearing the working dress she'd forgotten to change and looked divine.

'No,' he said.

'You kissed me, Bart!'

He pushed past her and she ran after him into the hall, where he stood looking up at the picture. Then he whirled and swept her round in the passageway beneath the decaying stairs. He opened a small back door and led her through it.

They stood in an overgrown garden. The first storey of the house was level with the ground here at the back. Tombstones grew out of the tangled weeds.

He took a great deep breath. 'I shall be buried here.'

'*Me*, Bart. Look at *me*.'

'This is our place,' he said. 'We're damned from the church we built. Deuteronomy. Unto the tenth generation. All this was ours.'

'Bart, look at me.'

But he ignored her, touching a pale headstone with a light hand. 'My mother is here.' He moved on: his family. 'Ranulf, my father, the last Master. It's a good place when the sun shines. Somebody will bury me here.' Watching him move between the stones, Laura sensed peace.

She wouldn't let him exclude her, coming after him and touching his elbow.

Suddenly he swung round and stared down the valley in the dawn. 'God, you are beautiful,' he said in an enraged voice. As if he hadn't noticed Laura's beauty at all.

She looked down the valley too. From this angle, behind the house, the fort above Myrtleberry Hangings looked further to the left and she could see more of Wind Hill behind, on the far side of the valley's curve. Where the hills dipped towards Lynmouth she could almost see the sea. The modern road, invisible at this distance, barged through the amber line of Countisbury promontory fort that the sun picked out – she could just discern the break.

'Bart. You can change your destiny.'

He pointed down the valley's cleave. 'This is *our* place. Our family motto is *Adsum*. Here I stand. My ancestors built the clapper bridge to join the forts. We were the men who created the real world, Laura, who built things with our hands and hearts.

124

We were engineers here two, three, four thousand years ago, when the Pervane clan were just witchdoctors lording it with their incantations, worshipping oak trees and gold knives, burning men and women and children alive in great wicker baskets for their God. And Watersmeet was a vast grove of sacred oaks.'

He pulled Laura into the trees, kneeling on the frozen ground as he explained. 'Every dry summer, the turf on Exmoor shrinks and the old stones reappear. Huge patterns are revealed that in the wet you'd never know were there, the White Ladder, henges, stone circles. Burial chambers are everywhere right in the heart of Exmoor, those vast earthen barrows you see on the skyline.' He pulled a yellow tussock of grass from in front of a low, pointed stone. Almost worn away, as though hard Lynton slate stone were as soft as soap, a faint outline remained: two vertical lines, one capped, the one on the right joining the ends of a curve.

'They look like letters,' Laura said.

'TD,' Bart said. 'It's not a headstone, it's a Saxon boundary marker. A claim a thousand years old. TD, *Torr Denu*: Torr's valley. And long before him. Watersmeet was ours from the dawn of time. Can't you feel it?'

'These people aren't you.' What she really wanted to say was: What about *me*?

'Torr was a Saxon name, taken up by our family – wisely – after the Celts lost the battle of Penselwood in 658. It's the Saxonized form of the Celtic name of Toher, bridge, or bridge-builder. The place now known as Tarr Steps, which we built, was named after us. Oh, we were great bridge-builders.

At a bridge in Parracombe repaired in the last century they found a TD stone sealed inside: *Toherus Delineavit*. It's Latin – two thousand years ago the Celtic Dumnonii tribe had sent their Druids into hiding, in deference to Roman wishes, and we were the masters again. *Toherus Delineavit*. Toher built me. Do you see now? We loved Watersmeet, Laura. This was where we came home.'

Laura said softly: 'Can't you escape?'

He looked at her contemptuously. He didn't brush the dirt off his hands. 'None of us escapes what we are.'

She hid a smile. 'You kissed me.'

He said slowly: 'You're just playing with fire.'

'Well then!' Laura flounced away. She stopped. He didn't come after her, so she went back. She pretended contrition. 'I'm cold, Bart.'

'We'll go inside.' She pushed in front of him and went first so that he would see her walk. The sun had risen behind them, stretching their shadows ahead of them and illuminating the back of the house between a web of bare black tree branches, the grave markers sticking out of the grass. She sensed him look to one side, and turned to see one headstone standing apart from the others – the name still seemed almost incredible here, in this place so precious to the Barronets: LUCY PERVANE.

'Lucy,' Laura murmured, going back. 'The same girl in the picture?'

'Covered in flowers,' he whispered.

Below her name Laura made out *Requiescat In Pace* – as though the full words had a different meaning in this context than the conventional abbreviation.

'She does not lie here.' Bart's emotion was fierce and Laura loved to hear him speak in such a voice.

'She found no Christian burial,' he said.

'The girl who died of love?' Laura was excited.

'Lucy Pervane has gone to the sea, where there is never peace.'

He steered her to a side gate and pointed. From here, this one place, the Severn Sea could be glimpsed in the vee of the cleave, like the petal of a pale, blueish orchid delineated by the hills.

Laura leaned into his shoulder, looking up into his eyes. 'Do you hate all women, Bart?'

For a moment she thought he would put his lips to hers again, but he opened the gate and pulled her after him by her wrists. She began to laugh as she swung from side to side behind him. He crossed the carriage circle – Blackbird did not shy from him – and swung her up into the saddle.

'Go, Laura.'

His hand was hot. She hung on to his fingers, still laughing until he snatched them away.

Blackbird galloped through the trees. Laura hung on with her eyes half closed, trembling with excitement. His kiss didn't lie. He loved her. He loved her more than Watersmeet, it was *Laura* he saw, not this stupid valley. She had discovered her power over him.

Laura had hooked Bart – and been hooked, but that was what she wanted. She understood even his love for Watersmeet that so limited his horizons. She made sure she rode out where she would be seen, places he was likely to be, the forest paths between Hellebore and the river, his favourite pools where she might surprise him any moment as spring came. She identified with his desire to be left alone, to be his own man, realizing that he was even more of a prisoner than she. But that silver needed cleaning – she imagined sitting there with the Silvo on the table and the bitter tang of it in the air as they rubbed away together with the yellow dusters.

She also realized that in a way he hated her, for disturbing his hardworking routine, for being cleverer than he was, for arousing complex feelings in him that he had lived very well without. So he had decided to ignore her. She didn't see him anywhere, although sometimes she *knew* he was there.

One afternoon she was out walking with Francis and he followed her eyes above the treetops. Hellebore was invisible behind the green canopy.

'He's been called up. Postman said so.' Francis loved to catalogue Bart's losing battle with the authorities. She remembered the buff OHMS envelope on the table last November. Bart had repudiated his registration papers, and the whole outside world at war, just as he repudiated her. She bit her lip.

'Will he have to fight in the Army?'

'The North Devon Regiment of the Royal Devon Yeomanry, Papa's old outfit,' Francis said casually. He neither approved nor disapproved; it was nothing to do with him.

'My father's too,' Laura said. 'He was nearly killed at Okehampton Range.'

'Fully motorized nowadays,' Francis said, 'self-propelling field guns.' Laura couldn't have cared less what they were, and she doubted if Francis knew

much more. His concession to the war was to wear
suits with padded shoulders and a straighter, more
military cut, and spend three evenings a week with
the Lynmouth Home Guard. Actually he was getting
quite good at it, but she hadn't stopped giggling the
first time she saw him in part-denim dress and field
service cap, without even a revolver in his button-
down holster, carrying a pig's-snout gas mask – God
help his asthma if he ever had to use it. Francis
always took his duties seriously. 'You'd laugh on the
other side of your face if Hun parachutists landed.'

She couldn't imagine Francis being bayoneted, he
was much too sensible, but she was worried about
the parachutists coming for Bart. He'd fight.

The war was suddenly real to Laura. Sybil had
asked Francis to Sunday lunch and Ernest was
carving a small shoulder of lamb, his knife clinking
on the bone, when the shrill scream of an
overstressed aero engine sent them all, except
Ernest, running outdoors to see black swastikas
thunder overhead. The engine of a damaged bomber
returning from a raid on Swansea trailed black
smoke, red lines dribbled back down the perforated
fuselage. Francis, holding her protectively in his
arms, said it was hydraulic fluid, but it looked like
blood, and she was sure it was.

As the sound of the plane had faded, they had
talked excitedly among themselves, then returned
to the dining room to find Ernest still sitting in the
carver chair, the sweat pouring down his face,
terrified and exhausted. His hands shook too much
to continue and Francis had finished carving.

'Will he have to go?' she asked, as they sauntered
along the riverbank later. Now that she believed in

the war, it might come roaring between these peaceful trees any moment. She twined a daisy in her fingers.

'Oh, my darling, the Barronets always were a law unto themselves. Apparently his name isn't on the latest electoral register, so officially he doesn't exist.' The stem broke in her fingers, and when she flicked it into the water Francis took her hand. They leaned on the wooden handrail of the Ash footbridge looking down into the river, and he slid his arm around her. The trees looked so green, as though their leaves had been freshly washed, and the forest floor was carpeted with wood anemones.

'I don't want you to worry about anything, ever,' Francis said, giving her shoulder a tight squeeze. Laura felt so guilty.

And she did worry. Everything was so calm, but now she seemed to see signs of Bart everywhere – a rabbit snare, a footprint here or there, peg-holes bored in the smooth rock where the overflow from Dumbledon Pool sluiced down, and sometimes trout or salmon hung there to be preserved as gravad lax by the fresh running water.

She went down to Watersmeet Manor much more often. Uncle George could always get his hands on flour or sugar, once a whole haunch of venison, his larder was always fully stocked – what the hotel couldn't supply, the farm did, and he was always pleased to see her. Sometimes he gave her a lift home in his black Humber, running illicitly on red agricultural petrol, the engine misfiring and Uncle George joking and jolly the whole way. He helped Laura out and carried the haunch of meat for her. Ernest thanked him profusely for it but looked worried in case the government man came back. Sybil made tea for Sir George and they all sat around in the parlour to entertain him.

'A piece of gutter fell down from the roof near my bedroom last week,' Laura said.

'I can do it,' Ernest said, shaking his head.

'It's cast iron, and twenty feet up.' Laura looked pleadingly at Sir George. 'Could you ask one of your men?'

He patted her knee jovially with the heel of his palm. 'I'll send Silas first thing tomorrow. Anything I can do. Pleasure.' He finished his tea and got up with a smile. They watched him drive off.

'There was no need to ask him,' Ernest said. 'I could have done it.'

But Laura was pleased with herself.

Old Silas came by a couple of days later. 'You'm putting us ter no trouble, I were coming by this way afore.' He had served the Pervanes all his days. Some said he was one of those men whose life Sir George saved, dragging him out of the gas-cloud of Loos on a rope. He carried a broad canvas holdall called a turkey, his trousers were held up with cord, and countryman's leather buskins were strapped around his gambers above his brown boots. Laura held the ladder while he went up. Silas was a painstaking worker and seemed to take hours. Her bored eye was caught by a toothed steel trap glinting in the holdall. It had the strongest spring on it she had ever seen.

'Whatever's that for, Silas?' she asked, pointing.

He finished up his work in a trice and retreated quickly down the ladder, closed up the bag and held it against his chest. Then he didn't say another word to her, just nodded more or less politely, touched his cap and hurried off.

'What a strange man,' Sybil said, when after supper Laura described what she had seen.

Ernest sucked his pipe. 'Of course he didn't want her to see.' He sounded embarrassed. 'Sir George is having trouble with poachers again. It was a mantrap, what else.'

'But I thought they were illegal.'

'They're illegal because they exist, Laura.'

Sybil said: 'But whatever would Silas want with such a dreadful thing?'

'I should have thought that was obvious. A man with a broken leg can't steal.

'I'm sure Sir George knows nothing about it,' Sybil said.

Laura was certain that Uncle George did know.

The next day they roasted the leg of venison for lunch, and it was delicious.

During the afternoon Laura saw Bart in the woods and rode up to him. It was that easy, when he wanted to be caught.

The moment had come so suddenly she didn't know what to say. He was wearing a dark red shirt and maroon cord trousers. He must have been irritated by the way his hair hung past one eyebrow, it needed cutting. He touched Blackbird's muzzle gently and let her sniff his palm. A couple of limp coneys dangled from the snare in his other hand. Laura sat awkwardly in the saddle.

'Laura.'

'Don't worry!' she said. 'I only came to warn you.'

He nodded. 'I know about the traps.'

132

'Oh, thank God!' She made to jump down from the saddle but he touched her knee.

'Laura,' he said, 'don't come to Hellebore Woods. Be careful.'

He was using the traps as an excuse. 'I haven't seen you for months,' she said miserably.

'I won't be caught, I know every tree, every root in the valley.'

'So do I!'

'No, you don't,' Bart said.

'But what would make Uncle George *do* such a thing?' she wailed. 'I saw it, the spring was so strong it had to be set using a special lever, you'd never pull it off. You'd have to lie there until they set you free. I can't bear the thought of you suffering, Bart.'

'Sir George knows he'll never catch me. He's just doing his duty.'

'Duty? Are you all mad?' She leaned forward. 'If you were hurt, I'd know it.'

He was amused. He was determined not to understand her. 'Listen, thank you for warning me.' He was thanking her as a friend. 'I do appreciate it, Laura.' Such ingratitude – and such an assertion of independence – made Laura want to kick him. The lock of blond hair over his forehead infuriated her.

She tugged the bridle out of his hand. 'Oh, go away! If you're so clever, you don't need me.' He concealed his surprise, but she saw a new expression on his face. She thought it was respect.

He watched her turn Blackbird away, and his eyes followed her as she swept back her hair and rode off between the trees, looking back until she could not see him any more.

She decided to avoid him. She'd fight for him by making him suffer until either he faced up to the fact that he *did* love her – and she was sure that in his heart of hearts he did – or he lost her. All she had to do to make him jealous was to let herself see more and more of Francis, getting past the walking-out stage, letting him court her seriously. And it was serious.

In the formal garden of Watersmeet Manor they sat drifting slowly to and fro in the sofa-swing looking at the gnarled old Monterey pine, watching the waterfalls splashing down the Hoaroak rocks, the sun swaying its diffused light across Laura's face beneath her parasol. Francis ran his finger down her cheek.

'I do love you, my darling,' he murmured, and she turned towards him. Francis glanced towards the house, where from easy chairs in the modern extension eyes supposedly closed in post-prandial slumber would doubtlessly be fixed on the young lovers – the Sunday lunches, Home Guard activities permitting, had become regular swaps, one week at the Bensons', the other at Sir George's invitation to the Manor, where the food was better. Francis tasted Laura, he drank Laura, he couldn't get her out of his mind, the shape of her dress, the way the hem swirled as she turned, the curve of her ankle into her shoe. Laura's smile: her pale arms in her pre-war summer dress, its hem taken up almost to her knees, the shoulders lifted and waist pulled in to show off the fuller bust that was so fashionable, and so feminine. She rested her wrists casually on his shoulders.

He glanced back at the picture windows.

'Let them,' she said. He pressed his lips to hers.

She raised her eyes to the trees that seemed to flow up the sides of the valley.

'I can't believe you're so beautiful, I'm so lucky,' he whispered.

She just laughed, and waved away an irritating wasp.

'You're all I have in the world,' he murmured into her shoulder, then inhaled the scent of her. 'My Laura, my goddess. I don't care when I'm with you.' He gripped her waist. 'I do love you so much.'

He slid his hand down her arm as she stood up. A Bechstein harmony wafted over the garden – Uncle George was an expert player – his music mingling subtly with the steady hiss of the waterfalls. Then he hit a wrong note and Francis winced.

'I don't know why he still tries to play. Arthritis.'

'It's therapeutic,' Laura said.

'That must be it.'

'I love to hear him play,' she said. He followed Laura inside. Her parents were just going, but she stayed on with Francis. Sir George Pervane winked at her as he returned to the keyboard. 'Glutton for punishment, eh?'

'You play beautifully.'

'I used to. This is Mozart.' He looked at her fondly while Francis left the room for a moment. 'I see how my son feels now. He's an introvert. He needs a girl like you. Damn.' Another wrong note, Uncle George made a face, and for a moment he really looked quite fierce. He shook the small dark Old Ruby bottle on a mat on top of the piano, but it was empty. 'Ask Francis to get me another bloody bottle of port from the cellar, would you?'

She found him in the orangery. Francis held both her hands. 'I wish we had more time alone,' he said, then the old man called impatiently and he pulled up a trapdoor in the tiled floor, so expertly matched into the grooves that Laura had never noticed it though she must have crossed here hundreds of times as a child. So the legend of the cellars built over by Roderick Pervane was true after all.

'Grandfather got very odd in his old age,' Francis said. 'By all accounts I don't think he was quite right in the head for the last ten or twenty years of his life. I don't remember him, of course.' She followed Francis down into the dark and at the bottom he turned on an electric light to illuminate a tunnel of earth clad at intervals with enormous slabs of stone. 'Actually it's a labyrinth,' Francis called back, going round the corner out of sight.

It was a game. Laura hurried after him, and of course he was gone. Several tunnels radiated out like spokes between the grey slabs. The place had been put to a practical use: mushrooms grew in sacks along one wall. In a broader place Laura found wine racks.

Hands slid around her waist from behind, and she gave a little squeak of terror and pleasure as Francis nuzzled his face against her neck.

He laughed, holding her hand reassuringly, and selected a bottle of port, coated with thick grey dust down one side, from the long rack. 'I suppose the old boy – Grandfather – got frightened of the dark,' he smiled. 'Legend has it these slabs are an old ring of standing stones that got silted over by the river ages ago. As soon as he inherited the property my father put in the trapdoor but the cellars have never been good for anything.' He held up the bottle. 'Except wine at exactly the right temperature.'

They went back up into the daylight and Francis opened the bottle. Uncle George drank the glass in one. Laura thought he was probably closer to self-inflicted gout than arthritis.

'In my youth,' the old man told her assertively, 'I was a bloody brilliant player. Threw it all away.'

'Wine, women and song,' Francis said, looking at the Art Deco clock. 'I've got to get down to Lynmouth, Father. Parade at eighteen hundred hours.'

Sir George stopped playing and held out his glass. 'Francis never had a youth. Come on!'

Francis took the bottle from the piano and refilled the glass.

'To the brim, man,' George said.

Francis overfilled it so that a couple of drops slopped on the pale carpet. Uncle George laughed and put his arm around Laura's waist, bent forward and she pulled him to his feet. They walked to the broad windows and he gestured with his glass.

'I'm going to have an ornamental fountain put in. Twenty-four hours a day, Mozart concertos powered by water.'

Laura said lightly: 'Not by port?'

He laughed heartily, he loved someone to stand up to him. He was playing a dangerous game, putting Francis down.

'You see, he's my only son.'

Sir George was a different man without Francis in the room. He relaxed and stopped tugging at Laura's ribs like an old lecher. To people he liked he was overwhelmingly generous, but he needed to

137

own them. 'I shout at him because he's my boy, Laura, and I . . . well, he's mine. It is not easy to be Master of Watersmeet. People have expectations.' The door creaked and he said quietly: 'Put salt on the carpet, my boy, then just leave it. Help yourself to a drink. Laura?'

'Just a small one.'

'I've got something to show you,' Sir George said roguishly. He led her by the hand into the spacious circular Adam hall of the elegant, older part of the house with its black-and-white chequer floors and curved interior doors, the exterior walls painted a pale orange, lit by curved fanlights and curved windows. The ceiling was an artfully contrived dome with the gallery serving the upstairs bedrooms encircling it at the first-floor level. Laura was not so familiar with this part. Sir George opened the door to a room she had never been in: because of the broad Chippendale directoire pedestal desk with its back to the window she guessed he must use it partly as his study, which instinctively made it almost sacred in her eyes because of her father and *his* study – not a place for women.

'My inner sanctum.' With its dull pale-blue and dark-blue walls it was a very cold and masculine room. It revealed a man she had not suspected existed – a lonely and insecure man, not at all the rough, likeable old bastard he pretended to be. She saw a few big pictures mostly in simple frames, but not the sentimental photographs she expected. Laura realized that the dark cabinets and wardrobes that she had mistaken in the corners were in fact keyboard instruments, upright pianos, pianolas, a pedal-powered organ, a harpsichord with black keys.

Sir George said: 'Shall I play my virginals?'

The old devil was trying to make her blush. The simplest tricks worked best, and such was the power of Sir George's personality that Laura did feel her cheeks colour.

'The favourite instrument of young ladies,' the old man said. He flicked out imaginary coat-tails in the fading light and grunted as he sat. The virginal was an oblong box on a stand. He opened it and began to play tinkling, unresonant notes. Francis came in and put his arm around her shoulder as they listened. He nibbled her ear while Sir George struggled with the keyboard. Laura pushed him away.

Francis whispered: 'I've simply got to go. Don't let him steal you while I'm gone. Love you.'

Sir George struggled to play a modern tune but the virginal didn't have enough octaves. He held up his hands and cracked his knuckles. Laura's eye was drawn to the ornate gilt frame of the picture above him, and the plaque that identified the sitter as Phineas Pervane.

Phineas was a young man with an intense, eager face, the thin tallness that all the young Pervanes seemed to share, a fine figure, proud and graceful in his old-fashioned black broad-brimmed hat, black coat, black knickerbockers. Below a white stock he wore pointed black shoes with his Christian name woven by the artist in the daisy-speckled grass, and he was holding up a spray of red roses as though they were to be a gift. Behind him, Laura saw part of Watersmeet valley holding the sea in its curve like the petal of a pale, blueish orchid. The head of a King Charles spaniel, pink tongue lolling, panted loyally up at Phineas' knee from its invisible body hidden by the frame. The proportions of the picture looked all wrong – much too tall.

Laura realized that it was the same painting as Lucy's at Hellebore House.

Lucy's picture had been torn in half.

This was the other half, here – here at Watersmeet Manor.

Laura stared spellbound. The virginal tinkled and twanged, and suddenly Sir George cursed and started again.

Laura said: 'Why –' She bit her tongue. In her innocence she had almost given herself away completely and said: '*Why was the picture at Hellebore House torn in two halves?*' – this to the kindly old gentleman who had done so much for her, whom she liked, who set mantraps in his neighbour's woods.

Sir George finished playing the piece, sat back and slammed down the lid with a laugh.

Laura said: 'Who was Phineas?'

He snorted, and she realized she should have complimented him on his playing. He didn't even look at the picture – so it was familiar to him too.

'A dreamer.'

'What did he dream?'

'That a Pervane could marry a Barronet. That love could forgive all, forget all. Her name was Lucy. Lady Lucy Barronet.'

'Was she very beautiful? Don't you have a painting of her?'

'Not a single one. For all I know she was very ugly, my dear, beauty is only in the eye of the beholder. Lasts but a day. She died long ago, unremembered and unmourned.' For a moment he had the grace to look uncomfortable. 'Except by my father's elder brother.'

'Who was he?'

'Laura, he was Phineas.'

He looked round as something gave a metallic clang out in the drive. Silas was poking about under the hood of the Fordson tractor with a petrol can and a length of rubber siphon hose. Sir George swore and slammed open the window. 'Is that for the wasps' nest? Use paraffin, not petrol, you bloody fool! Do you want to blow yourself up?' He closed the window and turned back to Laura with a smile, their previous conversation ruled finished.

'Was Phineas so deeply in love?' Laura couldn't let such a potent romance go. 'Did Lucy really marry him?'

'Oh, yes. It couldn't end well, and it did not. They tried to defy fate.'

'Fate?'

'That a Pervane is always a Pervane, and a Barronet is always a Barronet. Phineas and Lucy dreamed . . . what young people dream. That love could conquer time. That love, not hate, could bring our families together. Wars aren't won by love.'

'Did it really end so badly for them?'

He cracked his swollen knuckles again. 'We are what we are. Our fate cannot be denied.'

Laura was sad. 'And so the picture was torn in two.'

He asked steadily: 'How did you know that?'

She struggled not to colour. 'I simply guessed, that's all.'

He glanced at the picture, then back at her, and nodded slowly. 'It ended the only way it could.'

'But it's all over now, isn't it, Sir George?'

'Yes.' He smiled painfully at his fingers. 'It's all over now.'

The next time she saw Bart, he took her by surprise. She was carrying Blackbird's bucket of water into the stable, it was dusk, her thoughts were miles away. Then his shadow moved amongst the shadows and she almost screamed his name.

He spoke quietly: 'Laura.'

Blackbird tugged peacefully at her haynet.

Bart turned on the light and Laura flinched. She had spilt the water and she could hear it trickling in the floor drain.

'They'll see us,' she said. The lights were already on in Paradise House behind her. The rainwater tanks were empty so the spigot in the stable was dry. He picked up the bucket and went out into the dimity to refill it for her from the goyle. When he returned Laura was sitting on the stool, having found the wood still warm from his backside. So he had been waiting for her. She knew he really needed to see her, he had passed the time sitting here whittling a piece of wood – a freshwater fish, perfectly detailed even to the scales scored with finger markings, expertly picked out with the tip of the knife. At first she was sure it was a trout but the tail was forked; a young salmon parr then, not yet ready to go down to the sea. She slipped it into her apron pocket. As he returned he turned the light off. He crossed the golden darkness and she heard Blackbird drink; she kept her eyes wide and gradually the glow faded from her retina, but she could see nothing.

142

She sensed him turn.

'Francis adores you,' he said.

She smiled with closed lips so that he shouldn't see the gleam of her teeth.

'Really? Does he? Why does that concern you?'

'You're making a fool of yourself, and a fool of him.'

'You're the one who's . . .' Laura couldn't trust herself to say it. 'Who won't recognize what he feels. Oh, Bart, why won't you admit it?'

He said: 'I'm wed to the valley.'

'I hear you've been called up.' Her voice trembled. 'You'll have to fight.'

She heard him give a low laugh, unworried. 'If I keep quiet, who will ever know I am still here?'

'One day, Bart, someone will touch you.' She reached out into the darkness.

'But not you.'

'You'll know what you'll have missed,' she said to the dark, 'and you'll have to face it. Maybe not me.' Again she couldn't go on. She clenched her fists on her thighs. 'You'll have to go one day, that's why I'm frightened.'

His voice came from by the manger. 'I am wed to the land that should have been mine,' he said sadly. 'Here I stand.'

She swallowed. She could just discern his outline now.

'Laura,' he said hopelessly. 'Even if you were Helen of Troy and even if I loved you.'

She grabbed at his last words. 'You know what I feel for you.'

'Then you know I don't feel the same for you.'

'I know it but I can't accept it.'

'You still aren't quite serious, Laura.'

He leaned down and touched her face, then licked his fingertips. She splayed out her fingers on her legs, pulling her hands up her body and pressing them into her breasts as hard as she could, causing herself pain that he could not see.

'You can't step off the world. You can't just hide in your own nature, Bart. One day something *will* touch you, and then you'll wonder, is *that* all I am?'

'Without you?' he mocked her.

'I'm telling you the truth and you're lying to me. Yes, without me.'

'Don't hurt yourself, Laura.'

'You hurt me.'

She curled her hands in her lap and looked down. She tried to keep him at least talking of love. 'What happened to Lucy and Phineas?'

'You found out his name.'

'I want to know everything,' she said simply. How else could she know *him*?

But she felt him shake his head. She couldn't see him, she couldn't touch him, but she could feel him. He was already turning away from her.

'You wouldn't want to hear.' The girl who died of love.

That wasn't the point. She didn't care what she heard; just to be with him. She jumped up, she couldn't bear to sit for a moment longer while he prowled around her like a caged animal. She had a flash of insight.

'Bart, I can set you free.'

Now he must admit it, enclose her in his arms, his hand in the small of her back, cover her with kisses. She saw his dark form, in the paler square of the doorway, turn. Then suddenly she could not see the doorway at all, he was standing so close to her. 'Laura. I don't want to hurt you.'

'You never do anything else.' She stood with her head down.

'I do not love you.'

'Is that all? I see. Then that's that.' She pressed her fists to her cheeks. 'Say it again, Bart. Say it *again* and *again*.'

She felt him shake his head.

'You're just frightened,' she said. Then she said: 'Bart? You *are* frightened of me.'

He said clearly: 'I do not love you, I do not care for you. I don't want to be good friends with you, I never want to see you again.'

She said nothing. She hated him more than she could say.

He waited. She wished he'd just get out, if this was all he'd come for.

'Are you all right?'

'Go. Just go away.'

He waited.

Laura sighed. Her eyebrows drew together, her lips stretched, but not in a smile. A silver line flowed across the lower half of her sight.

'I hate you.' Perhaps that was what he had wanted her to say, because she saw him move in the doorway, and felt that he was gone. 'I hate you!' she screamed. She ran after him.

She fell against a tree and cried her heart out, and he didn't come back.

'You don't see so much of Francis now.' Her mother, speaking to Laura, glanced at her father. They sat alone around the table in the dining room at Paradise House and Laura twined her fingers in the napkin that lay in her lap. She reached out without meeting their eyes and finished her water. Ernest leaned over and without a word refilled her glass with wine.

'Laura waits for rationing, and then she diets.'

'I'm just not hungry. I don't like potato soup. I do see him.'

'But not as often.'

Laura considered what he had said as she cleared away the soup plates. Perhaps Francis, too, thought she was rejecting him. If so, it had changed him for the better. He embraced her passionately when they met, putting his arm around her when they walked, stroking her upper arm with his hand as they sat by the river, lying back in the grass with her looking up at the sky. It was pleasant. Once he rolled over on his elbow and began to kiss her, his hand caressing her hair, her shoulder, then slipping down and touching her breast as if by accident, then kneading through the soft material, and her nipple had gone terribly hard. She'd sat up, embarrassed, but only because she had liked him doing it and it was wrong. He did it the next time too, drawing in a breath with each squeeze. A harnzee, a grey heron, swept down the valley and crouched in a dead tree like a pterodactyl. She saw a kit, the buzzard on four-foot wings shaped exactly like a Spitfire's, circle against the drifting clouds watching for rabbits below. A red squirrel skittered along a branch and Laura sighed. Francis' fingertip slid down to her tummy-button and she knew where he was headed next. She wanted him to. Her knees were pressed tight together and her dress was clamped between her thighs but she longed for him to touch her and reassure her and whisper that she was lovely, and treasure her.

'But you don't see Francis as often,' Ernest repeated as Laura put the plates round for the stew.

'Do we have to meet twice a day just to keep you happy?' She went to fetch the stew-pot from the kitchen.

'Darling,' he called after her, 'I hate to sound clichéd, but I really do want what's best for you. You're my own daughter. Don't try to be so hard.'

Hard. Laura stopped by the kitchen window and remembered that evening in the stable, with Blackbird peacefully chewing her hay, while she first talked like a reasonable person with her nocturnal visitor, then begged, then pleaded with him, and her chin trembled. She remembered laying her heart bare with words, which meant so much more than had she opened her legs to Francis' fingertip. She did hate Bart. He had abused her, and he had done it deliberately with words, which hurt most of all. She had meant what she said. So did he.

The scales had fallen from her eyes, she had cried that night into her pillow, devastated by his hardness. She had felt the iron fist behind the velvet glove, the real Mr Bart Barronet. She wouldn't forgive him for that, a man who could treat her like that. And in a way she didn't forgive Francis for it either. She was off men. Yet she'd had to laugh when Francis had turned up with a bottle of champagne in the wicker picnic hamper next time. Francis always did the right thing. He even drank almost as much as she. But she hadn't let him kiss her breasts. He had understood, and he hadn't touched her at all, except a peck on the cheek when they said goodbye.

And he always noticed what clothes she was wearing and complimented her. She was going through all her old dresses and skirts, taking them up, letting them out – it was amazing how much material the old pleats had wasted. While she sewed it was nice to think of him noticing.

Laura shook herself and lifted the pot off the Aga with the oven gloves, carrying it through to the dining room.

Ernest ladled rabbit stew, dumplings, peas onto his plate and began to eat. 'Well, what do you think of the latest news?'

Some new frightfulness of the war. 'What news, Father?' Laura took one of the dumplings and tried to avoid the peas.

'About Sir George Pervane.'

Laura stopped with her spoon halfway to her mouth.

'I haven't heard anything about Uncle George.'

'I thought you saw Francis this morning? Oh, my darling! He came over. He was looking for you. Terribly worried, poor chap. When we heard what he had to say, we told him he'd find you in the stable.'

'What did he say?'

'We assumed he'd talked to you, dear,' Sybil said, with a warning glance to Ernest.

Laura admitted: 'I wasn't in the stable, I was probably picking the vegetables for the stew.' Actually she'd been walking in the woods, trying to get her thoughts in order.

Ernest said: 'Francis drove Sir George to the Lynton Cottage Hospital at nine o'clock this morning.'

Laura didn't move. Pictures flashed through her mind, Sir George turning round in the church pew when Clara was married and giving her a smile with his kindly eyes; Uncle George cracking his knuckles and complaining about his arthritis; *they dreamed that love could conquer time, they dreamed that they could defy fate.*

'What happened, Daddy?'

Ernest rinsed his mouth with wine. 'There was a Meet of the North Devon Staghounds yesterday – you must have heard them, they gathered at Rockford, outside the inn. The racket those hounds put up.' The NDS pack were a cross of bloodhound and the yellow southern hound, over two feet tall at the shoulder, with deep chests and powerful jaws. 'The harbourer roused a warrantable stag from covert with his herd. Magnificent beast, ran towards Deercombe, then doubled back and nearly ran into Francis – that roan of his took to the air. Francis reckoned the stag's antlers spanned three feet – probably four, in the spread. The velvet just dry. And what a look in his eye! Then in the mêlée he was off up the combe towards the open moor, and Francis said he didn't reckon he'd stop before Simonsbath.

'But, you know, those hounds don't give up. They don't carry a head like foxhounds, they're individuals, they don't pack together until they close in for the kill. First one couple picked up the scent and gave tongue, then they all got the line. Sir George rode to the top of Brendon Common and reckoned they'd turn the stag east, that he'd go to ground in Doone valley, using the water to throw them off. Sir George galloped the field down there, just to find the hounds chasing back the other way. The stag was cleverer than the men, he'd doubled back to the west, and Sir George had to turn everyone back uphill.

'The stag outran them on the open moor towards Exe Plain; he dropped down from the skyline and they reckoned he'd turn down Farley Water, but he was already going up the far side by the time they got there. So they trailed after him all the way up on to Cheriton Ridge. By the stone-age hut circles he dropped down to Hoaroak Water and splashed a mile or two northward to refresh himself and throw off the hounds. But Sir George and his men spied him coming out of the brake below Roborough Castle, then glimpsed him again at Hillsford Bridge, heading downstream straight for Watersmeet Manor. The water confused the hounds, the chutes and waterfalls were impossible for the horses, so they rode down the county road and gathered by the Manor listening to the baying of the hounds echoing down the Hoaroak. The hounds arrived and milled around. They'd lost him. The stag had gone to soil somewhere, his antlers flat against the surface of the water, only his nose showing, and they'd passed him. Sir George rode up a few yards over the rocks to Lucy's Pool then turned, shaking his head.

'Behind him, Francis saw the water heave. He shouted. Up into the sunlight, showering drops from his antlers and his coat shining like beaten silver, the stag rose from his hiding place in the pool behind

Sir George. Springing from rock to rock the stag found a way up the bluff, teetered, then disappeared over the top into Hellebore.

'Sir George just stared. A Pervane had not set foot on Barronet land for half a century. But the horn had morted and the hounds were streaming uphill between the trees. He hesitated, then followed the huntsmen up. What else could he do?'

Ernest helped himself to another dumpling and chewed slowly.

Laura had forgotten her plate of food. She let the fork clatter on her plate. Ernest glanced at her.

'The stag was trapped against the very walls of Hellebore House, which is a ruin up there, Laura, the old haunt of the Barronet family. You saw Bart Barronet the day Clara was married.'

'Oh, yes, I remember.'

'None of them ever cared what decent people thought, those Barronets. The old Master had a wonderful feel for a stag, though. He would never have let this happen.'

'What did happen?'

'Well,' Ernest said, 'it seems that the huntsmen arrived along the drive with whippers-in and riders and hunt followers all together, and the pack was snapping and howling for blood. But as they moved in, the door opened and a man walked down the steps in a maroon coat and old patched trousers held up with rope.'

'Bart Barronet,' Sybil said. Her cheeks were flushed. 'He stood between the hounds and their prey.'

Ernest said: 'A hound snapped at him and he picked it up and broke its neck in his hands. One of Sir George's best hounds! With Sir George watching, and all his friends gathered around him. Bart wouldn't let them have the stag.'

Laura knew; he would have comprehended the terror of the exhausted animal as though it were himself.

'I don't want to hear,' she said. 'I don't care.'

'Bart Barronet ordered them to get off *his* land. 'Sir George couldn't back down. Everyone knew that. He used his horsewhip on Bart Barronet.'

Laura asked: 'Was Bart hurt?'

'Only a little blood. Drink your wine, it's excellent. You're no longer a little girl, Laura. That's better.'

'But Sir George is a kind man. Why did he do it?'

'To save face. He had no choice.'

'What did Bart do?'

'He just stood there and took his punishment. That type always do – proud of spoiling the sport of others for the sake of their own inflated self-importance.' Ernest chased a smear of rabbit gravy around with the last piece of dumpling on his fork, then put his knife and fork together and wiped his lips. 'He's had it now. By saving that animal he's made new enemies and drawn attention to himself. His appeal as a conscientious objector will be turned down for certain. The Justice of the Peace is a keen huntsman. They'll take him and shape him up and make him fight. He'll have to report to barracks with the North Devons forthwith, you'll see.'

Laura's lips tasted bitter when she pressed her fingertips to them. She turned calmly to her father. 'What about Uncle George?'

'He took a nasty turn in the night. Obvious what

the cause was. They're keeping him under observation in hospital for a day or two.'

'And the first thing Francis thought of,' Sybil said, 'was to come and tell you.'

'I'm sorry I was out, Francis,' Laura said as soon as she saw him.

He dropped the dry leaf he was cracking between his fingers, staring at the dippers working the stretch of mingling waters by the Manor's garden, and took both her hands in his. 'I wanted you to be first to know, that's all.' They both knew why. Suddenly he hugged her urgently, wrapping his arms around her. He was so much taller, 'You're everything to me,' he said in a rush. 'My whole world. My darling.' Behind him she brought up her hands to his shoulders and pressed her head against his chest.

'It's very serious,' he said. 'My father has had an apoplectic stroke.'

'Oh, Francis, I am so sorry.'

It was already getting dark as they walked along beside the river. 'There's so much he never told me.' Laura found a boulder and sat on it, taking off her shoes and drawing her feet up inside her skirt, resting her arms around her knees. It was the sienna peasant skirt, very full, and he could just see the semicircle of her pale toes under the hem. She was wearing a leather belt and thick cotton blouse that was beginning to look very white in the fading light, her hair raven black. Her smile showed a gleam and he realized that she was very aware of his approval of how she looked, and knew his thoughts. He longed to embrace her again.

153

'You heard what happened? It was terrible. I've
never seen my father behave like that before. Like
a different man.' He chucked a pebble. 'What do
I say? I've never quite trusted him but I've always
had faith in him – that he'd always try to do the
right thing. But yesterday it was as though he had
a different man inside him who had to come out.
I'll never forget him bringing that horsewhip down.
And the grunt of approval that came from the men
behind us. The blood across Barronet's cheek. The
men pushed forward when they saw that, you
know, wanting more. My father raised his whip
again and that's when he – like this. Twisted. I had
to hold him in the saddle. But in ten minutes he
felt better again. Laughed it off.'

The river reflected the sky; an aquamarine serpent
gliding between the ochre trees. High up along the
valley walls the furze made clouds of chrome
yellow.

'But it was a stroke.

'He always takes a glass of water to bed. That was
how he warned me. Our bedrooms are close, on
opposite sides of the house. His faces south, towards
Hellebore, mine towards Lynmouth. Only the gallery
landing between us. I thought he'd just knocked his
glass off the bedside table. He does get through
rather a substantial quantity of alcohol in the
evenings, so he always wakes up thirsty in the night.
Dehydration and alcoholic insomnia.' Francis was
trying not to let his feelings show but they did.
Laura took his hand in her own and had never felt
so close to him. He sighed.

'Then the glass pitcher fell on the boards with a
dreadful crash. I just lay there, half awake, listening

to what sounded like an awful struggle. That's what it was, of course – him struggling to warn me he was in trouble. Then the bedside table crashed over and I knocked on his door and went in. Sheets, broken glass, water everywhere. He was lying there trying to talk to me. And I knew that stupid feud had killed him.'

Laura straightened her legs and slid off the rock, almost treading on his shoes, and put her arms around him silently.

But Francis was a man of words; he described waiting, not knowing what to do. 'You'd have known, Laura, hot water, tea, sandwiches. Something.' They'd almost paid to have a telephone line put in before the war, but now there was no hope of arranging that sort of work. 'He couldn't move down the left side. His mouth was all crooked. I couldn't bear to leave him in the night to fetch the doctor – suppose he died alone? I sat beside him for hours but, of course, he couldn't say a word. And neither could I. My own father, I must have felt *something*. At first light I went for the doctor and we had him in the cottage hospital in no time at all.'

They walked back across the grass towards the Manor.

'But a lot of people have strokes,' Laura said, 'and they recover. Aunt Lily did at Minehead. The brain's a funny thing, it makes up for the damage somehow.'

'It turns out he's had something like it before. They call it a transient ischaemic episode. This time he's going to die.'

'Francis, I wish there was something I could do.'

He pulled the blackout curtains and flicked on a few lights, yellow bulbs glowing in the frosted glass hemispheres that hung from chromium-plated chains at each end of the long room. He struck a lingering chord on the Bechstein, then went to the bar and uncorked the Old Ruby: 'Let's drink the sort of toast he'd understand. To the old swine.' He drank his glass in one, plainly hardly tasting it.

'Francis, you're talking of him as though he was already dead.'

He stood in the centre of the floor. 'You know what a difference this makes to us.'

Of course she knew.

He called to her: 'We don't have to pretend any more.'

She found a spot to sit on the sofa. She felt very adult leaning back watching him across the drink in her hand. But suddenly adult was not what she wanted to be. She wished it were simple again.

'I haven't been pretending,' she said.

Still he didn't say he loved her. He said: 'I've always thought you were terrific. Ever since I saw you dive into the ice. The way your skirt clung to your body.'

'God, Francis, I was only eleven, twelve.'

'And I was fourteen. Even then. I've been committed to you for so long.'

'That's a sweet thing to say.'

He dropped into the sofa beside her. 'I feel so many things because you're here. You know what you make me feel.'

She was pleased. 'Francis, you're coming on much too strong.'

'It's that simple.'

'What time did you say visiting hours are at the hospital?'

'I love you.'

There it was. The three little words from Francis Pervane.

He searched her eyes urgently, his hands on her forearms.

'Soon I will be Master of Watersmeet. I know I'm jumping the gun. I know it's not decent with him not dead and all that. But you're driving me crazy.'

She put down her drink before he spilled it. He touched her chin and made her face him. She looked down. At last he just kissed her anyway. She curled her hands around the back of his head. He took his mouth away and looked at her, then kissed her again, her eyelashes fluttering against his cheek. His fingers counted her ribs. He dropped his lips to her throat and she caressed the top of his head with one hand, her other arm lying out palm up across his back. He buried his face in her blouse and his fingertip rotated gently around her tummy-button as though it were a precious coin. Then his hand slid down over the woollen skirt until his wrist lay across her pelvic mound hidden beneath the weave, his fingers spreading halfway down her thigh. He drew them in, gathering a handful of material, and the hem slipped up over her knee, over her smooth pale thigh, and his hand turned underneath the hem and gently rose. She stopped its progress with her own hand over the bunched material.

'I can't stop,' he said, 'I want you. Let me touch you. Please.'

She lifted his hand to her lips, not letting him go

any further, but left her skirt where it was, so that he could see part of her legs beneath him, sharing his pleasure in her femininity, feeling emotions of great tenderness for him.

'It wouldn't be right.'

He looked at her yearningly. 'Put me out of my misery. I'll do anything for you. Oh, let me.'

She pulled the hem down over her knees. 'I must be getting home.'

'This is your home. Stay with me.'

'Francis,' she laughed, flattered.

. . . But she didn't stay. She walked back home under the stars and came back to reality, washing-up piled on the draining board, and a mountain of ironing that wasn't finished until the early hours. Afterwards she switched on her bedroom light and stood in the open window smoking a forbidden cigarette. The smoke trickled deliciously in her nostrils, she remembered Francis' passionate entreaties and how much he had wanted her, and swept the hair out of her eyes. Then she stubbed out her cigarette, got into bed and cuddled her pillow.

Francis told her that Sir George Pervane didn't want her to see him as he now was. Though he was regaining partial control of his left side it was a great burden and when he talked he sounded completely drunk. Laura wrote to him twice a week but he never replied; he had his pride; he wanted her to remember him as the man he had been. He didn't expect to live.

The stags were belling and roaring in the woods below Summer House Hill in October when the old man crossed over to the convalescent home in Lee Road. He could have gone to the Watersmeet Falls Hotel, which had the staff and facilities to look after him, but there were too many people he knew. His left eye watered constantly, as though he were weeping. Below he could hear the cliff railway clicking and slamming at the top station, the balancing water gushing into the tanks. The ornate iron street lamps had been taken down and through the bare branches of the trees lining the road he could watch the military traffic driving through Lynton. That was where he saw his first jeep, his first female officer in uniform, his first gum-chewing American sailor. His life revolved around such details now.

He could just, if the pretty little nurse consented to pull his bed round, see up Watersmeet Cleave as far as the old iron-age fort that rose up from the valley wall like a bald head. Below there, somewhere in the depths on the far side, was Watersmeet Manor. He never wanted to go back.

But his revenge, and he was no longer its master, worked its way slowly but surely along the old-boy network towards his enemy. Sir George Pervane didn't try to stop it. Sometimes it seemed that everything he had ever been as a child, as a man, as a father, led up to the moment when he raised the whip. Now he wanted no more, and he longed to leave his body.

The yellow telegram ordered Mr Bart Barronet to report forthwith to the North Devon Regiment at the Exeter Training Depôt at sixteen hundred hours, Monday 2 February 1942, or face the consequences. The Regiment was currently attached to 45 Division, part of the GHQ Mobile Reserve, a lower establishment division with a home defence rôle, but there was talk of attaching it to a Guards Brigade and Sir George knew what that meant: they would be trained up for real fighting. Perhaps Africa, or Burma. Perhaps for the Second Front, an opposed landing somewhere in Europe, across beaches raked with gunfire.

For the first time in a thousand years the House of Ruins would stand empty.

Victory. Victory.

Once a week Ernest Benson drove up to Lynton by God knows what effort, his thigh clamped by an iron strap to the boards, in his properly licensed trap with little Laura's black horse between the shafts, and very skittish too at being made to plod all the way round via Barbrook to avoid the hills. Ernest smuggled half a bottle of malt whisky and two glasses under his rug.

'Little Laura? They're neither of them children any more, George.' The two men sat staring out of the window, one in a wheelchair, the other propped up in bed. They were equals now.

'I don't want to get in Francis' way,' grunted George. 'It's all his responsibility from now on, Watersmeet, Laura, the hotel. Francis knows his duty.'

'Do you think they'll do it?'

'Get spliced? Not in my time. He'll wait until I'm safely under the flowers, I know him. Then he'll ask her. Will you give your permission?'

'She's nearly old enough not to need my say-so, George. Besides my girl's always been quite certain of her own mind. And Francis has gained confidence. We hardly recognize him. The Home Guard work, the farm, the hotel, it's quite a burden. He's put in a terrific effort.'

'He is a good boy. He has guts, he never ran away. I wish I'd encouraged him, Ernest, not always knocked him down to make him stand up. It's me who's the damned fool. I wish I'd been kinder to Francis. I wish.' He moved his hand back and forth meaninglessly on the coverlet. The slate wiped clean.

Ernest looked at George slowly dying and hoped his own end would be quick.

Of course, Laura didn't care in the slightest that Bart had to leave Watersmeet. It was time he did his bit for his country. But *this* was his country. Well, everyone else had to fight in the crusade against evil and risk their lives in places they'd never heard of for what was right. The sooner he went the better, as far as she was concerned. He was part of the past.

There was frost on the ground the day he left.

She saw him from a distance: a lonely, broad-shouldered figure moving through the trees, a kitbag dangling from his hand. He wasn't wearing gloves or a hat, he must have been freezing. And he wasn't carrying a bag of sandwiches or anything – perhaps he could get something at Barum station. She didn't call out. She was frightened she'd get angry with him and say something she didn't mean – or something she *did* mean. He didn't look back, and she watched until he was gone.

Soon he seemed so long ago, the man up the hill,

that she had almost forgotten him, a part of her childhood she had put behind her.

Francis saw her almost daily, and he always had that special smile for her, a sort of spring in his step when he saw her – he sent Silas Giddings over with the petrol-driven British Anzani that ploughed as much ground in an hour as Laura could dig over in a week, and Francis personally brought her seeds, or a sack of fertilizer, or hay for Blackbird. They couldn't imagine how they would have managed without him. He'd *blossomed* was the best word Laura could think of, and she did think of him quite a lot. Without his father around, Francis was a different man. He worked hard, played hard, snatching a goodbye kiss from Laura almost casually as he hurried off – she almost felt neglected. Perhaps he had found another girl. No, it was simply that Francis was standing on his own two feet. Under his management the Manor farm had been upgraded from *B* status to *A* for outstanding by the District Committee of the Ministry of Agriculture. He more than quadrupled his acreage of land for the wheat and barley that were so desperately required, by cutting down scrub woodland and hedgerows, ploughing up virgin moorland, and in early May he took advantage of the dry spell to burn off the dead fern and thorny furze along Cheriton Ridge. Afterwards it looked like the blackened spine of some vast dinosaur, but within days the first grass was putting through shoots. The ridge would support twice as many sheep this year as last. He'd done a wonderful job, approaching problems calmly and sensibly, keeping his head, and Laura admired him for it. When the manager of the Watersmeet Falls

Hotel was tragically drowned in a sea-fishing accident, Francis oversaw the running of the place himself. This meant that when he came for a meal, or occasionally she went over and cooked for him, he often as not fell asleep in her arms afterwards. It was rather touching; how much someone so intelligent wanted her and trusted her. She looked down at his sleeping face and brushed the hair tenderly off his forehead. He did look dashing. He snored: she was fascinated. And his socks needed darning too. She gently transferred his head from her lap on to a cushion, putting his feet upon the sofa and slipped off the offending sock, working with needle and thread, glancing at him from time to time, feeling just like wife and husband. Then she covered him with a blanket and went home.

Sometimes she wondered: *Will he really ask me to marry him?*

Francis visited his father at the convalescent home most afternoons, going the long way round through Lynton on his way to the hotel. Now that Francis was in command, they'd never been closer. The old man insisted on hobbling with a stick, but the effort plainly exhausted him. He'd lost stones in weight, his fine hearty suits hung on him like sacks. He'd developed a passion for toffee and Francis went to endless trouble to obtain the stuff for him. Francis watched his father hobble aimlessly around the common room, his knuckles sticking out around the knob of his stick, listening to Francis' local news with his head cocked on one side and his eyes vacant.

'You've done well, my boy,' he said, 'I am proud of you.'

And then it happened again: he twisted and Francis caught him. Although he appeared fully recovered in half an hour, he was grateful to find himself back in bed, and showed no inclination to leave it again.

Going home Francis stopped the car in the trees and walked to the edge. He stood staring out over Watersmeet. His need for Laura was simply irresistible. Her laugh, her hair flying as she turned, the light in her eyes, the talcum-powder smell of her body, and her heat. God, he desired her! He could hardly think straight when she was in his mind, just wanted her. He thought she honestly didn't understand what she was doing to him: to hug her, to kiss her, to stroke her, though probably pleasant enough for her, was a torment to him because it had to stop.

He found Laura at Paradise House, wearing a broad-brimmed straw hat, working in the garden. Sybil looked up from the kitchen table where she was preparing the lunch. Francis slammed the car door and hardly glanced at her, his face set, his gaze fixed on Laura working under the almost vertical sunlight, all harsh contrasts, the trees brilliant above and black below. She turned and the hat cast a weave of fine shadows down her face, the pale half moons below her eyes, the surprised smile trembling on her lips.

'God,' he said anxiously, 'you're beautiful. I haven't slept last night.'

Her eyes searched his.

'For thinking of you.' Francis shook his head. 'He's still alive. Come out with me today.'

She didn't say anything he expected and had

prepared answers for – *It's much too sudden, I
couldn't possibly, I haven't got anything to wear* –
she simply rested the hoe against the netting and
went into the house. He waited on tenterhooks for
ten minutes; then half an hour, standing in the
solarium, slapping his hat against his leg. Sybil
looked in once, and later Ernest wheeled himself
by outside, looking at Francis through the glass and
giving him a surprised smile as though he hadn't
known he was there.

'Let's go,' Laura said, and Francis looked round
with such an expression of relief that she nearly
laughed. She was wearing the lavender summer
dress that he loved, with a pleated bust and
everything else so smooth it looked almost sheer,
with a lovely flow to it as she walked. Her hair
looked like black silk. Her hand was so hot that she
had wiped it on her handkerchief before coming in,
but now as he reached out for her she felt that his
hand was just as hot, and she could hardly contain
her excitement.

They got in the Humber and he drove up the
winding track over the cliffs above Dumbledon Pool
and the lime kilns to Watersmeet Manor, then up
the county road. Instead of turning left, as she had
expected, he let the car free-wheel downhill
towards Lynmouth.

'I thought you visited your father every morning.'

'Not this morning,' he lied.

'You're such a torrent of conversation today.'

'I've got a surprise for you.' She had already seen
the wicker hamper on the back seat. 'We'll have
a picnic on Lynmouth beach. With champagne.'

It was silly, but Laura felt tears in her eyes. It

would be the first time she had left the valley in years. The Humber coasted down the road cut in the rock cliffs high above the river, the hanging woods above them obscuring the sky, the treetops below affording only glimpses of the foaming waters. Then the valley walls receded and the sky opened up to show Lynmouth and the sea. They passed a row of houses then Francis turned in by the church and parked beside the hotel.

'Only ten minutes, I promise you.' He opened the bonnet, unclipped the distributor cap with his handkerchief and pulled out the rotor arm without which the engine could not start, as demanded by wartime regulations, and slipped the small copper-tipped rectangle in his pocket. It didn't take a moment; he came down here so often, Laura realized enviously, looking around her.

The Watersmeet Falls Hotel was built in the Swiss style, with thick ground-floor walls of local stone, the second and third storeys in red cedarwood rising to deeply overhanging eaves and a steeply pitched roof. Laura stood on the patio looking over the river, remembering Clara, then went inside. The foyer was much busier than she had expected, mostly men in uniform and their wives, often in uniform too, with shiny wedding rings. *Guests are reminded that baths must not be filled with more than five inches of water*. Civilians wore utility clothing, with strangely narrow lapels and no turn-ups, the girls, smoking in public, wearing very short skirts to save cloth, with narrow hips and aggressive squared-up shoulders. Amidst all this drabness their lipstick, the colour of beetroot juice, seemed lurid to Laura, and her keen eyes picked out ladders in their silk stockings. Some poor girls had to wear frumpish-looking woollen hose. Laura wanted to hide herself in a corner, feeling almost obscenely privileged to be so well dressed, so well fed, so untouched.

Francis came out of the office and took her arm. 'Are you all right?'

'I haven't been away from Watersmeet for so long. It seems so strange.'

'Horrible, isn't it? Our finest hour.' He fetched the hamper from the car and they walked down past the bridge and the Granville House Hotel. As they passed Lloyds Bank the manager waved through the window. Walking between the houses, they glimpsed the women below the back steps washing their clothes in the stream, then going past the Beach Hotel Laura paused by the ivy-clad Rising Sun. She leaned on the parapet watching the river sweep through the tiny harbour. The flow had undercut the deep gravel banks. Fishermen were unloading baskets of lobster, crab and skate for the Savoy Hotel on to the cobbled ramp. A terrier barked at the black twelve-foot conger eel hanging from a gaff. An ARP warden stared at Francis suspiciously from his lookout post atop the Rhenish tower, then recognized him and called down a good afternoon.

Laura took a deep breath of fresh salt air. 'I feel better already.'

'You see all the rowing boats have their oars removed? Regulations.' He pointed along the beach and Laura saw the barbed wire she had not noticed before, and three-pronged things like the jacks schoolgirls played with together, except that these were formed of massive slabs of concrete as tall as a man.

'Tank traps,' Francis said. 'Though any Nazi tank commander would have to be crazy to land here, surrounded by thousand-foot hills, it's a natural fortress. But you can never tell. People do crazy things.'

'Do they?'

'It wouldn't be the first time. In the ninth century the Vikings landed a big force here, they meant business, pulled up their longships on the beach. The Saxons retreated to the ancient forts.' He pointed up Countisbury Hill above the Tors Hotel. 'At the right moment they rushed down and slaughtered the lot. Nearly a thousand men.'

'*Toher delineavit*,' Laura whispered. 'Toher did it.'

'I beg your pardon?'

Laura shaded her eyes. 'The sun's so hot.'

He took her hand. 'Come on.' They walked past the bottom station of the Cliff Railway to the sandbagged Home Guard checkpoint. The tin helmets had come through, and the men had rifles with bayonets. In the hot air Laura could clearly smell the blanco on their belts and gaiters. They stood to attention and saluted Francis, then went back to their work checking papers. 'There's some talk of banning these coastal areas completely,' Francis said, 'no visitors allowed at all.' He helped her down on to the western beach and they sat on the rocks overlooking the tidal swimming pool. Laura leaned back on her elbows and held up her face to the arch of the sky. The champagne cork popped. 'To us,' Francis said.

Laura drank. Her mouth filled with bubbles and she gasped, then laughed while Francis thumped her back. In front of them was the pool with the boulder in it and she remembered standing on top, all the other kids trying to push her in. Then someone had knocked her from behind and she plunged out of her depth in deep salt water.

'I want you to marry me,' Francis said.

He'd done it at last. It still took her breath away.

Francis held up his hand. 'I don't want you to answer straight away.' Laura shaded her eyes, the sun was so fierce, the cliffs shimmering in the glare.

'I *shall* make you happy,' Francis said. 'Your happiness is everything to me.'

She hardly knew what he was talking about. She was delighted. Should she string him along, say she'd give him her answer tomorrow? What should she say?

'It's so sudden. I'm only nineteen.'

'Nineteen years and ten months.' Francis was impatient. 'That's nearly twenty. Plenty old enough to know your own mind.'

'What did my father say?'

'I haven't asked his permission,' Francis said simply, 'I'm asking yours. I want *you*, not him. It's only your word that matters, only your happiness that is important to me.'

But did she love him? She had every reason to.

'Laura, I love you. I swear it.'

Laura drew a deep breath.

'Yes.'

He kissed her.

'You spilt your glass,' he said, 'when I asked you.' He refilled it. 'To us.'

'To us!'

He still hadn't removed his jacket despite the heat, he must be baking. He pulled out a jeweller's box – *his* jeweller's box, with his name on it – from his pocket. 'I nearly forgot.' He held it and let her lift open the lid, watching her eyes. Inside was a beautiful gold engagement ring set with a single glowing diamond. He slipped it on her finger and watched as she held it up to the sunlight, where it glittered and flashed.

She thought: *I shall remember this for ever – this moment when he has just asked me to marry him and we sat on Lynmouth beach and drank champagne.*

'Francis,' she said, 'for God's sake let me take your jacket off.' He wanted to fold it but she dropped it on the rocks behind them and loosened his tie, put her arm around him and rested her head in the hollow of his shoulder. He was wearing a white shirt.

By nine in the evening Lynmouth still seemed to lie almost transparently around them under the midsummer sky, and she never wanted to leave. In the Palm Court room of the Watersmeet Falls Hotel a girl was trying to sing 'We'll Meet Again' like Vera Lynn. Francis turned the Humber up the Watersmeet road and the shadowed valley air struck chill on Laura's sunburn. She didn't want to go back. The light faded as the valley walls rose around them and they crossed the clapper bridge to Watersmeet Manor. He stopped the motor, opened Laura's door and swung her down.

'Your hand's hot.'

'My cheeks feel glowing. I've caught the sun.' She walked to the river and patted cold water on her face. She hoped he wouldn't caress her shoulders, they were very red. His hand felt like sandpaper as he turned her towards him.

On the stones where the waters met, with a splash Francis suddenly knelt in front of her. Holding her hands firmly in his, he looked up at her. 'We must do this properly.'

Laura giggled but he held on to her, pulling her back to him as she laughed.

'I'm serious,' he repeated, and then she did respond.

'Yes, I know, Francis.'

'This is Watersmeet.'

He squeezed her hands so tight they hurt. 'Laura Benson, to you I plight my troth, to be yours for ever, I swear.'

Laura shivered.

He stared up at her.

To Francis Pervane, she repeated his words, with his name, her voice small in the deep cleave of the valley, and realized that she was not sorry. She looked around her with a sigh: it was very beautiful, and for a moment she felt at one with everything she saw: the hills, the trees, the mingling waters.

Laura ran all the way home, but her parents had already gone to bed.

She didn't sleep a wink. She lay looking at her engagement ring gleaming in the moonlight. It was too precious to wear in bed. She wrapped it in tissue on the bedside table but she couldn't bear not to see it. Then she simply had to get up and slide it slowly over her finger and clasp her hands between her breasts, staring from her window at the end of the most wonderful day of her life, her white nightdress shifting and fluttering in the wind from the hills.

Her parents were already eating breakfast when Laura breezed brightly into the dining room, having finally fallen asleep at six o'clock, and Sybil flashed her a hostile look. But Ernest waited patiently. Laura put her hand on the table, and the ring glittered.

'So he plucked up the courage at last,' Sybil said.

Ernest covered Laura's hand. 'Darling. Congratulations. We're so happy for you.' He kissed her and examined the ring. 'It's beautiful.'

'You never know a man until you marry him,' Sybil said. 'Or know yourself for that matter. Laura, you're so young. But I wish you all the luck in the world. To be in love is a frightening thing.'

'I'm not at all frightened of Francis. Look what a lovely ring it is.'

Sybil folded her napkin neatly but her chair scraped with an ugly sound when she pushed it back, and she almost ran out. They heard her crying in the hall, then the door of her little knitting parlour closed.

'Don't worry,' Ernest said, 'she's worried about me, not about you.'

'Daddy, I feel so guilty. I shouldn't have said yes. I should have thought about it but I couldn't wait.'

He patted her hand. 'Francis can look after you much better than I can. That's the reality of the situation. You're doing the right thing.'

Laura began to clear up the dishes.

Francis kept his word. He always did. Because he

loved Laura, he waited for his father to die. Not that he thought of it in such callous terms, but he knew he must move out from his father's shadow before Laura could be truly his.

Still she would not let him bed her. He respected her for withholding herself, but in her ability to withdraw from him when he was hottest, she seemed wilfully cruel to him. She wasn't; she was a woman. The more feminine she was, the more she hurt him, and the more he loved her.

Francis was glad Laura was getting by far the better part of the deal. She brought him little money, little property. Sir George had always had his eye on that portion of Paradise Woods abutting Hellebore land but that didn't matter to Francis, it was all in the past. He, on the other hand, brought much to her: he would soon be wealthy, what with the hotel and Pervane's the jeweller, twelve hundred acres of woodland, and several hundred acres more of prime farmland at Higher Lyn, not to mention grazing rights over huge tracts of unfenced moor. So he did not feel ashamed to be cementing their relationship.

Sir George suffered another stroke before the new hunting season started, and Francis' words came true. His father never came home. Laura saw him one last time, the day Francis drove her to Lynton to tell him of their engagement. The old man wanted to put his teeth in and Francis called the nurse. Laura waited on the landing, looking out of the open window at the busy village scene below her. One of the soldiers working under the raised bonnet of a jeep in Lee Road whistled up at her. Then she was called into the room where Sir George was half lying against propped pillows. His eyes moved. Laura put her hand next to his but he couldn't take it. 'Other side,' Francis whispered. She went round the foot of the bed feeling awful, Uncle George's kindly blue Father Christmas eyes following her, then when she touched his good side his hand curled like stiff cardboard around hers. Suddenly he smiled, showing all his teeth. It was a generous, almost completely vacant smile.

Francis said: 'Father, I have asked Laura to be my wife, and she has accepted.'

The hand fluttered in Laura's. The old man was trying to pull himself up. His eyes hardened with the effort as he struggled, not moving from Laura's. She got her arm around his shoulders and lifted gently, willing him up. At last he was sitting upright.

'Nrrg.' Sir George tried desperately to speak. He sounded as though he'd drunk a whole bottle of Old Ruby.

'It's all right,' she whispered, 'don't tire yourself, Uncle George.'

He wrestled a breath into his lungs then gripped her with fierce strength and approval.

He said clearly: 'Now you are a Pervane.'

Satisfied, he said no more.

Sir George Pervane was buried on top of the hill at St Brendan's, next to the grave of Roderick his father. *Hic Iacet*: Laura watched his coffin jerking lightly on the slings as it was lowered into the soil, that corpulent body dwindled to half its weight of a year ago. An astonishing number of mourners had come, mostly old men, staff from the hotel, and some handsome middle-aged and younger women. Old Silas was there, the tears streaming down his face, and that got all the women going, even Sybil. The last time they had all been here together was when Clara was married, but Clara had not come today, too busy with her new life, no doubt. Laura shed a tear as she dropped in her red rose and turned away dabbing her cheeks beneath her black mourning veil. The burned skeletons of furze bushes still stuck up along Cheriton Ridge towards the ranked moor-lines of deep Exmoor: mauve, purple, violet marching into the haze of clouds clustered above the rim of the earth.

'I believe in the resurrection,' Ernest said calmly. He had jarred the excruciating knuckle that stuck out of his pelvis on the way up in the trap and his face was grey with anguish. Laura touched his shoulder compassionately. It was all loss, only love was gain. She turned to Francis standing in a black overcoat at the graveside. He threw his handful of earth into the pit and turned, pulling on his glove, taking Laura's hand in his, Sir Francis Pervane, Baronet, Master of Watersmeet.

'Blow hard,' he ordered, and the huntsmen who waited blew a long wavering mort into the wind. As the people dispersed Laura returned alone inside the church.

She waited for a while in the box-pew where she had been sitting with Francis three years ago, when Clara was married. Married not for love. Laura still didn't understand her clever, crazy sister. She walked down the aisle and paused at the tomb of Ranulph de Barreneau and Resda his wife, the Wolf and the Fox, staring at their battered stone faces, the fingertips chipped from their clasped hands.

Now you are a Pervane.

The door boomed behind her and she turned. 'Francis. You startled me.'

'I've said goodbye to them all.' He smiled and walked jauntily down the aisle, clasped her hand in his. 'We shall be married here.' He kissed her ear.

'Francis, where were their bones scattered?' She touched the stone lid.

'By our naughty ancestors?' He shrugged. 'I don't know. Outside, I suppose. Probably trampled into the earth.'

She shook her head. 'I don't want to be married here.'

He said soothingly: 'As far as I'm concerned the whole silly business is dead and buried. I'm not going to repeat my father's mistakes. I won't be ruled by the past, Laura, it's the future that concerns me.'

'I still don't want to be married in this place.'

He laughed companionably. 'You're the boss. Wherever you like.'

'I'm so cold.'

He kissed her mouth, right there against the tomb, and she felt the cold stone pressing into the small of her back like a reminder of mortality. She hugged Francis desperately, almost crying, grateful for his warmth, his love. Her life felt so small. He rubbed her sides, pinching her.

'God,' he said, 'God I love you.'

She drew deep breaths. 'When will it be?' She nibbled his lips. She thought she felt his thing pressing against her hip like a hard lump even through his overcoat, but it might have been something in his pocket. It wasn't. She reached up on tiptoe, caressing his hair, knowing how excited he was – and she was, yearning for the warmth, the companionship. 'When will we be married?'

'When the estate's wound up. Six months. I don't know. After Christmas. Say you love me.'

'Kiss me again.'

'What are you trying to do? Drive me out of my mind?' Then he laughed, and swept her outside into the chilly wind, the walnut-and-leather warmth of the Humber, and drove her home.

The details of the ritual swept Laura on. Both she and Francis wanted it to be a private affair, and wartime conditions simplified the guest list enormously. Laura decided that the banns were to be read from the church of St John the Evangelist on Countisbury Hill, just above the great promontory fort Francis had pointed out when he asked her to marry him. She had written to Clara telling her the good news, and eventually got a letter back in the tiny handwriting so familiar to her from the Gondwana stories that Laura felt a rush of nostalgia as soon as she saw the envelope, and stood by the kitchen table turning it over in her hands. Then she opened it.

Clara had lots of news. Rob was now an education officer working in the Barum council offices at Castle House and he was an important man. Laura read aloud – she had been peeling potatoes with her mother. Clara had given up her WVS job. 'She says she's going to have a baby!' Laura exclaimed.

'What does it matter,' Sybil said, 'we'll never see it.'

'Wait. Oh no, she says she won't be able to come to my wedding because February is getting near her time. Well–' Laura could hardly hide her disappointment – 'we always knew she wouldn't come anyway. But she says – she says she'd like to see me at Christmas! We're going to have a family Christmas!' cried Laura joyously.

'How will she get here?' Ernest fretted when he heard the news. 'They should never have closed that railway. The buses don't run on time. Does she expect me to pick her up?'

'They can ask the driver to let them off on the county road near Watersmeet Manor, and I'll bring them here in the trap,' Laura said brightly. 'I wonder if she'll be awfully fat?'

Clara did show a bulge, but she was tall enough to look substantial, almost intimidating, rather than plump. Laura hardly recognized her half-sister as the bus pulled away. Her straight brown hair that had hung down to her shoulders – Laura smiled, remembering all the fuss and palaver curling it – now was cut short, giving her face a blocky, mannish look. She looked older, like a woman who knew her mind.

Rob held out his hand to Laura. 'I've heard so much about you,' he said cleverly. Cleanshaven, with a shiny jaw, he was already turning away as they shook hands, picking up his suitcase. 'Is this the vehicle?' He crossed the road and hefted the case on the back platform, walked around the trap, slapped Blackbird's neck. Then he looked out over the valley, inhaling through his nose.

'We can't stay long,' Clara said tenderly, 'Rob misses the traffic. He won't sleep.' She grunted as she got up beside Laura. They drove along the black cleave of leafless trees under the pale winter sky. There was snow on the hilltops.

Laura made conversation: 'I suppose it all looks very different to you.'

'Nothing's changed.' Clara eyed Laura's fur. 'How is my mother?'

'Subtly accusing me of the crime of being young.'

'And in love. Congratulations.'

'Congratulations on your baby,' Laura said awkwardly.

It must have snowed more in the night – in the morning the hilltops trailed their white mantle into the trees. Still Laura had hardly talked to Clara, who stayed for hours in her old bedroom. Rob came between them whenever they got together down-stairs. Laura was confirmed in her dislike of him by the way he walked around as though the place wasn't quite up to his standards, hands in his pockets too, and he didn't know anything about horses. Francis arrived for the roast turkey lunch with all the trimmings and Rob talked to him about the 1937 Education Act. In the afternoon they exchanged brightly wrapped parcels under the Christmas tree in the hall, its tip reaching up the stairwell almost to the railing of the upstairs banisters, the candles that decorated the branches shimmering as darkness fell before four o'clock teatime. Rob started yawning. 'He didn't sleep a wink last night,' Clara said. 'Wake up, dear, or you won't sleep tonight.' She watched Laura and Francis, who sat on the floor by firelight, holding hands.

Then Francis had to go home, shrugging on his raincoat, and everyone went to bed. Laura finished clearing up, then locked the front door. She paused with her hand on the key, then instead opened the door and looked out. The rain had turned to snow and the valley glowed with the stuff, making the night pale and magical, everything utterly still and silent under the whirling flakes that flew like brilliant moths into the porch light, drifting in grey curtains through the distance. The river looked like a black snake winding through the scenery, cutting it in half.

Clara said: 'So you're making the same mistake I did.' Laura span.

Clara was coming slowly downstairs. The yellow, even candlelight from the tree made her nightdress, which was pink, turn an odd sort of bruised colour. She seemed terribly tired, battered and defeated, yet the pancake cream on her face made her features almost devoid of expression.

Standing under the electric hall light, Laura closed the door.

Clara parted her legs and sat with a grunt. The stair squeaked and both girls noticed it: she'd forgotten. But she stayed where she was, a tired adult.

'Rob's asleep,' Clara sighed. 'I was going through the Gondwana stories. I was remembering how it was when I was young.'

'Aren't we still young?'

'No. Being young is when we had dreams, and they came true.' She shifted up one step, as if to make it again as it had been between them when they were children.

Laura walked to the foot of the stairs. She was wearing a dark blue dress that matched her eyes. 'Turn out the light,' Clara said, and they sat on the stairs illuminated only by the glow of candles on the Christmas tree.

'What did you dream?' Laura asked.

'At first? Of marrying Francis.'

Laura said instantly: 'There was never anything between you and Francis.'

'I would have married him like a shot, if he'd asked. Love him?' She shook her head. 'But I would have been a good wife, I know my duty. Instead, he's got you. Fair enough.' But her eyes glittered with bitchy vindictiveness.

Laura's head span. Clara who was unhappily married wanted Laura to be unhappily married too, so that Clara had made no error of judgement, so that unhappiness was inevitable fate, no fault of her plainness or pinched nature. Clara in the end wanted her dreams to fail; she didn't have the courage, in real life, to risk everything, and *then* fail. She had consciously rejected them, left them here at Watersmeet.

Clara said: 'I thought it would be different for you. But you're just like me. You are marrying the man you do not love.'

'That's a lie!'

'I watched you and Francis. Believe me, I speak of what I know.'

'You don't have the faintest idea what I feel!' How could Clara ever know what she felt for Bart, or what she felt for Francis?

Clara said calmly: 'Laura, he took me to bed.'

Laura thought she was going to be sick.

'Not Francis, you idiot,' Clara said gently. 'The other one.'

Laura stared into the candles in Clara's eyes.

'Bart,' said Clara simply. 'I wanted you to know.'

181

Laura shook her head. She put her hands in her hair.

'I went up there,' Clara said. 'Years before you ever thought of it. *The wrong way.* I loved him. I still love him. I'll love him until I die.'

Laura murmured: 'Did he love you?'

Clara didn't answer that.

Even though she cared nothing at all for Bart, Laura was so jealous that she wanted to shake Clara's shoulders until that self-satisfied grin was wiped off her face. She never wanted to see her half-sister again.

But she had to know. 'He didn't . . . did he?'

'*The wrong way,*' Clara said proudly. 'I just stood in the trees and he came out of the house smiling and said hallo, the most handsome young man I'd ever seen in my life. Laura, this was when you and I still slept in the same room. I fell in love. Such a torment of happiness. I went back and back and back. I put my arms around him, I'd never let him go. He led me upstairs to bed. And we.' The candlelight speckled her eyes, she was reliving the moment. Laura wanted to die.

Clara said: 'And we made love. He was very kind and gentle. I was so shy, I had goosepimples, I was trembling all over. I gave myself and he took me. Once, twice, three times.'

Laura's hands dropped into her lap. Her face wrinkled up.

'Why didn't you stay with him then? Why didn't you set up your own happy home together and make love with your bloody lover every day and night instead of sneaking back and lying to me?'

'Sssh,' Clara hushed her. 'Lies? There were no

lies,' she murmured. 'He would never lie. No, Laura, he didn't love me. He was just using me.'

'Oh, you fool.'

'Aren't we all? I'd do the same again. I've never been so happy. I loved him and I lived for each moment with him. But he didn't. I knew it. I knew he was going to break my heart one day and yet I couldn't stop dreaming. I used the body God gave me to be his whore. That was why I couldn't have you in my room any more, so that I could – you're right – sneak back without anyone knowing. I gave myself time after time to keep him, I learned all the tricks. I thought maybe I could keep him by bearing his child. I risked everything. But nothing happened, and all my dreams fell into the dust.'

She heaved a sigh and sat forward. 'I don't know what love is, Laura, I've only known the half of it. To feel it returned . . . it must be the beginning and the end of the world. It terrifies me. I'm contented now, Gondwana's long gone, every little girl grows up. Happiness is too dangerous.' She patted her stomach. 'I'm bearing Rob's lovely baby, and I wouldn't want to ask for more.'

'You're defeated,' Laura said. It was the cruellest thing she could think of to say.

'No,' Clara said, 'I'm contented.'

'You're wrong about Francis.'

Clara stood up. 'You always did play dangerous games. Go on, Laura, be selfish, go riding without a hat, get your silly head knocked off.' She lifted her nightdress around her knees and plodded to the top of the stairs. 'Goodnight. Rob won't sleep if I'm not there. We'll be leaving early in the morning, don't worry.'

She left Laura sitting on the stairs.

But Laura was up earlier, because she didn't sleep a wink. The valley was a white, silent world curving up to a heavy yellow sky. The river chuckled under the plumes of grey mist that rose between the motionless trees. She milked the animals and fed the chickens and a threadbare cat who was shivering under the outhouse, licking wet snow off her paws with magisterial distaste. Laura cuddled her but Maxine refused a sip of fresh milk, then drank a saucer Laura left. While the family ate breakfast Laura fed Blackbird and harnessed her to the trap. She didn't want to talk to Clara any more. Laura felt confused and exploited; she'd let Bart Barronet make such a fool of her and she hated herself. But he *hadn't*, had he? He hadn't taken *her* to his bed, as he had poor Clara who hadn't meant a damn thing to him. The tears threatened to flow into Laura's eyes.

She drove Clara and Rob, who talked the whole way, to the county road, Clara sitting there like a statue without a word – what was he afraid she would say? The Western National coach came labouring up the hill almost immediately, not the one they had hoped to catch but the one before, running late. Rob shook hands and Clara leaned down from the step and pecked Laura's cheek.

'Goodbye, darling,' Clara said cheerfully, then looked back at the snow-covered valley. 'Watersmeet decked out in virgin's apparel.'

Laura watched the coach depart in a cloud of fumes. She hesitated then drove the trap a short way after it up Hoaroak Cleave, hitched Blackbird to the guardrail and walked down to the stream, beginning the climb up into the woods on the far side. Her gloves were soon soaked and her feet were freezing. Clumps of wet snow slithered off the trees and her breath hung about her in the misty silence. Once she saw tracks in the snow, the slotted prints of deer.

She came to the top of the bluff and turned along the drive to Hellebore House. She stood surveying the empty fortress, marvelling that he was not there. All the windows were boarded up, showing how hard he had worked: only one or two planks had sprung and half-hid the remains of birds' nests from last spring. Even the door was boarded, the boards sealed with a massive oak beam, and the steps looking dangerously smooth with snow.

She went round the back, through the side gate. The headstones were featureless lumps and she couldn't even remember which was Lucy Pervane's. Then she turned and there, between the white hills, she glimpsed the sea. Laura closed the gate and left. On the road a police car passed her going the other way. She didn't see it turn left behind her over Hillsford Bridge and she wouldn't have cared if she had. The driver engaged first gear with a crunch and the car lurched down the track to Hellebore House. It bottomed on the carriage circle, the rear wheels digging down and spraying slush, then mud. While the driver cursed and rocked it back and forth two armed policemen got out and stood gazing at the house. The third, who was the local bobby, looked from one to the other with the satisfaction of a man who has been proved right.

'Told'ee wuden't be yur,' he said.

The church of St John the Evangelist lay almost a thousand feet above the sea, and the wedding party wound its way up from Paradise Woods, upward through Horner's Neck Wood, into the clouds.

Ernest drove, with Laura sitting beside him. 'You make me feel very proud,' he whispered to her above the sound of Blackbird's clopping hooves. 'Little Laura, Lady Laura, I have always loved you the best.'

The sheep on Trilly Fields looked like balls of fog bumbling in the sea-mist. Because Watersmeet turned parallel to the coastline for the last few miles of its course, the enormous bulk of Countisbury Hill lay between the valley and the flat waste of sea. One of the little pageboys dragooned from the Lynmouth Primary School opened the gate – the other one, evacuated from the East End, was missing his mummy and sat frozen – as Ernest turned the trap down the main road from Porlock to Lynmouth. The church appeared between billows of cloud in the tiny vale across the road from the Blue Ball Inn, where Francis' Home Guard company would doubtless have refreshed themselves on landlord John Haynes' thin wartime beer after their long climb from Lynmouth.

Laura thought Francis looked very businesslike in his uniform and his buttoned-down holster, containing a Webley revolver, swung heavily as he turned to snatch a glimpse of his bride. He looked so lonely standing there amongst the yew bushes outside the church, all of them bent over to the right as though the sea-wind were still blowing, making him very tall against the low doorway. Laura knew he was looking at her. She wanted to wave but she couldn't. Then the mist rolled over them. The trap stopped.

They could hear the sound of the organ playing faintly through the thick walls.

But more solid, in the distorted world of the fog, was the rumble of ships' engines pulsing and fading down on the invisible sea, seeming to come from all around them, the mournful sirens echoing, and the loom of Countisbury lighthouse far below rotating giant white spokes of light into the gloom.

Laura was all in pure white; Sybil had dug out lots of old chiffon and tulle. A white veil covered her face and she carried a posy of snowdrops. No bouquet of wild flowers for her. Laura could have cried; Clara had wanted to hurt her, but Laura was sure she was doing the right thing. She loved and needed Francis – seeing him waiting so anxiously had convinced her – the warmth she felt, and that knitted tie pulled just a little too tight, convinced her that she knew him through and through. The days of their future were all ahead. Laura was too impatient to wait for the tarpaulin to be put over the wheels, she bundled up her frock in her arms and jumped down. Sybil had already unstrapped the wheelchair. Laura put her hands around Blackbird's muzzle and kissed her. It was all so easy. Time seemed to pass in slow motion.

In the church the woman organist pedalled the Casson's patent Positive Organ with extra vigour as soon as she saw Laura. Laura tried to look demure; they couldn't see her face behind the veil anyway. The free-standing candelabra had been lit and moved forward, the light was so dim. Francis looked as tall as the top candle. He had put his gloves in his hat. She gripped his hand fiercely.

'I love you,' he whispered. And they were married.

187

She sensed someone in the doorway behind her but knew that no one was there, because she had already looked. And there was no other sign, Blackbird did not whinny, no draught stirred the pages of the hymn books. Her last chance, if she had wanted to take it, she let go of her own free will.

'I do.'

Francis kissed her. It was not a social kiss, it was hot and passionate, greedy with hunger and promise, and that was what she liked. 'I love you,' she whispered back to her husband, and clenched her fingers so tightly on his hand that she felt her bones crack.

Outside, Bart stroked Blackbird's neck and let her lick the sweat off his hand as he looked back at the church. No sign of his fury showed on his face, or in the gentle sweeps of his palm across the horse's silky black coat, carefully groomed this morning, groomed by *her* hand. Then he strode away downhill. He hoped she would find contentment with Francis Pervane. He bit his lips. He knew her better than she knew herself. He heard a bicycle on the hill, its whirring spokes, and hid, then crossed the foggy road at a run.

Yet everything about Laura was a mystery, he couldn't understand her. Let Francis know her, have her, possess her. She terrified Bart. She awoke so much in him that she hurt him. He could have undressed her and taken her there in the great window with Watersmeet laid out beneath them. With Laura it wouldn't have been an ending, but a beginning.

The church had been swallowed in the mist behind him. Watersmeet suddenly revealed itself as he dropped below the cloud line. Here was his mistress, unspoiled nature, Watersmeet, *his* world. He knew her. He knew the moods of her seasons, her trees and flowers, he knew by heart the sea-trout pools where the peal spawned, he felt in his bones when the elvers were running. He knew the rhythms of solstice and equinox. There was a name for it: home. Watersmeet was his. So he fought his own war.

He had seen the writing on the wall: the Regiment's training association with 32 Guards Brigade ended and the heavy self-propelled Bishop guns arrived. The unit was attached to 1 Canadian Division, the Bishops were already being waterproofed with Bostik sealant and submersible cowlings fitted, and they started practising firing over the heads of advancing troops. When Bart saw tropical kit being unloaded into the quartermaster's stores, he knew the Regiment was very shortly to take part in a landing operation abroad, and it wasn't his war. It was *theirs* – he wasn't frightened, he was angry at what they were trying to do to him: to make him like other men, ordered and obedient. He had no choice but to go absent without leave. He simply evaporated from a night exercise in Hertfordshire, threw his rifle off a bridge but kept the fine Army boots, and crossed country living on his wits like a hunted animal, a rôle in which he felt perfectly at home. He had already seen the police visit Hellebore, so he knew it would be safe for a while. He had come home.

He found Laura so beautiful – not only in her slightly discordant features, her mouth that did not quite match her eyes – but in ways that mattered most, the flicker of laughter in her even when she was angry or hurt, her vulnerability, her unpredictability. And he denied he loved her.

Arriving down in Lynmouth Laura saw that even the Watersmeet Falls Hotel, where the wedding reception was held in the Palm Court, was bedevilled by shortages of the smallest things now – but not of luxuries; shellfish, salmon served up on brown bread, sea-trout, André's famous bouillabaisse, even venison. Laura was touched by efforts everyone had gone to – the old boys of the Home Guard had formed up along the path outside the church, standing to attention, and they wanted to loose off a volley but it wasn't allowed, and they didn't have any swords to make an arch for the bride and groom to walk under, so they gave three rousing cheers and flanked them proudly to the waiting car.

'You'll have to dance with them all,' Francis warned her so gloomily during the brief ride downhill that she laughed and hugged him.

The acoustics of the Palm Court with its polished wood ceiling and hardwood floor, the few surviving palms ranked between the tables along one wall, were so good that they did more than justice to the hotel-sized Big Band sound of Carmen Cavallero. After the first dance Laura kept on dancing and Francis didn't take his eyes off her. Everyone was asking her, there was a bloody queue of them. Francis chatted and smiled. He was not a social person, he had done this for her, and when she was over the other side of the room he longed for her to come back to him. He glanced surreptitiously at his watch, then cut in and danced with her again, trying to enjoy himself. She let him hold her closer than anyone else, her face shining with perspiration, she felt like a glowing coal. He would give all this show up in a moment for her, just to hold her, alone, no one else, and he saw from the way she looked up into his eyes that she knew exactly what he was thinking, and that she felt the same.

Laura hardly knew any of the people here. All that must change. She wanted to share Francis' life completely. It was a help that everyone was so kind and introduced themselves. Lord Fortescue kissed her hand and called her Lady Pervane. Laura laughed. She supposed she was.

It was a shock to realize it was dark. Tony Fewkes-Carson, the best man, made a suitably crude speech. Laura nibbled a shrimp canapé, the only food she ate all evening, surrounded by plenty. Francis checked that one of the staff would drive Laura's parents home as arranged, the trap would be delivered tomorrow. Tears filled Laura's eyes as she kissed her father goodbye, then her mother.

Francis wrapped her cloak around her and Laura suddenly realized how cold it was outside: the fog had cleared and everything was totally black. Not a single light showed in Lynmouth. Francis started the Humber. A few drunks hammered on the roof and Tony slipped on to his backside on a frozen puddle.

'Time to go home,' Francis said, driving. She giggled and tried to stop him changing gear. She kissed his ear then wiggled his earlobe with the tip of her tongue. The car went swaying along the road, then turned down, crossed the clapper bridge and passed through the white gates, and Laura became serious as they passed where the waters joined. Watersmeet Manor was her home now.

She surveyed its long black shape in the gleam of the headlamps. 'Carry me across the threshold!' she demanded. He was very strong, swept her up easily, and she hugged his neck and kicked her legs as he knocked open the door with his shoulder. She wasn't quite sure what would happen next.

He was. He carried her upstairs, breathing heavily, and she wondered if he'd have to put her down. Then he followed the circular landing round to a room she had never been in before: it was her bedroom and contained a double bed. There was no open fire; the Manor was centrally heated.

'You'll have to wait,' Laura whispered.

'Yes. Of course.'

He went out and closed the door. Laura took off her dress and laid it over a chair. Then she crossed to the bed and turned down the covers. The eiderdown was decorated with a pink flower pattern which she disliked. It was probably his mother's; Francis never liked throwing anything away. She tested the bed gingerly, she did not feel at all passionate. She wished she hadn't sent Francis out, she wanted to hold him in her arms. Wearing only her shift, she combed her hair in the mirror. Should she call for him? She stood there naked. She wanted Francis to see her. The door opened and she turned.

'I wanted to undress you,' Francis said.

She felt awful; it had never occurred to her. She had spoiled some plan that he had been looking forward to. She slipped across to him. 'Let *me* undress *you*.'

He stood motionless. Only the first of his buttons

192

was awkward, the rest came easily. She caressed his chest with the palms of her hands, stroked them upwards, so that her fingertips sent the shirt slithering from his shoulders. She counted his ribs lightly down with her long fingernails, then with a quick motion released his belt, and he undid the fly buttons himself, his trousers dropped away, the waistband fell across her toes. She pulled his head down on to her mouth and lifted herself on tiptoe, her nipples rippling up his ribs, so that she gave a small gasp of passion.

Francis moved to reach behind him and turned off the light. Suddenly he took command, taking her hand and leading her to the bed. Then in a voice husky with desire he said the words she longed to hear, taking her in his arms, 'My Laura, oh my Laura, I love you.' He didn't try to seduce her now, to build her up with caresses, she was his wife. He lay on top of her and pushed forward with his knees so that her legs were parted. She felt the pressure of him pushing and pressing and then thank God everything was slippery and he slid inside her while she lay gasping with relief. Then gradually she felt him dwindling and realized it was over, it had actually happened, and that was all it was.

'My love,' he murmured, lying beside her, 'my lovely Lady Laura Pervane. Now you are Mistress of Watersmeet, and I am Master.' He pinched her playfully, but his voice was serious.

PART THREE

Mistress of Watersmeet

What was wrong with Francis? Laura felt baffled and guilty. She had wanted to make him happy, and he was. He was so damned happy and likable her every provocation was water off a duck's back to him – he made her sick. She provoked him to make him come alive. But he did love her.

All happy families resemble one another, but each unhappy family is unhappy in its own way. That had long been true of the Pervanes and the Barronets, united and bound together by hatred – and by Watersmeet. *All happy marriages resemble one another, but each unhappy marriage is unhappy in its own way.* Yet Laura had everything to be contented about, Francis often passed the whole night in her bed, in her arms. But she did not seem to attract him as she once had. Sometimes he fingered the seams up the back of her stockings, ran his hands up her legs; but he already possessed her. He thought she was happy and would have been amazed to know she was bored.

She did not love her husband and never had. Without meaning to, he made her feel guilty about herself. She felt so empty. He came to her bed with her, but he was gone if she woke wanting him later. He liked her to wear a nightdress because it was more sensual. It took Laura months to realize that he found her naked body intimidating. So she wore the nightdress even when he wasn't there, in case he came in. Nothing in the world was more hurtful than that kiss goodnight at the top of the stairs.

They settled into the routine of a married couple, a good deal more loving than most, she supposed: he grinned with genuine happiness to see her when he came down to breakfast, pecked at her cheek, asked her what she was doing today. Like two people playing husband and wife on the wireless. For the first time in her life Laura didn't have enough to do. A daily, Mrs Pawkins, a brave soul whose husband had run off in the thirties and was said to be living with a chorus girl, plodded loyally up from the hotel and did most of the housework for Laura, and the laundry was trounced by a modern electric machine.

She wasn't sure where she had gone wrong, but she was certain it was her fault. Love conquered all – didn't it? So she set out to conquer Francis properly. She wore pleasing clothes, she cooked his favourite meals, she made sure she finished her work organizing the conversion of the Manor garage to a stable – Sir George had rarely ridden for pleasure, and like him Francis kept his roan Haymaker up at the Hunt stables on Higher Lyn Down, a hell of a climb on foot – before Francis came back from the hotel or wherever he went all day, she had a bath, she ran out to meet him, and made it obvious that she was pleased to see him; that she was doing everything for *him*.

Yet Francis was a man. His emotions were different. The more she advanced, the more he retreated into himself. And yet he loved her. He liked sex with her, he liked her company, he thought she was fun. Love, sex, companionship and fun.

These words meant different things to them. Romance, glamour, change. So Laura went off her food; she was too fat. She wanted to cut her hair, but Francis came in when she had the scissors in her hand and he was horrified. 'You mustn't! It's your best feature.'

'Is it? You never have said so.'

He buried his face in her curls and made love to her, right there on the floor, before she could even get her clothes off. She stroked his cheek tenderly.

'I do love you,' he whispered. 'Promise me you won't cut your hair.'

'I promise.'

'Ever.'

'Not until you want me to, darling.'

'I never want you to,' he said seriously. 'I never want you to change a thing, my Laura, my wife.' She loved him to talk like that, and lay contentedly with her eyes closed while he got up. Then he was gone, and she wondered how she had failed him.

She worked hard on the stable, getting Silas to help her with the heavy work, but he didn't approve and wasn't much use – that piece of oak wasn't right, too heavy; but that length wouldn't take the weight, anyone could see that; she'd have to use two-inch galvanized nails on that manger and they didn't have any. Didn't she know what a tenon-and-mortice joint was? Laura learned. He was faintly alarmed when she taught herself to solder the pipe for water, and he was horrified when she looked up in a book how to rig the connections for an electric light. Then she started learning how to get Silas going, so that he *wanted* to help her, making him think for himself until finally the old boy's enthusiasm matched her own. They were both sorry when the work was finished and Laura hung Blackbird's haynet from the stape.

'Thee bist bringing 'orze over now, Lady Pervane?'

'My name is Laura, Silas.'

He shook his head confidently. 'Thee bist Lady Pervane, Mistress of Watersmeet, my lady, whether'ee like it or no. Thee can't take that away from him.'

'From who?'

Silas settled a stem comfortably in his mouth. 'Thy husband, lady.'

'Oh, that silly old title isn't really so important to him, is it?'

Silas said over his shoulder: 'Lady, doan't thee *know*?'

Over supper Laura said: 'Francis, I really feel I ought to do my bit. There must be some work I could do on the farm.'

He smiled. 'You're forgetting who you are.'

'Or at the hotel, then. You're always saying how short-staffed you are. I have a good head for numbers, I'm a good organizer— '

'No,' Francis said, wiping his lips.

'The place needs some push. I have willpower, Francis. I get my way.'

'This is your place.'

'We never go for picnics any more, you never take me out. I feel like your princess locked up in a tower. You always go out and I never do.'

'That's not fun, it's business. You know perfectly well you can go out whenever you like. There's the Wild Herbs Committee.'

'You always take the car,' she pouted.

'You can't drive,' he pointed out.

'I can learn.'

'It's six cylinders, Laura, and more than twelve horsepower.'

'I could learn to be good enough.'

'There's only one thing you need to be good at,' he murmured, reaching for her, 'and you're good at that already.'

But later she thought: *so why am I not happy?*

Her energy, like her emotions, was pushed back inside her; into want.

He took her all too much for granted.

So she took Silas' 12-bore shotgun and shot the peacocks, that had been a fixture of the Manor for the last hundred and fifty years, where they had always roosted on that particular branch of the tree, from her bedroom window. Francis rushed in while the gun was still smoking. For a moment she saw, quite literally, fear in his eyes. She had meant to be as matter of fact as he: I couldn't stand the racket they made. I couldn't stand them soiling the lawn any more. We kill chickens and eat them, don't we? But instead she cried, the tears welling up in her eyes and overflowing down her cheeks, and he rushed across the room and took the gun and held her in his arms. He didn't try to make love to her or do anything tactless, just held her.

It was too late. She already knew how he really thought of her: not as an object exactly but as something different from him, a woman, someone he could never comprehend however much he loved her. There was no longer any point of contact between them.

Francis had dutifully excluded her from his life
– his man's world – so she began to exclude him
from her interests. Throughout the spring she took
to riding alone, since she was left alone. Francis
watched her go. He knew she was rebelling against
his authority, but she did not have his sense of
righteousness. He *knew* he was in the right, whereas
she felt guilty that she was unhappy. He was doing
what was expected of him. He waited patiently for
her to settle down.

Laura was haunted. Once she thought she saw
Bart in the woods.

Francis arranged a surprise. He appealed to Laura
by giving her a pretty present, a box done up with
crimson ribbon. She had just come in wearing a
hacking jacket, her hair dragged smoothly back into
a knot, and she didn't seem particularly pleased to
see him.

Then she saw the gift box on the Bechstein.
'That's not for me, is it?'

'Who else?'

She sat on the stool and pulled the bows open.
Inside was a sapphire necklace.

'To match your eyes,' he smiled.

It was nice. She tried to look more pleased than
she felt. It didn't mean as much to her as she wanted
it to mean – once she would have killed for such a
gift. She still wore her father's watch; now she hung
the expensive, real jewellery dutifully around her
neck and let Francis go behind her to fasten the
clasp, as he so obviously wanted to do. He stroked
her neck but she couldn't respond. She knew that
Francis was being artificial; he was not giving her the
gift out of strength but from weakness. She had

dreamed of a man with the courage to be formed by his own passions rather than one who was dominated by what society expected of him. Marriage to Francis had taught her he was prosaic. He was *safe*.

He poured the tea. 'Did you enjoy your ride?'

'Yes.'

'I do wish you'd wear a hat.'

'Oh Francis, do shut up!' she said angrily.

He looked at her in the mirror above the fireplace, hurt by her outburst. She niggled at the necklace as though it were too tight.

'If you *will* go riding through the woods,' Francis said, still stroking her neck, 'I must tell you that Bart Barronet is on the run from the Army.'

'My God,' Laura said.

'He's been AWOL since the end of January and they haven't caught him yet. Desertion is a very serious offence. He must be desperate, and he's probably dangerous.'

She murmured: 'But do you think he'd dare come back here?'

'He'd be out of his mind if he did. Why? You haven't seen— '

'What would *you* do if you saw the poor man?'

Francis sounded baffled by her question. 'I'd do my duty. I'd arrest him on the spot, then turn the cowardly swine in to the proper authorities.'

'Just because he doesn't suffer from asthma?' She was sorry at once. 'I didn't mean— '

'I know what you meant.' He fingered the cool necklace, her warm smooth skin. His gaze softened. She brushed him off impatiently.

'Cowardice wouldn't bring him back here!' she said.

'What, then?'

'Courage.'

Francis stopped. He asked her directly: 'Why, have you seen him sneaking about?'

'No. No, I haven't seen him sneaking about.'

He looked down and struck a note thoughtfully on the piano. 'The Pervanes have always known their duty.'

'But we're free of all that, Francis! Free of the past.'

She might not have spoken. He ignored her, for the first time ever. 'Laura, you are a Pervane now.'

'Yes, of course,' Laura said immediately. 'Of course you are quite right.'

But when she turned away she saw, in the mirror, Francis eyeing her thoughtfully.

Laura rode out and saw her parents most days. They'd cut back on the kitchen garden a lot even though she'd sent Silas over with the rotovator. They ate hardly anything. Her father was always pleased to see her, but he seemed weary, like a man who knows his duty is done. Sybil was often in her solarium reading a book – something she rarely did before – her silver half-glasses perched on her nose, her hair like Laura's, swept back into a bun: but greying, with little hooks of short hair sticking up like a fuzz, whereas Laura's looked sleek, pulled back black and shiny as fresh tar. Sybil watched her fondly: Laura still moved distinctively as always, lithe and quick, graceful but determined. There was no sign of a baby yet, but she ought not to ride so much, or so fast. She poured her a tumbler of lemonade and they sat on the white cane chairs amongst the litter of kneeling mats and secateurs, packets of Sutton seeds, Laura resting the ankle of her long riding boot across her other knee, with the scent of growing things all around them under the glass.

'You mustn't worry about us,' Sybil said gently. 'I know you do. But we can live without you, you know, darling.'

Laura had finished her lemonade and jumped up already. 'I'll send Silas over to do the heavy digging.'

'We don't eat like horses, you know.' Sybil wished she could tell Laura that she listened to the wireless with Ernest in the evenings now; that this vast, irrelevant cataclysm gripping the world would soon be over. 'All the news is of victories now. There will be a Second Front this year, or if not, next year. We thought,' Sybil confided, confident it would never happen, 'after the Armistice, we might buy a villa in the south of France. Somewhere near the beach, where it's flat. Ernest could easily manage the Croisette, see the harbour, and of course there's the casino.' The sun was already dropping behind the hilltops. *Suppose they aren't here to come over and talk to?* Laura thought, almost panicky. They thought it was perfect between Francis and her. Francis would keep her under control.

Laura turned by the door. 'Are you sure there's nothing I can do for you?'

Sybil said indulgently: 'Just give my love to Francis, dear.' She didn't suspect a thing, thank God.

Laura swung into the saddle and rode home towards Watersmeet Manor. On impulse she went down through the trees towards Dumbledon Pool where she used to swim. She stopped near the cliff-top.

He was down there.

Him. She was almost certain. Bart was there.

Then she glimpsed him well enough to be sure. He did not look at her, and she did not move. Then she couldn't see him any more, but her eyes followed where he must be up through the shimmering treetops on the far side, towards Hellebore.

She tightened the reins, and Blackbird backed away from the cliff-edge, the horseshoes clinking on the boulders, and turned towards the Manor. She made Blackbird walk the whole way. She hardly remembered dismounting or brushing down; she went upstairs. She sat on the dressing-table stool, staring at herself.

She ought to do something. She went and ran her bath.

Suddenly the front door slammed and Laura was still steaming in her bath. She must have slept. Francis came in taking off his uniform jacket, baring his teeth in that odd way a man did when he pulled off his tie.

'Full to the brim, not very patriotic,' he grinned. 'You look rather pale. What's the matter?'

'Is poached fish all right for supper?'

'Whatever suits you, my darling.'

She shrugged and closed her eyes.

He said: 'It's not this bloody flu, is it?' She wished he'd stop talking and get into the bath with her, let the water overflow on the floor, lose the soap.

'No,' she said, pulling the plug and wrapping herself in a towel, 'it's not that.'

Francis always dressed for dinner, so she supposed Sir George always had. She wore her dark blue dress with the plunging crossover neckline trimmed with white lace, the sapphire necklace. Mrs Pawkins from the hotel had peeled the potatoes and put the fish on to poach before she left, all Laura had to do was take it out. Its taste was as unsatisfactory as she felt.

Francis looked at her across the candlelit refectory table and spoke softly. 'Tell me, darling.' He put out his hand, palm up, halfway across the table towards her. 'Tell me.'

'I don't know myself.' She pushed the flaking fish around her plate.

'Reach out,' Francis said. 'I'm here.'

If only he wasn't so kind. She shook her head. 'I'm just in a mood.' But she almost reached out to him.

He said: 'Is it— ' he glanced at her eagerly.

'How can I be?' she said bitterly, 'when we don't sleep in one another's arms, we sleep in separate bedrooms?'

That was unfair. He used his hand to pick up his fish knife just as she reached out. He recommenced eating, head down. Laura kicked herself.

'I'm sorry, Francis. I hurt you.'

'Not at all.'

'I didn't mean to, I'm sorry.'

'You didn't! For God's sake shut up,' he said, and she looked at him in surprise. There was a glint in his eye. He threw down his knife, then his fork, on his plate, and she flinched with each clattering impact. The fork span towards the floor, and they waited, but it landed soundlessly on the carpet. He got up and walked to the door, then turned and went back to the sideboard, pulled out a bottle of port, and drank a glass, staring at her.

She curled her hands in her lap, lowered her head. 'Francis,' she murmured.

He waved her away. He was a weak man aroused. She went to him and put her arms on his shoulders, but he pushed her away, quite hard, so that she bumped against the corner of the table. He hadn't meant to do it, didn't realize he had. She had let no sign of her pain show on her face. He put the bottle back in the sideboard, then picked up the fork.

'I'll come to your bedroom tonight,' he said, and went out.

She cleared up the plates then stood in the kitchen, rubbing her hip. She didn't want to go upstairs at first; she didn't want to feel more inadequate than she already did. She could hear Francis in the lounge so she went through into the hall and stared up at the wonderful circular balcony, the ascending loop of staircase, then backed away, opened the door to the old study and went inside. It was dark; she clicked on the lights and limped across to stand beneath the picture of Phineas Pervane, the elder brother who would have inherited the titles and estate that went to Sir George's father.

Laura had rearranged the room. Sir George's horrid old Chippendale directoire desk was relegated to a corner, she'd put round sprays of flowers, placed the virginals in another corner, and the harpsichord with its black-white keys was under the painting now.

She stared upwards.

Phineas looked out at her from the torn picture for his love, Lucy Barronet, Lady Lucy Pervane, who stood covered in flowers in the other half of the painting that hung in the hallway of Hellebore House, the wagging tail and haunches of a King Charles spaniel at her foot; the same dog whose head, with pink lolling tongue, panted adoringly at Phineas' knee in front of Laura's eyes. She remembered Sir George saying: *They dreamed that love could conquer time.*

Laura went upstairs. She undressed, put on her nightdress, and combed out her hair like a dark cloud. She got into bed and read for a while, then Francis came in. She could smell Old Ruby on his breath, so she knew he'd gone back for another glass. He turned out the light and they made love. Because the alcohol had slowed his reactions, by the time he finished she actually felt quite aroused.

Tonight he did not leave her. She lay awake with her arms around him, listening to the black rain fall. It was not enough. She knew what she ought to think, ought to feel; but she knew now what she must do.

Still it was raining the next morning when Laura, dressed in a shining black waterproof cape, a black sou'wester protecting her head, rode up through the dripping woods towards Hellebore. There were the vertical rocks of the bluff, the withered oak jutting out from them high above the hissing stream, the crumbling gateposts with the broken stone buzzard on top. She turned along the drive and stopped below the rain-streaked façade of the house, the front doors still battened closed and braced with that huge oak beam.

She left Blackbird to graze on the fresh spring

grass and walked slowly up the steps, half expecting that the battened doors were a trompe l'oeil and would open, but the oak was real and solid as a rock. She tugged, then pushed with her shoulder before stepping back defeated, shut out. As she retreated back to ground level, she could feel water running down inside her collar.

She walked round the side, opened the gate and went through. Back here the grass had grown wild, already with seed heads, peppering her waterproof to the waist with husks as she walked between the drenched tussocks, the dripping heads of campion, foxglove, spurge, and strange plants whose names she did not know. The headstone of Lucy Pervane was beaded with moisture. *Requiescat In Pace.*

Laura turned and looked between the hills. Today the sea, glimpsed in the vee of the cleave, looked grey and smooth, slick as a mackintosh. Then she crossed to the back door, twisted the handle, and went inside.

She was at the back of the hall, beneath the staircase where the little children started the fire. Her nose wrinkled at the smell of damp, her footfalls were muffled on the dusty boards, she could hear water dripping inside the walls. 'Bart.' She cleared her throat, and called his name again. Then she went to the stairs and climbed the creaking risers, taking off her sou'wester and slapping the drops off against her knees for courage. At the top stretched a long corridor. She chose the first door on the right.

So it was true.

The room was dominated by a four-poster bed. Laura could not bring herself to touch it. She imagined him with Clara. She imagined Bart letting her seduce him, taking her, using her, while she lay holding her legs as wide as they would go, because she loved him, and her dreams had come true.

But Laura remembered Clara's whisper on the stairs: *They don't come true.*

Laura couldn't bear it. She strode forward and snatched at the fabric. A whole drape peeled away with a popping sound as the rotten stitching gave way, and fell on to the mouldering rug at her feet, She stared at it, then ran.

Downstairs, she followed winding passageways through a warren of storerooms, pantries, kitchens, servants' quarters below ground level. Everything was deserted, but he was here, or had been. She could sense his presence, the real Bart Barronet, she was getting closer.

She found a coat hanging on a hook and in a scullery, in the plane of light from the skylight above, a half-empty jam jar stood on the table next to a jam-smeared knife. She rubbed a few crumbs of bread between her fingers, still soft. On the small iron Bodley stove, a stockpot steamed languidly, rabbit stew, she could smell it, strong and rich. She shouldn't be here. The sensation of trespass was very vivid. She actually looked over her shoulder, but couldn't resist the door beyond. It was his larder: a few pots of yeast and brown bags of tea, no sugar, he wouldn't have a rations card, but plenty of home-made honey, he must have a hive somewhere. She marvelled at what she was finding. If she didn't tell Francis, she'd become an accomplice against her own husband. Laura decided the only sensible thing to do was to pretend she'd never been here, and she turned stiffly towards the door. And screamed as a hand gripped her shoulder.

'Bart!'

His face was dark, all shadows. She stared, compelled by his fury. His hair was ragged, still growing out its Army cut, brown and gold. But his steady, tawny eyes hadn't changed. She looked up into them and she really believed that he could kill her.

'Bart, it's me.'

'Long ago,' he said, 'it was sworn that a Pervane would never again enter between these walls. You are a Pervane now.'

She swallowed her anger. 'Do you really think I'd tell Francis you're here?'

'I don't know what you'd do.'

She said gently:'How long can you stay here? You can't keep running from them for ever.'

He actually laughed. 'You don't think the local police would give me away? Besides, when the village bobby comes up on his bicycle, you can hear him puffing half a mile away up the valley.'

'But they'll keep coming back.'

'I know.'

He took off his coat and suddenly she realized how wet through, cold and weary he was.

'You couldn't make me hate you,' Laura said.

He gave her a relaxed, friendly smile. He had tried.

They sat at the table. How much had changed. 'Why were we never like this before?' she wondered.

'You didn't belong to Francis before.'

'I don't belong to Francis!' she cried impulsively.

He looked at her without a change of expression.

'Lady Laura Pervane, Mistress of Watersmeet. Yes, you do.'

She admitted: 'My heart doesn't.'

'He's a good and proper man, and you married him good and proper.'

'I'm not talking about marriage.'

'I am.'

'He doesn't deserve me. I can't tell him I don't love him. I don't.'

'I'm so sorry,' Bart said firmly. 'Laura. It's all for the best.'

'Second best.' She propped her elbows on the rough wood, her hair over her hands. 'When you came in, I realized that when I'm with him I don't feel anything. Friendship. I don't think he could ever hurt me, not unless he really tried. But you could. You hurt me now you are here. I wish I could see you better,' she said defiantly, 'can't I turn the light on?'

'Hush,' Bart said. 'Don't talk.'

She didn't dare just get up and do it anyway, as she would have done if he'd been Francis. She felt so sorry for Bart. The Army, the police, the real world, would get him in the end.

'If only you hadn't saved the stag,' she said miserably, 'they would have left you in peace. Why did you do it?' She pushed back her hair. 'Why did you have to be so stupid?'

Now she did see his eyes gleam. Bart said: 'Once, that wild red deer was only a few hours old. His mother had abandoned him, or been killed. I fed him milk from a baby's bottle, and one day I let him go. Now he leads the herd. Did you ever see such a beautiful animal?'

213

'Perhaps I will, one day.'

'Be careful,' he said in a voice totally without sentiment.

She laid her hands on the table. 'Bart, I feel so guilty. I don't know why I came here. Francis is so sweet. I must be mad.'

He reached out and took up both her hands in one of his. 'You must never, ever come here again. Please.'

'I could bring you food. Sugar, flour.' She was trying desperately to get him to acknowledge her in one way or another. He squeezed her hands lightly, and Laura said abruptly: 'I know you took Clara upstairs.'

'She didn't mean anything to me,' he said swiftly.

'Does that mean I do?'

For a moment longer he looked at her, almost an endless moment. She had opened the collar of her black waterproof and he could see the pulse in her throat, sensed her heartbeat, felt it pumping in her cool wrists, her quivering hands. Her hair was pulled back and tied, making her look so smooth and elegant, but he wished she would let it fall. There was something so tense about her, somewhere her fun and laughter had gone, her little-girlishness. She was serious. Marriage had changed her inside. Beneath that waterproof cape she was still slowly changing, like a chrysalis into a butterfly, a valley metaphor that made him both pleased and sad. He knew what he felt about her.

'Let us talk,' he said.

Laura trembled as he pulled back her chair politely and helped her up, led her back along the twisting passageway she had come down. She wondered if he was going to lead her upstairs to the bed, and whether she would let him?

He did take her upstairs, but only as far as the entrance hall where he pulled her over to the picture of Lucy.

'No one can defy fate,' Bart said softly. 'No man, no woman.'

Sir George Pervane had told her almost the same thing. Laura was wiser now. 'Bart, our lives are our own. We're free to make of them what we will.'

They looked up at the girl with the Mona Lisa smile, the painting of a girl in love. She knew what she wanted. Behind her Watersmeet valley fell away into a haze of wild flowers. And yet her husband was missing: Phineas, down in Watersmeet Manor.

Bart spoke softly. 'This painting is unique. It was commissioned jointly by the two families, the Barronets and the Pervanes, on the occasion of Lucy Barronet's betrothal to Phineas. The artist was their friend, Arthur Hughes, who knew the young lovers well. He was hardly older than they. A genius, and this is his last work. He died young, having completed only the figures. So Watersmeet was painted in by one of their wedding guests, John Brett. Rosetti, leader of the Brotherhood, who passed most of his visit out of his mind on chloral and laudanum, told Brett it was his finest work, better than *Val d'Aosta*. Well, some of the best work in art, if not in life, is by committees. If it were ever made whole again, this work of art would be worth a fortune. But it was a tragedy, the story of young Pre-Raphaelite lovers defying the manipulations of their parents.'

'Where were they married?'

He didn't look at her. 'The church of St John the

Evangelist. The sea on the one hand, and Watersmeet on the other.'

Laura said nothing.

'Phineas and Lucy dreamed of bringing their two warring families together, uniting them by marriage. Their child would be of the two bloods met, like the meeting of the two rivers, and peace would come to the valley of Watersmeet.'

'As it now has.'

'As it now has,' he said, and touched his scarred cheek thoughtlessly. 'They were very clever, committed in their idealism. I think Lucy was the natural leader, the down-to-earth one. Of course Lavinia Barronet told her daughter that if she married Phineas and became a Pervane, the Barronet family would disown her. I don't mean disinherit, lose out on a few bob and some of the family silver, I mean she would cease to exist as far as they were concerned. Lucy could not change her mother's mind, and the matriarch's words were not a threat or a warning, they were a promise. Lucy defied her mother and married Phineas, all for love, and became Mistress of Watersmeet. And conceived a child.'

He was shivering. She touched his chest: his shirt was still damp. It was the white shirt with the black buttons. 'You're cold!' she said. 'You'll catch your death.'

He took her elbow and led her outside. A high, diffuse sun was breaking through the white sky, the grass was already steaming, she inhaled the intense green scent of growing things. She felt Bart's hands on her shoulders and she began to unbutton her cape. He hung it over his arm and turned his face up to the sun.

'The union seemed to be successful. The two families seemed to come to an uneasy reconciliation apart from Lavinia, and Lucy's elder brother, who had inherited Hellebore— '

'What was his name?'

'Bart,' said Bart apologetically. 'It's a name that's been handed down through our family for centuries.'

'But what of Lucy's baby? You aren't going to tell me something dreadful happened?'

'No,' Bart said, 'she and Phineas called their son Adam.' He looked away. 'That's the end of my story.'

She rested her cheek against his shoulder. 'Tell me everything. You and I wouldn't be standing here if that was the ending. Everything would be perfect.'

He took her arm as he walked her down the drive. 'It seemed that the feud was over . . . but they did not realize that of course a feud knows no peace. One evening at Watersmeet Manor when Roderick, Phineas' younger brother, was staying there for the holiday season, the weather was so hot that it finally broke into a ferocious rainstorm. Thunder and lightning. You know the way the trees roar. And Phineas carried a candle to his bedroom . . . Phineas leans over the cradle-bed where Adam is already asleep, about two years old, in a white nightgown embroidered by the women and still too long for him. His tiny hands are clutched above his head, eyes staring, tongue black between bulging lips, strangled and lifeless. When Phineas screams, no one hears him. He picks up his tiny son and cuddles him, trying to bring him back to life. Under the body he finds Lucy's handkerchief. The scent of rosewater she uses, which fades so quickly, is still strong. In that one moment, Phineas loses his mind. *Once a Barronet, always a Barronet.* What is he to think? Did she never love him – was this her dreadful revenge? In his sorrow he believes what the murderer meant him to – he hates Lucy, and his own life. Everything he fought for and won falls in ruins around his ears in the storm. Raving, he snatches up the bottle of medicinal chloral that made them sleep, that gave them such wonderful dreams, and drinks it down to the dregs. And so Lucy finds them, the bodies of her son and her husband together.'

Laura swept back her hair. 'She must have lost her mind too.'

'As she knelt beside him she saw her handkerchief and must have understood that Phineas had lost faith in her, that their love did not conquer all but was itself conquered. She embraced them together, son and husband, and saw what Phineas had missed: wet footprints by the bed, French windows open to the balcony and the body of the dog, the loyal spaniel, who had died trying to defend the baby. A grim scene. And then, behind her, the door opened.'

'And the Pervane clan gathered,' Laura said.

'They blamed Lucy. Roderick Pervane especially. *Once a Barronet.* Lucy must have been frantic. In a stroke she had lost everything she believed in, her son, her husband, everything. Roderick threw her out of the house there and then, into the storm.'

Bart stopped. They stood on the top of the bluff, where the driveway curved. He had a head for heights that made Laura wince: he parted the nittal bushes and revealed the bend in the river far below them, the rooflines of Watersmeet Manor amid the pattern of formal gardens in the natural amphitheatre. Bart said in a low voice: 'I don't know what she must have felt, that night she spent alone in the wind and rain down there.'

'But surely Roderick— '

'He was a Pervane,' Bart said. 'Dawn found Lucy shivering in her soaking clothes, climbing back to Hellebore House. Where else could she go? She came along the drive here and pleaded for forgiveness from her own mother. But Lavinia would not take her back in. She spoke only four words to her daughter: *You are a Pervane.* Lavinia's hand was done up in a bloodstained bandage, she had caught it on some thorns in the rose garden the day before. But the blood still ran, just as it does from a dog bite, and the truth hit Lucy: her own mother was the murderer. Better dead than a Pervane. Insane with jealousy, she had strangled her own grandchild in his cradle.'

Laura could not hide her shudder of revulsion. 'Do you believe that?'

'Lucy believed it.' He walked Laura to the peak of the bluff, to the very edge, and stood staring out. 'She threw herself over the edge. Here. Just here.'

Laura opened her eyes and glimpsed the pools and waterfalls of the Hoaroak Water hissing and chuting down there towards Watersmeet Manor. 'Oh my God, I understand now,' she said. 'Lucy's Pool. That's where her body fell.'

He shook his head. 'It's much worse than that, the pool gets its name because she used to go

swimming there, not because she died there. She
never reached the water.' He gripped Laura's upper
arm in his hand like a vice, so that it hurt. 'Go on.
Lean out. Trust me.'

He held her on the edge as she forced herself to
look down. Between the pointed toes of her riding
boots she saw the vertical rock face falling away
– but she couldn't see the water. The leaves of the
old oak tree clinging in its cliff-niche obscured the
pool.

'The tree saved her!' said Laura, relieved.

He pulled her back.

'You see, I trusted you not to let me go,' she said
mischievously. 'So a Pervane can trust a Barronet.'
He didn't smile. She said: 'And you trusted me not
to give you away to the police, so a Barronet can
trust a Pervane nowadays.' She looked at him
earnestly. Then her expression faltered.

He said: 'She fell amongst the branches of the oak
tree, which held her. Neither was Phineas dead.
Chloral is a hypnotic, God knows what nightmares
he had experienced that night. But hearing her
screams, he ran to save her. No one would aid him,
neither Barronet nor Pervane. Phineas climbed
down there to her. How he did it without a rope
I do not know. Although at first he believed she was
almost unharmed, beneath her voluminous dress her
injuries were terrible. Her spine was broken across
the bough beneath her. Yet he had never seen her
look so beautiful. She was dying, and who knows
what entreaties they whispered to one another?'

'Was she in agony?' Laura asked.

'She felt no pain. As gently as he could Phineas
carried her back up, somehow scaling the cliff, and

then carried his love down in his arms to the rose-covered summerhouse at Watersmeet, by the river's side, where she died.'

Bart sighed.

'Phineas entwined a wreath of twigs and flowers into a beautiful death-boat to launch her spirit on the waters, where she would drift to heaven like the Lady of Shallot. Then he fetched their baby from the house. Adam would have looked as though he were sleeping as he was laid in his mother's bosom amongst the flowers. Phineas carried them out to the sweeping waters and waded into the darkness. I do not think he could bear to let her go, and he was swept away with her.

'Their bodies were never found. They lie where there is never peace,' Bart said, 'on the face of the everlasting sea.'

Laura understood. There could never really be peace between Pervane and Barronet. Even Bart could do nothing about that.

But Laura murmured: 'Perhaps they reached the Happy Isles at last.'

'*Requiescat in pace*,' Bart said, but shook his head.

Laura tossed and turned in her sleep beneath her hot, damp sheets, and next day stared uncomprehendingly at the grey mid-morning light pouring from the clouds sweeping above the treetops. She pulled on a gown over her nightdress and knocked on Francis' bedroom door, then went in anyway. His pyjamas were discarded, cold, and there was a note on his pillow: *Gone hunting*.

She washed and dressed in a white blouse and her maroon summer skirt then went downstairs.

Gratefully, she saw the coffeepot still on the warmer. Francis returned as she was yawning, still rubbing her eyes and pouring her second cup, and the sound of the wind was suddenly very loud. She saw dried leaves eddying in the porch, then he slammed the door behind him. He was dressed in riding clothes, still carrying his horsewhip, and he looked furious.

'Missed him!' he said.

Then he crossed the room and embraced Laura, burying his hands in her hair, turning her face up, covering her lips with his. This was the Francis she had known. He wanted her, she could feel the excitement running like a chemical through them both.

'Let's go upstairs,' he said.

'But Mrs Pawkins.'

'Don't be frigid, who cares about Mrs . . .' he gave Laura a scorching pre-marital kiss, squeezing her bottom with his hand. She spilt her cup, started mopping it with a dishcloth, but his hand closed over hers. As they went upstairs he pinched her sides playfully, and she could feel his eyes on the backs of her knees, the seams of her stockings, thank goodness she had checked they were straight before she came down. Laura looked backwards urgently. She still wasn't sure what had come over him but their relationship was full steam ahead again. More than full; his fingers were trembling with desire as he unpopped her stocking tops and she could feel the warm, indecent panting of his breath on her thighs.

'Francis don't.' But she wanted him to. Her skirt kept getting in his way and he got quite angry with it. She longed for him to pull it off so that she could hold him. When he grinned down at her, she wondered what he saw. There was something quite vacant about his eyes, he was concentrating on what he felt lower down. Then he pressed so hard that she heard a cartilage in his knee crack, and his face changed. She had almost never made love in daylight before; never seen that look before.

'You're beautiful,' he hissed, 'you're mine.'

She turned her face away as he collapsed across her. All of a sudden tears trickled from the corners of her eyes.

'Have I hurt you?'

She shook her head. He covered her thoughtfully, victoriously, with a sheet.

He said: 'The police raided Hellebore at dawn this morning.'

'Oh?'

'Armed military police. A few local bobbies.'

Laura waited with her heart in her mouth.

'The fools missed him,' Francis said. 'He escaped, this time. But— '

'You went up to Hellebore House yourself?'

'Yes.' He smiled at her cockily. 'Why not?' He laughed. 'And he ran away from us!'

'Oh Francis, you shouldn't have gone. You could have been hurt.'

She hardly heard herself. Once out of the fifteen hundred acres of Watersmeet woodlands, she knew Bart could hide out anywhere over a hundred square miles of open moor. They'd never find him. Laura was appalled. The wind rattled the French windows. She already heard the hiss of falling leaves and imagined the wild conditions on the vast slopes of the uplands, where snow might fall from October until May. She closed her eyes.

Francis stood and pulled the sheet off her, stood looking down at her, her creased skirt, one knee bent, a shoe missing, her opened blouse. There was desire in his eyes, but also a kind of contempt, easy satisfaction. Until he wanted her again, he did not need to respect her. She wanted to give herself, but he wanted only to take her.

'There is no Barronet at Watersmeet for the first time in a thousand years,' he said. 'It's done.'

Laura imagined Bart's loneliness up on the moor. What would he eat, where would he sleep? Did he have clothes to keep him warm? In her mind's eye she saw him staggering along exhausted, blowing on his cold fingers, snatching sleep in a byre, or huddled for shelter in the lee of a sheep-stell. Francis was looking at her.

'If he's got any sense,' Francis said with his confident insensitivity, 'he'll give himself up to the authorities before he starves.'

Laura knew Bart would never give in. Clara had, and look how unhappy she was. Laura had too, and look how unhappy *she* was., She wiped her eyes. 'Do I have to sleep in this room any more?' she asked.

'This is your room, my lady.' Francis knelt on the bed and kissed her lips. 'I love you.'

He jumped to his feet. 'Get dressed! I'll take you out to lunch at the hotel. Lobster soup, fresh salmon! And I think I will celebrate with a cigar.'

Laura closed the door behind him and leaned back against it. She understood her position exactly.

That afternoon, Francis was with her every

moment – she could not even feel guilty eating such a fine meal, although rationing was so tight for most people, because she was so worried, and of course Francis asked her permission to light up a Havana, which he did with every sign of uncomplicated satisfaction in the gentlemanly ritual his father had taught him, crinkling the dark cylinder against his ear to check for freshness, the silver clippers to cut the end, the removal of the gold band. He kept her occupied the whole time. And of course she loved Lynmouth; the freedom. And she could not get away the next day because it was Sunday so her parents were coming to lunch, and there was no Mrs Pawkins coming to free her of the cooking chores.

But Francis always went to Barum on Monday mornings to check on the jewellery business, and that was Laura's opportunity. She saddled Blackbird, dressed in a warm riding habit and tied her hair, and rode up on to the moor, going *the wrong way* into the woods through the tall gate topped with formidable spikes, past Hellebore and the bluff where Lucy had jumped to her terrible fate. Laura dug in her heels and set Blackbird prancing onward up to Cheriton without a pause. But she rode only a short way along the ridge before stopping hopelessly as the wide moorland opened up ahead of her. The bleak scenery was so vast and empty that she knew she would never find him.

Blackbird wanted to gallop, but Laura turned her around, and held her stiffly back to a trot all the way to Watersmeet Manor. Francis had returned early from Barum and the Humber was already parked outside the stable. He was curry-combing his roan gelding, Haymaker. Laura thought that

Haymaker might be a rig, because his thing dangled when he saw Blackbird. The mare played up for all she was worth, kicking dust from the gravel and whickering. Laura dismounted and tied Blackbird out of sight.

'I was just going out,' Francis said, disappointed. 'It's much too windy.'

'Is that so? I thought I might ride up to Hellebore.'

Laura unknotted her headscarf, realizing he *believed* in the feud he had once derided – now that he had won it. 'Why on earth do such a thing? Hellebore can't have any good associations for you. Your father had his stroke there that eventually killed him. Let it go, Francis.'

He put his arm around her. 'You're right as always.' He kissed her and she almost pulled her head away, wondering if he was right that she was frigid – the word he used so casually had all but passed her by when he first said it, but now it kept coming back to her. She liked his caresses because they made her feel close to him, but she took little pleasure in their commencement. Obviously she ought to, so she pampered him with a little laugh of pleasure when he squeezed her waist tight. It was the first time she had lied to herself.

'I must see to Blackbird!' she said.

'I have a little present for you.' Francis pulled a flat box from the rear seat of the Humber. The wind tried to snatch it like a wing. 'You were right!' he laughed. 'I won't go riding today.' He gave her the box in the calm of the stable. 'I was going to do it up in coloured paper and everything.' He watched her eyes. She opened the top and pulled out a long black dress. Obviously non-utility, it must be highly illegal: the material was plain but sumptuous, the cut old-fashioned, with flounces and pleats and all the forbidden things. It must have cost a fortune.

'Suppose you'd been caught!'

'There's nothing I wouldn't do for you,' he said honestly, and waited for her to embrace him. So she did.

That night Laura lay awake listening to the wind. It was rarely strong in the valley: like tonight, in a storm it gusted and eddied with temporary violence, making the treetops roar, and very occasionally a freak cyclone could be sucked down to flatten trees as if a giant hand had been wiped against the slopes, but most of the wind passed over the hilltops to make that smooth, steady gale across the moor. She got up and listened to the rivers: the deeper rumble of the Lyn, the lighter, higher sound of the Hoaroak's leaping waters. There were no trees in the Exmoor Forest, probably not since the bronze-age farmers and miners chopped them down for their houses, hearths and smelters three thousand years ago. But one famous tree remained: an oak tree marking an ancient boundary long before recorded time, *the* Hoar Oak, said to have been re-planted in the eleventh century by Ranulph de Barreneau, which fell just before the Restoration from sheer age and rottenness. It was replaced by Sir Lionel Barronet four years later in token of belated loyalty to his sovereign, who stripped him of his rights as lord of the manor and Warden of the Forest nevertheless. This tree fell during the First World War, and the new sapling had been dedicated by Bart's father Ranulf in a ceremony on New Year's Day, 1917. From this tree deep on the

227

moor the Hoaroak stream, which rose somewhere nearby on that huge, remote and treacherous plateau called the Chains, derived its name.

Laura held the luxurious dress against her. It seemed unfaithful, in the face of such a gift, and the sapphire necklace, and Francis' obvious love, even to wonder where Bart was hiding out. But she was sure she knew. He would have gone to the source of the Hoaroak Water that flowed clear to Watersmeet. He was in the Chains. She mustn't go to him.

She got up early and dressed, wrapping herself in her black woollen cape against the cold, tying down her soft-brimmed hat with a white headscarf. Holding her long black boots in her hand, she actually crept into Francis' bedroom and stood there at the foot of his bed, but he was too exhausted from his lust of last evening to wake. She went downstairs, made sandwiches and stole a bottle of rum from Francis' cellar, then rode out. The valley fell behind her, and she could see the colours of the trees along the valley walls in bands, like a microcosm of the seasons: bare black branches near the valley rim, autumnal yellow and gold below, green clinging along the rivers' sinuous loop. Leaves swirled round her at Hillsford Bridge like the flames of a gigantic, cold fire, but Cheriton was bare and grey, and the wind was a steady pressure. Blackbird's nostrils flared as she scented the wild space of the open moor along the spine of the ridge, and Cheriton fell behind.

Emptiness surrounded Laura, a windswept vista giving no hint of the dangerous pools, pits and bogs which pocked the marching horizon-lines after the recent rains, and the clouds seemed terribly close above her head, and fast. She didn't know which way the sun was. A cloud streamed over her, wet grey mist; she licked the moisture from her lips. A few sheep were dotted here and there, Francis' Exmoor hornies, then she was past them, the ground still rising as the ridge climbed and merged into the Exe Plain. She stopped at last, the wind a smooth unvarying thunder in her ears.

In front of her and below was Exe Head, the source of the river that gave Exmoor its name, starting its long journey to the south coast and the city of Exeter. Six hundred yards to the right, the Hoaroak Water rose and flowed to the north. But for this narrow causeway of tawny wind-thrashed molinia grass and rush, all England to the west was an island. She knew he would be here.

She let Blackbird walk across slowly. She had entered a different herding. The few sheep scattered about were Highland Blackfaces. Chains Barrow, the ancient burial chamber, rose against the skyline ahead of her. But first the ground fell away into a deep combe – Short Chains Combe, with its strange, primitive stone settings. The stream flowing northward was narrow enough to step across. The steep slopes rose around her as she followed the water down, grateful to be out of the wind. A couple of Exmoor ponies saw her and moved politely aside, never frightened of a human on another horse. Long Chains Combe, cut by its own brook, plunged from the Barrow to her left, and she could discern the bronze-age field outlines and maybe half a dozen of the round hut circles on its slopes. Where the streams met, Bart Barronet stood watching her.

Behind him was an old bothy hanging crookedly on a grassy eminence, where he must be living. The drystone wall of a sheepfold once enclosed the hut on three sides, but now it was collapsed to a ruin. There was not the slightest sign of life, except for him. She dismounted and walked shyly towards him. The wind ruffled his hair. It was the first time she had met him away from the Watersmeet valley; she despised herself as she approached him step by step across the boggy ground, all emotion exposed, vulnerable.

He turned away from her to stare at the hulking mound of Chains Barrow silhouetted against the clouds, and Laura wondered how much he hid in his heart.

'There's so much we don't know. I don't believe they always built them on the skyline,' he said. 'The ones in the valleys got swept away sooner or later, that's all, silted over, grown over, hidden by trees. It's only here on the high moor that we can see their remains.' He turned back to her. His face carried the scar of Sir George Pervane's horsewhip down one cheek. 'Laura, won't you ever leave me alone?' he demanded gently, and she saw the torment she caused him. But also the pleasure she gave him, the lift to his morale. 'You've taken a fearful risk coming here.'

'To meet you,' she said with the simple truth she never seemed able to manage with Francis. 'I had to know that you weren't hurt.'

'I am hurt.'

Still he didn't move, the water flowing over his boots, a pitcher hanging from his hand. His cheeks were covered with dense, pale stubble that couldn't conceal his scar. She realized that he had been happy until she came.

He spoke in a low voice. 'The Chains are covered with dangerous marshes and swamp-holes. You risked your life.' For him.

'I brought you some sandwiches!' She held them out in their greaseproof paper wrapper.

He stared at her with surprise, then roared with laughter, a warm and generous sound. He touched her shoulder, suddenly serious.

'Who knows you have come here?'

'No one,' she promised, 'I am at your mercy.'

'No,' he said, scanning the skyline anxiously, 'I am at yours.'

'I would never give you away!' she whispered.

Trust and concern; all this was close between them, and Laura could not bear it. She felt he was another part of herself, except he wasn't. Her nipples, sensitized by Francis' hands and lips, itched against her brassiere unbearably, and her face flushed red-hot with guilt.

'What a horrid little hut!' she said, looking away from him.

'Do you want to see it?'

'Not much.' But he held out his hand and she took it, jumping the stream, stood beside him clinging on, still not looking at him. He bent down and filled the pitcher.

'I brought you some rum in case you were thirsty,' she said.

'That's very kind of you.'

She said quietly: 'You know why I am here.'

He put his arm around her shoulder, and his finger to his lips, their faces that close. It must not be said.

Then he walked her amiably up the slope. He wanted her, she could tell. She tried to calm herself. Nothing terrible would happen to him, would it? They didn't shoot deserters did they? Maybe they would return him to his unit if they found him. But his unit was with the Eighth Army in the fierce fighting in Sicily. Perhaps the war would be over in a few months and everyone would forget and the world would be normal again.

He said as they walked: 'How is the valley?'

'What?' She wanted to talk about them.

'Watersmeet.'

She shrugged. The same as always. She remembered about the colours of the trees and told him. Bart gave a tight little smile of familiarity; he was seeing the valley, not seeing her. And yet he was as aware of her as she was herself. Laura was so distracted that she almost fell. *She* was real, not Watersmeet. The valley was nothing, it had no feelings.

He pushed open the bothy's plank door with his foot.

'I love you,' she whispered. 'You know what I feel.'

The door banged wide as if he hadn't heard her. Inside she saw a hovel, stone walls stiffened with crumbling ochre cob, hardly larger inside than a garden shed, one tiny window sealed with paper. Not even big enough for a bed, only a hammock strung between two beams. The floor needed sweeping and the blankets felt damp.

Bart said: 'You don't know what love really is.'

'I do!'

'No, no,' he said, turning away from her, rejecting

her. He would not look at her. 'It's over, Laura.'

'It's not over. There's nothing to *be* over, according to you.' She wouldn't give up a second time. 'I'll bring you supplies.'

When he still said no she started making an inventory of what he would need, going through his things, picking them up and dropping them, only one pair of socks, no woollen jumper, no vegetables; but he still had his stack of Army saucepans and a big brown bag of tea. She would not let him change her mind, and at last he crossed his arms and leaned against the wall looking at her with amusement. She folded his jacket angrily, not looking at him, except out of the corner of her eyes.

'I'll come tomorrow, Bart. I won't be able to fetch much but I'll do my best.'

He chuckled, shaking his head. 'In that case, you might bring some boiled sweets with you.'

She gave a small smile of satisfaction, went outside and he ducked after her. He whistled and Blackbird came trotting over. Laura put her muddy boot in Bart's hand and swung into the saddle.

'I knew you'd be there,' she said. 'I just knew.' She looked around her. 'You're almost free here, aren't you?'

'Why are you doing this for me?' he asked, holding on to the horse's bridle.

'I told you!' she said.

He let go the bridle as though it were hot, and Laura rode off.

She couldn't help a smile spreading across her face as Cheriton Ridge unreeled beneath her and the sea and Watersmeet rose into sharp view beneath the hazy far-distant Welsh hinterland. Bart was a different person away from the valley and she had stamped her personality on him, made him notice her, react to her.

When she got home Francis was also returning from a ride. Haymaker was lathered. Francis kissed Laura's cheek and asked her if she had enjoyed herself, and she thought:*Would I really have been unfaithful to him?*

In practice, it seemed such a desperate thought.

She rode back the very next day. All her energies had been consumed with thinking about Bart – his lonely struggle to avoid her, to deny her, to deny his feelings for her. She hardly ate supper, and went to bed early. When Francis came to her room she said she was too tired. He was so sweet: just meekly said he understood, kissed her goodnight, and left her feeling restless and like a cheat. It was wrong and dishonest not to tell Francis that she did not love him, but she knew she did not. She liked him and she knew she was lucky, but the smoothness of her life was driving her to despair. She was starting to hate, not Francis, which was impossible, but Watersmeet. Because of Bart. Today when Bart looked at Laura he saw her as she was, passionate, ambitious, vulnerable, beautiful – *that* was what she saw in his face, and that he knew how dangerous she was to him. Yet he had to see her again. He had admitted that too. If he escaped Watersmeet he had nowhere to go but Laura.

She had to see him, today, now.

As soon as Francis was out of the house she stole another bottle, this time of whisky, found a plucked and drawn chicken in the larder, wrapped it and put it in a string bag together with some ham, a loaf

234

of bread, a tin of Huntley & Palmer biscuits. If Francis came in, what would she say she was doing? She didn't have the faintest idea, and he didn't come in anyway. She rode up on to Cheriton Ridge. There was no sun today, the moor was windless and chilly but very clear. She cut across the Chains a slightly different way and topped the last rise, then the combe fell away beneath her, revealing the huddled stones of the hut circles below Chains Barrow and the little bothy standing on its grassy eminence, a grey filament of smoke rising absolutely vertically from its chimney into the motionless air.

Then she saw little shapes moving across the ground. It was like watching a silent film running, with the vast grey moorland for a screen – all the men closing in on the bothy were the size of toys below her.

They were policemen.

The spikes on top of their helmets gleamed grey like the sky. Laura wanted to scream a warning. The uniforms of the military policemen were grey-green like the grass, but the bands on their arms stood out like painted blood. She could hear the shrill piping of whistles, seeing senior officers in blue, one in khaki, standing by a big half-track vehicle beside the stream. She watched horrorstruck as a group of men appeared, dragging Bart out of the bothy, fighting furiously with him, clouting the door frame with their shoulders, she saw the jagged white splinters show. He fell on one knee and they beat down on his head with their fists, so that his blond hair hung slick and red. He shook them off, broke through the cordon and ran uphill towards Laura, staring up at her, impossibly far, and then two

235

policemen in blue cut in from the side. He knocked them down and they stayed down. The other bobbies made a half circle, forcing him against the stone wall of the bothy. He tore a plank from the door and used it to hold them back; all in the silence of distance, which seemed to make it all the more awful to Laura – the tiny struggling figures, the soundless blows. She couldn't bear to watch – but she couldn't turn away. The little figures closed in on Bart's white-shirted form and brought him down with truncheons.

Then he staggered up, pouring blood down his face, and Laura whispered to herself, begging him to escape: *'Run away!'*

Instead Bart turned to face his tormentors.

But he looked back at Laura one last time. He must have thought she had betrayed him.

Laura was horrified. She couldn't weep. Her hands tightened the reins without her realizing it and as Blackbird obediently backed away, the soft, grassy edge of the combe rose to obscure the scene below. The two policemen Bart had knocked down still had not moved, tiny blue out-stretched crosses. Perhaps he had killed them. She hoped so! The men milling around Bart were cuffing his wrists, roping his legs like an animal. The last she saw of him was his white shirt, then there was only grass and emptiness.

Laura's throat swelled. She rode not knowing where she was going. That look. She would never have betrayed him. Then she realized that she had. Yesterday Francis had followed her.

Francis Pervane did not trust her. He had

betrayed Bart as he was bound to do, a Pervane, to a Barronet. Francis would see it as justice.

He knew of Laura's interest in Bart – did he guess her feelings for him? She doubted that. For Francis it would be bad enough that she, a Pervane, had shown kindness to their enemy.

Laura was too angry to cry. She and Francis were finished. She untied Bart's string bag of food from the saddle and let it drop as Blackbird jumped a ditch. Her bound hair thumped against her back. She had lost Bart, she had nothing to live for. She crossed the Hoaroak Water and rode past Hellebore to the top of the bluff, paused, then spurred on down the track, the trees racing by her until the high, spiked gate blocked the way in front of her, closed. She kicked on, lifting with her knees, and Blackbird jumped.

Laura saw the group of men on the far side too late. Blackbird landed amongst their scattering shapes, men in Army uniforms. She reined in. Dust hung in the still air around them. Such was her emotional state that she looked at the uniforms almost with loathing until she realized that they were foreign. The shade of khaki, its cut, the deep-dish shape of their tin helmets, their boots with heels, everything was different. The wet collars and armpits of their fatigue shirts: the sergeant had been marching them double time. Most of all the direct way they gawped at her, thumbs hooked in belts, jaws moving soundlessly, chewing gum. Americans. The war had come to Watersmeet.

'That was quite a jump,' the young sergeant said admiringly, picking up the map he had been scratching his head over and slapping off the dust

237

against his thigh. Then he looked at her more closely. 'You sure you're okay?'

Laura nodded.

He nodded too. He had the brightest blue eyes she had ever seen, a wide supple mouth, even white teeth shifting the gum from side to side, but most of all that intelligent blue gaze, honest and patient, straightforward in his appraisal: he saw a real English lady who kept her emotions reined in as tightly as her horse. He turned on his heel and looked at the gate, then turned back. He shook his head.

'Six foot if it's an inch,' he murmured, not letting her go, 'and downhill.'

'Come on, Jerry,' the one called Cory complained, always worrying, 'we gotta get moving.'

'You don't know where you're going to, Cory,' said Jerry out of the corner of his mouth, without turning. 'Take five, men.' He just stood looking up at her.

'For sure it's uphill,' muttered Cory, swinging off his pack, unlacing his boots.

'Everywhere's uphill,' Jerry said. He hadn't taken his eyes off her. The girl on the horse spoke in a low, English voice.

'Are you the American unit staying at Sir George Newnes' old place in Lynton, Hollerday House?'

Jerry grinned even more widely. 'Military secret, ma'am.'

'Everything's a military secret,' Cory grumbled nervily. 'I'm pooped out, Sarge. Christ, lookithat, size of my blisters. Now I know what they mean by walking on the water.'

'Shut it,' Jerry snapped. 'Way to go. Two minutes!'

'Keep your hat on, Sarge.' They were already picking up English slang.

Jerry ignored him.

'Sure,' Jerry told Laura politely, 'Newnes' old house.' The man who built the cliff railway and put Lynmouth on the map at the end of the last century; these violent young killers couldn't possibly know or care. 'And when we're finished with it,' Jerry grinned, 'we're going to blow it up. Just for practice.'

'If we ever find the way back there,' Cory groaned. He lay with the other demolition experts against a grassy bank, flexing his feet, his eyes closed and mouth working a square of cheese, but Jerry stood looking up at Laura. Suddenly he held out his hand. 'Sergeant Ellis, at your services, ma'am. I gotta get these creeps moving. Field exercise, mapreading, these guys got no idea. You'll be seeing plenty of lost souls like us from now on, I guess. This is Watersmeet, right?' He noted the slim feel of her hand beneath its soft glove.

Laura pointed. 'You can't see it, but you'll find a path in the trees over there. That'll get you home.'

The men's easy camaraderie, their griping and bitching, Jerry's wide-open eyes, had been a breath of fresh air for Laura, and she had recovered her calm. The last she saw of Sergeant Jerry Ellis as she rode on was him finally looking away from her, kicking Cory's boots and shouting, 'move it, you— '

Laura walked Blackbird into the stable. Francis came out of the house and watched her but she was too angry to speak to him. He went back indoors. She fed and watered Blackbird, sponged her down, and brushed neatsfoot oil over the chipped front of a hoof: she must have caught it on one of the gate spikes. She had been that close to destruction, and suddenly Laura felt sick with fear. Suppose Blackbird had come plunging down on those formidable spikes? All for Laura. She threw her arms around the horse's neck, ashamed of herself, taking off her hat and pressing her forehead against Blackbird's trusting, innocent heat.

Francis was waiting for her in the hall. Laura ignored him and went upstairs to her bedroom. She closed the door quietly behind her, pulled out her suitcase from under the bed, and started packing.

Francis knocked on the door.

She didn't reply.

He came in.

He stood watching her. 'Come on, darling.' He touched her and she shrugged him off, busily opening drawers, pulling her clothes out of the wardrobes, moving around him without looking at him. She glanced at him in the mirror and saw he was grinning, his arms folded, so plainly amused by her behaviour. He even helped her by picking up a few perfume bottles and dropping them in the case, such was the confidence of his complacency. He didn't seriously believe that she would really leave him.

Laura grabbed the bottles out. 'Just go to hell, Francis.' She put them back on the dresser until she was ready for them.

He leaned his shoulder on the wall, arms folded, ankles crossed, the gleaming black toecap of his shoe jutting languidly into the expensive carpet. His mind was racing. He knew he was fighting for his marriage, but he knew he would win. Like all women Laura was foolish and impulsive but ultimately she knew what side her bread was buttered on. She had been very stupid. Laura wasn't the type to run home to Mummy and admit her failure, and she had nowhere else to go. Not even any money of her own, the bank accounts were in his name.

Laura kept glancing at him in the mirror. He couldn't believe that she could love anyone but him, because he had money, property and a high opinion of himself. But she could. She might be married to Francis Pervane, but she loved another man. It trembled on the tip of her tongue to tell him that, to destroy the bland ignorant veneer of his self-satisfaction, to reveal how much more of her there was than he knew.

Francis indulged her temper patiently.

'I know exactly what happened,' he said, when her pace began to slow.

She turned guiltily, but he only meant that the police had been up and told him what happened. 'They hurt him,' she said, trying to make him understand. 'They beat him with truncheons and I think he might have killed one of them, or at least hurt him badly.'

Francis knew how to handle Laura. 'It had to end this way,' he explained calmly. 'I followed you yesterday. I know I shouldn't, it was wrong, but it's all for the best. It was in your own interest, Laura. Who knows what might have happened? So I informed the police where I had been. I didn't mention your name! You're safe, Laura. Only that Bart Barronet was hiding out in Long Chains Combe. That was all. It was my duty – as your husband,

and as Francis Pervane. That man did not really
deserve your sympathy.'

Sympathy. Laura struggled to suppress her
emotions.

She would become like Francis himself. She stood
by the French windows and forced herself to fold
a dress calmly.

'You're quite right of course. I must have been
out of my mind.'

Francis smiled.

'But Bart will believe that it was you who
informed the police,' he said.

Laura put the folded dress neatly on the dresser.
'Yes,' she said. That was the first thing she had
realized. 'Yes, I know.'

'And that is the way it had to be,' Francis said
reasonably. 'For our sakes, Laura, the sake of our
marriage.'

'Our marriage,' she said flatly.

'Because I do love you.'

'Yes, I know that too.' It was true. But in his
arrogance and jealousy he thought that only his
feelings were fixed, and hers were malleable.

'Tell me what better way I could show it. I know
you better than you know yourself, Laura, and what
is right for you. I want you to be happy.'

He stood there, smiling, determined to keep her.
He treated her lovingly, tolerated her pretending to
pack, because she was trapped, totally his. He could
even own her feelings, because Laura's submission
and her allegiance as his wife were what he thought
of as love.

Francis said: 'I want you to learn to be my wife.'

She looked down. Francis didn't know what real

love was, and the good side to that was that he didn't believe she really loved Bart. He was quite unable to imagine what she really felt.

'I am your wife,' she admitted.

He embraced her. She stood limply in his arms.

He kicked the lid of the suitcase closed. 'All this packing nonsense is finished.'

He kissed the top of her head. Francis knew that Bart was in deep trouble: his assault on the two civil police officers had made the military law offence of desertion, resolved by court martial and probably sentencing to the military prison in Colchester, into the much more serious civil charge of attempted grievous bodily harm. He would be tried in the Crown Court at Plymouth; he would go to prison for sure, and they would throw away the key. Bart was out of the way, finished, and finished too was Laura's strange, unhealthy fascination with him, so that Francis was safe – safe where the Pervanes had always felt most threatened – from the Barronets. He was overjoyed, and he knew he was forgiving Laura more easily than she deserved. But he loved her.

He lifted her face and kissed her lips. They didn't move.

'My darling,' he whispered, 'I forgive you.'

She didn't close her eyes. He dropped his hands lower, kneading her. She neither stepped away nor forward. But he knew she'd come round.

When he was gone Laura closed the door softly behind him.

She stood in the centre of the room, turning slowly in circles.

She heard Bart's voice whisper: *You don't know what love really is.*

Didn't she? She was learning. She'd let her husband down by taking food to a man he considered his enemy. By being in love with that man, doing anything for him, even if he wasn't in love with her. But even if Bart hated her, he was her life. Francis had grounds for his jealousy. The fault was all hers.

She started to unpack.

Then Laura flung herself down on her bed, weeping bitterly.

She learned to be obedient, to subordinate her own identity to her husband's interests. It wasn't hard; it was so comfortable that it was difficult to think sometimes, as day followed day in the routine of her life, that there had ever been anything more. She organized the house, she got involved in local charities. She didn't provoke Francis any more. They settled into a contented marriage. Francis came to her bedroom from time to time, quick and considerate, and sometimes as she lay there in the dark she remembered . . . but it was gone. It was odd that for all her indifference, Francis could take such ecstasy in her mere presence, mere body. *She* was not important except as a receptacle. It should be enough; a man who loved her. Christ, she was lucky! For the first time Laura took the coach and went to see Clara and her little daughter at home in Barum.

It was a neat, narrow road of rippled concrete with a pavement on each side planted with bare saplings. Laura, walking with a wicker basket over her arm, looked around her. The houses, all semidetached with en suite garages, had bow windows and mansard roofs that swept down at the side like protective wings. She found the number, opened the little paling gate and walked slowly up the concrete path through a tiny front garden dug up to winter vegetables, a few square feet of patriotic carrots and potatoes, a bush of brussels sprouts that had caught the frost. There was no door knocker above the letter box – the postman delivered to the door here – only an electric button. Laura pressed it and heard a tune play faintly in the house.

Clara opened the door, her face red and jolly, a child wriggling in the crook of her arm.

'My God,' she exclaimed, and actually stepped back a pace, 'you look awful! Come in, come on in. Don't fall over Perdie's bloody toys, she's crawling. Here, hold her, I'll put the tea on.' Laura took the unfamiliar weight of the little girl clumsily. 'Don't worry, she'll probably bawl!' Clara closed the door behind Laura and pushed past a lot of hanging washing into the kitchen, slammed a kettle on the gas, cursed the damp matches. Finally the smelly wartime pressure gas ignited its dull blue flame. There was a table, pale blue hoop-backed chairs, pink tile walls and cupboards with blue doors the same shade as the chairs. 'Do you want to go in the front room? Rob won't come in here because of the mess.'

Laura shook her head and tickled Perdie under the chin. 'She's lovely.' The corner of Perdie's mouth turned down, her enormous eyes turned up towards her mummy, filling with tears.

Clara frowned and snatched her up. 'Yes, isn't she? You little horror, you've done your nappy, haven't you.' She thumped her down on the table and spoke through the safety pins in her mouth. 'I think I've got another bun in the oven. Not sure yet.' She looked up at Laura between the kicking pink legs, then said nothing. The kettle whistled.

Laura filled the teapot, unpinning her hat and taking off her gloves as she sat. Clara was growing her hair out again, a brown gloss with a faint curl to it, no longer over-washed and hanging limp but spreading out attractively across her shoulders. She was apple-cheeked and had put on a lot of padding around the hips and bust. Slinging Perdie over her shoulder she poured the tea and plumped down opposite Laura, then hesitated. 'You don't mind . . .?' She unlimbered a breast and latched Perdie on to the big brown nipple. 'Saves on Cow & Gate, helps the war effort,' she explained. 'You aren't supposed to be able to have another doing this. Bloody rubbish.'

'How's Rob?'

'Just promoted, took the course and exams in Plymouth. Bombed flat! We can't imagine.' She lit a cigarette, coughed. 'I'm doing part-time at the British Restaurant in Boutport Street, meals for people on war work. It isn't used as a theatre any more, since the fire. It's a way of meeting people. And the Mothers' Union is running a neighbourhood crèche. How's Watersmeet?'

'Quiet. I've wanted for years for Francis to let me help out at the Watersmeet Falls Hotel . . . We get a lot of Army exercises in the woods now.'

'And the deserters hiding out.'

'Yes,' Laura said, 'a few of those.' She picked up her basket. 'I don't know if you can use these.'

'Eggs!' cried Clara. 'There must be a whole dozen.

Oh Laura, you are a sport.' She put them down on the table and the two of them sat sipping their tea.

'Tell me how things really are at Watersmeet,' Clara said.

'The hotel job didn't come off,' Laura said in a rush. 'I know I could have made a go of it, I'm sure I could, but you know how conservative Francis is. An hotel can't have a female manager – a *female manager* is a *landlady*, and Francis wouldn't have it. Not that he put it like that, he didn't even tell me he'd advertised the post just before Christmas – for a professional manager at last. A man.'

'Laura – ' Then Clara said: 'Ouch!' and looked down at the baby fondly. 'Isn't she greedy?'

'Francis' sort of man,' Laura said rapidly. 'Mr Sayle is London trained, Clara, a decorated war veteran – I can hardly object – he had his right foot blown away by a stick-grenade in Sicily last summer. The Ministry of Pensions sent him to Roehampton to be fitted for a wooden foot complete with a shoe, and now he glides along the hotel corridors as good as new, I should think, so polite that you want to wash your hands after speaking to him, and he's a tyrant to the staff. Yes, he knows how to run hotels efficiently, all the fiddles much better than I do, but I could have learned. The staff hate him and André – you remember André the chef who kept the place going for years – he's at the Royal Fortescue now – well, the good thing about it is, I see a lot more of Francis nowadays – because he's at home nearly all the time and it's – wonderful. Clara – he's so caring and sweet. And I – ' She began to cry, and now they had started the tears simply rolled down her cheeks.

'Laura, slow down, dear,' Clara said kindly while Laura fiddled in her handbag, powder compact, lipstick, coach ticket, everything but: Clara looked about then found a fresh handkerchief in the full side of her brassiere and handed it over. Laura blew her nose.

'I – I can't help it. It's so terrible, Clara.'

'Tell me how things *really* are at Watersmeet.'

'They've sent Bart to Dartmoor prison.'

Clara pulled little Perdie off her breast and flipped it back inside. 'You've had enough.' She explained: 'If I let her sleep in the afternoon I get no peace in the evenings.'

'And in the mornings you're at the British Restaurant.'

'The night shift comes in. Tea and two slices. Then there's all the preparation to get ready for lunch.'

'Oh God.'

Laura squeezed the handkerchief angrily in her fist.

'Take it easy,' Clara advised. 'You always were your own worst enemy. Flying off the handle. Just take things one at a time. I know what you're feeling.'

'It's not the same,' Laura said. 'It feels like the end of the world.'

'You're so self-centred.' But now Clara sounded almost amused, almost envious of this fault. 'You'll just have to learn to forget him.'

'I can't.'

'You mean you won't,' Clara pointed out.

'I won't!' Laura said fiercely.

Clara nodded to herself, then sighed. 'It all seems so important when you're young, but *that* passes soon enough. Gradually it doesn't seem important any more.' She stopped. 'It's eating you up, isn't it?'

Laura was instantly worried. 'Does it show?' She opened the compact and examined herself in the mirror, dabbed her cheeks.

'You don't have to do that for me. I'm not Francis,' Clara said, then replied: 'No, only to another woman. A man would never notice.'

'*He'd* notice.'

Laura sat there with her hair tied back, smooth and black, her fully exposed face seeming all the more pale and vulnerable. Clara tried to look at her as a man would: she looked perfectly beautiful. No wonder Francis was so madly in love.

But Laura was talking about Bart. She said in an awful voice: 'He's been sentenced to ten years' hard labour. One of the policemen has only just returned to duty.'

Clara tried to be comforting. 'He'll be out in seven, if he gets a good-conduct remission.'

'That's for ever too.'

'Laura, forget him.'

'It's a cruel sentence. The harshest prison in the land, and he'll be out on the chain gang, breaking stones. He won't survive. Locked inside prison walls, prowling a tiny cell when all he loved was Watersmeet. He'll come out a broken man.'

Clara ran her finger round the rim of her saucer. 'He's used to being a prisoner.'

Laura said: 'But he was so nearly free.'

'He'll never be free of you.'

'If only that was true,' Laura said desperately. 'I don't think he cares for me at all. Yet I feel he does. It's like a cut that won't stop bleeding. It hurts.'

She pressed her hands in her lap, then looked around her. 'I wish I was you!'

'Perhaps when you and Francis start a family.'

'Never.' Laura's hands whitened.

'Does Francis know this?'

Laura said simply: 'He couldn't possibly imagine. I don't hate him, but I don't love him. I suppose we'll have children, he does his job. If there's one thing Francis knows it's his duty. After him there's no more Pervanes, unless I give them to him.' She glanced up, tear-reddened eyes over white hands, implacable.

'Phew,' Clara blew out between her lips. 'I'm glad you and I are friends now, that's all I can say.'

'It was Francis who sent Bart to prison. He followed me. My own husband, but I don't blame him, I blame myself. I was foolish, but Francis was just being what he is. I can accept that. I married him.' She made a conscious effort to relax, finishing her tea with a tight smile. 'Bart said to me:"You don't know what love really is, Laura." ' She paused. 'But now I do. Look what I've done to him!'

'Are you going to see him?'

Laura stared at her, then shivered, pushing the palms of her hands down her woollen skirt as though she were ironing out creases. 'I couldn't. Francis told me Bart believed it was *I* who betrayed him. Laura Pervane. He'd be bound to believe that, wouldn't he, Clara?'

'You mustn't see him,' Clara said positively.

Laura said: 'Why not?'

Clara stared at her, astonished. 'Ah,' she said. 'Now I understand. So that's the way it is. Still is.'

'If I didn't go I'd never forgive myself.' Laura

smoothed her skirt, smoothed it again. 'You've got
a nice house, and Perdie's gorgeous. But don't you
ever wonder, Clara?'

'Wonder?'

'What it would have been like. What might have
been.'

Clara got up, Perdie in one arm, and embraced
Laura with the other arm, so that their cheeks
touched, hot and close, for a single moment.

'Stay here tonight,' Clara said. 'The telephone's
in the hall, you can call the Watersmeet Falls Hotel.
They'll send a messenger to tell Francis not to
expect you home until late tomorrow. There's a
coach leaves for Tavistock at five a.m., if you're
really serious.'

'I am serious,' Laura said.

'Then you're a fool,' Clara said.

Five o'clock in the morning at the bus station on
Barum's Strand was bitterly cold and dark, and still
the coach had not arrived from the depôt to collect
the small unhappy group of travellers. Laura wished
she had brought a heavier coat and flat shoes. The
wind off the Taw river, that black pit whose
invisible waters slapped noisily at the hollow iron
pilings of the railway bridge behind them, carried
flecks of snow on its icy damp breath, smelling of
the sea. Suddenly the bridge signals clacked noisily,
and everyone looked round, but it was only the milk
train from Ilfracombe going to the Junction station.
Bromley's restaurant was closed and when Laura
asked for something to eat in the canteen of the
Town railway station nearby, the officious woman
with a handkerchief tied over her hair said she

would only sell tea or sandwiches to service personnel. Still the coach did not come. Laura faintly saw the statue of Queen Anne forming against the brightening sky, the square chimney of the electricity station behind trailing horizontal smoke across the rooftops. By now the tide was out and the Taw estuary was an empty wasteland of sand and snow. Then an alert old woman in a white scarf, carrying a terrier whose head stuck out of her travelling bag, exclaimed 'At last!' as the Western National coach appeared, pulling round the square, then turning in the road with difficulty because of the producer-gas trailer it was towing. The conductor got down and poked the contraption with a rod, and a belch of fumes blew out.

Fumes were leaking inside the coach too. The sliding windows were kept open by common consent despite the freezing draught. Laura rested her head against the window-sticker telling her how much petrol the gas-bus saved, and tried to sleep. The men had to get out and push on every hill. She woke each time they heaved themselves back in, smelling of slush and sweat, stamping their boots in disgust. The conductor told them to be grateful they had a ride at all.

The coach slithered into Tavistock just as the bus to Buckfastleigh via Princetown was pulling out. Laura got the last, threadbare seat. The olive-green bus groaned and stuttered and stank its way up the steepening hills into a white glare: the rolling, open snowfields of Dartmoor. Granite tors stuck up like eruptions of black teeth, so different from Exmoor. The road was barely passable. They seemed to see the prison ahead of them for hours, a grimy grey fortress hanging between snow and sky, before the bus finally pulled up and Laura and a few other women climbed down into this featureless nowhere-land. Most of them were carrying baskets which the warders searched. Then the iron doors clanged closed behind them, shutting out the light, and Laura forced back the impulse to stare fearfully over her shoulder, to let the sense of claustrophobia grip her.

She had come all the way here; she wasn't going to back out now.

But for the first time she wondered what she would really say. She would have to speak to Bart through a screen of wire mesh. The men were marched in on the other side. The women leaned forward to chatter cheerfully, or cry, or argue, but Laura sat staring through the empty squares of wire in front of her. He wouldn't agree to see her even now.

Then the door clanged and he was led in. The warder, with a hand on Bart's shoulder, sat him opposite her and stood back, watching them. Bart was thinner, harder. He stared her straight in the eyes as though the wire were not there.

'Oh, Bart,' she said, 'oh Bart— '

'Laura.'

He took her breath away. 'How do you feel?' she asked. 'Are they – how are you?'

'Degraded.'

This emptiness between them was awful.

She gabbled: 'Are they looking after you?'

He didn't bother to reply. 'I know,' he said, changing everything between them so effortlessly: as though an electric current had come on. She could never be bored in his presence, never really pretend.

She almost broke down. 'I didn't – I didn't mean to – give you away– '

'I *know*,' he said, and she could almost imagine his hand closing over hers, the heat and comfort of it, but the wire was between them. They sat like statues on the uncomfortable stools.

'I didn't tell the police. I would never have done.'

'I know that,' he said gently.

She shook her head, baffled. He believed in her innocence when all the evidence pointed to the contrary. Still he wouldn't answer. Laura's mouth trembled.

He said: 'Because I . . .'

Her eyes glistened hopefully. He looked away and swallowed. They were so close. She'd had a hell of a journey; and all he could do now was hurt her. He forced himself to pull back.

'Are you getting enough to eat?' she was going on bravely, 'I wish I'd brought you something. I was thinking of you.'

He said: 'We're finished, Laura.'

She didn't hear him.

'I beg your pardon?' But she knew what he had said.

'We are finished,' he said. 'I've finished with you. I knew the first day I saw you . . .'

'In the woods . . . in the rain.' She tried to smile, remembering. 'I saw the look in your eyes. That terrifying, wonderful moment . . . I was sixteen.'

He shook his head. 'No. Leave me alone. Laura.'

'You do care for me. I'm looking at you and I can see it.'

'You must go,' he said, staring down into his calloused hands, 'never come back here. Why did you come? You've got Francis.'

She drew a breath. 'Don't break my heart.'

'Why do you make me suffer?'

'Do I?' she asked eagerly.

'We're mad— '

'Out of our heads!' Her fingers touched the wire. How she longed to stroke his face to fix the moment.

He murmured: 'From the very first day.'

'I knew it.'

'Forget me.'

'Forget *me*,' she whispered through the mesh. 'Can you do that?' He looked away, then back at her, drinking in every moment of her. 'You can't. *I* can't. Are you really sitting there so calmly? Aren't you breaking your heart too?'

He didn't answer. For an instant she really feared he would still say no.

He nodded.

'Say it Bart.' He couldn't. Men couldn't, they couldn't admit it. They couldn't love, couldn't feel in the same way women did from birth as naturally as breathing. Laura was hardly aware of whether she was comfortable or not, whether her legs were crossed or her shoes hurt. All her feeling was concentrated on him: the light on his hair, that look in his eyes. However far apart they were, he didn't have to be alone. Say it.

He kept silent.

She demanded: 'Why are you so afraid of me?' She didn't mean it that way, but that was how it slipped out.

'We're all prisoners,' he said, looking around him.

She saw through his eyes: the wire, the stone, the row of pathetic figures, the women beside Laura in cheap overcoats doing their best for their men. Some of them had pressed their hands against the mesh. Laura did the same.

'Prisoners,' Bart said quietly. 'Not just me. Francis is. You are. Prisoners of name, of time, of fate. Of parents, of marriage. Of our human emotions.'

'Of the valley,' Laura cried at him openly between the palms of her hands on the wire, 'of Watersmeet.'

'Forget me.'

She said:'I don't love Francis.'

She saw the pain in Bart's face. He pressed his hands against the wire, his flesh bulging in white squares, almost touching hers. She pressed back, feeling the weight of his strength against the wire.

'You must be loyal to . . . to him, Laura.'

She shook her head. Bart couldn't possibly understand that she didn't hate Francis, but that her husband was not *enough*. She wanted to elope with Bart, and be free. But he was in prison, and so was she.

Bart pulled his hands slowly back from the wire. 'You must get away. Just pack a suitcase and go, go anywhere.'

'I tried it and it didn't work. It isn't that simple.'

'Be what you are. Be Laura. The real Laura hidden beneath the Mistress of Watersmeet's skin. Your beautiful skin.'

A warder blew a short pip on a whistle. 'Time!'

'Forget me,' Bart said hurriedly. 'Go and *don't look back*.'

'I can . . . not forget you.'

He said cruelly: 'I thought you'd show more spirit.'

She looked around her at this dreadful place where Bart was incarcerated.

'You won't survive here,' she said. 'The valley is your place.'

He smiled. He was tougher than she thought. 'I shall endure.'

She knew it was impossible.

The warder stepped forward impatiently. Laura realized that all the other women had left. The convict prisoners were being filed out, the empty room echoed to their two voices.

'Bart?' she whispered.

'You will forget me.'

The warder took his elbow.

Bart stood. 'You must never come back here.' He would be in prison for the next six years and more, and she would not see him or hear from him again.

The warder pulled him away. Then Bart did what he had told Laura never to do: he looked back at her. 'Laura. I loved you always.'

The door clanged shut and he was gone from her life.

Laura sat without moving, drained of all emotion. What would keep Bart alive was his love for her.

'Come on, dear,' a voice said, 'you'll miss your bus.'

It was one of the warders. By the light of the naked bulbs she couldn't see his eyes below the peaked cap, but his voice was kind.

'Thank you,' she said gratefully, climbing to her feet.

'Are you sure you're all right?' he called after her.

Laura didn't look back.

She waited in the white glare with the other women. There was snow over her shoes and the cold was bitter. Her coat seemed to suck it in. She clenched the lapels closed under her chin, staring along the empty white ribbon of road where the bus would come. She didn't dare stamp her feet in case she spattered her stockings or broke a heel. She breathed her own breath in and out like steam through her scarf to keep her warm, her body beginning to shiver, then to tremble uncontrollably, and she had never felt so cold in her life. She was exhausted. And the other women were laughing and smoking together, talking about the numbers of coupons for stockings or how to take the fishy taste out of whalemeat with onions. Laura's tears pulled icy ribbons down her cheeks and she began to walk, not waiting for the bus. It seemed to draw up alongside her almost immediately.

The conductor opened the door and leaned down.

'Where do you think you're going then?'

Still walking, she looked at him without comprehending.

'There's nothing ahead for five miles,' he said. 'Come on, love, get in.'

She hesitated, then he put out his hand. 'Come on,' he said, and pulled her up. The driver crashed the gears and they moved off. She found a seat and must have slept through the long descent into Tavistock; with a jerk she realized that the streets were all around the windows, then the smelly bedlam of the bus station, people hurrying to join the queues, buses pulling out in fountains of blue fumes, shouted orders, people wrapped in blankets sleeping in the waiting room, men in uniform smoking cigarettes, yawning, joking in groups, or standing alone staring out at the street.

She recognized the Barum coach at once: it was the same one she had taken this morning. The conductor welcomed her with a yawn. As she plumped back into the window seat, the familiar tarry smell, she closed her eyes with a sigh of relief. The bus shook as more people came aboard.

'Hey. Excuse me.'

A bright face she did not know had recognized her. Clear blue eyes crinkled with smile-lines around the edges, an open face with a wide mouth revealing fine white teeth, short sandy hair – he had taken off his officer's cap to wipe his forehead with an ironed white linen handkerchief. His Class A uniform looked brand new, still so stiff that it showed the tiny holes left by the tailor's pins. He put away the handkerchief, smiling at her confusion, and stuck out his hand.

'Watersmeet. Jerry Ellis. Hi. Mind if I sit down?'

PART FOUR

The Serpent

'Please yourself,' she shrugged listlessly.

He hefted his kitbag up on to the rack and swung his lean frame into the seat beside her as if they had been friends for years, so familiar in his attitude to her that Laura was offended. She turned away from the brash American and examined the busy town passing the window. His reflection beyond hers was grinning at the back of her head unabashed.

'We met last year,' he said, 'don't you remember? Your horse jumped that gate and landed among us like a bomb. The guys thought you were amazing.'

'I've had a very rough day, Mr Ellis. I'd prefer to sleep.' She glanced at him. He was still smiling. 'There are plenty of empty seats,' she said pointedly.

'Lieutenant.' Not *left*enant, lootenant. 'I packed away my sergeant's stripes, promotion comes fast in a war. War suits the ambitious.'

'And you are very ambitious, Lieutenant Ellis?'

'Please,' he grinned, 'call me Jerry.' As always with American accents, it was impossible not to think of film stars. But he was in full colour: that pushy blue gaze. And a faint sting in her nostrils of – it must be cologne. But it was the tiny bitter lines around his eyes and mouth that made his face interesting.

'Laura,' she said.

'Sure, I know that, I asked around. The Mistress of Watersmeet. Wow. Sounds great, Lady Pervane. All that history. Like a fairytale – for kids.' He offered her a cigarette, but she shook her head. He said: 'I am a child of the proud and ancient city of Portland, Maine.' He held the Swan Vesta between two fingers and flicked it alight on the thumbnail of the same hand. The flame glowed in his eyes.

She gazed from the window.

'I'm afraid it isn't quite such a fairytale if one lives there.' She roused herself. 'Is this your first trip to Europe?'

'I lacked the opportunity to travel before.' He said it so seriously, like at a job interview, that she had to laugh. 'Say – you don't *mind* if I smoke?'

'Yes, I do. Put it out at once.'

He actually moved his cigarette respectfully towards the metal ashtray cupped on the seatback in front, and she realized he was unused to women's company; a fighter.

'Got me,' he said, leaning back ruefully. Still those tiny, bitter lines, even when he smiled. A minute or two later he put the cigarette out anyway. The coach had left the suburbs for open country and the cold sun travelling like a cheery red beach-ball above the snowy skyline of Bodmin Moor picked those lines out, unstitching him, making him look tired and much more mature. She wondered if he had suffered in the war, what sights he had seen in his brief life in this foreign land.

She imagined Portland, Maine: huge smoothly contoured automobiles cruising slowly along wide streets, low buildings rising towards a business district swarming with life, steaming drain-covers, a network of elevated railways racketing and roaring through the valleys of glass.

'I remember . . .' Jerry murmured, his eyes closed, 'how my father's breath stank on Friday nights when he got paid. He had back-Maine teeth and muscles in his arms you couldn't hold in both hands, he was a union man, Great Southern and Western Maine, riding the rails all his life. It was Mom brought us up, mostly.' He crossed himself. 'I was the sixth of seven boys. Big family, Mom's Catholic, right? Eight of us children altogether in the shanty trailer, only the last was a girl, Allie, she died in the crib, and Pa kind of gave up after that. Six sons grew up. Ah, Mom.'

From the way he spoke Laura thought she had died. 'Is she − is she still alive?'

'Sure, and kicking, you bet. But my brother Paulie got meningitis and passed on when he was seven years old. That was plenty old enough to be frightened of what was happening to him, to understand it when Father Aaron called again and hung around. That was the last time Paulie's eyes opened, and Mom was holding his hand.' Jerry put back his head and pulled out a tiny gold crucifix along with the identity tag around his neck. 'Nine-carat real gold, Lady Pervane. Rubs a little smoother each year. After the fire at Marty's Empy the old feller retired and Mom got them cheap in the sale. Six of them, one for each of us boys of hers going off to fight. Five's been sent back.'

'I'm so terribly sorry,' Laura said.

'The twins both together, in the Pacific, not the same ship, but the same battle. Ed's was sent back from Burma, he was the brightest of us, got two kids of his own. Sam crashed his trainer into New England woodland, it was eight, nine weeks until a hunter's bird-dog found his body, but that little old gold crucifix was still there and it got sent back. Rick was hit by a drunk driver just along the road, Mom heard the sirens.' His gold cross twinkled between Jerry's fingers in the last, flat light of the sun. 'She's never going to get this one sent back to her. Couldn't let Mom down.' The bus shuddered and jerked, then stopped. Jerry swore a word which Laura had never heard in public before, then said: 'Sorry, ma'am. Or should I always call you— '

She hid her amusement. 'Just Laura.'

The conductor called for all hands to get them up the hill. Jerry and the other men got out. Laura turned, watching his bobbing head through the back window as he pushed, the crewcut sandy hair darkening to brown with sweat despite the white streamers of his breath. The coach halted on top of the rise and the men jumped back aboard. Jerry wiped the traffic grime off his hands, grinning for Laura.

And he opened up his world for her.

'After my father hurt his back I had to get out of school, and I was never going to make it to college. I could run fast though, look, see,' he slapped his knees jutting out into the aisle, 'long legs, I could always beat the other guys goofing off in the surfside running races, hard sand, running like the wind. But Joe, the coach at High, said you've got to be pigeon-footed to run really fast. Education is the route to self-improvement, not washing up at Chet's Diner – the dried-on egg's the worst – or working for dimes pumping gas. One of the regulars for a top-up and a cleaned windscreen was the dentist, Mr Mayo, Mom knew him from church, he'd extracted her wisdom tooth that went sour. She told him about her bright youngest son working nights to put himself through college, reading Melville and Hawthorne resting his heels by the cash register between calls, and he began to take an interest in me. Al Mayo was splitting with his partners and setting up on his own, so he needed an orthodontic assistant, you know, answer the phone with one hand while mixing amalgam with the other. I knew he drank, but that just meant I had the afternoons free for study. I was the best assistant he ever had, I just about ran that practice single-handed, and I kept him literally on his feet until Mom got to hear about the drinking. She was teetotal and since Rick got run down she'd hated alcohol worse than sin. She said if I worked for that Mr Mayo one more day I needn't bother about coming home that evening.'

'So you joined the Army?' Laura prompted him.

He looked at her with those bright blue eyes.

'Not at once,' he said. The coach shuddered and stopped again, and the men got out to push. Laura stared out at the darkening landscape of a short winter's day, not even teatime yet, and she realized how thirsty she was. Jerry's words had flowed therapeutically over her, yet she found she could remember most of what he'd said. He was exactly what he appeared: ambitious, proud of what he had learned, taking pride in his efficiency, talking about himself clearly and well, reassuring her, a good companion to distract her mind from her troubles. She smiled, it had honestly meant a lot to him when the dentist said he was the best assistant he'd ever had. Jerry was honest: his manner as open and unforced as the smile on his face which hid nothing from Laura.

When he got back aboard, she said: 'Let me guess. But for the war, you would have got Al Mayo to pay you through dental school, and ended up owning the practice.'

Jerry laughed. 'I'd want more than that.'

'What more?'

'Just – more.' He smiled his irresistible smile.

But Laura insisted: 'What more is there?'

'You don't give up, do you?' He looked at his dirty hands, then gave up on them and turned towards her in the gloom. 'Money.'

'Is that all?' she mocked him.

He didn't laugh. He didn't even smile. 'A house with brick walls, a pretty wife with a hairstyle and the latest clothes, and next year's Pontiac standing in the drive.' His voice was totally serious, almost messianic; he believed in the American dream. 'My kids playing on a quiet leafy street with the sound of lawnmowers. Church on Sundays, and clothes bought new, and shoes that fit. An all-electric kitchen with a dishwasher. The life. The *life*.'

Laura felt abashed by his obvious sincerity. 'I didn't mean to sound . . . the way I did.'

He chuckled, then looked straight at her. 'Sure you did,' he said frankly. 'You've never been hungry. I guess you've always got what you wanted, one way or the other. Isn't that true?'

She changed the subject. He was on leave. Most young men of his age on a four-day pass would jaunt around the clubs and brothels of London or Bristol or Plymouth for a good time, but Jerry was different. He was *serious*, and his idea of a good time was clean, fresh air and the leisure to read military manuals before taking up his new post. The coach pulled into Barum and he asked if the way to Instow was over the bridge, so she guessed he would be reporting to the Combined Services Operations Unit base there next week. Mrs Pawkins' nephew had volunteered at Appledore, just across the water, to join the Landing Craft Obstacle Clearance Unit operating from the explosives and demolition school, and she guessed that Jerry would most probably be something to do with the landing exercises being held on the vast sweep of Woolacombe Beach and at Northam Burrows.

She asked: 'I hear you explosives experts really did blow up the old Newnes house last year.'

He grinned. 'A fine and perfect job.'

'Handling explosives must be a very skilled profession.'

'And knowing where to place them. Knowing where to look for them. And how to render them harmless.' Once the landing beach was secure, an invading army would race to secure the bridges that the enemy would try to blow up; there would be booby-traps in every town, every village. He winked at her and swung his kitbag down from the rack. 'If we hurry,' he said, 'we can beat the transport curfew and get to Lynmouth tonight. I'm staying at the Watersmeet Falls Hotel.'

'But that's an extraordinary coincidence.'

He helped her down and they crossed to the smaller Lynton coach. 'Now I'm an officer on an officer's pay, I do things in style. I fell in love with the area last year. Watersmeet's not a million miles from Maine – woods, valleys, seafood. General Eisenhower goes riding on Exmoor, you know that? I guess you don't read about it in the papers, but there's more Americans in Devon these days than there are Brits . . .'

A row of pallid bulbs cast a thick yellow gloom through the musty interior of the coach, and now that the blackout regulations had been eased somewhat a few Barum streetlights flickered past the netted windows. A half moon stained the gathering hills with blue luminescence. Jerry offered her a Camel cigarette, and this time she accepted. She told him how before she was married she used to stand in her open bedroom window smoking oval Passing Clouds, wafting the smoke outside so her parents wouldn't know. She talked to this handsome, earnest young man of her own age from halfway across the world about everything but her unhappy marriage, her loneliness, and Bart.

The coach stopped in Lee Road and they took the Cliff Railway slanting down through the trees, Jerry leaning on the railing looking out with white knuckles as the rooftops of Lynmouth rose around them. He had no head for heights. Laura, standing apart from him, caught a last glimpse of the rocky western beach, the smooth outline by deep blue moonlight of the tidal swimming pool, young love and easy promises.

They walked out into the road. The sandbagged Home Guard post was gone and there was talk that the units would be stood down entirely. Jerry pushed back his cap with his thumb, swung his kitbag over his shoulder and walked after Laura with one hand in his pocket. The Watersmeet Falls Hotel swung into view ahead of them, the river cascading beside it dwindling upwards into the Watersmeet valley like a silver road climbing to the moon.

Jerry spoke for the first time in a long while; he had to clear his throat.

'It's beautiful,' he said.

Laura shuddered, but he only thought she was cold and breathed out a long white streamer, agreeing. There were no ghosts in America.

When she stopped on the bridge before the hotel he said: 'Sure you won't come in for a drink?'

She turned and shook her head, then pulled off her glove and held out her hand politely. 'I can walk home from here. Goodbye, Lieutenant, and thank you for being a good companion on a bad journey. I hope you enjoy your leave.'

The royal brush-off. He shook hands tolerantly. Her hand was warm and light, and he could feel the ring on her finger. She looked over her shoulder and he sensed her reluctance to go.

'Sure about that drink?' he said.

'Quite sure! she said.

'Maybe I'll see you around,' he called.

She glanced back over her shoulder as she crossed the bridge. He watched her turn along the Tors path, his eyes following her tiny figure illuminated by the river until she disappeared in the trees. Then he drew a deep breath.

Laura was woken by voices outside. She rolled over and scrabbled up her gold-plated watch from the bedside table, beside her rings and the empty glass

271

of water, then squinted at its sentimental little face. It was past nine already, and she had been so tired that she had forgotten to draw the curtains. From the winter-blue sky above the valley walls sunlight slanted past her French windows to touch the lawns with green between the white shadows of the trees.

The voices laughed, carrying that slight echo she associated with the area outside the stable. Laura wrapped herself in a dressing gown and stepped out on her balcony, its tiles icy cold to her bare feet. In the bright scene below her Francis was immaculately dressed in jodhpurs and black riding jacket. A horsewhip at his hip, he was standing by Haymaker, cheerfully talking shop with Lieutenant Jerry Ellis.

She had refused his offer of a drink because she really didn't want to get at all involved with a chance acquaintance from a bus ride. And she had been nearly dying of thirst; she wondered if he had seen her, last night, slip down to the river as soon as she reached the trees and drink from her cupped hands by moonlight. She suspected he had.

She looked down at the visitor coldly, not wanting to like him. He was taking advantage of her. Jerry wore a green woollen vee-neck pullover, sharply creased slacks and rugged US Army boots. That little speck of nine-carat gold glinted at his throat. He bent down and examined one of Haymaker's hooves. Doubtless he knew all about horses too. It really was an incredible cheek to come up here.

Laura went in and drew her bath, broke off a chunk of solidified pre-war bath salts – at last all those unused Christmas presents were coming in useful – and dropped it in curiously. It lay underwater like a nugget of green glass then gathered its strength, put out filaments and began to melt. She tossed her gown and nightie in the corner, piled up her hair under a cap and inhaled the luxurious scent of the bath salts, then tested the temperature with her foot and slipped under the bubbles with a groan of pleasure as the aches and pains of yesterday washed away.

What *was* he doing here?

She reviewed what she had told him; nothing she shouldn't have, *nothing* of her unhappiness.

She turned off the hot-water tap with her toes. The bath was white enamel, Victorian, freestanding and vast, with the familiar blue streaks beneath the taps, but the Manor had been re-fitted with expensive stainless steel water-pipes, the latest thing, in the early twenties. She heard the kitchen door slam below her and realized that Francis had invited Jerry inside. She lay there, bothered, then added more hot water. But she was still bothered.

Finally she swore the same word Jerry had used yesterday and heaved out the plug, put on her pale blue woollen dress and combed out her hair, bunched it up and clipped it back. The man who had spoiled her bath was sitting at her kitchen table, and Francis was frying bacon.

'Darling,' he said, kissing her, handing her the spatula, 'I believe you know Lieutenant Ellis.'

'Hardly,' Laura said coolly. 'He travelled back with me on the same bus from Barum last night, that's all.'

'All the way from Tavistock.' Ellis stood with that wide, innocent smile on his open face, his hand extended. 'Please call me Jerry.'

Tavistock. Jerry had said *Tavistock.* Francis hadn't noticed.

She transferred the spatula to her other hand and shook hands perfunctorily, then turned the smoking bacon and put the pan on the simmer plate. Francis had put four slices of brown bread in the Aga's oven to make toast. 'I don't think you'll have any more trouble with that lameness, sir,' Jerry was saying. She listened to their man-to-man talk with half her mind while she cooked. She had to admire Jerry's way of handling Francis: he was very deferential and respectful. *Respect* was a key word with Francis, and Jerry, playing the polite guest, always gave way when Francis interrupted, yet he got his own point across through flexibility and persistence. Laura wondered: *How did Francis get so old?*

Francis put his horsewhip down on the table, sitting with his legs crossed, leaning his elbow comfortably over the back of his chair. Laura put the teapot down in front of him.

'I was surprised that you stayed on with Clara yesterday, dear,' he said.

'I just felt like it. I hadn't seen her for so long and it turned out we had so much to talk about.'

'Women,' Francis explained. 'My wife hasn't been quite well for some time.'

'What nonsense!' Laura said.

'I hope it's nothing serious?' Jerry said, obviously concerned.

Francis bit into his bacon sandwich and shook his head. Laura poured the bacon-fat miserably from the frying pan into a dish. She and Francis were starting to conduct their relationship through third parties. Francis was looking to Jerry for an ally

274

against Laura. *Women.* She didn't know what to do, what she *wanted* to do about it. They ought to have a serious sit-down, work-it-out talk. But Francis had been brought up to treat words as unnecessary chatter, loading the dice on the woman's side in an argument, while she was afraid what truth might spill out of her mouth. She now desperately wanted their marriage to work, because she was so frightened of the alternative; when it came down to it the thought of admitting failure, even privately to herself, was horrible. The valley seemed to close in on the windows of the house.

She pulled her chair to a corner of the table, sipping her tea and watching the two men, observing how Jerry manipulated Francis like a customer, as if Jerry were a salesman earnestly pitching a product. Which Jerry was: his product was himself. The boy would go far. Francis looked at the clock and gulped his tea.

'I must be getting on.' He had to ride up to the farm to meet assessors from the District Agriculture Committee.

'I'll be on my way too, sir,' Jerry said. They shook hands. 'Could you direct me to the Rockford path?'

'Lady Pervane will show you.' Laura nearly burst out laughing: he couldn't even call her Laura. Francis changed his cravat for a dark green wool tie, tightly knotted, and checked the Rotary badge pinned to his lapel. He kissed Laura's cheek with his hand on her shoulder, saluted Jerry, then they heard him ride away.

Jerry looked at her across the table.

'Said I'd see you around,' he said. 'Don't worry, I'm going.'

'You've got a nerve coming here,' Laura said.

He'd half risen to his feet, but now he sat back with that smile of his, still looking at her.

'Why?' he said.

Laura couldn't answer.

'Listen,' he said cockily, 'I work with women all the time, half our drivers are women, more than half the support staff, so let's get it straight. Nowadays a man and a woman can be friends. Just friends. I like you, and that is all.'

She didn't reply.

'And you like me,' he said.

She went to the sink and started the washing-up.

'Sure you do,' Jerry said.

'If you keep making such silly talk, you'll have to go.'

'Just point out the way to Rockford.' She started to feel intensely annoyed with him.

'I will, when I've finished this.' Her hands were covered with suds.

He said nothing for a long time. Neither of them wanted him to go. She put the plates in the rack and he took them out, wiping them with the drying-up cloth.

He said: 'Last night. It seemed so dark after you left, that's all.'

'Oh.' So she had not concealed her loneliness and unhappiness from him after all, and that was the real reason he had come sniffing around.

But he said: 'Francis is a lucky man.' He folded the cloth over the Aga rail, and she realized he *didn't* know. He was an idealist.

Jerry watched her dry her hands. Even something so prosaic was interesting when she did it: he knew

276

he was putting her on a pedestal. Soon he must go back to the war, and he might be killed.

'I'll put you on your path,' she said, swinging a coat over her shoulders.

But he followed so slowly that she found herself showing him around the grounds, the oasis of formal gardens nestling in the bend of the river. Here was the tall rusting frame, Jerry effortlessly doing chin-ups from it, that had carried the swing-sofa where Francis courted her all those years ago before the war, and she remembered Bart saying it was exactly where the old summerhouse had once stood, where Phineas launched Lucy on her death-boat to the sea, the everlasting sea, and willingly accompanied her. Jerry slapped the old rust off his hands with a laugh as she stared over the river running at winter height and then he fell silent, listening to her, watching her face: her heat, the emotional dimension of her, the power in her he sensed when she talked of Watersmeet.

But he didn't look around him as she spoke. It was Laura he could not take his eyes off.

He said: 'You obviously love the valley.'

Laura no longer bothered to hide her unhappiness. 'How little you know.'

'But you and your husband— ' Jerry stopped, realizing. 'I just assumed – you seemed so happy and in love. This lovely place. You must have thought – you make me feel like the worst sort of heel, coming here.'

She stared across the water, Lucy's Pool, the waterfalls, up the rising wall of red rock white with frost to the skyline of white trees: Hellebore.

'You don't know what love is,' she said.

He gazed at her, seeing Laura as a real woman at last. He searched her face, then kissed her lips for the lightest, briefest moment. She almost jerked away, then he felt her lips hot on his, her fingernails on the side of his neck.

She looked down, stepped back meekly, so vulnerable that his heart ached. He'd gone much too far.

'I'm sorry,' he said tenderly, following her. 'I didn't mean to do that. Hell, yes, I *did* mean it.' Something very like pain crossed his still-smiling face. He didn't know what he was selling, he couldn't act with her.

She looked over the river. She didn't move.

'I'd better go,' he said.

'No,' she said impetuously, turning. They stood six feet apart. Snowdrops and primroses were pushing through the frost all around them already, in Watersmeet spring arrived almost before winter had a chance. 'Yes,' she said, 'you'd better go.'

'I didn't mean this to happen,' he said. Something moved in his eyes.

She threw back at him: 'Yes you did.'

'Sure I did, in the woods, or yesterday on the bus, when you were anybody, until I got to know you. Until now. I wanted to kiss you on the bridge last night, and I'm glad I just did kiss you.'

She avoided his gaze, then pointed upriver without looking. 'To get to Rockford keep going straight on past Paradise House, my parents' house. Just go.'

He said something or other; she didn't answer him. He waited ten seconds, fifteen, then left her standing alone on the grass. She watched him until the trees hid him.

Laura ran back to the house. She wished she hadn't done the washing-up, she could have done it now. She looked for the vacuum-cleaner to busy herself with but Mrs Pawkins had done a proper job yesterday and the carpets were immaculate, even the pale grey expanse of Wilton in the modern Long Room that showed the slightest mark was perfect, the fire neatly laid in the wide stone mouth of the fireplace ready for lighting. Laura looked for the matches. On the gleaming rosewood of the Bechstein stood a parcel, a *gift*, wrapped in brightly coloured paper. Her heart froze.

A card was tied to the red ribbon.

She reached out and turned over the card with her fingernail. Francis' handwriting.

To my darling wife: with all my love, on the occasion of our first Wedding Anniversary.

Yesterday. Laura felt sick. Yesterday had been their first wedding anniversary, and she had gone swanning off to Dartmoor. How *could* she have forgotten? Maybe she had meant to hurt Francis without consciously realizing it. The day had been just as important to her, but she had celebrated it in the way that meant most to her: by going to see Bart. Laura felt frantic. She had wanted to be caught; the relief of it. It was time Francis knew. She pressed the back of her hand to her mouth. She really thought she was going to be sick. But still she could not stop taking Francis' love, wondering what that mask of glittering paper contained: too small for another dress, his gift was bound to be jewellery, not sapphires this time, or diamonds, the package was too large to be a ring at all. He was determined to keep the charade going. Maybe to him it wasn't

279

a charade. He wanted – only her, and his gifts were genuine. She slipped her finger through the bow of the ribbon, then lifted it weighingly, but the ribbon parted.

She picked up the naked package, heavier than she had thought, and held it against her. Suddenly her fingers tore at the paper, she couldn't resist the sense of anticipation, of knowing she was *treasured*.

It was a heavy gold bracelet, highly ornate, Victorian, set with rubies. It was gorgeous. Laura could not help but slip it over her wrist. This was how much he loved her: it looked priceless.

'Where did you go?' Francis said from the doorway, where he was watching her.

'I didn't hear you come back!' she gasped, and fingered the plundered bracelet guiltily.

'Lieutenant Ellis didn't know anything about horses after all,' Francis said. 'That shoe came off at the farm, so Silas dropped me back.' He picked up the gift-wrapping, crumpled it, threw it in the grate. 'Where did you go?' he repeated, taking a book of matches from his pocket, not looking at her.

'This is the most beautiful present you've ever given me.' She crossed to him, holding up her wrist with the bracelet to show him, but he knelt and struck a match.

'It was my grandmother's.'

Laura shivered. Sir Roderick Pervane's young wife: Lady Pervane, Mistress of Watersmeet, and her son George who was eventually born in baby Adam's place. Had she known her husband, in unholy alliance with Lavinia Barronet, was a murderer? Perhaps she hadn't wanted to know. Laura doubted even if Sir George or Francis knew

– or admitted to themselves that they did. She dared say nothing.

Just before it burned his fingers, Francis touched the match to the paper.

'Where did you go?'

'To see Clara,' Laura said defensively.

He watched the growing flame. 'Are you sure?'

'Ask Clara.'

'And get the truth? That boy said *Tavistock*. Tavistock. *That* I believe.'

'Yes, Francis, I did go to Tavistock.'

'To see . . .' Francis wouldn't even say Bart's name. 'Dartmoor. You went to Dartmoor yesterday. I'd wrapped up my grandmother's bracelet for you. I waited and waited.'

'I did go to Tavistock, but I turned round there,' Laura lied. 'I felt guilty about the way Bart Barronet had been treated. I felt his suffering was my fault. But then I realized I was a Pervane.' She was going to embellish her story with true details of the smelly bedlam of the bus station at Tavistock, the buses pulling out in fountains of blue fumes, inventing only hesitation, a decision to turn back, but she had said enough. *I realized I was a Pervane.*

She held her tongue, and Francis nodded.

'You deny seeing him?' he said.

Laura denied seeing Bart.

'Thank God.' Francis shuddered, and Laura realized that he was so jealous of Bart that his life was dominated even by his absence.

'Francis, it's all right,' she whispered, 'I'm here.'

They were kneeling together staring into the fire.

Francis said: 'I do love you.'

'Francis, Francis.'

He gripped her wrists passionately, speaking into her face. 'If you ever tried to go there again, I would kill you.' He pulled her head against him hungrily. 'I love you so much, Laura my darling.'

On the first really warm day Laura rode Blackbird up on to the moor. She didn't dare go *the wrong way*, it simply wasn't worth the bother if Francis should ever find out, it would hurt him too much: so she took the county road, and not until she was past Cheriton and there was no risk of meeting anyone at all, let alone anyone who would know her, did she loose her hair and let Blackbird stretch out into the wonderful wild gallop southward down the ridge. Laura had escaped Watersmeet, she was sixteen again and she had never been in love, she had no power to hurt or be hurt: just for these few minutes of freedom, the spring sun was flying above, her hair pulled out in the slipstream behind her was probably tangling itself to hell, and she didn't care.

She reined in on the Exe Plain, Blackbird snorting and stamping, and made her walk to the edge. Below them was Long Chains Combe, and the bothy where Bart had hidden out had been vindictively knocked down, its walls a circle of scattered stones already looking strikingly similar to the humped, time-eroded circles of the bronze-age village beyond. Nothing was known of these people who built their homes in the Mediterranean warmth of Exmoor three or four thousand years ago, their lives and loves, even their names were lost: long before Barronet, before Torr, even perhaps before Toher, the bridge. Only their stones remained, and their ransacked tombs. And their children. And their children's children.

The wind from the sea blew around Laura.

They knew what she knew: that day after day, a life had to be lived. They knew, as she did, that there was something deeply erotic about a man's passion. Francis had actually threatened to kill her, or perhaps he meant kill himself, and she had felt terribly excited by the power of that. She gasped with passion as he took her, using him as he used her, then while he slept across her afterwards she found herself weeping, despising herself for making him suffer, for not being able to love him more. The routine of life went on.

Laura shouted. The moor, vast, empty and potent, swept away her voice as though it had never been.

She must return to Watersmeet.

Instead she rode down to the bothy and picked up a stone. Six years at least must pass before Bart would come out of prison, and she would keep her promise not to go there. Tears misted her eyes: she felt she spent all her life living up to what other people wanted her to be, and that was so much less than she wanted to be. Jerry Ellis would have loved her, if she had given him the chance.

She rode back to Watersmeet Manor, and as the walls of the valley rose around her, enclosing her, the wind failed, and she was back home.

Of course, Francis turned on the radio every morning while they ate breakfast. Very early on the morning of 6 June, Allied forces landed in strength on the northern coast of France.

Francis, unshaven, stopped chewing. 'Laura!

Listen to this!' An opposed landing was the most difficult of all military manoeuvres, he informed her.

Later they heard that all the bridges over the Seine, and many of those across the Loire, had been blown up by Nazi bridgemasters before they could be defused by the specialist teams parachuted into the spearhead of the Allied advance; casualties were very high. That boy Jerry Ellis would be in the thick of it, Francis reminded her.

'Yes,' Laura said, 'I suppose so.'

That was a Tuesday, and on the following Sunday it was their turn to go to Paradise House for lunch. She thought how much older her father looked, losing his hair, but Ernest's grip was as strong as ever. He pulled himself upstairs each night on his massive arms, step by step on his knuckles, rather than forsake Sybil's bed. She couldn't carry him any longer, but to Laura her mother looked no less strong, her unshiny hair and powdered face perhaps a little greyer, and the lines around her beestung lips were pinched into an expression of sour irritation, but those eyes were still sensuous, full of life: the most startling, vivacious feature in someone self-controlled to the point of immobility, those lovely, gentle sad blue eyes.

'Hallo, Laura,' Sybil said in the hall, and Laura *knew* she knew Francis was not the man in her life. Did it show? Only to another woman. They could hear Francis outside, wearing the red, black and green ribbon of his Defence Medal, chatting cheerfully with Ernest about the Home Guard stand-down fixed for October, then Ernest going on about the liberation of France, and Laura breathed a sigh of relief.

Sybil took her sherry into her solarium, and Laura followed her. In this her own room Sybil relaxed, turned her face up to the almost vertical sun: the valley glared around them under the steep light beyond the panes, each silver leaf green below, each tree growing, to their sun-adjusted eyes, from shadow as black as night.

'Rob Stall sent me a telegram,' Sybil said. 'Clara had her baby boy last Thursday night, eight pounds and kicking. He did not inform me of its name.' She looked at Laura. 'I hope they will invite me to the christening this time.'

'Will you go, this time?'

'What have we done wrong? I loved Clara, but she treats me like this. We did everything for her. And she married that frightful Rob.' She sipped her sherry. Outside on the lawn where the lunch table had been laid, the men were on their second glass, both of them still wearing a jacket and tie under the hot sun. 'I must say, Laura, you're looking very well . . .'

Laura knew what was coming and looked away so that Sybil did not say it to her face. 'It would make Ernest so happy to have grandchildren of his own. You know what I mean. You're his real daughter. He never cared for Clara.'

'It's Clara I feel most sorry for.'

'And Francis.'

'What about *me*, mother?' But Sybil looked at her steadily. Laura had her duty to do: at least one little Pervane, preferably several, or else their good work might be all wasted. They didn't care about Laura or Francis, only the blood.

'It would make him so happy, dear,' Sybil repeated: as if Laura would be guilty by not having children.

Perhaps she was right.

Laura started thinking about children.

'You don't understand how awful it is,' Sybil said suddenly, 'being old. Everything is behind you.'

'That's Francis' third glass,' Laura warned. 'Isn't lunch ready?'

She helped her mother carry out a cut of cold ham and a potato salad to the table. Laura sat coolly in the shade of a parasol knowing she'd burn in no time if she wasn't careful, but the others sweltered in the direct heat of the sun, and the linen tablecloth was almost blindingly white. The wine, one of Ernest's precious clarets, was bleached almost as pale as rosé in the sparkling glasses, and the silver cutlery, blue and green in reflection of the sky and forest, flashed startling spears of sunlight.

'Monty will hand us France on a plate,' Ernest said, making a mouthful of ham go a long way, 'he'll be knocking at the German border in a month if that Yank colonel lets him.' Laura knew he meant Eisenhower, whom he detested for his unfairly rapid promotion.

'The Germans are still not our natural enemies,' Francis said.

'Ernest has *still* got this bee in his bonnet about retiring to the south of France,' Sybil explained.

Francis liked it. 'Good idea.' Ernest helped him to more wine.

'It's nice to have these pipe dreams,' Sybil said calmly, and Laura could see she absolutely hated the idea, 'but they're just dreams, after all.'

'The man who broke the bank at Monte Carlo,' Ernest chided her with the hopeful words of the old song.

'Ernest is already overdrawn on the bank of miracles,' Sybil said icily, looking at him with bruised, loving eyes. 'Just to be alive.'

Ernest winked at Laura. 'What do you think? Your opinion always meant most to me.'

Laura heard herself say: 'If I wanted something, really wanted it, I'd do anything to get it.'

'There you are,' Ernest said. 'The Hôtel les Ambassadeurs it is. You're a lucky man, Francis. She has her mother's ruthlessness.'

'Lucky?' grinned Francis. He had drunk enough to pick on words. 'Lucky? With that bloody place still standing?' He raised his knife towards the obscuring woods, and Laura knew he meant Hellebore House.

'Pass the wine, darling,' she said, and kept the bottle at her end of the table.

Francis couldn't get Bart out of his mind. 'The place should be burned. Can't be sold, even though he is just a common criminal. The property is held in commonage, we can't get at it.'

Laura listened to the familiarity of that bitterness. Had her parents seen how similar he would become to them? Was that the reason she had found herself marrying Francis – immortality for her parents? The perpetuation of their echoing voices, their own bitterness. Didn't she have any will of her own?

Francis looked round for the wine. Sybil pulled the bottle from Laura's fingers and passed it to him.

'He'll be a broken man when he comes out of prison,' Francis said. 'What do you think, dear?'

Laura glanced up at him. 'Yes.'

'Laura always agrees with me. Don't you, dear?'

Laura smiled.

287

'Why should a man like that be left with anything at all?' Francis fretted impotently. 'A man who deserted his country.'

'He'll be sent back into the Army,' Ernest said.

Laura said: 'But surely there won't be a war by the time he comes out.'

'The Russians,' Ernest said, 'the French.' He also had drunk too much, but Sybil looked interested and amused. The men were making fools of themselves again. 'The Yanks. Somebody . . .'

Laura looked at her mother encouraging them: was this lying, unhappy creature what she too would become? Yes, if she was not already.

'The war will never end,' Francis said. Francis' war.

Laura looked at them, even herself, seeing them all sitting around the table as if from the outside, father, mother, husband, wife, the civilized flashing of the sun off the family cutlery, and felt a sensation of horror creep up her spine. The valley walls overhung her, heavy with summer; the motionless air almost suffocated her. She excused herself and walked to the goyle, immersed her wrists in the freezing water, splashed droplets over her burning face.

'It's just Laura,' Francis slurred, 'having one of her days, you know.'

It was shameful, because men were fighting and dying far from home and the girls they left behind. Monty was not going to be knocking at the German border in a month, or even two.

One morning – it was the same week as the Home Guard stand-down parades – a letter arrived

addressed to Sir Francis and Lady Pervane. It caught
Laura's eye in the pile of other letters because of
the US Forces Mail sticker. It had been opened by
the censor.

It was from Lieutenant Jerry Ellis. She was sure
of it, and stood by the kitchen sink with her
fingertips pressed to her mouth, feeling quite dizzy.
She had not realized how much it meant to her that
he was still alive: that tiny gold crucifix had not been
sent four thousand miles home to the old woman in
Portland, Maine after all. Really she'd never doubted
it. Jerry was a survivor if anyone was.

But the good handwriting of the address was
decidedly shaky, even though she could see the
ruled pencil-feint he'd used to try to keep the lines
straight. Laura's hand trembled and the urge to slip
the envelope into her apron and read it secretly in
her bedroom was almost irresistible. But she was
determined to be fair to Francis, and took it through
with the others to his study.

Wearing battledress, he was working on his speech
at the big directoire desk before setting off for
Lynmouth. He took the letters and while he worked
through them she waited by the desk in an agony
of suspense.

'Ah,' he said, coming to it and opening the
envelope at last.

'Is it from Lieutenant Ellis?' Laura asked, calmly
sipping her tea. 'I saw the sticker— '

'Captain Ellis,' Francis informed her, then read
quietly.

Laura was desperate.

If he'd been promoted, he'd probably been in the
thick of the fighting. The Nazis were putting up a

furious resistance, wires across the road, mines, booby-traps. Laura asked: 'Is he well? What does he say?'

'He's been wounded. "Somewhere in France." You liked that country boy better than I did, Laura, I found him rather too full of hot air. Bit of a wide boy. Didn't know a thing about horses.'

'How seriously wounded?' Laura was afraid her voice had given her away.

'Read it yourself.' Francis shrugged and held out the note between his fingers. He didn't rate Jerry. Laura's feelings could not have been better camouflaged than by Francis Pervane's continuing obsession with his beaten enemy, Bart Barronet.

At first she could hardly read the letter. Jerry had been shot in the side and shoulder. He was at the convalescent hospital in Southampton. The letter said little; little could be said. Kind nurses, no pain, own fault. His writing: the patient effort that had gone into the forming of each letter. He should get convalescent leave in about a month. There was no infection and he was very fit. Laura remembered him in the garden doing effortless chin-ups on the frame of the sofa-swing.

A month. It seemed an unendurable length of time stretching out in front of her. Perhaps, anyway, he wouldn't come. She knew he would. Suppose Francis was in? He would monopolize the conversation, and she would have to sit there being polite while the minutes trickled away. She became so irritated with Francis that she could hardly bear to sit in the same room with him. Everything about him was boring and predictable, the way he dressed, his mannerisms, the way he held her upper arm when he kissed her goodbye going out, the way he slammed the door and called out 'I'm home!' when he returned. He was eating much more than when he was young and self-consciously tormented by anxiety and desire, now comfortable to put on weight, while she was eating less to keep herself in trim. She had not noticed, before, the sucking noises his mouth made as he chewed his food, and she wished he would trim the hairs in his ears. How could she ever have thought he was handsome? The veins were breaking in his cheeks and nose, just like his father's had. Yet she knew how lucky she was to have him. At least Francis loved her, whereas Rob Stall cared not one whit for Clara, and played around. But Clara had Perdie and little Johnny to love. Laura counted the days until Jerry Ellis would come. Nothing would happen, she didn't love him, he didn't love her, he was just randy, but she was dying to see him, to see how he had changed, to hear all that had happened to him. To see that wide smile crease his youthful face just because he saw her. He'd want to kiss her, she wouldn't let him. She hadn't meant to last time. She crossed off the days down the last week of the month.

Jerry didn't come.

He wasn't booked in at the Watersmeet Falls Hotel, she'd checked. She could hardly believe it. She'd been so sure. Not a word from him. Perhaps he'd booked in at the Granville, the Lyndale or one of the guest houses, but no, he wouldn't do that, the Watersmeet Falls Hotel was the most expensive and the best and it was never in his personality to do anything cheap: *Now I'm an officer on an officer's pay, I do things in style.* She checked again with Mr Sayle personally, and however much she disliked the new manager, he was efficient, and no one by the name of Ellis was booked in. Quite definite.

She already regretted writing to the centre in Southampton casually putting it forward that, if Jerry was passing, he might drop by. Obviously he wasn't in the slightest interested in her, any more than she was in him. This time their friendship would be meticulously correct. Besides, it was such a long time. A lot of water under the bridge, and men were fickle. But she had not thought that of Jerry.

Three days passed, then four. She gave up looking for him from the window of her knitting room on the first floor. She put on her cape and walked by the river amongst the bare trees, the mossy boulders with water sliding between them. She saw Jerry Ellis coming up the path from Lynmouth long before he saw her. He was walking without a care in the world, just as she remembered him, carrying his kitbag over his shoulder, his cap tipped back by his thumb, one hand casually in his pocket. Laura felt her face flush with heat, and she was angry with him for being so unchanged. She pretended to be absorbed in the river's flow.

He stopped with a jolt a dozen paces from her. Still she wouldn't look at him, and he wouldn't approach her: a lady alone with her thoughts. That was how he thought of her, a real lady, some sort of English goddess on a pedestal. Instead she was flesh and blood.

Laura turned towards him and rushed into his arms.

He dropped his kitbag and met her in the middle,

his arms around her, her velocity lifting her off her feet against him, their mouths pressed tight.

She gazed into his eyes. She could feel him shaking.

'Toothpaste and cologne,' she taunted him.

'What?'

'I love your smell. Fresh mint toothpaste and— '

'Puppy-dogs' tails.'

'Mind reader,' she said tenderly, running her little finger down his smooth-shaven shiny skin from his dark sideburn to his jaw.

'The bad news is, Laura, I've only got thirty-six hours. To get to Dover. I can't stay, I've travelled for a day to spend an hour with you. I'm joining my unit in northern France tomorrow.'

'Jerry, that's not fair.' She touched his side, his shoulder. 'Where is it? Surely they must give you longer.'

'Not now the German cities are starting to fall. It's hellish.'

'Don't talk about it.'

'The buildings are just shells, shells of ruins. We give them the chance to surrender or die, and they choose death. I don't know what it means any more.'

She could feel the small round pucker of skin through his jacket, just beneath his ribs where the bullet had entered. 'It doesn't hurt,' he said. 'I just wanted to see you all the time. I dreamed of you.'

'Did you?'

'I wanted you to feel for me the same I feel for you.'

'Did I? In your dreams?'

He said: 'You were happy and loved your husband.'

She pulled away from him.

'I thought you'd forgotten me.' He followed her earnestly. 'I can't get you out of my mind, sleeping or waking, you're in my blood.'

She searched his eyes.

'Watersmeet,' he said. 'I dream I see Laura Pervane, your face, your body, the way you move, you. Simply you. I see you in the valley, the trees, the river. I'm in love with you.'

'In your dream.'

'For real.'

They both knew it was true. They could see it in each other's face. Their eyes, mouths, hands, every move they made, acknowledged it between them. She desired him and trusted him. He held her gently, almost reverently.

'No one's ever felt like this before,' Jerry whispered, 'the way I feel about you.'

'Take me with you.' She didn't want to think about Francis: she couldn't think of him, her whole world was in Jerry's low voice.

'All the while I was lying there in pain,' he murmured, 'all I thought of was you. In the train coming down, in the bus. Only you. Laura, this can't be happening. I love you. I've got to go. One day we'll laugh at this, that I could be so in love with you.' He was kissing her face, she was gripping his upper arms with all the power in her hands. They were standing between a red sandstone boulder and the river's flow, out of sight in the rocks, a black screen of trees towering around them to the sky. He clasped her against him.

'I'm so lonely without you,' he admitted. His eyes were still lovely and pushy, undefeated, incorrigibly full of hope. And yet she knew he needed her heat, her passion, to force him on. In so many ways love was unromantic, calculating, summing-up, seeing the other partner more clearly than ever before.

'We'd make a good team,' Laura said.

'It's love I'm talking about.'

'Don't talk.'

He kissed her.

'If only you were free of Francis.' He nuzzled her with his lips.

She said distantly: 'I am free of him.'

Jerry looked earnestly, seriously into her eyes.

She said impatiently: 'There's so much I do feel about him. I feel guilty because I've treated him so badly. I've made him suffer, he's drinking, I'm turning him into what he once despised most. I should never have married Francis; it was greed, doing what my parents wanted. An escape. And he's so kind, little gifts, and big ones, this bracelet, important ones, he's thoughtful and tender, and he does everything a husband should. Yes, so much I feel about him.' She stopped hopelessly. 'But nothing I feel for him.'

Jerry said quietly: 'Does he love you?'

'Yes, he does.'

'And you're still married to him, Lady Pervane.'

'You like saying that, "Lady Pervane".'

'You're my lady. My English rose.' He kissed her lips, and she returned his kiss hungrily with her mouth.

'And if I did leave him?' she whispered.

He didn't reply, then held her tight against him,

and rested her head on his shoulder. Her eyes were wide open.

'Oh, Laura,' Jerry said. 'This is so wrong. I might be killed tomorrow.'

'Stop saying that!'

'Don't forget this is Uncle Sam's uniform I'm wearing.'

'To hell with Uncle Sam. This is *us*.'

'I'll come back.'

'Promise me.'

He lifted her head gently. 'I can't face losing you.'

'Now you have promised.'

He paused. 'I've never broken a promise,' he said simply. 'But, Laura, you won't be happy in America. Look around you, this beautiful place. Watersmeet.' He tried to explain industrial ugliness to her, its mighty indifference. 'I have no money, no class . . . You really wouldn't like living in a trailer. I truly am a simple small-town working joe.'

'I don't care. All the things you say I shouldn't like about you are what I *do* like you for.'

'I'm telling you what I am,' he said honestly.

'Do you have to be so honest and truthful? I trust you. Just hold me.'

He held her. She could feel him against her breasts, his frame taut and fit, slighter, leaner, but as vigorous as she hoped; *different*. Part of her was horrified at herself, the sensuality of her body, the coolness and calculation she felt in the logical side of her brain; but her other half simply longed for Jerry's contact, his company. And she had not been unfaithful to Francis in the way that mattered: it wasn't as though Jerry had entered her. Whatever they might say, he had to go back to the war today.

'Are you ambitious enough, Jerry?' she whispered.

'Yes,' he said, burying his face in her hair, 'my God yes!'

And if he had demanded to make love, she would have sighed and let him, there and then, though she didn't want to because the rocks were cold and hard, it would have to be quick and uncomfortable . . . she must be so careful not to make him into another Francis. 'I treasure you, Jerry,' she said softly, running the palm of her hand over his short, sandy hair.

'Trust me,' Jerry said, caressing her. But he didn't go too far, glancing at his watch, the bloody bus; and she sensed that something else too was stopping him.

'Jerry?' she murmured.

'Nothing,' he smiled.

'You don't have anything secret between us?'

'Only how much I love you.'

'But you can't truly love me if there's something you haven't told me,' she said, beguiling and adamant.

'I do love you,' Jerry Ellis told her directly and without frills. 'I am yours until the day I die. Truly.'

She looked up into his eyes, those pleasantly pushy, bright blue, salesman's eyes of his. Their thoughtfulness, their hope. She believed in his simple morality, obvious ambition, strange sense of humour. He wouldn't make love to her, she was sure, because she was married. But he wanted her so badly that she could feel the electricity running up his body, and she knew she could have seduced him even now, when he had to go, so that he missed his bus and was late reporting back to his unit, the worst crime in Jerry's book. For her.

He looked back over his shoulder. 'Just remember, whatever happens,' he said. 'It was because I couldn't face losing you.'

And she knew he'd come back.

As always, once she had the courage to make it happen, she knew it was right. Laura had started the day determined to be fair to Francis, but when she found herself propelled into Jerry's arms – her real feelings revealed to her, everything she kept hidden and repressed – she knew she was right to do what she was doing. And how level-headed she had felt, her mind calm and clear – and when she said *And if I leave him?* she knew that leaving Francis was what she had been thinking about and deciding on for a long time. Ever since seeing Bart in prison.

Away from Watersmeet, she could be free. Totally free of her past, to be herself. There were no ghosts in America.

She lay in her lonely bed, staring at the invisible ceiling. Divorce would be messy and painful, but Francis had forced her into Jerry Ellis' arms; he had brought his fate on himself.

But still, temporarily, their life continued in its almost contented rhythm. She interested herself in hotel management, and Francis did not complain. It was almost as if Francis were deliberately giving her no cause to fall out with him, no fault to find. Safe with Jerry's presence warm in the back of her mind, Laura knew her behaviour appeared increasingly difficult and arbitrary, but Francis refused to be provoked. She asked him impossible questions, showing up his ignorance. Sometimes she left the washing-up, or was deliberately clumsy, crashing the plates, or gave him food he didn't like, ashamed of herself – and yet still found herself doing it. Sometimes she sat alone in the kitchen with tears trickling slowly down her cheeks. She cleaned the silver at the most inconvenient times, or just sat with her own supper in front of her not touching it, watching him eat, drawing attention to herself. Francis was so loving she could have killed him. He was worried about her losing weight. She lost more weight. She criticized his drinking. She lay in bed dying for his company, and when the door quietly opened on a dim glow of light and his shadow came to lie beside her she petulantly complained that he had woken her up. And when he considerately left her alone she hated him more, jeering at him to herself for respecting her feelings, for not being more of a man.

As winter passed the war was winding down, casualties falling away, at least among the Allied troops. She followed the news eagerly – the Battle of the Bulge was a nasty surprise, then the German towns were falling one by one, razed to the ground by bombers, thank God, and rendered relatively harmless to the invading troops.

The sight of men fresh out of uniform walking awkwardly in ghastly demob suits and cheap shoes, knocking on doors for work, became a common sight in Lynmouth as the hotels geared up for Easter and the start of the holiday season. News censorship eased, the papers were full of smiling faces. Still she had not heard from Jerry. Vast numbers of American and commonwealth troops were being shipped home on the great ocean liners to be demobilized and returned to civilian life in their own countries. The chilling thought occurred to her that he had been lumped in with them; it was all too likely. He had no money, he might be trapped in Maine just as she was trapped in Watersmeet, half a world away. Perhaps he could arrange to have himself discharged in Europe. But then how would he get home?

Nothing escaped Francis' spying eyes. She looked off colour and she ought to see the doctor. A few weeks later he even suggested she come up on a business trip he was taking to London, they'd make a holiday of it, a change of scene would do her good – and she refused, panicking in case Jerry arrived while she was away. There would be only one conclusion Jerry could draw from her absence.

At the last minute Francis said he didn't like to leave Laura alone in the house. He would ask Mrs Pawkins to stay with her.

Laura laughed and reassured him that there was nothing in Watersmeet that could possibly cause her concern.

Francis kissed her goodbye. He was wearing a Prussian-blue pinstripe suit with a Watersmeet blood-rose neatly folded in his buttonhole, black tooled leather brogues, a black mohair overcoat despite the warmth of the day, and the bowler hat which she handed him. She watched his tall, slim figure, more elegant than ever carrying a silver-topped cane, walk out across the gravel to the waiting car. He turned and waved. She waved back cheerfully, and she didn't sleep that night, unsatisfied and yearning. Next morning she gave up breakfast, waiting for the postman's van to come, running up to the postbox as soon as she heard its drone pull away up the county road, flicking impatiently through the letters. Nothing in his handwriting.

All day she roamed the house, waiting for Jerry, but he did not appear.

Tomorrow Francis was due back and Silas was picking him up on the afternoon 2.50 from Barum's Junction station. Francis had told her to expect him for tea.

Laura fell asleep on the sofa.

When she woke, with a crick in her neck, it was morning of the last day, and the postman's funny little van was just a fading murmur.

Today. It had to be today. Rubbing her neck, she rifled the envelopes hungrily, then pressed her lips together. Nothing.

She had to get out of this house. She couldn't face saddling up Blackbird so she walked alone through the dense, shimmering green glare of the woodlands. She was wearing her yellow cotton summer dress with the low-cut neck, the shoulder straps no thicker than her little finger, the dark blue hemline brushing gracefully against the tops of her calves as she walked. This, the dark blue jacket she carried over her shoulder, her handbag, her flat-soled shoes, all matched: she could run away today. The drumbledranes that had supplied them with honey through the war buzzed drowsily around their hives, then the Manor was behind her and she found herself following the track that led to Paradise House.

She found her mother pruning in the rose garden, crouched on a green rubber kneeling mat, her hands

protected from the thorns by thick green gloves. She
was wearing a gardening smock and a wide-brimmed
straw hat. She glanced at Laura then carried on.
Laura watched silently, unacknowledged.

'You've been crying,' Sybil said, closing the
secateurs and clicking the safety latch.

Laura stirred. 'No, I haven't.'

Sybil braced her palms on her knees and grunted,
then held out one imperious hand instead, and
Laura helped her up.

'Don't say you've not been crying when you have
been crying.'

'Don't keep trying to bully me.'

Sybil raised her eyebrows and her eyes gleamed
for a moment beneath the shadowing brim. Then
she asked: 'This mood is because Francis is away,
I suppose?'

Laura swallowed.

'You're too old for me to hug,' Sybil said, turning
away.

Laura followed her to the house. It seemed very
cool and dark in the hall. Sybil was tugging off her
gloves, then she carefully removed her hat and
placed it by the silver post-tray on the armoire,
started checking her swept-back white hair in the
mirror for wayward strands. Her immobile,
sunbrowned face looked as wooden as a Red
Indian's. Then she smiled, and actually touched
Laura's neck with her warm hand, her thumb
resting against the lobe of Laura's ear. 'He's resting,'
she whispered, with a roll of her eyes at Ernest's
study. She was shorter than Laura usually thought
of her, as if, unnoticed by Laura, she had suddenly
grown older.

'Resting in the morning?'

'He's not so strong as he thinks.'

'Will you really go to France?'

'He thinks so. He's in touch with a valuer about selling this house.' Sybil twisted Laura's wrist and looked at her watch. 'Time for elevenses. I baked some biscuits yesterday.'

'I won't stay.'

'Go on, a cup of tea won't hurt you.'

'I've got to get back to the Manor.'

'I've just remembered, this came for you.' Sybil lifted a white envelope off the tray and held it out, looking at Laura steadily. Jerry's handwriting. Laura snatched it, examined the envelope feverishly. Laura Pervane, c/o Paradise House; she had pointed the place out to him. Jerry, bless him, missed nothing.

Then she cried: 'But it's *ancient* – the postmark is dated last week!'

'It arrived a few days ago. I didn't realize it was so important.' Sybil's gaze was measuring.

'Oh, it isn't important,' Laura said lightly. The envelope was burning her hands. She knew why it was not sent to Watersmeet Manor: so that Francis would not open it – Jerry was not to know that Francis would be away.

'Laura,' Sybil said very gently, 'please come and have a cup of tea and a biscuit with me. Please . . . I'd really like you to. Sometimes one gets a little lonely and . . . feels how good it would be to talk sometimes.' She lifted her shoulders tentatively. Laura was free to reject her as usual.

Laura hovered. Then she nodded and forced the envelope into her handbag.

'You see,' said Sybil, pouring boiling goyle-water into the teapot, 'I saw the look in your eyes when I handed you that envelope. It is about Francis, isn't it? I know how selfish you can be.'

'Only by your incomparable standards of selflessness, Mother.'

Sybil closed the door. 'Everyone says you're like you father, but that's not true. We're just the same, you and I. I can read your eyes, I know your heart. Because I've been in that place, Laura. I loved a man.' She swilled the pot, poured out the tea into two elegant white teacups with gold rims.

Laura remembered what Clara used to claim: mother really loved Alex, *her* father, Sybil's first husband. 'Alex Summers. Mother, I know,' she said quietly. 'And you were driving when he was killed.' She almost reached out to her mother. 'I'm so sorry.'

'Driving?' Sybil laughed, 'wherever did you get that from? A woman, driving, before the First World War? Even if it were socially acceptable, which it was not, I doubt I could have found the strength to turn the steering wheel. Besides, driving was all oil and dust and horrid stink in those days. No, Alex died of septicaemia, three days after a visit to his Harley Street dentist to have a bad tooth removed. It's true I loved him enough to marry him and of course I thought I would die when he died. He was terribly strict, he gave pattern to my life, it was he who brought me to God's love. It seemed that I would never recover from my grief, or ever want to look at another man. Then I met Ernest, who loved me, and still does, and needed me, and still does. And I do hold him in the most enormous affection.' She turned a biscuit between her fingers.

'It was I who advised you to marry Francis. Not because, or just because, he would be Master of Watersmeet. But because you told me you loved him. Do you remember?'

'I remember.'

'You couldn't lie to me. But . . . you did it, by thinking of someone else, didn't you?'

Laura shrugged.

'Is that man the author of the letter?'

Laura shook her head.

'Someone else? And you love him.'

Laura didn't reply.

'And he loves you, I suppose.'

'Yes, it seems he does, Mother.'

'I see.'

'I know you must be horrified at me but I can't help it.'

'I believe in love,' said Sybil sadly, looking down at her teacup, the same words she had used years ago when they were sitting here, when Laura was thinking of Bart. 'I just wanted you to be happy. Though I thought Francis was no good for you, I thought you loved him. And that is what matters. Because love conquers all, darling.'

Laura lowered her eyes. 'I'm afraid I can't believe in your religion, Mother.'

Sybil said: 'I don't mean God's love. No, I was thinking very much of this world. I meant Ranulf Barronet.'

Bart's father: the hereditary Master of the North Devon Staghounds until his death, falling from his horse, and Sir George Pervane's usurpation of that position. Laura had never seen Ranulf but she had a flashing half-awareness of a scarlet riding jacket, a tall whip of a man with a wolfish face and eyes with pale lights in them; she must have been very young when she saw him, perhaps held in her mother's arms at a Hunt Meet.

'It wasn't Alex I loved, Laura, and still love,' Sybil confessed, 'it was Ranulf. You'd been born but when I should have been happiest, with you, I found myself saddest. You were not an easy birth, my darling, I was torn, and I could not seem to recover. Ranulf was the most handsome man I'd ever met. I know this must sound silly to you, and I was wholly to blame. I simply fell in love with him. How Ernest didn't find out I shall never know. Perhaps I should have told him, though it would have broken his heart.

'There is a house in the Hellebore Woods, little more than a ruin now, but once it was a great house. Ranulf lived there alone, except for his servants and his young son, Bart. The boy was never allowed to meet me, or to know of my existence. It was not, you see . . . not a social contact. He was never to know what his father— ' her face creased with shame – 'his father and I were doing upstairs.'

Laura stared at her tea. It was not how she liked it, her mother always added too much milk for Laura's taste, she never learned. Feeling resentful, Laura flushed it down the sink, without even being noticed she then refilled her cup with a stronger brew from the pot. She was shaken.

Sybil calmly sipped her disgusting tea. 'I wish I could say that I had fallen in love with a man who was a saint. But Ranulf was a cruel man. He treated me cruelly, and not just me. His son, apparently, was defiant and self-willed, and Ranulf couldn't do

306

anything with him. He employed tutors to break the boy: Latin and Greek, mathematics and logic, ostensibly to educate him, but really to crush his spirit. That's the way to do it.' Just for a moment she sounded oddly, curiously, like the Punch and Judy professor on Lynmouth beach. 'Oh, Laura, I can hear the beatings, the boy's screams, still. But when Ranulf touched me, I was powerless. I loved Ranulf; *but he did not love me*. I would have died for him, but he would not have lifted a finger to save me.'

'Did you stop seeing him?'

'He stopped seeing me. Once he even passed me in the road by the inn at Rockford without a sideways glance. Men are swine.'

They sat in silence.

'I trust this man,' Laura said.

'Then you'd better read his letter. So that you can be a swine to Francis.'

Laura reached forward with her hand to touch her mother's across the table, but Sybil pulled back, folding her arms across her breasts. 'Don't you *dare* feel sorry for me,' she said.

Laura couldn't bring herself to open the letter in her mother's domineering presence. She pulled on her blue jacket walking down the hall, then her fingers started struggling with the stuck-down flap of the envelope even as her feet tapped down the steps. She almost tripped, forced herself to stop, reading the letter in the merciless glare of the sunlight across the lawns. She winced, moving under the swaying shadows of the trees. His slanting blue handwriting.

The date was six days ago.

Oh God, she'd missed him. Jerry would be waiting for her at the church on top of Countisbury Hill – St John the Evangelist, where Laura was married – at midday, *today*. It was nearly that now. Panic filled her. She must wash her hair. But there wasn't a moment to spare – she must hurry to catch him at all.

She ran, but she couldn't keep up that pace for long: it was a climb of almost a thousand feet through the trees. She took off her jacket and concentrated on climbing. Her swinging handbag annoyed her. Shafts of vivid light swirling with motes and spores stood around her, streaming between the gnarled trunks that supported the dappled canopy of leaves. Stones slithered from beneath her shoes and bounded downhill, then span out into space over the great Chiselcombe cliffs above the river now far below, and she saw she was coming on to the open, windy hilltop, following the ridge up to Trilly Fields, running again on the footpath through the grass as the slope levelled. She arrived at the main road breathless and flushed.

Jerry was waiting under a yew hedge on the dusty path to the church. For a moment she wondered if it was really him because he was wearing civvies, a cheap too-tight grey suit, she could see he'd been travelling in it all morning because it was so creased. But his shoes were shiny, his sandy hair well trimmed. She stopped, uncertainly, half a dozen paces from him.

'You look totally beautiful,' he said, sliding his arms around her, but she saw the flash of guilt in his eyes. Her sides panted as he kissed her, then held her tight against him.

'Why didn't you write before?' she whispered angrily to his chest. 'I waited for you and waited . . .'

He didn't answer, just buried his hands in her hair. She had not even realized it had come unbound, curling like a warm wave down her back.

'I was trying to persuade myself that I didn't love you,' he said. Her breathing stopped. 'But I do,' he said.

They stood like this in the shadow of the hedge.

She put her hair up, the familiarity of the gesture giving her time to think. She was showing the damp patches under her arms, but he kissed her upraised elbows, watching her with admiration.

'Shall we walk around the churchyard?' he suggested. 'It's very peaceful.'

'I'd rather not,' she said.

'Let's have a drink.' She swung her jacket over her shoulder and they walked down towards the Blue Ball. 'I'm still technically in the Army, but it's all over bar the shouting,' he said, holding the oak door open for her.

'Then you're a free man,' Laura said.

Jerry's smile became a little strained. He ordered a glass of lemonade for her and a pint of beer for him. They sat at a dark little table in the corner, a dull arrangement of dried flowers in the grate where the fire had been, the little windows seeming very bright.

'Well, this is it. I have to make a confession,' Jerry said. He hadn't touched his beer.

'You can't back out now,' she said.

'I love you,' was all he said. 'God help me, I do. There's something I have to tell you. It's because I love you – for our sake – I'm determined not to take advantage of you.'

'You sound awfully serious.'

'About you.'

'Oh, Jerry.'

'But there was another woman in my life once.'

Laura understood completely. There had been another man in her life once. She dropped her hand casually on to the bench between them and Jerry grabbed it, pressing and squeezing her fingers, close contact, and she knew Jerry's feelings for her hadn't changed one whit, though their upper bodies had to sit the social six inches apart above the tablecloth. Beneath it his leg lay warm alongside her thigh, cheap grey twill against sheer silk stocking.

'You don't have to tell me,' she said very quietly. 'I was in love with a man a long time ago, really in love.' She closed her eyes.

'And that's how it ended?'

'It ended.'

'He's gone?'

'Yes, Jerry, he's gone.' She opened her eyes and smiled. 'It's all in the past.'

He said: 'I told you about my life before the war. When I was working at Chet's snack bar. But I couldn't tell everything. Chet's was on the boardwalk by the public beach, quite a trip from Mom's, white sand, blue ocean. Just a boy, seventeen, eighteen. The place had a big concrete park out back for truckers to pull off the Interstate, and that kept the place on the go out of season. But

310

summer was the real time. You'd think you were young for ever, the way the sun came off that sand, and the smell of Coppertone oil through the open windows, and girls in one-pieces with their legs all oiled brown, speckled with white sand to the knees, and their noses red, hanging their hands off the shoulders of their guys and giggling at everything they said, and the guys knocking each other about. But good-natured. And they'd come in for clam cake or go running up into the dunes. They were good buddies. Ended up in Europe, mostly, and too many won't come home.'

So far Laura had listened patiently. 'What are you trying to tell me?'

'Beverly— '

'She was your girl?'

'Bev was the short-order cook. She had a mouth full of more white teeth than you ever saw in your life, freckles, red hair, big sleepy eyes with long lashes. In summer she wore her shirt knotted under her breasts, legs that went up to her chin, and she wore slacks that were tight as skin. You know what happened.'

'You fell in love with her.'

'No. I thought I did.'

'Did you tell her you loved her?'

'When she got pregnant she was going to get rid of the kid – just like that. And maybe it had happened before, too. I knew what she was, I was working for Al Mayo in the surgery by then, making my way. But I went back to Beverly.' He touched the flash of gold at his neck. 'I believe in sin. I couldn't face what she was going to do. If you marry me, I said, we can keep the kid.'

'So that's why you married her? And you really went ahead with it?'

'It was the right thing to do.'

Laura couldn't help her bitterness. 'Jerry, you are a fool.'

He glanced at her with that complex look in his eyes and again she reminded herself that he wasn't naïve. He was honest.

She twined her fingers through his, trusting him.

'We got married in the big Roman Catholic church. Mom was there, Ed and the twins, Sam, and Rick who got killed by the drunk driver. Bev wore white, she'd always wanted to get married in church, she was bowled over. Nothing showed, you see. And then we moved into a trailer of our own, a lot nearer to Al Mayo's, away from Mom. I still worked the gas station nights to make the pay up to feed three; after ten no one came in for hours at a time, I could sleep. I had to leave Bev alone in the trailer.

'Bev lost our baby. She *said* she lost the baby. I know what she really did but I couldn't face it. I said that we'd be happy when we had a house.

'Bev was full of life, she always wanted a good time, but I always wanted to get on in the world. In the end there was no point where we touched, and all we saw of each other was rumpled bedclothes and ashtrays under cigarette butts. It wasn't fun. But she was having fun. I was too blind, or too tired, to see it.'

'She must have been a complete monster!' Laura hated her.

'Now, I don't know,' Jerry said firmly. 'It was my fault as much as Bev's. Anyway, she found another man and moved out. He was an auto mechanic with

312

a couple of rooms over the workshop. Proper rooms, not tin walls and a tin roof. That was then. I don't know where the hell she is now. Anywhere.' He took out a packet of Camel cigarettes, offered her one, then helped himself and lit it one-handed with casual authority.

Laura said: 'Why do you want to know where she is?' A cold hand closed slowly over her heart. 'You aren't saying it isn't over between you, are you?'

'I don't feel a damn thing for her. Only you.' He looked at her steadily, then nodded in affirmation, and she couldn't doubt him.

'You haven't drunk any of your beer,' she said. He looked at his glass as if he'd forgotten it, then drank half the watery brew down without pleasure or distaste.

'You're worrying me,' Laura said. 'If you don't know where she is . . . surely you send her alimony?'

'The Army sends her part of my pay, that's the standard deal. I could find out where, I suppose. But it isn't alimony. We— '

Laura closed her eyes.

'You see, Laura,' he said, 'Bev and I are still married.'

Laura buried her hands in her lap. She said something about the flower arrangement, how pretty it was, she couldn't bring herself to look at him.

He, looking down, said how sorry he was. ' . . . knew you'd be upset.'

'Divorce her. I'll divorce Francis.'

'I *can't* – for the same reason I married her.' Again he touched that flash of gold. 'Laura, I am as upset as you are.'

313

She stood up, catching her hip on the table's corner. For a moment the pain was excruciating and she felt her eyes prickle with tears. 'Upset? What makes you think so?' She wouldn't let him touch her, not pull back her chair, hold her elbow, anything. She found the ladies' lavatory and closed the door behind her, then freshened up alone, staring at herself in the yellowing, flyspecked mirror. She could not imagine how she would begin to cope. Francis would be back in an hour.

When she came out Jerry was still standing there looking tragic. He followed her outside.

'I suppose you have to catch your bus,' she said.

'I don't care about the bus,' he said.

She turned. 'I trusted you!' she shouted. She crossed the road, a horn blared.

He had to wait then ran after her through the churchyard, the backdrop of Watersmeet spread out behind and below them like a map, his jacket flapping in the cold wind from the sea. Laura was shivering as she walked across the open grassland of the cliff-top; she couldn't yet see the sea, only feel the wind. It seemed to blow right through her. A fulmar soared. Jerry followed her doggedly, then as Laura's pace eased he came up and walked silently beside her. She was crying, almost exhausted. He took her jacket and draped it over her shoulders to keep her warm.

Laura stopped. The lighthouse was far below them, Lynmouth Bay as dark blue as her jacket and the hem of her dress, the river winding through the tiny village below seeming no wider than a blue thread. Over the Severn Sea rose the thin line of the faraway cliffs of Wales, pale buff in the sunlight and mist.

'Change it!' she demanded. 'Give up your faith. Divorce her.'

'Laura, I can't do that.'

'You and your bloody principles. Give them up, can't you?'

'I never thought you were this hard.'

She flicked her seaward gaze at him. 'That's what you like. You need, Jerry.'

'The truth is I love you. My life doesn't mean a single thing to me, without you.'

'Then force it to mean something. Or are you going to be Mommy's boy for ever?'

He stared at her, then shook his head. 'I *can't*. I never meant to lie to you. I just never guessed I could feel this way about a real woman. A woman I can never have.'

They stood on the plunging hogsback curve, seagulls drifting tiny and white on outstretched wings over the wrinkled expanse of the abyss. Jerry gazed into Laura's pale, rigid face.

'Laura, we'll get better, won't we? We'll forget all this and it won't be so bad . . . Watersmeet . . . And one day we won't feel a thing . . . won't we?'

He kissed her but she did not respond. She had to go back.

'I love you . . .' he called after her.

She looked over her shoulder with a mocking flash of her dark blue eyes.

Then as she walked away she heard him calling after her in a voice she had never heard from him before, normally so reasonable and soft-spoken, a shouted oath hoarse with passion.

'I'll come back for you, Laura!'

She kept on walking.

His voice from the cliff-top followed her. 'One day I'll be rich as hell, rich as sin, and then I'll give it all up for you and come back for you.' He shouted her name again and again, until she could no longer hear him.

PART FIVE
Hellebore

The last year had probably been the happiest of her father's chairbound life. Limited to fifty pounds' currency allowance between them, Ernest and Sybil took a room for a fortnight at the Hôtel les Ambassadeurs, still with German bullet-holes in the walls, in the tiny and unfashionable – and cheap – seaside village of Juan-les-Pins. Ernest passed the warm Riviera evenings inside the little casino overlooking the dusty square, betting on the two-franc tables. The gamblers were professional, mostly older ladies of somewhat faded elegance, both hands crimped across the tops of their handbags, eyes watchful: when they won, they left, and when they lost, they left. Just when Sybil thought Ernest had got the bee out of his bonnet, that they had run out of money and were coming home, he informed her that he had won enough to keep them for another week. He employed a man to push him up the hill, while Sybil stayed reading in the hotel room. That week became a month, and he began to call his winnings *earnings* again, sometimes hiring a taxi to take him to the big casino at Nice, or the one by the harbour at Cannes, promising Sybil that they could afford a suite at the Hôtel Carlton if they wished. Then he switched from the two-franc tables to the five-franc tables and lost all he had won. That was the luck of the game. He was still exultant. He would sell up their house and return permanently next year. 'Steady' seemed to have recovered all his youthful energy. What a magnificent time they would have!

A Midlands family made an offer for Paradise House, and Sybil warned Ernest that if he bought that villa he dreamed of overlooking the sparkling Mediterranean, he would live there without her. She would not leave Watersmeet.

Laura was sure her mother would win this battle of wills and pull Ernest back into line. Francis, coming and sitting on the edge of Laura's bed, urged her to intercede with her father and insist he stop the sale. Francis hated the idea of a new family moving into Watersmeet; Paradise House must belong to the Pervanes. He couldn't understand Laura's indifference.

As Laura had predicted, Ernest took Paradise House off the market for Sybil's sake and cancelled the sale. They would not move to France.

Laura had occupied her time learning the piano, and as always when she really determined her mind to do something, she made fast progress. But already this winter of 1947 was on record as being the worst of the century, and although the Manor's central heating – converted to run on wood because of the acute shortage of coal – had been turned full on, so that several of the priceless curved Adam doors had dried out and cracked, this old part of the house with its high ceilings never seemed to get really warm. She gave up practising in the study, where the cold made her fingers clumsy and intractable, and the painting of Phineas Pervane loomed above her.

If only you were free of Francis.

And she replied: *I am free of him.*

But Jerry would not free himself from Beverly. He could not divorce her. He could not pay that high a price for Laura.

Poor Francis. Laura had tried so hard to come to love him. Yet he still obstinately refused to become a part of her life.

Blizzard followed blizzard. Snow covered the windows; it seemed that the valley might gently fill up to the brim with snow and that Watersmeet would simply disappear, frozen in time, below a featureless white continuation of the rolling moorland. No one would ever know of them: their lives, their loves, even their names would be lost.

Motorists were already rationed to ninety miles' worth of petrol a month, but now almost no tankers were getting through to Devon because of the weather, and food rationing, already tougher in peacetime than it had ever been during the war, meant people had no stocks to make do with as supplies were cut off entirely. Some villages were almost starving. It was as though the war had never ended. Francis knew that hundreds of his sheep were dying in their stells up on the moor, but there was nothing he could do for them.

In the Manor, the lights went out early in the evening as the power lines came down at last. While Francis donned winter clothing and went out to investigate, Laura practised 'Für Elise' on the Bechstein by firelight, and she always remembered the glowing pattern of the flames across the polished rosewood at that moment when the door opened on a flurry of snow.

Francis stood there, looking for an instant

ridiculously like Old Father Time, all in white, holding his shepherd's crook in snow-muffled mittens, snow bristling over his deerstalker and the shoulders of his cape, ice caked thick on his boots. He stared at her then put out his arms and tracked ice and slush across the carpet in soundless grief.

'Laura, your father is dead.'

The firelight, 'Für Elise', and the ice-cold touch of Francis' embrace.

'Don't touch me!' she said. 'You'll mark my dress.' She didn't want to show her feelings in front of Francis. 'No,' she said.

He dropped his hat and cape by the fireplace, grabbed her hands. 'It was very sudden – it was an accident.' His tone was hectic; he really looked as though he might cry himself, if she did not.

'An accident?' she said numbly. 'What sort of accident?'

'Let yourself go, my darling. I'm here.' Francis knew his opportunity had come and he held her tight, making her remember this moment with her head against his chest. 'I'm here,' he repeated. Only Francis; only him.

'How – how is my mother?'

'She's coping marvellously. You'll want to go, of course. I'll walk with you. Laura, I am so terribly sorry.' There was no doubting his genuineness, although as always it was self-serving.

The tears in her eyes treacherously threatened to fall: she had loved her father more than she knew. She needed him, and he was gone. Francis followed her upstairs to her room, watching while she pulled on warm woollen leggings, then baggy black trousers which she tucked into her boots, and the black pure

wool cape. If only he had left her alone, she would
have cried. She'd lost the gloves which went with
the cape; but Francis found them in a drawer. He
threw her anxious glances, as if afraid she wouldn't
bear up emotionally, still playing the part of her
feelings, bending her to his will. She didn't want
him to come, but he was determined to stand by her.

Outside, his torch-beam rippled over the white
trees standing in the darkness around them: the
motionless intensity of silence, night, then the sound
of their footsteps ploughing through the snow.

'Now I am all you have,' murmured Francis. 'I
won't let you down, Laura.'

He insisted on supporting her elbow – and once
he did save her from a nasty skid. Their torch-beams
jumped cones and circles of light across the
snowdrifts like standing waves all around them,
sculpted and deserted by the wind that had
disappeared, now with only their voices to dislodge
fresh falls from the tree-filled darkness above.
Twenty minutes' fast walk became a long, slow
trudge for over an hour before they saw the orange
glow of a candle in the window of Paradise House
ahead of them, and they paused to catch their
breath.

'There's no hope of getting the doctor up to
certify . . .' Francis said.

'We'll have to have telephones put in,' Laura told
him. 'We can't go on like this.'

Francis leaned across on his stick as if for a private
word with her, but Laura walked on. 'I had to lay
him in the outhouse – it's good and cold in there,'
he called, then ran clumsily after her. 'Strange –
how little he weighed,' he said. 'One always expects

them to be so heavy, don't you think?' He tried so hard to communicate, to get in touch with her: to make her be what he thought she ought to be.

Laura remembered her father's weight so clearly: his left arm locked around her neck, the straightforward unscented smell of him, tweed and pipe-tobacco, and both the hardness of his muscles and yet the way his left thigh flopped dependently against her as she lifted; she was part of his body.

Francis hugged her.

'It's too cold!' she said, pushing him away.

She made him stamp the snow off his boots together with her on the porch, then Laura opened the front door. The coolness of the hallway struck her immediately: Sybil had already turned down the heating. Laura put her boots tidily on the mat but kept her outdoor clothing on. Sybil was sitting in the solarium, a single candle burning in front of her, the black glass repeating its glowing image a thousand times around them.

Laura sat on the wrought-iron bench beside her mother.

'The house will be yours when I die,' Sybil said. 'Yours and Clara's.'

'I'm sure it's much too early to think of that,' Francis said.

Sybil ignored him, as if Francis was so without weight, without force, that he was not the one worth talking to. It was Laura she addressed. 'You see, your father was so very happy. Although we had decided not to sell the house, we had agreed to go to France for the first two weeks of July, and he was looking forward to it very much. He was making plans, working it all out in his head.' She smiled faintly. 'He was having a much better time than if he'd really gone.'

Laura asked quietly: 'How did it happen?'

'We took our afternoon nap together upstairs, as usual. I was still in bed when I heard a clattering, banging, going away from me, then the crash of his upstairs wheelchair across the wooden floor of the hallway down below. I found the door of Clara's old bedroom open, and so was yours, darling. I could almost still feel the heat of his hand on the handle where he sat looking in. Then he must have returned to the top of the stairs and – lost control for a moment – perhaps the wheel slipped over the edge. As soon as the sound ceased down below there was no other sound at all and I knew, I knew he was dead.'

'We all loved him,' Francis said.

'He wasn't a very lovable man.' Sybil studied her hands in her lap. She drew a breath, then sighed. 'There was never a day that he was not in the most hideous agony. Surely you knew! Death was a mercy for him, and it claimed him when he was happiest, full of dreams and expectations.' She looked at Laura. 'I stood by him to the end.'

'Of course,' Francis said, glancing between the two of them.

And with a frisson Laura wondered if he had known about her and Jerry.

Francis dealt with every little detail, and Ernest was laid to rest not in the churchyard of St John's on Countisbury, where Laura had been married and lost her lover, but instead at Francis' suggestion in the windy cemetery at St Brendan's, next to the bones of the Pervane family whose name Ernest had been so eager, and later proud, for his daughter to bear. The thaw had set in and everything was dripping, the grey snow sliding, but on Cheriton Ridge the ground was still frozen hard, the gravediggers must have had a terrible time, and Francis tipped them with a bottle of port. Laura dressed all in black, which suited her, with diamond earrings. The graveside ceremony seemed to go on and on for ever, the wind as cold as mortality, shivering the women's veils, Francis holding Laura's hand firmly inside his own, his head bent devoutly.

'Ashes to ashes, dust to dust,' intoned the minister, the same man who had married Clara. Laura glanced at Francis, startled to meet his eyes. He looked so staid, concerned and responsible compared to the man she had married, but he was still attractive, his eyes clearer now he was drinking less. He patted Laura's hand comfortingly, taking over the older man's rôle in her life. There was a problem with this: a father and a husband were two different things. But she had driven Francis to it. Still they had no children. Clara's elder children played around the graveside, and the lucky woman stood there as mothers do, with her mind turned half off as they ran up and tugged her hands or bobbed behind the headstones in an ecstatic game of hide and seek. Clara, holding the baby, looked staid and responsible, and her clothes were boring.

Francis should have married Clara, Laura decided, and got the woman he deserved, one whose faults matched his own nature. *She* would have given him children by now. Clara was content to find happiness and love in her children.

Laura found her mother's hand and squeezed it,

but Sybil did not respond. She insisted on returning to her own home tonight, even though she would be alone. Her determination not to show her grief was a matter of pride to the old woman: she dammed it back inside her, showing no sign of what she felt, and Laura was afraid to make the breach.

When mother dies, Laura thought, as earth thudded down on the coffin – a full-length coffin, though the man inside took up less than half of it – *there is nothing to keep me in the valley*. Was that really true?

Francis held her arm.

'You're more beautiful than ever,' he whispered.

She still felt like a young girl, the same Laura she had always been. But people were deferential to Lady Pervane, and when Laura had casually told Clara she must come down to the Manor for drinks after the service Clara's gratitude had been unmistakable, her acceptance almost shy – the kids would make a frightful mess . . . as though she thought Lady Pervane must be horrorstruck if a child's dirty shoe came anywhere near her smooth grey Wilton, her smooth grey life. Laura might feel herself childlike still, and vulnerable, but that was not how others saw her. They saw the Mistress of Watersmeet, and now no one seemed able to break through this claustrophobic shell to the real Laura beneath, not even Laura herself.

Sybil stared calmly down into the grave.

' . . . the sure and certain hope of the resurrection.'

Jerry . . . Laura remembered Jerry. More than a year had passed since she had received a letter from him, nothing since. More than a letter, it had really been a love letter, sent to Paradise House. Sybil, who thought Laura had given Jerry the push, had handed this unwelcome reminder to her without comment, not wishing to be involved.

Laura kept the letter in the secret compartment underneath the bottom tray of her locked jewellery casket. She could recall every word of his slanted blue handwriting as though she held it now.

Jerry had once said – she remembered his voice above the calling gulls – *We'll get better, won't we? We'll forget all this and it won't be so bad . . . And one day we won't feel a thing . . . won't we?*

She hadn't forgotten. She still felt a lot. She still remembered him backing down.

Yet he wrote that he *couldn't* forget her. Although now, *especially* now, he had set up his own dental supplies corporation, he was still in love with Laura. More so. Laura was delighted, it sounded as though Jerry were quite obsessed. Slanted blue words: his dreams of her, what she was doing, what she looked like, sometimes he thinks he sees her, a slim woman on the sidewalk, but then she turns and it isn't Laura – a voice laughing in a restaurant, but when he goes up to her it isn't Laura. *You are the one, only you. You are the centre of my universe.*

Laura had sat staring at the single, simple page of handwriting for hours. The letter ended with strange words. *Write me.*

Of course she never did. She had nothing she could say. But she hugged the Americanism to her, like warmth in times of trouble. He had said nothing about divorcing Beverly, he could not love Laura enough to pay that price. She knew he would not write again. But there, standing at the chilly graveside, the handfuls of earth dribbling six feet down on to the shining brass and mahogany, she remembered Jerry's voice when he knew he had lost her: *One day I'll be rich as hell, rich as sin, and then I'll give it all up for you and come back for you* . . .

She stood with Francis' arm around her, watching shovelfuls of earth thud down on her father's coffin until it was gone.

'It's all right, darling,' Francis whispered. 'Let's go home.'

Clara sat in the Manor's immaculate lounge sipping sherry. She was terrified of what the children would get up to and kept jumping up to avert some real or imagined crisis. The room was not designed for children: there were far too many valuables low down, glass and porcelain figurines on open shelves, a tempting bookcase, and Laura's reactions were all wrong – she put her glass down on a low drinks table where little hands could reach it, and of course Johnny got hold of it and sprayed medium-sweet oloroso across the carpet, but Laura just laughed. She crawled around with the youngsters on her hands and knees, chasing Perdie, who screamed with joy, and even little Andrew gurgled, kicking his legs, and followed their progress with his eyes, Johnny jumping on Laura's back like a mahout. A whole row of books went over and the chairs got knocked out of their places but Laura didn't seem to mind. Finally Clara leaned back tolerantly and watched Laura and the kids enjoying themselves wrecking the place.

Laura sat up, her legs to one side, her face flushed, panting, happy. Her hair had come undone and she swung it back out of her eyes.

'I'm only twenty-four!' she laughed. 'I'm still only twenty-four!' She begged Clara: 'Can't you stay for supper?'

'It's the bus,' Clara said.

'I wish you'd come again.'

'It's the schools,' Clara said. 'I wish we could.' She lined up the children to be kissed goodbye by Auntie Laura.

Laura fetched the torch and waved them off in the bus, holding a waterproof over her head against the drizzle drifting down, then walked back across the clapper bridge towards the Manor. The river was running high with meltwater, she could see the streaks of foam standing out of the dark, and the lights of her house with Francis' shape moving in the windows, clearing up, then his shadow came to the window and looked out for her. She flashed the torch so that he could see her. He was always spying on her, not as he thought proving his love for her, but as it seemed to her rather the opposite – proving that as her husband he simply owned her life. It was his male arrogance – 'I *care* about you' – and yet it was comforting. As Laura reached out her hand to the door, Francis opened it. 'I've cleared up.' He had, too, and the books were in the right order. He offered her a sherry, then when she shook her head poured himself a whisky.

'Darling,' Laura said, 'can we talk about us?'

'About us! Why on earth should we?' he smiled, and put his arm around her shoulders, taking charge. 'Come on. We'll have the cold meat for a late supper. I've put it in the dining room.'

He sharpened the knife, stopping conversation, then carved the leg of mutton with smooth sweeps of the blade. The wall lights were on, casting a glow through their pink-tasselled fringes on to the dark panelling.

'It wasn't really funny, you know,' he said, glancing up, 'letting them make such a mess.' So they were going to talk about *us* after all.

'I could have cleared it up.'

'But you didn't. I did. I'm always clearing up after you, aren't I, Laura?'

Laura stared at the ovals of dark meat rimmed with white fat on her plate. She wasn't hungry at all; there was an inedible lump growing in her stomach. Francis helped himself to another glass of whisky. 'Where's the redcurrant jelly?'

She knew that tone of voice, the way things were going. She kept her voice level. 'I'm afraid it's all gone.'

'You couldn't even do that properly.'

'I'll fetch the rowan jelly. I made some.'

'Don't bother. I'll eat it without.' He cut a lump of meat and chewed it with distaste.

'Francis. Please. Not now.'

He chewed for a while, then sighed, regaining his temper. He smiled broadly and suddenly came round the table, sat on the other chair beside her, held her hands in his, then kissed her forehead. 'You know how much I love my little girl?'

She didn't reply.

'Laura,' he said, 'I knew about him.' He kept his eyes on hers, raising his eyebrows, nodding his head. 'Yes, I did, you know. Your interest in that boy Jerry.' He turned her chair towards him, his legs apart almost enclosing her, and she could feel his breath on her face. 'I simply waited for you to get

331

over him,' he explained condescendingly, 'and you did.' He winked and kissed her cheek.

'Jerry?'

'I *knew*.' Francis kissed her lips. 'You're such a little fool, it's what I love about you. To know your heart is mine.'

He kissed her mouth, but she turned her head away. He put his palm against her jaw, turning her gently back to face him.

'Laura, my Laura,' he said, 'You've always been my whole life, you've always been there.' He touched his chest where his heart was. That was true; but for her it wasn't enough.

'I don't want to talk to you any more,' she said, getting up.

And he let her. He laughed. 'I love it when you're angry,' he said. He did, she realized: he derived passion from her emotions just as he derived it from her clothes, or the seams in her stockings, or looking at her breasts, or thinking of Jerry wanting her and failing, so possessive was Francis. And yet so without consummation in the act of possession.

She couldn't explain to him what she felt, if he didn't know. What they had together felt puny compared to what love ought to be. It ought to be the sun and the stars, not this paltry waste, this slow death. Holding back the sob swelling in her throat, she ran for the stairs.

'Darling.' He caught hold of her wrist, gently, not hard. An appeal. The sob filled her throat like a big red apple. 'Darling,' he said lovingly, wrapping her softly in his arms, 'don't you think I have feelings? You kiss me goodnight at the top of the stairs and sweep off to your bedroom like a princess. Why do you want to make me crawl after you, and make me treat you as though you meant no more to me than a sexual object? We could have so much more. It is always what *I* must do. Why don't you come and love *me*, Laura?' he called after her as she ran upstairs.

She slammed her bedroom door and threw herself down on her bed.

He was right of course.

He stayed downstairs drinking, then she heard the bathroom door upstairs, and a little later the soft thump of his bedroom door closing.

She combed out her hair and made up her face, dabbed perfume on her throat, and chose a filmy rose-pink nightdress with the keyhole neckline slashed between her breasts almost to her navel. She wore it for him. She wore her satin dressing gown of a darker rose, she wore her matching slippers. She crossed the gallery and went, as he had asked her to, and as she should have done before if she loved him, into his bedroom.

He was asleep. She could hear him snoring softly.

She knelt by his bed. His breath smelt of mutton. She whispered his name, she touched his chest. She lay on the covers beside him for a moment, stroking his face. His bed was softer than hers, with a dip in the middle. The room was airless. She raised the covers to slip inside, then went instead to open the window. She had forgotten to take her gown off, and she put her fingers on the satin cord to undo it, then found herself just standing there, staring into the dark, the dim hump of his outline in the glass, listening to the sound of his snoring. She stood there for a very long time.

She returned to her own bedroom and clicked on the dressing-table lamp, then opened the drawer and took out a sheet of notepaper, an envelope and a fountain pen which she uncapped. She began a letter to Jerry.

I have decided to divorce Francis.

Then she stopped. There was nothing more to say.

She sealed the envelope and addressed it Private and Confidential to Ellis Medical Supplies of Portland, Maine. It could go with the postman tomorrow.

Probably nothing would happen, Jerry would never have the courage to respond – a thousand good reasons.

But Laura had decided. It was like a huge weight off her chest. She had launched her boat.

She didn't expect a reply; neither did she get one.

Francis slammed down his newspaper on the breakfast table. Here was socialist Britain for you: no motoring for pleasure, the meat ration cut to hardly a bob's worth of scrag end a week, and guests would have to present ration books for hotel stays over two nights. Foreign holidays banned entirely, which was a help, but even so this latest idiocy would kill the peak of the domestic tourist season stone dead. The Watersmeet Falls Hotel was half empty already. There were some things even Mr Sayle, the manager, could not save them from.

Laura came in and he stood up politely. Just seeing her was always a thrill. He wanted to hold her and give her a good-morning kiss but he knew she disdained such manners.

'You've let the coffee get cold!' she scolded him.

'We're lucky to have coffee at all, the way things are going,' he said, turning to the small pile of letters beside his newspaper. He glanced up, watching her make fresh coffee, more than she would actually drink. She was very far from being a perfect woman. He decided to say nothing so as not to give her an excuse to flare up. She snatched up the paper and read it peremptorily. He was amused to see her looking at the financial news, matters of which she knew absolutely nothing, and remembered her asking him about the hotel. She was ambitious as well as temperamental.

She was wearing a cotton dress in the new style, with soft rounded shoulders and a pulled-in waist that showed off how slim she was. Her lips curled into a smile of cynical resignation. Francis dropped his eyes, opening a private note from a farming neighbour, a friend who did his turn on the Bench as a Justice of the Peace. Bart Barronet—

Francis sat up, watching Laura. Her expression did not change. Did she know?

Laura wondered what had got into Francis. As usual he was paying no attention to her, then suddenly he sat bolt upright as though someone had stuck a hatpin in his bottom, and his expression was so funny that she almost laughed. She struggled to keep her face straight.

'What is it dear?' she asked.

He waved the letter. 'Bart Barronet is to be released from Dartmoor prison. He has won full good-conduct remission.'

'I'm so glad!' she said involuntarily, out of simple humanity.

Francis eyed her. He had waited for her to 'get

335

over' Jerry, but Bart's return was a different matter. Jerry was just an average doughboy on the make and it had only been a matter of time before Laura saw through him, and now she had, but Bart was a Barronet. That was different.

On her finger Laura wore the Pervane wedding ring. Around her wrist she wore his grandmother's gold bracelet inset with blood rubies – Francis hadn't had to give her that, he had given it to her because he loved her. He loved everything about her, the tiny smooth mole on the inside of her thigh, the way she held her head, her eyelashes, even that expression on her lips. His wife.

'I wish you would continue with your piano lessons. You are not to see him.'

She actually laughed. 'Oh, Francis, don't be so silly.'

He put down the letter. 'I'm not joking. I forbid it. He's a broken man.'

Her response was not what he expected: she looked at things from the feminine point of view, and it caught him out time after time.

'If he's a broken man,' she pointed out, 'then he needs help. It must be awful for him coming home to an empty house. End this stupid feud between you. Go there, help him. Reach out your hand, Francis. You have the strength.'

Francis knew he didn't have the strength.

'Yes,' he smiled, pecking her cheek, 'perhaps you are right. I must get to Lynmouth.' He stood up and folded the note, put it in his inside pocket. 'Promise me,' he said quietly.

'Francis?'

'Promise me you won't see him.'

'Francis, must I promise you everything?'

He waited, relishing his authority.

'I promise,' she whispered.

'I didn't quite catch that,' he insisted.

'I promise!' she shouted.

'Thank you, dear,' he said, and she knew he wanted to make love to her. He thought making love was love. He brushed his fingers over her shoulder and she shrugged him off, but of course, that was what he liked. It gave him something to conquer.

'Good!' he said. 'Now we can be happy.' He kissed the top of her head and left.

Laura was furious.

But she controlled herself. She made herself sip her coffee, sitting with her elbows on the kitchen table, staring into the black liquid. Of course she thought about Bart. Little things, his terrible old maroon jacket, his eyes, his hands pressing on the wire. She couldn't imagine what attracted him to her, what had made him insist she must be loyal to Francis, though as it turned out she had been. Bart had even promised that Laura would forget him, but she hadn't. Now he was coming back.

Bart would never leave the valley, and Laura *must* leave: she was stifling. Her life was draining away minute by minute, year by year, on an invisible river.

Her coffee was cold. She tossed it down the sink. She would ride up to Hellebore House, that was all, check that it was all right for Bart's return – maybe a woman's touch, some flowers. She went outside and picked some past-their-best zinnias, plonked them in a jam jar on the kitchen table, and stood looking at them with her hands on her hips.

Bart wouldn't be there.

Face it. She would be defying Francis. Who did he think he was, trying to run her life?

She changed into jodhpurs and a silk blouse, picked a bunch of flowers from the formal garden by the river, and rode up to Hellebore House carrying them.

She found the crumbling house much decayed. The boarded windows were green with moss and creepers infested the walls. Dismounting, she left Blackbird to graze and went round to the back. The door she had used before shuddered open on rusty hinges, forcing aside a drift of leaves as she pushed her way in and crept round the massive staircase. The silence of the musty interior was intense, brilliant lines and stars of sunlight from board-joins and knot-holes laying their extravagant designs across the dusty floors, latticing the walls with light.

'Bart?' she called. But he wasn't there.

Sunlight made the picture of Lucy seem blinding with life: shining chains of long-stemmed daisies, Irish spurge, spurge laurel, hellebore, blood-roses.

She opened the door to Bart's room of treasures and stepped inside.

Beneath the dustsheets and cobwebs, nothing had changed.

But now the huge Elizabethan windows, boarded on the outside, were dark, reflecting only her own image. She walked amongst the splayed fingers of sunlight pouring through, rippling over her as she trod between the covered heaps of portraits, all those hidden faces; rusty armour, and the age-darkened pine carving of the pointy-bearded Spanish grandee, Don Juan Delgadillo de Spes, father of the bastard line claimed in his impotence as his own by old Jack Barronet, the necromancer.

If there arise among you a prophet, or a dreamer of dreams, and giveth thee a sign or a wonder, that prophet shall be put to death. He that is wounded in the stones, or hath his privy member cut off, shall not enter into the congregation of the Lord. A bastard shall not enter into the congregation of the Lord; even unto his tenth generation shall he not enter into the congregation of the Lord.

She went to the glass, knelt on the seat, and peered through a glowing knot-hole at the world beyond the pane, the immense view of Watersmeet; as though he owned it all.

She saw part of Watersmeet Manor far below, the tiny white gates and miniature jagged rooflines, she could even pick out the French windows of her bedroom.

Yes, as if Bart Barronet owned it all – all that was in fact Francis Pervane's. This was what drove Francis wild with despair in his victory: this power and *simplicity* of the Barronets. They held the high ground. Despite his prison sentence, despite the impoverishment and humiliation of his proud name, Bart Barronet had won everything. Except Laura.

Did Bart love the valley more than he loved Laura because it secured his domination of the Pervanes?

Laura took her eye from the window. She shivered. Did he really never love her any more than Francis? Did Bart use Laura merely to manipulate Francis, and tease him? Was he that callous?

Laura didn't know what she thought. She just wanted to be free and far away. To be her own woman.

She left the roses strewn across the table and left. The house settled back into its silence.

. . . Francis had observed her. Blackbird's hoofbeats passed him and faded downhill. He came out of the bushes and stood in the middle of the drive staring up at Hellebore House.

Laura stood on her balcony. The night breeze whispered softly in the trees, tugging her nightclothes, then fell so quiet that she could hear the hiss of meteors scratching the sky. She was looking upwards as if to watch them. But she was not. Above the treetops, candlelight had come to Hellebore.

The candle moved from room to room, and there was a regular, dull thumping sound she could not recognize at first. Bart was knocking the boards out of the windows. Then there would be an echoing clatter of loose planks falling on to gravel, silence again, and the candle moving across the unshuttered window.

Laura remembered to breathe. She looked over her shoulder. Francis was too dull to realize she did not love him, but he normally came to her room once or twice a week and they were both used to the routine. What had intrigued her was the change in his lovemaking since learning of Bart's return. Francis no longer thought solely of his own brief pleasure, he tried to imagine how Laura felt, to consider her. He had always been too careful of what he thought were her feelings: caressing her body to a state of half awareness, then always there was that disappointing moment of ecstasy for him that she knew was the end for her; but afterwards, holding him, she had always felt a lovely tenderness for him, and wished she could love him fully. They had so little.

Francis denied it. He cared for her too much. He lay kissing her breasts until all pleasure ceased and the poor things were numb. He stroked her until she was dying for him to get on with it. He treated her like china. She pinched his sides roughly, but he said 'Ow!' She clasped her hands behind his neck, pinking his skin with her long, lacquered fingernails, rubbing his face against her flesh, but he only pretended to enjoy it for her sake. Yet she had done it for him.

It was unbearable, living a lie.

Laura closed the drapes. Francis was not coming to her tonight. She took off her gown, flicked a brush through her hair and put a dab of cold cream on her cheeks. There were many advantages to sleeping alone: she got into bed and spread out her correspondence-course books on hotel management, put her HB pencil between her teeth, and began to study.

When the door creaked, it startled her.

'You've never regarded yourself as Lady Pervane, have you?' said Francis from the doorway. His expression was serious, sad. 'My greatest gift to you meant nothing. You don't have any class.' He looked almost frightened. He had been thinking, not drinking. He sat on the end of her bed in his pyjamas and dressing gown, and she moved her feet. Such dread as she heard in his voice deserved an honest reply.

'I just want to be regarded as myself,' Laura told him.

'Do you admire me?'

What an extraordinary question. 'I think you're very nice!'

'As a man?'

'You are a man.'

'All these books,' he murmured, 'you'll have to wear reading glasses soon. Darling, I know where you've been.'

'Been, Francis?' she said unconvincingly.

He looked straight at her. 'You broke your solemn promise to me. You went up to Hellebore House.'

'But he wasn't there!'

Francis sighed. 'He is there now. Bart Barronet was released this morning. I saw him get off the bus.'

She had to know. 'How was he?'

'Worried about him?' Francis shrugged. 'Why am I telling you this? Prison food must suit him. Hale and hearty as they come.' He couldn't comprehend it. 'A jailbird, a man with a dishonourable discharge from His Majesty's Armed Forces stuck in his pocket – he should have been crawling with shame. That place of his is a complete ruin, you know. He has no money. How can he feel pride in himself? Laura?'

But her mind was miles away. *Hale and hearty.* Laura understood. Bart had endured. She knew what that meant.

Francis watched her. He couldn't bring himself to say anything.

'Francis— ' she said. But the expression on his face stopped her tongue. It was such despair. He knew he was losing her. He clenched his fists powerlessly.

He was still wearing his dressing gown, his pyjamas, his slippers. But his hair was in disarray and his fingernails dug crescents of blood across his palms. He held out his arms to her. 'What do I have to do?'

She didn't know what to say. There was nothing he could do; it was all too late.

'Francis . . . we can't go on like this. It's over.'

He said eagerly: 'I *shall* make you happy. I shall insist.' His promise when he asked her to marry him, and perhaps the poor man thought the old magic would work again.

'I want a divorce, Francis.'

He laughed. He tried to pretend she was joking. He raised his hands above his head, chuckling with mirth, thin lines of blood trickling up his wrists.

'I want to go,' Laura said, 'I've got to leave.' With Bart back in Hellebore, she could never be happy, or safe from herself.

'Leave Watersmeet!' Francis exclaimed. 'It's our place. We're happy here.'

'I've got to be free. Free. Oh, Francis, not only of you, but of this beautiful, terrible place. Look what we've done to ourselves. You've got to let me go.'

Francis still couldn't believe it. He was still laughing.

She said: 'I'm sorry.'

She couldn't bear to sit there with him knowing so little of her that he laughed when she was most serious. She snatched her eiderdown and stood beside him for a moment, knowing that what was so clear to her was inexplicable to him. 'Oh!' she said angrily, and left him sitting there on her bed. She went downstairs and covered herself on the sofa, lay there awake, and tried to sleep.

The distant sounds of boards being knocked out,

of windows being uncovered, permeated her slumbers. She was up early. She hadn't rested well, and using the sofa's arm as a pillow had cricked her neck. She washed in the kitchen sink and went upstairs. Francis wasn't in his bedroom – he was still in hers, stretched out face down across her bed with one arm on her pillow as though it were her. His legs stuck out over the edge, his slippers had dropped off, and the soles of his feet looked white and faintly ridiculous. She dressed without waking him, put up her hair in a ballerina bun and slipped out.

It was as lovely in the fresh air as only Watersmeet mornings knew how to be, the narrow sky streaked with wandering clouds, the rising slopes in their complex, forested folds both massive yet shimmering like thin air. She had to get out from the Manor, and fortunately it was the morning of the week she usually saw her mother. Sybil insisted on these joyless visits to Paradise House for the pleasure of complaining about everything. But this morning in the hall Sybil simply held out a letter to her without a word. The stamp, the postmark, the handwriting, everything gave it away.

'I'll be in the solarium when you want me,' she said, and left Laura alone.

Laura sat on the sixth step. It squeaked.

Her name in his slanted blue handwriting. But the letter was very short – only one sheet of paper inside, she could feel it through the envelope, and knew it was the brush-off. She couldn't open it, she felt so rejected and miserable, but she couldn't bring herself to tear it up. She could hear Sybil listening, alert to every vibration in her daughter's emotions,

344

just as a fish is aware of everything that moves in the water. Laura jumped to her feet and ran down the hallway, then walked away outside without glancing back at her mother's figure staring after her from the solarium.

She went to a place she felt safe, sitting by the waterfall into Dumbledon Pool where she used to swim when she was a girl. The water rumbled and roared comfortingly past her boulder and she put her elbows on her knees, then opened Jerry's letter. She was confused for a moment by the sheet of high-quality corporation-headed notepaper that slipped out. Jerry's own company.

In his own handwriting, he said yes!

Laura put back her head. Everything was going to be all right. This was her passport from Watersmeet.

Here was the proof she needed of Jerry's love: he had launched his boat too.

I understand the sacrifice you demand of me, he wrote.

Had she demanded a sacrifice? Of course she had. How else could she be sure he loved her? With Francis she had learned her lesson as far as men were concerned.

You have destroyed my life, Jerry wrote. He couldn't live without her. *I believe in a better life, a life I can make better by my own efforts. We can escape. We can learn to be free.*

He had begun proceedings against Beverly. He was abandoning his faith for Laura.

Laura closed her eyes and held the letter against her heart. She must mean everything to him.

She slipped the letter into her brassiere, cupped

345

her hands, and drank thirstily from the waterfall.
She unbound her hair, splashed water over herself,
patted the icy droplets over her face and let the
beads trickle hither and thither down her sun-
heated skin. Then she scrambled back to the path.

A few stones skittered past her.

Francis was waiting for her up there.

He held out his hand to help her but she pretended
not to notice. His expression was wary, vulnerable.
By now he did believe she was serious, he saw it
in her eyes, her face, her walk, observing her as
never before as she walked away from him. He
wasn't laughing.

'We used to swim there as children,' he called.
'I suppose that's boring.'

'Did we?'

'At least talk to me,' he said. 'We'll sort something
out.'

Laura shook her head. It was a warm day, but her
damp hair felt freezing on her shoulders. She didn't
tell him about Jerry.

Francis' world had fallen apart, and he knew the
reason for it. What other reason would a Pervane
ever suspect for his undoing but a Barronet?

'Laura!' he said, and she turned.

'It's him, isn't it?' Francis accused her, and Laura
looked surprised. She was so clever, so desirable,
so brutally unpredictable. She was wearing her
cotton skirt and she looked lovely. But beneath that
beautiful shape was a woman. He gave her
everything, and she took it all, her appetite for love
was voracious. How he longed for her, loving her
even when she hurt him. But she couldn't be
allowed to lie to him any more.

346

'It's Bart who put you up to this,' Francis said flatly.

'No!' Laura looked genuinely shocked, but he no longer believed her.

'I know you better than you know yourself.'

She shook her head. 'My life with you is finished.'

'Oh yes, just like that!'

'It has been for years, Francis.'

He said quietly: 'Is there nothing I can do?'

'Let me go.'

'I love you so much and you don't see it.'

'What about me, Francis? What about what I feel?'

He frowned.

'Oh, Francis!' she shouted angrily.

He held out his hands. 'I love you.'

She pitied him, but she left him.

'Look at me!' he called after her on his knees. 'Look how much I love you.'

Laura returned to Watersmeet Manor. She went up to her bedroom and began again what she should have finished years before. She packed her suitcase. Tomorrow she would swallow her pride and return to Paradise House.

Francis' voice haunted her dreams. A little boy until the end, crying for his mother.

Laura murmured in her sleep, tossing and turning. This had been his father's room.

Strands of her hair fell across her face and she moaned, struggling, until her eyes snapped open.

The Manor was silent. Her room was a black wall: the intense dark before dawn. Then she heard scuffling noises. Outside? Blackbird stirring in her stable? Inside again now. Sounds of human movement, footsteps, a door creaking downstairs. She was too frightened to turn on her bedside light. She reached out for her dressing gown over the back of the chair and found it by touch, then knelt and swept the palms of her hands across the carpet until she located her slippers, sitting on the bed and forcing herself to pull them on properly rather than just tread down the heels. Holding her arms outstretched she walked through the darkness in the direction of her bedroom door until she felt the gloss-painted wood under her fingertips. Turning the handle, she stepped out on to the gallery. There was a faint smell of petrol. She clicked on the light.

Francis was standing at the head of the stairs, less than six paces from her. He was fully dressed, suit, shiny black shoes, a trilby hat rakishly on his head, a Burberry overcoat belted at his waist. His eyes were wild and exultant, and . . . relieved. He ran at Laura and grabbed her by the throat, kissing her, digging his thumbs on each side of her windpipe with a strength she had not known he possessed. He cried her name in an enraged voice. He wasn't trying to kill her, but that was what he was doing, choking her life away. Her strength fled, suddenly there was nothing beneath her, she lost her footing and fell out of his grip, tumbling over and over downstairs.

She lay with her cheek on the circular hall carpet, her bruised neck pounding. Through the cracked Adam door half open to the study she saw the picture of Phineas, Lucy's husband, tall as all the Pervanes. Laura felt herself fading into unconsciousness. When vaguely Francis' gigantic foot appeared in front of her eye, she could hardly recognize it. Her eyelids slipped closed and for a moment she floated in limbo, distantly aware of Francis kneeling over her, weeping as though she were dead: he thought he had killed her . . .

She tried to swallow; the second time was easier. She opened her eyes, winced at the glare of light. The illuminated fan-window above the double doors showed dawn, clear and fine, the glowing sky radiating pale pleats of sunlight above the treetops.

Laura dragged herself on to hip and hand. Her dangling hair brushed the floor. Something awful had happened: she remembered Francis weeping and how sorry she had felt for him. And the smell of petrol on his clothes. Her heart stopped. A thin spiral of smoke rose over the trees: Hellebore. Hellebore House was afire.

Groaning, she rolled to her feet and dragged the door open on the brilliant, beautiful morning. The yellowish-greenish back of an oodwall woodpecker showed off his characteristic, looping flight fast and self-confidently between the tree trunks, ringing out his call, *tuw-tuw-tuwk*, then silence, and Laura heard the valley echo the crackle of burning timbers from high above.

She ran with her dressing gown flapping behind her, splashing across the river, following the old fisherman's path for a way then taking the short cut up into the trees, digging her fingers into the mossy slope as she climbed. When she came to the track she ran with her hair flying behind her. Her breath rasped and she had to stop to cough. She should have taken the time to saddle up Blackbird. It was too late now. By now the fire would have taken hold.

She staggered on. The iron-tipped gate across the path was closed. She tugged at the latch.

A memory struck her: Sir George shouting through the study window to old Silas, who was preparing to burn out a wasps' nest – *Use paraffin, not petrol, you bloody fool!* Laura didn't know the difference, but she was terrified. Still the stupid iron latch resisted her scrabbling fingers.

'You're pulling too hard,' came a voice behind her.

Bart stood close enough to touch her, a massive presence of calm. He observed the wild, dishevelled creature in front of him, her hair across her face, her hands streaked with rust, and showed concern rather than surprise. His eyes hadn't changed.

'Bart,' she murmured.

But the sentence in Dartmoor had changed him, his face was leaner, showing distrust where there had been trust before, and muscles stood bunched in his shoulders and down his front beneath his white shirt. Over his left shoulder was tossed the thigh-length maroon jacket: he had been out since long before dawn, and a brace of hare dangled from his hand, slowly revolving, against the black trews he wore.

She gasped: 'Something terrible – my husband – fire! He's set fire to your house.'

Bart looked across the top of her head. 'The old place is stone, take him a while to set that alight.'

'He has petrol,' Laura wept.

Bart covered her hand with his and effortlessly pulled the gate open, the rusty hinges squealing. He dropped the hares and ran forward up the track, calling over his shoulder: *'Stay there!'*

She followed him, of course.

Almost at once she heard a loud explosion and a few seconds later a red fireball billowed slowly above the treetops, the flames rotating within the oily cloud, thudding and popping as they consumed themselves, the valley walls throwing back the sound. She could not bear to watch: she turned, and there was the abyss, she could see Watersmeet Manor calm and quiet below her.

At the top of the bluff she turned between the crumbling gateposts, almost exhausted, the sole peeling from one of her slippers and flapping as she ran.

The flames had taken hold so that the windows of Hellebore House shone like beacons beneath the pall of smoke. Birds fluttered between the naked joists of the roof, then whirled up, escaping. The wooden fabric was burning inside. Steam hissed, then there was another explosion and the front doors fell open, the flare silhouetting Bart crouched on the steps, the heat beating him back. He stood up and walked away backwards, slowly, not taking his eyes from the scene of destruction in front of him. Laura smelt the heat and the smoke emanating from him. Beyond him she saw history burning. More birds swept out from the roof between the smoking, shimmering chimneys, but she could hear the shrieks of some poor animal still trapped inside.

Laura screamed her husband's name.

Wreathed in flames, Francis ran down the steps, but not towards her. He was thinking only of the river. Towing fire behind his petrol-stinking clothes, he lunged past them without seeing.

They ran after him, and saw Francis plummet over the cliff-edge towards the river far below.

351

Laura stared as smoke and flames came shooting out of the void. Francis' body was caught in the oak tree, everything was burning. Long yellow flames danced above the rim of the bluff, and thick blue woodsmoke rose. There was no other noise now. The valley beyond was sunlit and peaceful.

Laura walked towards the edge, her hands clapped to her cheeks.

She gave herself up to grief for Francis, as she was expected to do. She made excuses for his behaviour, and blamed everyone but Francis. If only she had been a better wife, if only she had loved him more, all the usual recriminations. He became simplified and noble in her memory. The Coroner was a local man, as were the jury, and the inquest returned a verdict of death by natural causes.

Francis was laid to rest beside his father in the churchyard at St Brendan's on Cheriton Ridge, pointing towards the heart of the moor, where the grass he had planted was growing green and his sheep were grazing. It was a private funeral. Sybil stood beside her daughter as though they shared some kind of secret, rather than being really close: she kept glancing at Laura's face, Laura's tears. Afterwards Laura couldn't stand her around, and told Silas to drive the old woman home.

She stood alone with the minister by the open grave letting his comforting words wash over her, then saw him look past her, startled, and she followed his eyes to the lych-gate where Bart Barronet was standing outside. He just smiled, as though he knew her better than she knew herself. Bart reached out his hand to the oak palings and pushed the gate open, then he walked into the churchyard.

'Carry on with what you were saying,' Laura told the minister. The man could not utter a sound.

Bart came and stood beside Laura, looking down into the grave. His maroon coat brushed her sleeve as he dropped in a single red Watersmeet blood-rose. Laura gazed at the minister with such intensity that he began to speak to her, nothing important, the same old words.

Bart looked up at the church, then walked towards the building. With sudden force he knocked open the door, and strode inside.

'What should we do?' the minister asked Laura.

'Leave him alone,' she ordered. Bart didn't come out of the church. Before Laura left the churchyard, she went quietly and looked through the doorway, her face showing no expression.

She saw Bart Barronet standing with his back to her by the desecrated tomb of Resda de Barreneau, his ancestor, lover of Alder Pervane, resting his hands on her cold stone. He didn't turn, and Laura left him to his thoughts.

She walked home to Watersmeet Manor. From the county road she couldn't help glancing across the valley. There was nothing at all to be seen of Hellebore House now; only a few wisps of smoke still rose above the trees over there to show its location.

She stayed indoors for the next few weeks, hardly moving, barely thinking. When the solicitor who was handling Francis' estate came she dealt with him brightly and efficiently, then dropped back into her torpor. Francis' complex affairs – Watersmeet

Manor was also held in commonage – might take years to wind up completely. His will had been written so that had Laura given him a son, the boy would have received almost everything, but as it was Laura remained sole beneficiary. Everything was hers: the land, the hotel, the jeweller's, a substantial deal of money, and the Pervane name. For her lifetime.

With her, the Pervane name ceased.

Laura sat in the semicircular orangery, the sweet musky scent of the fruit giving the air a Mediterranean softness.

She went out walking. She avoided seeing Bart. She felt empty. Perhaps Francis had meant more to her than she liked to believe. She was not certain what her feelings were. Perhaps she felt guilty about Jerry. Still dressed in black, she put on her black-veiled broad-brimmed hat, and decided she would go and see her mother. They would have tea. She knew Sybil had not sorted out all Ernest's things yet, any more than Laura could face going into Francis' bedroom and starting to clear all his socks and shirts from the drawers, laying his suits out for charities . . . A nice cup of tea with her mother, and they would talk about, well, death. That wasn't what she wanted.

She walked up to Hellebore House.

She could smell the odour of burned stone long before she arrived. Bart was working with a spade in the ruins, she heard the clink of the blade coming through the trees, and stood by a tree trunk watching his figure toil. He was wearing a white shirt rolled up to the elbows. No fragment of wall stood higher than his head amongst the shapeless mounds of rubble, the debris of generations, and she wondered how much she had not known of all its secrets and mysteries. Yet suddenly she felt glad that she had never known, that the past was gone and laid to rest, and now her life lay in front of her. She was really free.

Bart was throwing out stones of a certain size into a pile. His energy was ferocious. She was sure he knew she was there, but he didn't stop. It was said that forty thousand ounces of silver had been lost, melted in the blaze . . . but all Bart seemed to care about was finding stones the right size, ignoring her.

Slowly Laura came forward out of the trees. Beds of nettles, bright green, were already growing out of the wood-ash and lumber; God knows how long their root systems had lain dormant beneath the masonry. Still Bart refused to notice her. He had taken off his shirt and the sun gleamed on his brown shoulders. She imagined him slaving on the chain gang like this in a Dartmoor quarry, the steady rhythm of his swinging arms, the growing pile of useless stones. Why wouldn't he acknowledge her?

She crossed the cinders of the carriage circle. From the corner of her eye she saw that the stables beneath the trees had been saved, and guessed he must be living rough there.

'Bart,' she said, and he stopped, waiting patiently. Now she didn't know what to say; the rubble beneath her feet was still warm, and smoke drifted faintly around them, but it smelt so strong that she could not trust herself to speak. She looked at the piled stones to ask what he was doing.

He held out his arms. Laura stiffened.

He called: 'I am going to rebuild Hellebore House.'

She gazed around her. She didn't scoff. He meant every word, but it seemed incredible to her that he just couldn't see when he was beaten. No one could ever rebuild Hellebore House. It was finished.

He dropped his arms to his sides without taking his eyes off her, seeming to understand what she was thinking.

'Not as it was.' He swung, pointing to one side. 'Over there, beyond Lucy's memorial stone. Do you see the sea? It will be a round house, with walls of stone and cob, and broad windows . . .'

She shook her head, not listening to his stupid dream, and his voice faded.

'Come here,' he said.

'I came to apologize,' she told him.

'I know why you came.'

She took a last step forward. 'It doesn't mean anything, just because I came here,' she said.

He touched her hair and it came unbound in a sudden unfolding rush, a silky weight that seemed instantly to gather the sun's heat within the circles of its locks, and he took her in his arms.

She gasped with passion, her hair hanging back on to the stones and greenery, pulling him onward, making him think he was doing it himself. His fingers slipping inside her black dress from her shoulder to her breast, soft and white and cherry-red in his hand and between his lips, her buttons popping willy-nilly and the two of them still having to stand, the nettles all around them spoiling everything.

'Bart,' she murmured, kissing his lips, standing up on tiptoe, pressing back with her fingers on his chest. He leaned back into the undergrowth, taking her pale body on top of him, her hair trailing over his face as she sat back on his thighs, her heels hooked under his knees, totally naked with him now, letting him see her breasts, her cleave. She already knew she possessed him. He would climax even if she let him go no further. But she let him raise his thighs and she slid down, writhing her hips to take him deeper, biting his hands. 'Look at me!' she said, 'look at me. I love you,' she whispered. His head was twisted back, the tendons standing out in his neck, and he groaned. It seemed so hard for a man. She touched him, caressing him tenderly, until her own body took her by surprise, shuddering and thumping with warmth in gorgeous waves, and with each one she slumped lower over him, exhausted.

He was lying looking back at the valley, the top of his head on the ground. An upside-down view; but she wanted him to pay attention wholly to her, and pinched his sides angrily.

'Only me,' she ordered, looking seriously into his eyes. She should never have allowed it to happen here. He would not talk of love.

'You beauty,' he laughed, and she did feel sorry for him when she saw that his back was a mass of nettle stings. He lay down on a straw palliasse in the stable and let her rub his back affectionately with dock leaves; and by the time evening came, when he sent her away, she had quite forgiven him for his lapse. But not for laughing at her. Neither of them had given everything. He was still not hers.

PART SIX

The Flood

'How pleasant it is of you to pay us a visit, Lady Pervane.' Tristram Sayle, the manager of the Watersmeet Falls Hotel, his oiled hair slicked flat, his black moustache pencilled on his upper lip, strode briskly into Reception with his hand extended. He took up Laura's hand, allowing a suggestion of firmness in his grip, showing her who was boss down here. 'If only you had given us a little more time . . .' he reprimanded her with a charming smile.

Laura said: 'That was deliberately not my intention, Mr Sayle.'

He bent to kiss her hand with smooth good manners, lingering to give himself time to think, which enabled him to observe the fortune in rings that clustered her fingers; diamonds, rubies, the Pervane bracelet encircling her slender wrist. Her long nails were buffed, not lacquered, to a soft pink glow, and she wore a dark brown Dior hourglass suede coat trimmed in fur the colour of burnt umber, which brought out how blue her eyes were. And how cold.

She pulled her hand away.

'Let's take the pleasantries as read and get straight down to business, shall we, Mr Sayle? she said, and he covered his feelings of disquiet with a smile. This young woman – he was old enough to be her father – was more formidable than he had anticipated. He

361

had much to hide, if only she knew it; life had been very comfortable for him down here.

'As you wish,' he said a little less politely. He opened the door to his office, limping a little now to remind her of his wooden foot for his country, but she walked straight past him. She was wearing perfume; something lovely. The signals he received confused him and he didn't know how seriously to take her. She unpinned her burnt-umber hat and dropped it on his desk, then stood at the broad window that lay behind it, against whose glare visitors to Mr Sayle's office had to narrow their eyes to see his face. He hovered with his hand on the doorknob, unable to get past her to his chair. 'We have to make do with a very small office, as you see,' he smiled accusingly.

She glanced at him then returned her attention to the view: the black hills, the salmon run, the river running past the steep-backed cottages into Lynmouth harbour, and the Rhenish tower with the jagged grey expanse of the western beach beyond. 'It was a very poor season,' she said. 'Poorer even than I expected.'

'I'm glad to be able to welcome you personally,' he fawned, 'I was just going on holiday for a couple of weeks . . .' She glanced at him again and his voice dried up. He didn't understand what was happening, his sophisticated manner always worked on the female gender, his wide steady eyes and humorous pucker in the corner of his lips assured them that he was a man of the world, a ladies' man, but he wasn't getting through to this one at all. It was humiliating. He croaked, then instead rang the bell and a maid came from the Palm Court tea-

rooms, Mavis with the red lips and the wink in her
eye. 'Lady Pervane?' prompted Mr Sayle in a
trembling voice. Still she said nothing.

'Tea or coffee?' piped up Mavis.

'Not now, thank you, Mavis,' the woman by the
window said. 'I'll call you when I want you.'

Mavis nudged Mr Sayle and he nodded her back
to the tea-room with his head, dismissing her. He
closed the door and wondered what to do with his
hands, trying to recover his calm.

'Now, what *can* I do for you, my lady?' he asked
patronizingly.

'You can clear out your desk.'

Tristram Sayle realized that he had made a serious
error of judgement. The woman was not at all as
he had thought her. He flushed red to the tips of
his ears.

'Are you mad!' he said, putting his fists on his desk
and leaning across at her.

She sat calmly in his chair. 'Let us make this
painless and plain, Mr Sayle— '

'Just who do you think you are?'

Laura arched her eyebrows. 'Your employer.'

He blustered: 'I can see you don't know a damn
thing about business— '

She interrupted quietly: 'I know when a business
is badly run. I know when I am being taken for a
fool. I am a woman, Mr Sayle, but I am not a fool.'
She raised her hand over his voice. 'Please don't
talk when I am interrupting. This is no longer your
office. I hire and fire who I like. You are fired.'

'You can't do that!'

'I have just done it.'

He looked from side to side. 'But you need me!'

Laura said: 'I do not need anyone.'

He looked at her implacable eyes, and could well believe that was true. He felt himself dwindle in the face of her feminine aggression. The old tricks didn't work. He didn't know how to fight her.

'Cigarette?' He hitched his trouser legs and sat on the edge of his desk, surveying her appreciatively. 'Let's be reasonable.'

'No, let's not be reasonable.' She looked impatiently to her watch, and he was amazed to see that she wore a cheap gold-plated job strapped tightly on her wrist. She opened her bag and took out a legal-sized envelope such as solicitors and accountants use. 'I have a good head for figures. You're an idiot, Tristram. You've been on the take for years.'

'That's slander,' he warned her.

'For years! And my husband knew about it, but he didn't have the guts to get rid of you. I do.' Her tone was withering. 'He knew how you treated the female staff, how they got jobs, and why they didn't, and he tolerated it because boys have got to stick together, haven't they? Let me assure you, that has changed.'

'Look,' Tristram begged her, 'you're making a mistake. Let's get down off our high horse, consider the broader view, and we'll talk about it over supper, just the two of us, right?'

'You're and even bigger idiot than I thought.' She uncapped her Waterman's Chinese laque pen and signed a cheque which she had prepared earlier. 'That includes your fortnight's holiday pay, and ends any association between us. The Granville will put

364

you up tonight.' She glanced up enquiringly when he didn't move.

'You're really going through with this?' he asked, astonished.

'I always go through with what I've started,' she said, holding out the cheque. 'Goodbye, Mr Sayle. On your way out, ask Mavis to step in. There is a small matter of mislaid till receipts to discuss.'

Oh, how she had stirred them up! She remembered their pale, shocked faces as she settled matters that Francis should have sorted out long ago. There were some she trusted: the sub-manageress, Hilda, a quiet but presentable woman, obviously knew her job and was promoted. The manageress of the Palm Court room, which was run as a separate business for tax reasons, had been on the take for years and was dismissed, her responsibilities handed to Hilda. The bar was left as it was under Lloyd, the bachelor. When it was all over Laura, who saw that she had forgotten to drink the tea someone had brought her, pinned her hat on straight, checked in the mirror, picked up her gloves, and prepared to leave. The sacked staff were standing around in the lobby like sheep, still in shock: there had not been such a bloodletting for many years. They drew back, then someone came and opened the door for her, and she stepped out into the fresh air. She had done what had to be done.

Laura realized that her heart was hammering. She had successfully concealed everything she was feeling inside her: men had bloodhound noses for weakness. She had been terribly afraid, but the right words had come to her tongue when she needed them.

By comparison Watersmeet Manor seemed so dull and enclosed, the heavy hills muffling her spirits; she was much too worked up to do piano practice or any of the makework tasks she once set herself. She couldn't get the excitement out of her head; she felt she would burst. Only the man who still defied her would do in her present mood. Confident now, knowing what she was doing, she rode up to Hellebore.

The round house was coming on; he'd got the circular foundations dug in before the frost. She could hear steel ringing on stone. She approached Bart with a shyness the staff of the Watersmeet Falls Hotel would not have recognized. His back, still brown, gleamed with sweat in the last rays of the sun, and the silver crescent of the pickaxe he wielded arced into the stone he was splitting, finding the flaw. The ringing note went flat as the stone cracked. He stepped back, satisfied, then in a swift motion turned, and she realized that he had known she was there: she was learning him better and better. But he didn't hug her against him.

'Where have you been?'

'At the hotel— ' she blurted excitedly, wanting to tell him about herself, to please him.

'Not all the time,' he said coldly. 'Why haven't you been here to help me?'

So he had missed her.

'Oh,' she shrugged with a smile, 'I had better things to do. You don't expect me to wield a pickaxe, I suppose?' She wanted so much to tell him of her success.

'I expect you to be with me.'

Instead of being angry, she kissed him earnestly. His lips were hot, his hair slick with sweat from his herculean labours, and she tangled it affectionately in her fingers. The temperature was rapidly dropping with such a clear sky.

'Mind you don't catch cold,' she said, wrapping his arms around her, hooking herself into the crook of his elbows, kissing his shoulders and his bicep muscles. 'Darling, you'll be amazed. I'm going to tell you everything I've been doing. I promise I won't leave a thing out.'

'While you've been playing at being a businesswoman,' he said, 'I've built the walls of the round house up to the three-foot level now, look.' He led her over, pointing with one arm, and she tried to seem interested. 'You can see where the doorway will be, Laura, and tomorrow I'll start levelling off for the sills of the ground-floor windows. I'll make the frames from hornbeam, they'll last forever . . .'

'But time passes so quickly.' She turned her head up: look at me.

He bent down and kissed her. 'Laura.' He said softly: 'We can't go on being apart.' She touched his cheeks with her fingertips, caressing his lips with her own, making their closeness last, knowing what it would do to him. Sliding her thumbs up his ribs, she brought the flat of her palms gliding down the curve of his spine, feeling his grip tighten, enclosing her, protecting her.

'Bart,' she murmured, 'I don't want to live here. If you really loved me— '

He said simply: 'I do.'

'We've got to make our own lives, our own

destiny.' She was sounding trite, like a woman in love.

'Our lives are here.'

'That was in the past, this is now.' She tugged him. 'It's important to me, Bart.'

'You are important to *me*,' he said at once. 'What does anything matter but us? Earthquakes in China, atom bomb tests, but all that means anything is the two of us, here.'

'Please understand.'

'Do we have to talk?'

She hugged him. 'This is a wonderful place here,' she lied. 'But I want so much more. I want company and friends, and— '

'To leave Watersmeet.'

'We aren't children.'

'But I'm here, and you would be far— '

She waited for him to realize that she was asking him to come with her.

He shook his head.

'Yes,' she said, 'you would, if you really loved me.'

He held her hair in the palms of his hands. The stars were emerging above the blue glow of the horizon. He put his forehead against hers. 'You and me, Laura.' She had to strain to catch his words. 'It's meant. It's ordained.'

She opened her lips.

'No,' he said. 'This is my place. Our place,' he added.

Her voice broke. 'You don't really love me.'

'God, Laura, I do!'

'Then— '

'I do want you.'

She waited.

'Is this how you treated Francis?' he demanded.

She was determined not to let herself be hurt. She smiled.

'If you go away from here,' he told her quietly, 'do you think you will find yourself? Is there anyone to find, Laura?'

'With you to love me and come with me. Us together. Yes.'

When he was about to say something more she just touched her finger to his lips. She knew how to make him say anything she wanted. The hilltops around them held the last of the light, fading. She tugged at his shoulders; his coat lay behind her on the broad wall. After the first frantic impulse, while they made love a languorous intensity came stealing over them, until she almost felt she was part of the earth.

'Laura,' he whispered to her, 'you're beautiful.'

She sighed eagerly, taking him, clasping him to her body and soul in the inexplicable moment, her arms and legs around him so that there was nothing of him that escaped her, making him her own, or so she thought.

She murmured, touching his hair, his ears, the long lashes of his tawny eyes. Then she kissed his lips pleasurably, feeling warm and contented beneath him. 'Ask what happened to me today,' she murmured.

'The long-awaited emasculation of Mr Tristram Sayle,' he guessed, accurately – of course.

She tickled him. 'I was the most frightful ogre down at the hotel. Don't sigh. It's me. I want you to know everything about me.'

'I do.' He yawned comfortably in her ear, sending an extraordinary tremble down her spine.

'Oh my darling,' she gasped involuntarily. 'You did that deliberately.'

'Don't talk about the hotel or anything like that.'

'But you'll be interested.'

'You'll have to sell it.' He sat up and wrapped her in his coat, not seeming to feel the cold.

'Sell it? The Watersmeet Falls Hotel! Why?'

'And the Manor. If it's to be real between us.'

'What could be more real than this!' She touched his naked thigh, kissed his hip. 'You're so stubborn. Anyway, I can't sell the Manor. Francis' last will and testament says so.'

'Pervane again.'

She called after him: 'Pervane is my name too.'

'Why are you doing this to me?'

It was so obvious she didn't need to say it.

'Love?' His voice came to her so quietly that she could hardly hear it.

'Let's scratch it in a tree,' she called mischievously, 'Bart Barronet loves Laura Pervane. Bart *does!* A heart with an arrow through it.' He finished dressing without a word. 'Don't be like that,' she said.

'Don't make me like that,' he said reasonably.

'Or what?'

'Or I'll tickle your toes until you scream for mercy.'

'You wouldn't dare,' she said, then screamed. 'Oh, oh, oh,' she gasped. 'Will I see you tomorrow?'

'It's Friday, so your mother's coming to lunch with you.'

'Join us,' Laura said.

He shook his head. He wouldn't go to Watersmeet

370

Manor. He was a stubborn stick-in-the-mud of a man
and he still wouldn't compromise.

'You'll have to, one day,' she told him, with that
light in her eye.

He searched for his pickaxe in the darkness. She
tucked her blouse under her belt and followed him,
rested her forehead on his shoulder. 'I'm sorry. I'm
not trying to hurry you. One day you'll find these
ghosts will be laid to rest. Trust me.' *You do love
me, Bart Barronet. You'll have to face it.*

He nodded at the humped shadows around them,
the piles of rubble.

'Ghosts never rest,' he said.

She remembered him saying: *As you see, I am
already possessed.*

'Bart,' she said, then stood on tiptoe and kissed
him.

'What was that for?'

'Nothing,' she said.

'Ernest never liked sole,' Sybil complained. He
didn't, so she didn't. 'He preferred halibut.' It was
a kind of grief, a sentimental celebration of Ernest's
habits *in memoriam,* even his bad ones. She picked
irritatingly at her grilled fish, pushing the peas
fastidiously to the side of her Royal Doulton plate
with the knife, and Laura knew she was
disappointed because they had been deep-frozen.
Her mother was a disappointed woman whose life
had deliberately been given up to coping. She had
made a pride and a virtue out of it, but it was her
daughters who had borne the burden. Now her life
was much easier than she pretended, the grocer's
van from Rockford called at Paradise House twice

a week, and Laura suspected her mother of buying Hovis.

'These aren't real peas,' said Sybil, squashing one beneath the tines of her fork.

'They're the latest thing.'

'The latest craze from America, no doubt, and they cost a fortune I'm sure. You can get them out of the ground for free.' Without Ernest to keep her in check Sybil wanted to pick fights, and it was unfortunate that when Laura's irritation with her mother turned to hot temper, as now, she usually got too angry and emotional to speak, a silence that had misled Clara more than once. 'And when you grow your own, dear, you know – they have more flavour.'

Laura cleared away the plates without a word.

'Talking of American crazes,' Sybil called through, 'we don't seem to have heard from your American friend lately. Dropped by the wayside.' She spoke this crassly in order to say things under the masquerade of closeness which neither of them now felt.

Laura stuck out her tongue at the doorway to the dining room. She took the bread and butter pudding from the oven, golden brown on top, and carried the sizzling dish through in oven gloves.

'Oh, I can't eat sultanas, dear.'

Laura found her voice. 'I'll pick them out for you.'

'Jerry,' Sybil said.

Laura found that she was able to think logically about Jerry Ellis.

'I don't think we'll hear any more from him,' she said.

'So you were just playing him off against Francis,'

said Sybil, nodding with self-satisfaction at her diagnosis.

There were times when her mother horrified Laura, and she thought: *Am I really going to be like her one day?* because she *could* see herself in the older woman – parts she wished to avoid. Sybil tried a mouthful of pudding then added more sugar, a provocation which Laura ignored.

'So you played your game, dear, and poor Francis blamed Bart Barronet. But you were the one to blame really.'

'Mother— '

'It's not your fault. Ernest spoiled you.'

'I wanted to love Francis.'

'These give me flatulence,' Sybil said, finding a sultana.

Laura said quietly, ashamed to feel tears welling behind her eyes: 'Is it true that you never loved me?'

Sybil's head jerked. She put back her spoon in her dish with a mouthful of pudding still on it, and stared straight at Laura.

'You were the one who broke us up. First by having you,' Sybil said steadily, 'then by not having you. Your father and I . . . we loved you too much. You were always the storm centre of our lives, child. Always noisy. It's so hard to be a parent. When you were gone . . .' She shook her head. 'We had nothing to hold us together.'

Laura touched her mother's hand. So it had always been themselves they thought about. *She* had never had any choice at all, their good little girl. Except that she had gone *the wrong way*.

'It was Bart, wasn't it?' Sybil said bitterly. 'He was

the only man you ever, ever thought of. And that
was how you got away with lying to us.'

Laura protested her innocence. She pulled back
a little from the table, putting more distance
between herself and her mother.

Sybil looked at her daughter, so elegant with her
sleek nylons crossed, and her diamond earrings
twinkling. Black suited her high colour. 'Thank God
Francis never knew you didn't love him!' Sybil said.
But he had known.

It wasn't Laura's fault. 'If only you had let me
be myself.'

'Oh yes? And who is *she*?' Sybil demanded,
refusing to take the blame. 'Men don't care.' Her
mother sounded just like Clara. 'All men want is sex
and food. Of course you loved Francis, dear. You
were married to him,' Sybil said smugly. 'Still,' she
smirked, 'now you have Watersmeet Manor. And
you do own the Watersmeet Falls Hotel, you've
done very well.' She explained: 'You're an attractive
prospect, dear. For the right man.'

Laura was startled. 'But I would never— ' She had
been going to say *stay*.

'After the seemly interval, of course.'

'You're matchmaking again.' Laura cleared away
the bowls, flicking the rejected sultanas into the dish
on the kitchen floor. The cat, Tigermoth, who sat
licking her paws in fond memory of the grilled sole,
regarded them with the same disdain as the leftover
peas. 'Not you too,' Laura whispered, stroking the
striped head fondly.

She sighed. If Sybil had once known what love
was, as she claimed she did, she had forgotten it
long ago, it was as long dead and buried as Ranulf

Barronet. To Sybil, it meant a good marriage. To Laura it was whatever it cost her. Sybil and Clara had given up; she would not. Bart knew what he wanted, but so did she.

Sybil came out and insisted on helping her with the drying-up, cornering Laura at the sink while she said what she had come to say.

'There really is only one possible choice. You mustn't take Jerry seriously. It isn't still going on, is it?'

Laura shook her head. 'I made it a little too difficult for him. He said he'd come back . . .'

'Don't they all! That's the one thing you can always trust a man to say.' Laura was surprised by the venom in her mother's voice: she was just smearing those plates with the drying-up cloth, and Laura knew she was going to have to re-do them later.

'I think he loved me,' Laura murmured, 'I think he really did.'

'He didn't send you those nylons, did he?'

'Everyone wears nylons nowadays.'

'That's all right. Laura, if you want to find happiness, the man you must marry is Bart Barronet.'

Laura laughed, as if dismissing the suggestion out of hand. 'I've never even thought of marrying Bart,' she pretended.

But Sybil spoiled it. She spoke no more of love.

'Think,' urged Sybil, 'you are a young woman in possession of a fortune, and you *must* want a husband. You're attractive enough. You have faults: you have more personality than some men would like, and you must learn to listen more and curb your own ideas. But I think . . .'

'What do you think, Mother?' Laura asked heavily.

Sybil's eyes were sparkling. 'My darling, think of it! You have the opportunity to unite the last of the Pervanes with the last of the Barronets.'

Laura stared at her, chilled. Still not a word of love.

Sybil sparkled: 'And, by becoming a Barronet, end the feud! A thousand years, Laura, perhaps more. To lay it at last to rest.' She gripped Laura's elbow. 'You. My daughter. Laura Barronet.'

'You don't know what you're talking about!' said Laura coldly, rubbing the plates mechanically.

'But isn't it perfect?' purred Sybil.

'I think it's awful!' cried Laura. Her mother was suggesting that she behave like Lucy. 'I'm not Lucy, all that business is in the past. It's just rubbish, Mother, can't you see that? Bart would never come into Watersmeet Manor. He hates this place as much as I do!' She said bitterly: 'It's the valley he loves, or thinks he does.' The old determined light flickered in her eye. 'I'll make my way in the real world, where important things happen. I won't be an ornament, I'll do something important and worthwhile, not stay stuck in this backwater all my life, playing Lady Pervane to yokels, a big fish in a little pool.'

Sybil interrupted the tirade. 'Many would envy you.'

'Not me!' Laura tried to explain calmly. 'Mother, you see, I discovered that some of the hotel staff were cheating Francis for years, and he must have known, but he put up with it. I'm not that sort of person! I *knew* I had to face them.'

'But you know nothing at all about the hotel trade.' Sybil was alarmed: Laura didn't understand what she was playing at. Sybil was no better informed about the hotel trade, but she was sure that it was a technical and expert business.

'I didn't need to know. I employed experts where necessary, and I had my own two eyes, my intuition. But could I actually go down there and face them, Mother? That was what I had to find out. It was all bluff. I was terrified,' Laura confessed, 'I couldn't eat anything all day for nerves, I could hardly think straight. I wanted to talk to Bart about it, but men have to feel they rule your life, so I knew it was something I had to work out for myself. I got rid of Mr Sayle, the manager, and suddenly he wasn't a clever or powerful man at all. They were so unintelligent, so clumsy with their petty plans and deceits. And now I've got a loyal, motivated manageress and the staff are working as a team. I've discovered what I can do, and I won't be tricked again.'

Sybil amazed Laura by kissing her. 'You're my girl, darling.'

'It feels wonderful, Mother, the whole world out there.'

Sybil gave a little grin and dropped her head on one side. 'Then you must ask yourself,' she said obliquely, with a sigh, 'whether Bart loves Watersmeet as much as he loves you.' With Sybil it was men all the time. That was all she knew about, and love was the end of the list. But times had changed.

'Mother, you'll see,' Laura said confidently.

But Sybil persisted. 'You are asking him to make the one sacrifice for you he cannot make.'

'Of course,' said Laura. She laughed: 'Aren't I worth it?'

'I wonder how much you really love him,' Sybil said. Then, almost too low for Laura to catch, she whispered: 'In the end it is all that matters.'

Laura was hurt. Of course she loved Bart. It was always she who had to go trailing up to see him, he never came downhill to her. She didn't want to talk to Sybil any more.

The white Jaguar ordered by Francis two years ago had at last been delivered, and Laura was learning to drive it.

'Home,' sighed Sybil on the way. 'It's nice to go,' she said as Paradise House appeared, 'but it's lovely to get back.'

How lonely the old woman looked walking up the steps. Laura waved goodbye, gunned the engine, and returned to her own lonely house.

Then she changed into slacks. The smeared plates would have to wait. She could have taken the county road and gone across Hillsford Bridge but Bart didn't like her to drive the car up, and she wanted to please him.

Putting on a long belted overcoat, she walked up the path through the trees with a robin redbreast, winter's bird, fluttering ahead of her hoping she would throw him crumbs. The Severn Sea sprawled in the indigo vee between the shoulders of the black hills, and the rib of Toher's promontory fort on Countisbury jutted against the twinkling lights of Wales. In the chasm below her she could see nothing of Watersmeet now, only the Y outline of pale mist rising off the rivers. It still felt wrong to come up here.

Laura waited shyly in the trees, watching him at work up a ladder. Now he had got the materials sorted and the basic work done, the curving structure was rising with amazing speed. Bart dropped down the ladder.

'I wish you'd brought the car,' he said, 'I could have used the headlights.' He wore only a light shirt, the sleeves rolled up, and pale cord trousers though the ground was already frosted hard: the climate was notably more exposed and wintry up here than in the sheltered valley. He didn't look at her. He took her hand and they stood looking at what he had achieved. The stone walls, bound with the mixture of clay and debris called cob, were some three feet thick and looked built to last for ever.

Laura realized this was his way of saying finally he was his own man, on his own terms. His pride excluded her, and she shivered with despair. What a fool she had been.

She was right to end it. It showed him she was in control. She demonstrated that she could stand on her own two feet, yet it made sense to have an amicable parting. That they could remain friends reassured her that they had never meant too much to each other.

But they had never been friends.

As winter hardened, further separating them, she saw him moving about less often, and no longer looked for him. She would not stay in the valley. What he did was his business. When she saw him by chance, from the road perhaps, or across the river, Laura acknowledged him with a very casual wave. Sometimes he nodded or touched his cap. They never spoke, polite strangers. It was better that way.

She had thought she feared loneliness above all, but in practice Laura was finding more than enough to keep her busy. Once she had committed herself to running her own business affairs, the growing flood of matters requiring her urgent attention distracted her from self-doubt. She hardly noticed the first brilliant green mist on the spruce trees proclaiming the end of winter, the flocks of birds returning from Africa, the spating rivers losing their red turbidity and dwindling back to summer levels. The world of Watersmeet was not a part of her.

She was walking in the garden, her head buzzing with exhaustion from a day of accountants' jargon, when she saw Bart on the other side of the river. He was quietly fishing. She stared at him from the shadow of the sequoia planted by Sir George where the summerhouse once was, the empty sofa-swing creaking softly beside her in the evening breeze, watching his expert fluid play of rod and line. Then he noticed her and they stared at one another across the bubbling waters. His line tugged taut but he flicked it away, packed up his things, and left without even calling out hallo.

One day a knock came on the door of Watersmeet Manor. She was going over the jeweller's accounts in the study, smartly dressed, her hair pulled back and her long legs crossed, left calf over right shin. She looked up from her desk in irritation, hating to be interrupted while she was working. 'You'll have to wait!' she called, initialling each page, writing notes to herself to follow up later on a separate pad. Everything had come to her since Francis' affairs were finally settled, and she had begun to understand her father's intoxication with gambling. But she, she told herself, was a good gambler: the cold, calm business of – not so much making money as obtaining power – enchanted her. She had the willpower and the determination to use people, and she was shrewd. Most of the men she employed weren't very good at their job, but they were learning very quickly to be better. There was the possibility of buying another jeweller's shop on the Quay at Bideford. The position was perfect, but . . . The knock on the door came again.

She went through the hall and opened it. 'What the hell do you want?' But no one was there, and now she heard a tapping on the study window pane. She saw an old man wearing a GPO cap and linesman's leather harness.

'We've put up the lines,' he called through the glass. When she lifted the sash window, he said cheerfully: 'An engineer will be round to put in your telephone for you, lady.'

She looked impatiently at her watch, then arranged for Mrs Pawkins to let him in and drove the white Jaguar down to the Watersmeet Falls Hotel. As usual she ate lunch there, hungry for company. She kept her own small, circular table reserved near the window, always perfectly prepared for her with a snow-white damask tablecloth, silver cutlery, and in the centre a damascene flower pitcher holding a single red rose. She ate lightly, listening to the hubbub of conversation at the busy tables around her, sipping her white wine from a frosted glass, watching the river flow down from Watersmeet past her window to the sea.

Salmon flashed in the foaming falls, and the guests at the other favoured tables along the windows pointed excitedly, but she had seen it all before. She lit a cigarette with a snap of her gold lighter, but simply couldn't resist the fresh strawberry ice cream.

People never saw her as the person she felt herself to be. Only Bart had. Other people saw the mask she wore. Mr Sayle had not seen through it, and if he had, he would have won. Once she overheard a waitress going into the kitchen say the word gold-digger. Was that how they thought of her? Only with Bart had she been truly herself. That was the one luxury she could no longer afford.

Laura put down her spoon, leaving her fresh strawberry ice cream almost untouched. 'Was everything as you wished, ma'am?' the little waitress asked nervously.

'It was very pleasant, than you, Maureen.' She made a point of remembering their names.

The girl bobbed and cleared away the full dish.

Laura drove home up the county road. Parts of it had been blasted through sheer rock, with only a narrow stone wall holding cars back from the drop. The road wriggled and jinked, widening abruptly, then narrowing unpredictably. Laura had disliked driving since a tourist coach almost scraped down the side of the car. When she got back to the Manor Mrs Pawkins was still there though it was past her time to go, and still in her housecoat too, her hands

fluttering with excitement. The telephone man had
been and gone.

'And it's been ringing,' Mrs Pawkins fluttered,
showing Laura into the study and anxiously pointing
at the device, 'that there thing's been ringing off
its hook!'

'Well?' Laura said calmly. 'Who was it? Didn't you
take a message?'

Mrs Pawkins looked offended. 'I didn't like to
poke my nose in, if you'll pardon me.'

She'd been afraid of the new machine. Laura
laughed.

'It was a woman's voice,' Mrs Pawkins admitted
suddenly.

'A woman?' The only person Laura could think
of was Clara.

'A foreign woman,' Mrs Pawkins said, and
shrugged on her outdoors coat. Fred Dissop, her
farmer friend, would pick her up at the gate. 'Now,
I've left bread and a nice piece of cheese at the front
of the larder for you. Promise you won't forget it.'

'I promise,' Laura said absently.

Mrs Pawkins put her head back round the door.
'It must have been one of them wrong numbers.'

Laura sat looking at the phone.

She picked up the handset and called Clara's
number in Barum. Rob's voice answered. 'Oh, Rob,
is Clara there?'

'She's out. Taken the kids to the Regal.' Laura
thought she could hear them in the background,
footsteps – then a woman's voice, abruptly cut off.
Not Clara's. Rob must have covered the mouthpiece,
but not quickly enough. 'They've gone to see the
Walt Disney,' came Rob's voice loudly.

Laura pressed the back of her hand against her mouth.

Then she said: 'I just thought I'd call. When does she get back?'

There was a pause, then Rob said honestly: 'You mean, you really don't know?'

'What, I don't— ' Laura listened, but the line went dead.

'Oh no,' she whispered.

Now she found she could cry, because the person she was crying for was not herself.

But Clara was perfectly calm. She sat on her bed in her old room at Paradise House, her legs drawn up under her tartan skirt and her arms around her knees, leaning back against the wall. She looked good, her hair curled in the latest on-the-shoulder style, brushed and glossy. Laura stood by the wardrobe. There had been no hysterics, no sudden rages against Rob.

'How could you live with it?' Laura said.

Downstairs Johnny had found the clockwork gramophone. Perdie and Andrew were singing to 'I've got a Luvverly Bunch of Coconuts' without a care in the world. The contralto trilling was muffled as Sybil closed the hall door.

'They are in love,' Clara said. 'My husband and his doxy are in true love, so they say. I was wrong, it is important. He met her on that Plymouth course during the war and I suppose I have been pretty irrelevant. It's so bloody humiliating not to have realized. Rob and I got on well enough, and we were good parents. Why me? I knew he'd had other women before but that was just . . . you know. Then I discovered I'd been living in the dark for years

– they can't live without each other, and so on.
When her husband died she moved up to Barum and
I saw them in the street. It was Rob's lunch hour.
She isn't pretty or anything, she's bloody ordinary,
except when she looks at him and then you can see
there's something. And in him too. I wish I could
have given it to him.'

'Clara, I'm so sorry.'

'Oh, I've got the kids, he's got the house, we'll
come to the usual arrangement, both of us will get
a share of nothing.' For the first time she sounded
bitter, and smiled brightly to cover it. She must
secretly hope for a reconciliation however much she
denied it.

'Wouldn't you rather stay at Watersmeet Manor?'
Laura offered.

'Mother needs me more,' Clara said reprovingly.
'She could hardly cope in this place alone, you
know. I've put the kids in your old room, hope you
don't mind. Of course, you're moving away from
us, aren't you?'

'Yes.' Laura fiddled with the wardrobe door and
it swung half open. 'You know I've always wanted
to. I can't make my career here.'

'And now I've come back.' Clara shook her head,
then jumped up and looked in the half-open door
at her old pile of stories, neatly tied up with string,
stored on the wardrobe floor. 'You didn't throw
them out after all. The Gondwana stories.' She
looked tenderly at Laura. 'You idiot. You always
were the romantic one.'

'Nonsense,' Laura said.

'Yes, you.' Clara closed the door. 'So you really
do think you can leave our valley.'

Laura didn't say *you did*. Clara had come back.

She wondered if Johnny, Perdie and Andrew whispered childish secrets alone on the dark stairs at night, and knew to skip the sixth step. But all that was past too.

'There's nothing to keep me here now,' Laura said. It had started to rain, and when she went into the corridor she could hear the water running in the gutters. Clara stood under the electric light in the centre of the room, her hair and shoulders brilliant, her face shadowed.

She said: '*Did* you learn to forget him?'

Laura said: 'Who?'

The kids came spilling out of the playroom downstairs, and Johnny swung Andrew up for the privilege of riding Laura's back like a mahout.

When Laura got back to Watersmeet Manor, she could hear the phone ringing even through the rain-starred glass. She hung up Blackbird's haynet and gave her a bucket of water in the stable. When she came out the phone was still ringing. She splashed across the yard, stood wiping her boots on the doormat. She crossed the hall picking straw out of her wet hair, then rubbed her hands down her thighs to clean them.

Then she picked up the receiver between rings and placed it against her ear. 'Yes?'

The line buzzed and a woman's accented voice came through, sounding very far away, very foreign. 'This is the United States calling.'

Laura picked up a pencil and put it down.

The transatlantic operator continued: 'I'm placing a person-to-person call to Lady Laura Pervane.'

'Yes,' Laura said.

The line clicked.

'Laura, it's Jerry.'

She could imagine his smile. He'd lost some of his drawl and his voice sounded deeper, more authoritative. All he said was: 'Am I wasting my time?'

She looked out at the rain.

'Francis is dead.'

There was a pause.

'That's pretty tragic,' came Jerry's voice, but he didn't bother her with condolences. 'I made you a promise, Laura.'

'I remember.'

One day I'll be rich as hell, rich as sin, and then I'll give it all up for you and come back for you. He was saying he was still in love with her.

'It's done,' he said.

He was a free man.

'Now you know how much you mean to me,' he said. 'You are my life.'

She lifted her free hand calmly through her hair, spattering raindrops on to her desk.

'Laura?'

'Yes, Jerry.'

'I want you to be my wife.'

She swallowed.

The line crackled. At last he had to ask: 'Are you still there?'

'Yes, I'm still here.'

'Am I wasting my time?'

'I don't know. I've got to see you.'

'I'm coming back for you, Laura,' Jerry said. 'Do you understand? It's all arranged. I've burned my boats for you. Don't duck out on your responsibilities. I love you.' He waited. 'Laura?'

'Yes.'

'Am I wasting my time?'

She looked around her; she listened to the rain pressing in close around the house, the age-rippled portrait of Phineas standing beside the misty window.

'No,' she said. 'No, you aren't wasting your time.'

He laughed aloud with relief.

'I'm alone, Jerry.' she said.

'Listen,' he told her, 'I can't be quite free until the end of summer but then— '

All Laura's hopes were dashed. 'I can't wait. I've got to see you. I don't know if I— '

'Listen, listen,' he whispered, so that she had to strain to catch his voice. 'Even if you'd said no . . . I would have come over. I've been trying and trying to get through . . . I took the Pullman down from Maine. I'm phoning you from Pier 90, New York. The *Queen Elizabeth* sails tonight, I'll be with you in six days.' He drew a breath. 'Just give me a chance. I've got business in London but I'll come to you first. I want to see you all dressed up.' She thought they could meet in London, or Southampton perhaps, but the line clicked. 'I'll see you at the Watersmeet Falls Hotel,' his voice said earnestly. The connection went *pip-pip-pip*, then emitted a steady burring sound, the dialling tone.

Laura stood holding the handset. Then she replaced it and stood looking down at her hands flat on the desk.

On Monday morning Clara walked the kids from

Paradise House past the Manor grounds to catch the Lynmouth school bus. She was worried about how they'd get on in their first day at the new school. Laura went out and waited with them, the boys looking awkward in their new caps and smart blue blazers, Perdie kicking at the hem of her long grey skirt just as Laura used to do. Laura kept glancing at Clara, dying to tell her about Jerry. It was difficult to imagine Rob being such a fool as to leave the attractive woman Clara had blossomed into in her middle age. The soft, modern clothes styles she wore suited her tall frame, she dressed simply and without show. Men had no sense. Her hair was lovely, and she was keeping it properly permed and salon-styled in case Rob turned up. Since her return Clara had got close with Sybil, softening the old woman up, getting her to do most of the household chores -- which Clara used to do – while Clara worked upstairs on her mysterious project. Laura reckoned it was just long letters to Rob. Clara had always been sentimental. Any realistic hopes she had of a reconciliation must be fading, surely.

They watched the kids get on the bus, and stood waving in the road.

'I miss my house,' Clara confided. 'I miss my road with the trees along the side, and people washing their cars. I know it must sound silly to you.'

'It isn't silly.'

'I hope Andrew doesn't eat all his sandwiches before lunchtime,' Clara worried. 'He does miss his dad.'

Why didn't the silly woman think of herself sometimes?

'I think I'm in love,' Laura said.

'I've known that for years.' Clara turned and they walked slowly back together towards the clapper bridge.

'I met a man in the war,' Laura said quietly. 'You didn't know about him, his name is Jerry. It's serious. I know I've had other men before but that was just . . . I've never slept with Jerry. He'd do anything for me. He was married but now he's divorced. He loves me, he did it for me. It shows he does love me and he does care about me.'

Clara leaned on the railing. 'And it's him you're going to leave us for.'

'He lives in America.'

'I see. What a long way away.'

Laura was anxious to explain. 'I can't sell Watersmeet Manor because of the commonage provision, but there's nothing in the covenant to say I can't give it away to an organization that will look after it, like the National Trust. I checked. They took over part of the Acland estate. The jewellery business is too big for local money to take on, but one of the London chains will.'

'True love.' Clara dropped a stalk of grass into the water. 'It's nice to be proved right for once.'

Laura frowned.

Seeing her expression, Clara laughed. 'I told you, you are the romantic one, you always did think you could get whatever you wanted. Look, do you mind if I borrow the car this afternoon to pick up the kids? I promised to take them to see the goats at the Valley of the Rocks.'

'You might as well take it now.' The keys were in the Jaguar's ignition. Laura stood listening to the sound of the engine fading between the trees, then walked back to the house along the river path. The sun would rise above the hillsides soon, and the still air promised a hot day. She saddled Blackbird, already wishing she hadn't let Clara take the car, and rode over to her farm at Higher Lyn. To increase its value she had recently invested in the top-of-the-range Fordson tractor with hydraulics and a power take-off. It had transformed the way the organization was run and made everyone realize that the old fields were far too small. Silas had retired and the new man, Dissop, was using the hydraulic backhoe to adjust the Saxon hedgerows. Bart would have been furious. Two Australian girls on a walking holiday waved to Laura and asked her the way to St Brendan's. Coaches carrying German tourists inched carefully down Countisbury Hill in the distance, the sun sparkling off their windows.

Laura stared across the valley, then rode down into the shadows and up the other side into the sunlight again.

To her inexperienced eye the round house looked almost complete. It was formidable what he had achieved – if only it had been worth achieving, this clinging to the past. And he had deliberately done it without her, denying her. She rode round: the oak door was hung, the windows glazed, the rough stones carefully pointed. Only a few roofslates were left stacked on the ground for when the circle of joists was complete – she saw him working to hand-form the last joist with an old-fashioned adze, a monumental task, and pointless in the age of circular saws. His figure seemed so small toiling against the vast backdrop of hills. He didn't know about Jerry.

* * *

391

Jerry said: 'I mean to have you, Laura.'

The evening air lay like a caress across her naked shoulders.

'I came three thousand one hundred eighty-nine miles across the ocean for you,' Jerry said.

The evening was as warm and still as only Lynmouth evenings, trapping the heat of the day between the hills, knew how to be. The tide was rising soundlessly to cover the beach and the lobster boats were returning up the harbour channel, each dumpy hull towing black ripples and a flurry of white seagulls across the motionless sea. Lovers of all ages walked by the water, and a terrier yapped at something trapped in one of the deep rocky pools, probably a skate, the troubled surface stirring and swirling. Soon the tide would cover the place.

He murmured: 'You're more beautiful than ever.' Her dress was off the shoulder in deep saffron yellow, the skin of her shoulders creamy white, the scent of her intoxicating. With her black hair swept back, the effect had stunned him. And the gold bracelet gleaming with rubies around her wrist was very plainly real.

She gave him a relaxed glance, enjoying herself. An Englishman would still have been talking about the weather.

'Ellis Medical Supplies' turnover nudged three hundred thousand last year,' Jerry told her. 'We cover the state. After Fed and State taxes I took home better than twelve thousand dollars . . .'

When she'd arrived at the Watersmeet Falls Hotel Jerry had been in the bar, absently popping olives. He'd stared at her, looked again, then exclaimed and run to her across the foyer, buttoning his sky-blue jacket. He stood looking into her eyes, holding both her hands.

'Laura, it's so good to see you! When you were late— ' he bit his tongue – 'I thought I'd sit where I could see you. I was early.' The social words tumbled out of him; but the yearning pain she saw in his eyes affected her most. He held her elbows and kissed her cheek. 'Oh God, you look great,' he said at last.

His wide white smile was just the same, and the lights in his unwavering blue eyes. 'You've put on weight,' she said, tapping her knuckles against his tummy.

'You're just finding fault. Ten pounds.'

'Twenty.'

'Okay!' There was an intolerance, an impatience about him that was fresh. A confidence in himself and his prosperity that she liked. He knew exactly what he wanted: he wanted her. That was when they walked out on to the patio and she looked at the sea, and he just looked at her. He didn't care where he was when he was with Laura, and she liked that too. When he went into the bar to order her drink she just stood there in the calm evening, listening to the rushing river.

He brought her a cocktail, the Watersmeet Falls Hotel was rare in having ice. He drank a cheap mild beer he'd got a taste for in the war, or maybe long ago. His sandy hair was cropped just as short. She let the silence between them draw out.

He said: 'She's gone, Laura.' And *this* was what made his face most interesting: those tiny bitter lines that his unhappiness and his struggle to succeed had bitten around his eyes and mouth. 'Beverly's gone, and I'm free,' he said. 'And by God, I do not know if I have done right.' He looked at her for a sign, and Laura did not give him one. 'I'm going to diet,' he said, 'I want to, I'm going to beat it.'

'What does your mother think, Jerry?' she asked quietly.

'We don't talk much.'

Laura said: 'You broke her heart.'

'I'm still a believer. I believe in you.'

She sucked the lemon from her drink. 'Let's eat,' she suggested.

He took her arm and again buttoned up his jacket as they walked through to the dining room: his silly pot belly embarrassed him, but not that he was the only man not dressed up in a dinner jacket. Few men as aware of themselves as Jerry were that tough. When the maître d' seated them at the best table Jerry grinned across the tablecloth at Laura with infectious good humour. He touched the silver damascene pitcher.

'My English rose, I love your thorns. You're quite right. The end of the affair was not painless. Satisfied?'

With a bow the maître d' offered him the menu and wine list but Laura waved them away. 'Fresh lobster with salad,' she ordered. 'And ask the wine waiter to prepare a bottle of Pouilly-Fuisse.'

'I can eat a dozen oysters,' Jerry said, forestalling her by raising his hand. 'I know, there's no R in the month, so I'll take Portuguese.' He even pronounced them Portugooses, like a joking Englishman, and made her laugh for the first time, as he had intended. He'd come a long way.

'We're still in love, aren't we?' he said.

'Give me time, Jerry.'

'Time,' he whispered earnestly, 'I served six busy years without you to get where I am now.'

The wine waiter, the little silver tasting-cup hanging on a chain around his neck, bowed to Laura and presented the wine bottle. Jerry tested its temperature with his hand. 'That's okay.'

'Everything I've done, I've done for you,' Jerry said, fixing her with his pushy blue gaze. 'I won't take no for an answer.' He clinked her glass. 'To us.'

The black windows held their reflections, glasses raised.

As they sipped the floodlights came on outside, illuminating the rushing white water below the hotel where the salmon leapt and flashed silver as they struggled upstream to mate and die. She ran her fingertips around the rim of her glass.

'So you've got your Pontiac in the drive now.'

'Cadillac,' he said. 'Impressed?'

'I have a Jaguar.'

He gave a bark of laughter. 'Let's run away tonight!' he said.

The lobster salad arrived, and the distraction gave them both time to recover. 'I didn't mean literally tonight. I do know what I want. I want you.' He held her hand as she picked up her fork. 'I love you, Laura. I treasure you.'

She didn't reply.

He said: 'Is it because there's . . . there isn't anyone else?'

'Good God, no!' She withdrew her hand and covered his. 'No. Of course not.'

'For you, I can change myself into a dinner jacket

like a chameleon . . .' He held his arms over his head as though to perform a trick.

'That's the last thing I want,' she said.

Jerry's smile was that of a man on ice so thin that his slightest movement might break it under him.

'Come with me,' he said.

She tried to make him understand. 'There's so much to do, so much to arrange . . .'

'I've lost everything for you, Laura.'

They ate unhappily. Of course he was right, but it was such a big step. He waved for their plates to be taken away. They both shook their heads at the pudding trolley.

'Let's talk outside,' he said. They walked by the river, which away from the hotel floodlights they could not see, only hear running beside them in the darkness.

'The more you hurt me the more I love you, Laura.'

'I don't mean to.'

'You *do*.' The street lamp on the bridge gleamed across his eyes as he looked at her. 'We both know the score, you can't have it all ways. You'll lose Watersmeet. But I'm offering you a whole new world.'

'I know,' she sighed.

'It's Watersmeet you love, isn't it?'

'I've never heard such rubbish!'

He said: 'Let me kiss you.'

She was looking down. He put one finger under her chin.

'Let me kiss you.'

'It's all got so terribly earnest and serious between

them,' Clara told Laura, flicking her cigarette ash into her saucer, 'though she does have lovely legs, I suppose.' In Clara's mind that explained everything. She knew in her heart Rob was never coming back to her.

'Another cup of tea, Laura?' Sybil said, putting off the rug from her lap and getting up from her rattan summer chair. Above them rain pattered on the solarium roof. 'What filthy weather. I don't recall a summer like it.' She waved the teapot.

Laura realized that the cup in her lap was still full, the two sweet biscuits lying untasted in the saucer. 'I'm sorry, I haven't finished this one.'

Clara stubbed out her half-smoked cigarette and lit another, looking at Laura.

'I'm putting the farm up for auction, lock, stock and barrel,' Laura said. 'I'm already in negotiation to sell Pervane's to a national jewellery chain. I'll be keeping the Watersmeet Falls Hotel.'

'Memories,' Clara said.

'The National Trust have expressed an interest in Watersmeet Manor.'

'All this, just to run away with a common salesman,' Clara said.

'I'm sorry for you, Clara,' Laura told her, and there was a silence.

'I hope she takes Rob for every penny he's got,' Sybil said.

'I don't blame him,' Clara said. 'I know it sounds silly but I want Rob to be happy.'

'You have the children to think of.'

'Yes, let's think about them,' Clara said brightly, 'and Laura, and everyone, but not me.' She made to stub out her cigarette, then noticed she had only smoked a few puffs. 'So lover boy has rushed back to America. He's still ditching his first wife, I gather.'

'I don't think this weather is ever going to stop,' Sybil said.

Laura insisted: 'Jerry Ellis and I will be married in Portland, Maine, in a civil ceremony. It's all arranged. We've set the date for September the first.'

'What if he's still married?' Clara said.

Laura said coolly: 'That's only a matter of finalization.'

'Finalization,' Clara said, 'I love that word. It's so romantic.'

'We very much hope you'll both come over and see us.'

'We'd *love* to,' Clara said. 'It is love, isn't it?' She got up so suddenly that Laura flinched, but Clara went the other way, and they heard her feet pounding up the stairs, not running, walking.

'I feel so sorry for her,' Sybil said. 'It's a difficult time. Why don't you go up to her?'

'No,' Laura said.

That night as she worked in her study she saw, for the first time, a light above the trees. The round house was inhabited.

She shivered. As July turned into August, the evenings were already beginning to draw in, to grow cold.

He must know about Jerry by now. If he'd any secret hopes, they'd been dashed. Bart must know, too, about Laura's departure, the signs were clear enough. The farm auction had been attended by a huge crowd, the buyer was an agent representing a consortium of City interests who promised to keep Fred Dissop on as the tenant, and not to break up the land for sale in different lots.

So Bart knew that it was almost too late, but still she didn't see him.

She walked by the river where she had often chanced to see him before.

He must know, too, that the National Trust had agreed to take over Watersmeet Manor and the covenanted lands. Francis, Sir George and all the Pervanes had schemed to possess the valley entirely for themselves; instead Watersmeet would belong to everyone. Even the furniture would be preserved tidily in its present arrangement, the sofa kept here with the armchairs facing it *just so*, an administration of ghosts. Groups of tourists would be led down roped-off walkways by uniformed guides. For a minute or two they'd pause at the great windows to glance at the Hoaroak Water splashing down to meet the East Lyn river. Anonymous visitors would gather on the lawns for Devon cream teas, and excited children Laura would never know would play and hunt for tiddlers in the dappled, ankle-deep streams. Francis would have been appalled, but he had brought it down on himself: all for love.

Laura sat on the sofa with the lights out, a whisky glass in her hand, the drink stinging her mouth. She put it down unfinished, shrugged on a cardigan and stood outside. The black trees and hills rose around her in every direction. High above, a single light burned.

She walked across to the garage and got in the

car. The engine started first turn. She drove up to the county road to Hillsford Bridge, then stopped to engage first gear for the gravel track that led into Hellebore Woods, and followed the tunnel the headlights made beneath the overhanging branches. It was the first time she had ever driven up here. She peered through the windscreen, wiping away the mist of her breath on the glass.

Where Hellebore House had been, even the grassy mounds and banks of nettles were disappearing beneath saplings and new foliage as the forest regenerated. The car ground to a halt. She killed the lights and walked. The round house seemed to grow out of the trees: the second-floor windows glowed with orange candlelight. A figure crossed the glass. It was Clara.

'You've been crying,' Clara said. It was morning and she stood on the top step of the stairs at Paradise House. The rain drummed on the sloping roof above their heads. Laura's hair hung in tails.

'You aren't so beautiful now,' Clara said slowly. 'I'm sorry. You brought it on yourself.' She held out her hand. '*It's your fault.*'

Laura put back her hair. 'I was going to wait until the rain stopped.'

'I understand,' Clara said.

Downstairs Sybil was cooking breakfast for the children, the old woman taking pleasure in her new responsibilities. They could hear the bacon frying and its warm, cheerful smell drifted incongruously around them on the stairs.

'Well, you'd better come up,' Clara said.

Laura followed her to the bedroom. The sound of

the rain was louder here. Notebooks lay open on the dressing table. The bitch was writing her Gondwana stories. Clara followed Laura's eyes, but made no attempt to hide her work.

She closed the door and leaned back on it.

'He's kind,' she said.

Laura stared at the sprawled papers without seeing them.

'Bart doesn't love you,' she said, 'he's just using you. How can you be so blind?'

'I want to be blind,' Clara said.

Laura was too hurt to speak.

'I have found happiness,' Clara said gently.

'For one night!' Laura turned in a circle. 'For a night or two.'

'He doesn't mean anything to you. You said so.'

'I hate him.'

'For a night, or for ever. What does it matter? For me it's enough.'

'You're lying!' Laura said.

'Can't you get it into your head? Clara told her. 'What passed between us is none of your business.'

Laura stared at her with a rigid face.

'If you want money and fame you've got to give everything for it,' Clara said. 'You knew.'

So he had not learned about Jerry from just anyone; he had heard it from Clara's lips, Laura realized.

They stood on opposite sides of the room, listening to the rain.

Laura was to meet Jerry at the Watersmeet Falls Hotel. He would arrive, having come by train from Heathrow airport and hired a car at Barum, during the evening of 15 August. At Watersmeet Manor that morning Joe Spanson's workmen had arrived to cover the furniture with dustsheets. With inches to spare he'd manoeuvred the lorry that would remove Laura's personal possessions across the clapper bridge and now it was blocking the drive. Laura had a canopy rigged from the porch to the rear of the vehicle to keep the worst of the rain off the men doing the loading, and made them put down sheets to protect her carpets from their clumping boots. The lorry had to be moved so that the dealer who had arrived to collect the Jaguar could get out, and the lorry's rear wheels sank promptly into the sodden lawn. The Jaguar dodged precariously around another car approaching the bridge; a worried-looking head in round tortoiseshell spectacles was stuck out of the Austin's window, but the Jaguar had already shot out of sight into the filaments of cloud drifting along the valley wall. The workmen were still heaving the lorry out of the rutted grass. The bonfire Joe had started earlier to burn the rubbish was making nothing but smoke that drifted around them beneath the dripping trees. Sweating and straining, splattered with the red mud churned up by the spinning wheels, Joe's men rocked the vehicle back on to the drive at last. The man in the Austin had to park by the stable, where Blackbird had stuck her head out to watch. He ducked under her neck, then approached Laura with his hand outstretched. 'Enjoying ourselves?'

'You must be Peter.'

'What absolutely frightful weather, isn't it?'

The expert on English country houses sent by the National Trust wore a plum-coloured sweater beneath his jacket. Laura showed him around. Peter carried a book of contents in which he noted such things as the particular Waterford glass used by the Baroness Le Clement de Taintegnies, handling it as preciously as though it were a reliquary. He attached a label to the trunk of the Spanish Camellia. He admired the gambrels and mullions of the old part of the house, but the modern part wasn't his period. While he scribbled notes beneath his mackintosh Laura's spirits sank, he was so intensely clever. She didn't know how to tell him about the summerhouse that had once stood where the tree now was, or how she could show him the shallow pool where Francis Pervane had knelt on the stones to plight his troth to her, for ever. She and this young expert didn't speak the same language. Going upstairs, he clicked his teeth with professional excitement at Laura's nineteenth-century bed: did she know those faded hangings were very possibly by Horace Vernet?

The original curved Adam doors in the gallery absorbed him. Laura wandered on. The dome echoed with the shouts of Joe Spanson's men, the din of hammers – the personal china was being packed into square crates, the few pictures she was taking stacked in flat boxes. She found herself in the study and stood there alone. She was saying farewell: she could almost hear Sir George's arthritic fingers struggling to conjure melody from the old keyboard instruments.

Peter came in and tapped the desk with his pen. 'Directoire.' He wrote it down in his book, the men carrying out the filing cabinets working around him.

Laura looked up at the portrait of Phineas Pervane, and Peter came over. 'Anyone we know?'

'No,' she said. 'No one.' The room stank of bonfire smoke as the wind eddied. Joe Spanson came in apologetically waving his hand in front of his face.

'This painting's no good, the proportions are all wrong,' Peter said, then peered more closely. 'I say— '

'Burn it,' Laura said suddenly, stepping back. She couldn't bear it any more. 'Joe, take it out and burn it.'

'Now, you can't possibly do that,' Peter said.

Joe stared at him then turned without a word, bunched his shoulders, and lifted the picture off the wall.

'Excuse me,' Peter said, 'I think that's a Brett – my God, I think it's a Hughes— '

'Get yur hand off me,' Joe said. He looked Laura in the eye. 'What you'm want done with this 'un, lady?'

'Burn it,' Laura said.

Joe took it out, and Peter stared at Laura. They heard the crackle of flames.

'It's all in the past,' Laura said. 'Just a love story.'

Peter ran outside and tried to snatch pieces of burning canvas out of the fire. Finally he gave up and just stood there with the smoke eddying around him, his suit drenched by the rain, staring into the smouldering pile.

'It was a Hughes,' he told Laura. Joe Spanson took his elbow.

'It wasn't real,' Laura said, 'only a lie. It doesn't exist.'

Joe Spanson jiggled the expert's elbow warningly. 'You'm heard the lady,' he growled, and then the Austin drove away, spraying gravel.

Laura went into the orangery, only to sit for a moment, then wearily closed her eyes. She basked in the stored warmth, listening to the rain rattle on the glass, the scent of ripening fruit around her. She made a mental note to leave Sybil a key and tell her to pick these oranges, lemons and peaches before they rotted away. As she got up to go she heard water insistently trickling, and realized the cellars were flooding. It was none of her affair now. She heard the lorry's tailgate slam and stood on the porch.

'We'm finishing,' Joe called. He looked at her, concerned. 'Drop you at the hotel, lady?'

Blackbird whinnied. 'I'm riding the horse back to my mother's,' Laura said. Blackbird would return to her old home beneath the clock at Paradise House until Laura decided whether to send for her. 'I'll walk down to the village.'

'It's a pretty walk, that,' one of the men said, who often took his children along the river path on Sunday afternoons.

Joe Spanson shook her hand and said goodbye.

Laura watched the lorry sway across the bridge. The smooth slope of water sluicing between the spans was breaking into foam. The horn tooted cheerfully and a hand waved back as the lorry turned up towards the county road, and was lost to her sight in a few seconds in the trees and rain.

She went back inside and put on her black waterproof cape, with a white silk scarf to stop the oiled cloth chafing her neck. She looked around her for the last time, then pulled the door closed and turned the key, locking herself outside Watersmeet Manor.

She rode Blackbird out of the Manor gates, but as they slammed behind her she reined in, pausing on the path to Paradise House. Blackbird stamped and pranced. Then Laura pulled on the right rein, sending the horse galloping across the lawns down to the river, across, and up into the woods on the far side.

He was sitting in his doorway at the top of the steps to his house. She didn't see him at first against the shadowed interior. His folded arms were bare, his elbows on his knees, and his hair was soaked. She jumped down and tucked the reins behind one of the stirrup-leathers.

'I can't see your eyes,' he called.

She came over and stood looking up at him, rainwater pattering from her broad hat-brim down her smooth, caped back, raindrops sliding down her cheeks.

'Did you?'

He didn't answer.

'Clara lied to me,' she said.

Rain dripped from her nose and chin, the lobes of her ears.

He must have been made of stone.

'She didn't lie,' he said.

Blackbird cropped the grass between the tree trunks. Beyond the round house the smooth low cloud was a grey lid pressing down over the valley. The bumpy skyline and the tall treetops were quite gone, and the rain hissed in the grass around them. She wanted to scream.

'You are beautiful,' Bart said in his lost voice. He was the only one who saw her as she really was.

'You know what I feel for you. And you love no other man but me.'

'Will you let her come up here in the rain?'

'I love you.'

'If that's true you know what you'll do.'

But he'd never leave.

She said: 'Will you hurt her too?'

'Yes.'

He stood up and came down into the full force of the rain and held out his hand to Laura.

She didn't let him touch her, because she knew her willpower would evaporate, and her life would go by. He dropped his hand to his side.

But he wanted nothing of her if he could not have all of her.

She took off her hat. The drops coursed down her naked face.

'Believe in me,' she said.

He swept out his arms against the immense natural panorama of clouds and hills around them.

She shook her head, willing him to comprehend her.

'Bart, come with me.'

'Go to your other man,' he told her quietly.

For a moment he thought she would stay.

God, she was beautiful: the real Laura, the one she denied.

Then she shook her head. He still didn't believe she'd really go.

Blackbird's hoof clanged on something buried in the grass and Laura looked down. It was the fallen gate: ADSUM. Here I stand.

She turned in the saddle, looked back through the

glowing cloud-mist between the trees. Only the rain.

For the last time she followed the path down to the spiked gate, pausing with her hand on the cold iron, then turned and looked back, but he did not appear, and their last chance was gone.

She let the gate clang shut by itself behind her.

Above Prideau's Pool the stepping stones stood out of the water like dark, gleaming Christmas puddings, each fronted by a creamy fountain of foam. As Blackbird scrambled up the riverbank the lights of Paradise House stood out of the sheeting rain. Laura put Blackbird in the stable and wiped her down, then crossed the drive.

'You look like a drowned woman,' Sybil greeted her in the porch.

Laura shook the water off. 'It's only rain. It can't last much longer.'

'I've seen the river flood much higher than this,' Sybil said. 'In 1924 the water covered the stepping stones.' She stood aside. 'Come in, dear.' But behind her at the top of the stairs Laura could see Clara, just standing there with inkstained fingers, not moving.

'I don't think so,' Laura said.

'Perhaps it's for the best,' Sybil said. 'The children have got awful colds.'

'Yes,' Laura said. 'I'm sorry I can't say goodbye to them.'

Sybil was almost crying.

'Come and see me, in a little while,' Laura said. She couldn't reach out to her mother.

She knew as soon as Sybil closed the door behind her Clara would return to her room, sit at the dressing table and happily pop a boiled sweet in her mouth, and continue the latest chapter of her wonderful, imaginary world.

'Don't go,' Sybil whispered.

'I'll write you,' Laura said.

Sybil pressed her dry, papery hands over Laura's, blessing her, or begging her not to leave. Nearly everything between them was without words. They spoke only of unimportant things. Neither of them said goodbye.

Laura waved back from the trees, then the door closed.

She followed the footpath over the high ground to Watersmeet Manor.

She found the rain had put the bonfire out; the melting ash stained the gravel with trickling black fingers in the fading light. The streaming waterfalls of the Hoaroak glowed tea-coloured with peat chafed from the high plateau of the Chains where Bart had hidden out so many years ago.

She stood looking up at Hellebore Cleave through the driving rain to the darkening lid of cloud.

He didn't love her.

She turned and walked north beside the river towards Lynmouth and the sea, and freedom.

Bart Barronet stood staring from the window, at the grey cloud beyond the streaming glass.

Watersmeet was hidden.

Somewhere far below him, he knew, the woman he loved was walking away along the valley he loved, to the sea. She was walking out of his life, and he knew that she would go through with it, if he didn't go after her.

Watersmeet: the flash of a salmon's scales, a

buzzard spilling and stooping from the blinding skyline. His heart's neighbourhood.

Again he looked out of the window. The rain worried him. He had never known such a long, heavy downpour in the middle of August.

Laura really was going to leave. He couldn't imagine living without her.

He put on his maroon overcoat and pulled on his boots, then turned up his collar and went out into the rain. The fog that pressed around him seemed solid, made of wet sponge. He splashed across to the toolshed and found a tarpaulin, and holding it over his head for protection sloshed his way down the drive, now a yellowish rippling stream.

Coming out between the ancient gateposts, he peered over the edge of the cliff.

Through the misty circle of rocks revealed far below him, the Hoaroak was running broader in its jagged channel than he ever remembered, the waterfalls falling slowly away from him in waves. In those ochre columns he glimpsed tumbling black flecks that must be twigs and small tree branches swept along on the flood. Lucy's Pool was clotted with debris.

Darkness hung in the fog up to the south, over the deep moorland of the Chains: the centre of the storm. Bart stared, the rain trickling down his face, understanding perfectly what was happening.

He splashed down the track to the iron-tipped gate that marked the limits of his property, knocked it open with his elbow, and left it swinging behind him.

The lower he descended in search of Laura, the

more water came rushing past him from the slopes above. The track began sliding away like a torrent, and when the wind stirred the treetops the forest deluged enormous drops on him from the sodden canopy of summer leaves.

Had Laura taken shelter at Paradise House?

He could see the Lyn river below him now, looking slow and solid, almost syrupy in its flow downstream over the boulders, the remnants of old landslides from the cliffs, that partially blocked its bed. Normally the river wended its way peacefully between these obstacles to form the pleasant pools at Prideau's and Dumbledon, but today only the peaks of the boulders showed, each trailing a huge fan of disturbed water.

He slid down the slope. Nothing remained of the stepping stones but a line of white fountains stretching away from him. Below them the overfall to Prideau's Pool dropped away, breaking into a white race of spray. The manila hand-rope was snagging in the current, snatching to and fro in great leaps above the fountains.

Beyond them, on the far side, he could see the lights of Paradise House.

He belted the tarpaulin around his waist, and water sprayed around him as he swung across.

On the other side he stood for a moment cooling his rope-burned hands on his knees, breathing deeply. Then water flowed over his boots. The river was backing up, overflowing the grassy banks, lapping at the smooth lawns.

It was growing dark, the cloud rising above the southern skyline showing absolutely black over the vivid green treetops.

He ran past the stable to Paradise House and hammered on the door. 'Laura?'

Clara opened it.

'We're so frightened,' she said.

'Is Laura here?'

She grasped at him, not answering.

'No,' Sybil said, 'she's gone.'

Clara said: 'She's *gone*, can't you understand?'

He stared at her.

Clara said: 'You've lost her, Bart. This is what it feels like.' Her face wrinkled.

The trees had almost lost their colour, standing like grey sentinels under the black sky. It was no longer possible to say where the lawns ended or the river began.

Clara held out her hands to him.

Sybil said clearly: 'Laura has gone back to Watersmeet Manor. She's probably sheltering there.'

'Phone her,' Bart said. 'The Manor's only a few feet above the river, you can see how it's rising, she'll be in danger.'

'Oh, don't be ridiculous.' But Sybil went to the telephone on the armoire, then put down the receiver after holding it to her ear for a moment.

'Oh,' she said.

The lights went out, and the hall seemed very dark.

'Where are your children?' came Bart's voice.

'Leave them alone,' Clara said. 'What's got into you?'

Now they clearly heard the roar of the river. Where the lawn had been rose a mass of jostling waves carrying a tide of debris with them, twigs and dirty foam, even a bumping tree branch.

'It doesn't matter,' Sybil said calmly, 'we have candles.'

Bart retreated down the steps and sheltered his eyes from the rain. The river was still backing up from the narrow section downstream. He didn't believe Paradise House to be in any serious danger, but the stable was already lapped by the river. Blackbird was there.

Bart turned back to the women. 'I can't do any more for you. I won't force you to do what you don't want to, but I advise you to get to higher ground.'

Sybil was calmly lighting a candle. 'You don't seriously believe— ' she said.

The candle's flame cast an orange glow down the side of Clara's face. She broke away from her mother and clung on to Bart with a strength that amazed him.

'I won't lose you a second time,' she whispered. She didn't understand; he loved Laura. Once he found her he would never come back.

'Goodbye, Clara,' he said.

He pushed her away and she put her hands to her face.

Paradise House was an island, the stables half submerged. He could hear Blackbird's panic-stricken whinnying as the water rose in her stall, the thumping of her hooves and the squeaking of the iron ring that secured her bridle rope to the wall. He splashed across and tugged unavailingly at the door. The pressure of the water against the boards on his side had seized the bolt fast. He strained at the unyielding metal, cutting his water-softened fingers on the sharp guides, but still the bolt would not move. Water swirled around his hips.

Then the bolt for the top half of the door, under no strain, slid freely, and pulled open. He heaved himself over the stuck-fast bottom half and found himself plunging forward into a mess of straw-covered water. Blackbird was rearing up, the rope that dragged her down as straight as a bar, eyes rolling, and it was the first time he had heard the odd, keening sound of a horse screaming in fear.

Floodwater poured in over the top of the lower door like water over a weir. He found a spade and hammered at the wood behind the submerged bolt. Splintering, the door gaped wide on inrushing water. Buckets, an empty tin of neatsfoot oil, bits of tackle were swept around him. Bart jumped on the rail of Blackbird's stall and caught her bridle, then laid his face against her eye, breathing over her flared nostrils, calming her. The rope slackened.

He unhitched the knot. Holding her mane firmly with one hand he swung on to her back. Blackbird shot towards the pale square of the doorway. Bart ducked, and then in a burst of spray they were through into the open air.

Where the lawns had been was a wild lake.

His last sight of Paradise House was of the upstairs windows glowing peacefully with candlelight. But his only thought was of Laura.

The path to Watersmeet Manor rose steeply. The pools far below were choked with surging floodwater and a chaos of tree trunks, dead sheep and something, incredibly, that looked like a car, all jammed against the boulders one after the other in a hundred small dams, and still it rained.

Bart slid down from the horse's back at the white

414

gate and stood there for a moment, gazing at the
old manor house silhouetted against the waterfalls,
stroking Blackbird's muzzle and letting her snuffle
his palm with her broad, soft lips.

Then he let go of her.

'Ya!' he shouted, windmilling his arms. 'Go! Go!
Free!'

He stood watching the horse disappear towards
the high ground of Countisbury. When he could no
longer see her black coat moving between the black
trees he knew she was safe, and ran towards the
darkened manor house.

The rain was so hard it was difficult to breathe,
and now he could discern the house as no more
than a pale outline of spray through the cloud-
burst. Part of the garden was a spreading fan of
water, but the curve of the Lyn river around the
house still showed its course in dull white foam,
not yet seriously overflowing in its bed. Beyond,
the Hoaroak Water fell forward in a solid conduit
of spray and the waters met with a thunderous
roar.

Surely Laura was sheltering here. Bart pressed his
hands and face to the orangery window.

For the first and last time since Lucy's vain
attempt to reconcile the families with love, a
Barronet had come to Watersmeet Manor.

He pushed forward with his shoulder and entered
the deserted room in a shower of glass.

'Laura!' he shouted.

Beneath the drumming rain the room was full of
the scent of lemons and oranges. He ran from room
to room, study, lounge, kitchen, calling her name,
then pounding up the stairs, circling the first-floor

gallery knocking open doors. Nothing, only empty rooms and the sound of rain, louder now.

He kicked open the last door. It was her bedroom.

The French windows were open, creaking on their hinges in the wind, letting in the sound of the rain and the river, raindrops spattering the carpet, soaking the curtains, so that the brass curtain rail was bent into a visible curve by their weight.

Beyond, he saw the rain-drenched vista of trees rising into the clouds towards Hellebore, and understood her.

He held his arms wide to shut the doors, but the wet wood had swollen. The landscape began to change: the great sequoia tree, with a full head of leaf, was leaning. Its roots came pulling one by one out of the lawn like fingers. As the trunk tilted and slowly fell outward the boughs and branches impacted the river's surface in a white explosion. The water piled up against the obstruction, then sluiced in a crescent across the gardens, swilling against the walls of the Manor. The empty house groaned.

Bart ran downstairs. Had Laura taken the county road or the river path? If she was walking the river way, then when the log-jam damming the cliffs by Dumbledon Pool collapsed, releasing its backed-up flow in a huge wave, she would be in terrible danger.

He tried to think like her: the road, or the river she knew and loved, however much she denied it?

The river.

If he crossed the river and ran down the county road, he could make up for lost time, call a warning down to her. Much of Watersmeet gorge had walls of sheer cliff, but there were ways to climb down, or pull her up.

He searched in the kitchen for a torch, dragging out the bare drawers on to the floor, leaving empty cupboard doors swinging wide. He could hear a strange echoing sound emanating beneath the house, water pouring into the cellars.

He ran to the orangery, its floor disappearing beneath cold swirling water even while its warm air still held the incongruous smell of oranges; he found nothing but a box of wet matches. Then a reek of raw earth came bubbling up from below and Bart sensed the floor dropping as he backed away, subsiding into the network of cellars beneath: Toher's Barrow, the silted-up Stonehenge of greywether stones long buried, long lost beneath the Manor, long forgotten, though not by the Barronets.

The floor of the Victorian orangery built by Roderick Pervane collapsed into the hidden labyrinth below. The sturdy iron posts distorted, popping, then the glass panes burst inward and came showering down in a sparkling, lethal cloud through the gloom, but Bart was already gone.

He left the front doors hanging wide in his victory, and splashed across the yard to the stable. In the corner, behind a sack tossed over a nail, a forgotten electric lantern swung from its wire handle. He pressed the switch, and a strong white beam lanced through the doorway into the silver curtain of rain. He pushed out into the rainstorm towards the clapper bridge, meaning to cross the river and climb to the county road that clung to the safety of the valley wall above.

In his room at the Watersmeet Falls Hotel, Jerry

glanced impatiently at his Omega wristwatch, for perhaps the hundredth time. He had grown unused to waiting.

He rang down to the desk again. Still no sign of her.

He had flown in by Pan-Am Constellation from New York, a luxurious but long and wearying flight; and then the shabby train journey onwards to Barum, bringing back so many memories of the war with its down-at-heel stations and cheap advertisements, seemed to go on for ever. He had to pay cash to hire a used Morris Minor automobile from the Mercedes garage on the Square.

Suppose she didn't come?

He mixed himself a whisky and parted the curtain with his hand, stood looking down at the river racing under the cold, rational glare of hotel floodlights. The rain was really chucking it down: as shiny as Hollywood chain mail in the beams. The river, fretting ten feet below the top of the deep stone walls that channelled its flow, carried brushwood and brambles down its smooth, swooping slopes of dirty water, so loud he could hardly hear the radio playing by his bed.

The BBC Third Programme was putting out Chopin, Water Music. He chuckled. Sure she'd come. He trusted Laura.

Laura wished she'd brought a torch. She'd thought she knew the path like the back of her hand, but the rain out of the darkness was so heavy that it was frightening. She was somewhere below the hanging woods of Myrtleberry Cleave. Streams of run-off poured down between the tree trunks from

418

the bald catchment of the iron-age fort three hundred feet above her, carrying away moss in great chunks, ripping deep channels in the soft red loam beneath. In the fading light these geysers looked as red and heavy as blood. She ducked beneath them where they spouted across the path, crying out as stones and gravel rattled across her back. Scrambling under the shelter of a fallen tree, she lost her hat and the rough bark snatched her hair-clip. She crouched, feeling the wood tremble as the river's flow tugged its branches.

Ahead, the river started to curve westward, running parallel to the sea hidden behind the high hills. In a short way the path rose; she ran along the crumbling banks and climbed clear of the river's flow.

The stone walls of the county road were holding back the run-off, channelling it down the roadway. The road had turned itself into a huge drain, and the track up to the single break in the wall was a roaring torrent impossible to struggle against.

Laura put up her face to the rain and began to laugh at her predicament, revelling in the power and excitement of nature.

Then light sizzled around her.

Upstream, closer to the storm, the lightning bolt was almost unbearably bright, the crash of thunder immediate. Bart paused with his hand on the iron rail of the clapper bridge, grimacing at the raw tingle of static. Beneath his feet the ten-ton stone slabs of the prehistoric bridge shuddered as a tangle of tree roots rose out of the darkness, and he jumped back barely in time.

He was trapped on the wrong side of the river. He could not get across to the road.

The water rose up his legs even as he dug his heels into the hillside, pushing himself back as the water came after him. The log jam at Dumbledon Pool had broken, the river was a mass of debris sweeping through his lantern beam where the bridge had been.

The Manor was being swept away. Paradise House must already be gone. He put his hands over his ears, blanking out an unbearable devouring noise, and watched the tangle of splintered planks, roof joists, tiles and bricks, remnants of shattered furniture, sliding silently past him in the tumult.

And something else.

It was the body of a woman.

Clara's pale face lay underwater, her body rotating in the flood. Against her stomach she clutched the body of her little girl in her white hands.

Bart pulled himself back as the water dragged at him. The same wave lifted her clear, and whirled her from sight.

Jerry sat at the bar at the Watersmeet Falls Hotel. He was wearing a dinner jacket to please her: he was sure Laura would arrive any minute, her face lighting up to see him as she opened the plate glass door to the foyer, calling across to him with a laugh as she shook out her umbrella. She'd been caught in the rain, nothing a hot bath and a glass of champagne wouldn't put right. He'd kiss her rain-beaded cheek, then her lips.

But still she didn't come.

He waited with the half pint of mild at his elbow, trying to resist a bowl of peanuts. He was nervous, and that always made him want to eat.

He kept looking round.

He took a handful of nuts and went to the phone, popping them into his mouth while the exchange connected him to Watersmeet Manor, but hearing only the hiss of an unobtainable line.

'I arranged to meet her here,' he told the barman.

'Best not to change arrangements once they're made,' Lloyd replied sensibly. Yes; but he didn't love her.

Jerry went to the window and stood there with his hands in his pockets. The river was running high enough that the standing waves almost covered the floodlights. The lines of foam glared in the beams, sending brilliant fans of light marching across the ceiling of the restaurant.

'It's rough out there,' Jerry called to the barman.

'It won't rise any higher, sir,' Lloyd said, polishing a glass, making an irritating squeaking. 'We lost the hydro-electric power several hours ago, but that's as far as it ever goes. The diesel generators— '

Jerry tried the phone again. This time it went completely dead in his hand. Even the hiss stopped.

'Those lights are going to go,' Jerry said, watching the bulbs flicker.

Lloyd was setting out candles along the counter and lighting them. His hands shook.

'Laura's in trouble,' Jerry said.

Then the lights did go out. Lloyd's hands shook so much that he extinguished the match he was holding, and Jerry realized that the man was terrified.

'If she's in trouble,' Jerry said, 'I'm not the man to back out.'

Outside, the rain had ceased. He sniffed the night air.

Jerry noticed one odd thing as he started the car.

Although the rain had stopped the river was still rising.

There was a reason for this.

The Chains caught the first of any rain. Rainfall across the high, flat plateau was always more than twice the Exmoor average, and the valleys running off this grim highland, like Watersmeet, had long been cut sharp and deep by the force of the water. On a sunny day it was difficult to imagine that Cheriton Ridge, for all its height, was merely the gap left uneroded between two streams, the Hoaroak and Farley, which joined at Hillsford Bridge and swept on to fall into the East Lyn river at Watersmeet. That more substantial river, too, was entirely fed by torrents cascading down from the Chains and its associated valley systems.

In tonight's freak cyclonic thunderstorm hundreds of millions of tons of water had fallen over the Chains, five inches in an hour. Lightning flashed through the misty lower layer of rainclouds from the massive thunderheads of the hidden storm above. The Chains was already waterlogged from the earlier rain, and the impermeable layer of iron, Exmoor's prize from prehistoric times, now kept the falling water on the surface. The level moorland turned into a maelstrom of tossing waves like the sea, searching for a way down. These light, foaming waves hissed across the smooth deer-sedge towards the rim as fast as a galloping horse, but the area was vast. It took a little time to get there.

Then the high combes began filling rapidly, the little streams sweeping along tussocks of grass, clumps of sedge, small stones. As the rivers gained weight and power, rocks were added, undergrowth and soil from the collapsing banks, small trees. Sheep and many smaller animals were sucked in as their places of refuge from the rain were carried away.

Lower down, full-grown trees began to fall, carried along like battering rams on the flood, motor cars, masonry, boulders as heavy as a man, all swept along willy-nilly, piling up at any obstacle in their path until it crumbled.

As the rivers frothed down the valley of Watersmeet, the narrowing gorge concentrated the force of the water. The hamlet of Middleham was already gone, all ten houses, no trace remaining. The old hydro-electric power station had been swept away hours ago, the heavy turbines and generators smashed out of the machine-houses like plastic toys. The steeper and narrower the cliffs of the gorge became, the higher the torrent rose up them: a depth of ten feet, now twenty, all roaring along at a speed of more than twenty miles per hour – great oak trees, vans, mangled coaches, fifteen-ton boulders driving through the dark towards Lynmouth.

And still the river rose.

The lantern's beam was fading, yellowing as its age-corroded battery failed. Bart jogged northward along the Horner's Neck path beside the east bank of the river. He whacked the lens against his hand and the bulb flared out brightly again. Where the path dipped down beneath the deadly swirl of the river, he made his own slithering path through the trees, whacking the lens each time the beam failed, but each time it returned more wanly. Finally there was not the faintest glow and the dark, the trees and the roar of the river enclosed him.

He reckoned he was on the outside bend where the river turned parallel to the sea. Everything had changed from what he knew, but he could only think of Laura.

Jerry peered through the Morris Minor's divided windscreen. The wipers clacked annoyingly to and fro, but he couldn't find the switch to turn them off in the dark. Leaves, twigs and running water covered the Watersmeet road as shown in the headlamp beams, and he had to navigate around the occasional tree bough deposited on the roadway like a Charles Atlas arm. The little car slithered on banks of sediment, the tyres throwing up gravel as they span round, the engine howling. Then the Morris would jerk forward, sending brown wings of spray flying in front of the headlamps as it picked up speed. The steering grew very light and vague as the pressure of the water lifted the underneath of the car, but he couldn't make himself slack off on the fast pedal. The destruction exceeded anything he had experienced. He was frightened of losing his nerve.

Jerry was afraid. But he had often been afraid – afraid of his first parachute jump into the darkness behind German lines in Normandy on D-Day, afraid when he and his team defused the booby-traps on the Remagen railway bridge, his fingers trembling on the sparking wires; afraid of losing Laura, of not deserving her. There was no shame in fear, without fear there was no courage. Without love, there was nothing.

Jerry was afraid of having nothing.

The little Morris jolted on a bank of greasy sediment across the road, the motor shuddered and stalled. The car rolled back, crumpling its rear mudguard into the stone wall. He pressed the starter button and the Morris strained without the engine starting; he'd forgotten to take it out of gear. His hands started to tremble. He punched the clutch and thumbed the go button again, the tiny motor grinding and popping but never quite catching, and he knew he'd flooded the carburettor, but he couldn't bring himself to stop.

The engine grunted, stuttered, then revved sweetly and he almost cried with relief. He'd had enough. Maybe Laura could have gotten through to the hotel somehow on her own. But as he turned the car, the bend in the road ahead disappeared in a torrent of filthy water, rolling stones and broken trees. The mass came sliding down the tarmac between the cliff and the stone wall. The car was flung forward into the wall. Staring through the windscreen Jerry thought the impact was surprisingly soft, then realized that was because the wall had given way. There was nothing much for him to see in the headlights, only the dim other side of the gorge. Filthy water was sweeping out past the car, falling into the darkness below, dragging the Morris with it. Jerry tried to open the door to get out but it wouldn't budge, wedged shut by the broken wall. He was trapped. Stones roared across the tin roof like a drum.

Jerry screamed, hanging on to the steering wheel as the front of the car tipped down, standing on the brake pedal with his back arched, seeing nothing whatsoever now through the windscreen as the Morris was propelled forward and fell into empty space.

The rising water had almost caught Laura at the closed-up stone building which housed the Lynrock Mineral Water Company. Now she scrambled up the path towards the Lynrock footbridge, finding her way along the streaming cliff by touch.

Lynrock Bridge was gone

Though sturdily constructed fifteen feet above the floor of the gorge, of rough-hewn beams bolted to six-inch iron girders, nevertheless it was gone, and a dull staircase of violent water loomed in its place, grinding its way full of boulders to the sea.

She stumbled on towards Black Pool Bridge, her path illuminated by flashes of lightning, where the gorge ran deepest. This footbridge was the highest on the river and the path on the other side followed a slope which she could climb – if she could get across.

Water sheeted over her from the roadway far above, knocking her to her knees.

It was the lights that brought her to her senses, shining out in a broad fan over the gorge, the headlamps of a car high above her. They moved, turning.

The roadway's retaining wall crumbled, brown

floodwater swept through in a great arc, spraying out as it fell. The car teetered, then with its lights still shining slid down to the river amidst a jumble of boulders.

Bart called her name over and over. He jumped a trench cut by the rushing water where the footpath had been and landed on his hands and knees in the darkness. Suddenly, from the far side of the gorge, headlamp beams fanned into the trees he was struggling through, surrounding him with a net of black shadows. He shaded his eyes. He was still undecided what to do when the lights plunged down, the illumination they cast racing away downslope of him to glow on the river.

He stared at the sight revealed by the vertical beams: the river flowing silver and white, sinuous and huge, like the scales of an enormous fish sliding downstream beneath the spidery outline of Black Pool Bridge.

In the motionless backwash of light he discerned the car trapped in the wedge-shaped slide of boulders and debris. It wouldn't last. The current streamed only feet beneath the headlamps which pointed into the depths.

At the other end of the bridge, a figure struggled towards the wreck of the car so precariously wedged a few yards downstream.

Her hair blew in the wind. She clutched at handholds as the earth slipped away under her feet.

Bart ran down to the bridge and laid his hand on the railing. Normally the wooden footbridge was thirty feet above the water, but now the foam lapped its boards.

Bart crossed the jolting, swaying structure towards her. The bridge skated on the top of the water like a wing, then snagged, and the water piled up like a wave. He felt the structure begin to bend as the velocity of the flood ripped it away beneath, spray leaping up.

As the boards were snatched from beneath his feet, he jumped on to the path and held out his hand towards Laura. There was only rushing water behind him, the bridge was gone.

He couldn't reach her. He drew back with his fingers still a yard from her wrist. The greasy soil slithered away under her shoes.

She stared at him, saying nothing. The illumination from below hollowed her eyes, her cheeks were streaked with mud. Her hands slipped.

Bart shrugged off his maroon coat. She saw that he wore only his pale brown trousers with the patterned seams and his white shirt, torn and soaking, half the buttons ripped off. Somewhere on the bridge he had lost one of his boots. He pulled off the other, and his socks. He looked at her and she saw he was enjoying himself.

Grabbing a tree root, he swung himself forward on to the treacherous debris with her and caught her wrist. The lights cast an eerie blue-green glow from the river up the cliffs and through the leafy underneaths of the trees, lit from below.

He pulled her towards him and they kissed.

The Morris Minor was up to its doors in rubble, one rear wheel caught against a tree, the front bumper crumpled on a boulder below. The wipers still worked, clacking to and fro ridiculously. Bart could see the man inside, unconscious or dead, no more than a shadow against the glass.

He swung Laura back on to the path and they stood looking down.

Now they could see Jerry slumped over the steering wheel, the back of his head pressed against the windscreen, his face on the metal dashboard. The seat had folded forward on top of him. More stones rained down and any second, Bart knew, the vehicle might somersault into the flood.

Bart leaned forward and reached out, but Laura grabbed his hand instinctively and pressed it to her mouth.

Bart reached for the tree root, and swung himself out on one arm over the debris. His other hand caught the rear bumper and for a moment he hung stretched between the two. Then he slid down beside the Morris, grabbing the metal tongue of the driver's doorhandle, his bare feet finding a purchase in the curve of the front wheel-arch, so that he stood up along the side of the car.

Jerry's eyes flickered.

Bart braced himself and heaved at the door. The car jerked lower. The river boiled over the front of the bonnet but the headlamps continued to shine underwater, sending down twin pillars of swirling light. The chromium handle bent in Bart's hand, but the door remained jammed shut. He couldn't shift it.

The car slithered down.

Bart sank to his knees in green spray. Laura screamed, but he couldn't hear her. His black silhouette raised a fist and smashed the windscreen to grab the man inside. Jerry flopped on to the bonnet in a shower of glass, the flood snagging at his arms and legs, then Bart dragged him up, holding him out towards Laura with all his strength.

Laura shook her head.

Jerry reached for her, his blood dripping on to Bart beneath him. Laura caught the arm of the dinner jacket then the weight of it increased horribly as the undermined debris slid slowly away, the car somersaulting outwards, transfixing her and Jerry in blinding beams of white light. Below, Bart stared upwards at Laura. The water roared over his head and the flood took him.

For a few moments green spokes of illumination flashed between the black boulders and falling foam, but Bart was gone.

They never found his body.

The sea stretched out in front of her, dead calm, toffee-coloured and ancient in the flat dawn light.

Laura sat on a boulder outside the Bath Hotel, too exhausted to move.

Lynmouth was gone. The ruins looked as though they had been bombed. Boulders as big as greywether slabs lay heaped in mounds. No boats remained in the harbour; no harbour remained. The Rhenish tower was gone. The sea was as wide as the sky.

All around her sprawled the gaping insides of buildings, rooms full of silt and rocks, floodmarks twenty and thirty feet up the walls, everything broken. Many buildings had been swept away entirely, battered by boulders as big as lorries. The Lyn river, now ankle deep once more, trickled meekly between its banks of pathetic debris to the sea.

Survivors, wearing overcoats as though it were winter, shuffled between the desolated buildings in a state of shock. A dog barked at a mound of rubble.

The Watersmeet Falls Hotel was gone, no trace of it remained. The Falls had been swept away, the bridges no longer existed – only planks that had been laid from boulder to boulder. The Lyndale Hotel looked as though it would have to be knocked down before it fell.

The chapel was a pile of stones spread out near a row of wrecked cottages.

The Beach Hotel had entirely disappeared.

The Rising Sun seemed miraculously untouched, but the Lifeboat Station had been washed away completely. The roof of the Bath Hotel was connected to the hill behind the building by ladders and ropes, over which the rescuers had worked. More ropes crossed the street high above Laura's head, showing the level the East and West Lyn rivers had flooded with their combined weight, where the fire brigade had swung across to save people from the riverside cottages. Of the road continuing to the harbour, nothing whatsoever remained.

A mortuary had been set up and was filling. Only half a dozen bodies yet, but they said the toll would rise to thirty dead, or more.

A man from the St John Ambulance put a blanket around Laura's shoulders and gave her a cup of tea brewed on a Primus stove. Jerry was having his head bandaged at the first-aid post at the foot of Lynmouth Hill.

She sipped, and the hot liquid burnt her lips.

Unaware of the blanket slipping from her shoulders, Laura walked towards the beach, and stared out.

Half a mile out to sea a remarkable sight awaited her. The trees carried downriver from Watersmeet, weighted by the stones and earth trapped in their roots, had planted themselves in the Severn Sea. Not just one or two, but hundreds, a forest.

Watersmeet had come down to the sea.

Postscript

No trace whatsoever exists today of Watersmeet Manor, Paradise House or Toher's clapper bridge, and all the elements of the story were swept away in the great Lynmouth flood disaster of 15 August 1952. The fire-blackened ruins of Hellebore House and the round house are not there. Neither are any of the characters portrayed in this novel. St Brendan's church on Cheriton Ridge was knocked down long ago, though some of its stones were incorporated into a more recent church a few miles to the east.

Watersmeet is again beautiful. The outlines of the prehistoric iron-age forts can still be seen, and Exmoor indeed hides a network of ancient bronze-age barrows and warm-weather farming settlements submerged in its soft, peaty soil. And it is also true that very long ago, the Severn Sea was a vast desert of red sand . . .

Today this peaceful valley is maintained by the National Trust. The lime kilns have been restored. The East Lyn river rises in Doone country, and in summer children play on the bend in the river where the gentle waters meet.

Lynmouth has been rebuilt.

In Lynmouth the sea never sparkles. The light flows from the land – northward from the high, bare slopes of Exmoor down the steep green secret valleys, finally coming to the seaside village huddled between ankle-deep streams and the unshining sea. No Watersmeet Falls Hotel of course; a car park in its place. The Rhenish tower was restored.

Surfers were sliding amongst the waves breaking on the beach where youngsters hunted tiddlers in the rocks, and the tidal swimming pool had been bulldozed in the interest of public safety. Lovers sauntered along the little Lynmouth Street shops: a bell clanged and the nineteenth-century Cliff Railway began its hair-raising ascent a thousand feet between the shimmering trees above the rooftops and satellite dishes, water spouting from beneath the carriage, people leaning on the railings waving down. Others filled the beer garden of the Bath Hotel or downed crab sandwiches and ale beneath the thatched eaves and whitewashed walls of the Rising Sun, watching the fishermen putting out their chalked boards along the pavement as the tide lapped the tiny harbour: mackerel, conger, shark, lines supplied. The huge Cadillac backed into a providential parking space, power-steering hissing in the tight turn, and the sunlight stared off the black paint and silvered windows. One of the fishermen moved his board.

The woman who got out of the car had not always been American; she had been British once.

Rainclouds showed jagged gold edges above the hills. She looked up the steep, tree-lined valley rising above the town between towering green bluffs.

God, it's beautiful, she thought.

She stood alone on the high bridge, staring up at the shallow silver stream trickling down from

Watersmeet, ignoring the ache in her side that no doctor's treatment could assuage.

The last of the sunlight shimmered off the vivid white cascades that rose up like a stairway between the ascending walls of the cleave. She had returned.

She tasted rain on her lips, and felt the real shock of memory.

'Blackbird,' she whispered, remembering the lovely black mare who had been the centre of her affections, feeling her simple love again as though it were yesterday – as though it were the last day before she was seventeen.

More Compelling Fiction from Headline:

FRANCES BROWN

THE HARESFOOT LEGACY

Turned out by her bigoted preacher father when he discovers she is pregnant, Liddy Nolan throws in her lot with Jem Granger, a gypsy prize-fighter who offers to be a father to her unborn child. Running away to the gypsies turns out to be no romantic adventure, and at first Liddy finds it hard to adapt to life on the road and a host of unfamiliar customs and laws. She also encounters hostility from the other Romany folk, who see her as an outsider, and this hostility increases when she inherits the haresfoot brooch that is a Granger family heirloom.

Despite these obstacles, Liddy retains her spirit and independence. Over the years, she and Jem raise a family together and follow the age-old gypsy routes, pitching their tent upon the common land and selling their wares at country fairs, and in time Liddy shows herself a true Romany at heart, earning herself an honoured place in the community.

But the happiness of the couple is marred by the past: Jem is haunted by the spectre of the unknown father of Liddy's firstborn, while Liddy herself fears that Jem feels pity rather than love for her. These misunderstandings come to a head against the tumultuous events of the Crimean War, and it is only through almost unbearable tragedy that Jem and Liddy finally acknowledge their love for each other and are united at last.

'A wonderful tale – (with) a good helping of romance and tragedy to give it true Romany charm' *Prima*

FICTION/SAGA   0 7472 3461 2   £4.50

A selection of bestsellers
from Headline

FICTION

A RARE BENEDICTINE	Ellis Peters	£2.99 ☐
APRIL	Christine Thomas	£4.50 ☐
FUNLAND	Richard Laymon	£4.50 ☐
GENERATION	Andrew MacAllan	£4.99 ☐
THE HARESFOOT LEGACY	Frances Brown	£4.50 ☐
BROKEN THREADS	Tessa Barclay	£4.50 ☐

NON-FICTION

| GOOD HOUSEKEEPING EATING FOR A HEALTHY BABY | Birthright | £4.99 ☐ |

SCIENCE FICTION AND FANTASY

RAVENS' GATHERING Bard IV	Keith Taylor	£3.50 ☐
ICED ON ARAN	Brian Lumley	£3.50 ☐
CARRION COMFORT	Dan Simmons	£4.99 ☐

All Headline books are available at your local bookshop or newsagent, or can be ordered direct from the publisher. Just tick the titles you want and fill in the form below. Prices and availability subject to change without notice.

Headline Book Publishing PLC, Cash Sales Department, PO Box 11, Falmouth, Cornwall, TR10 9EN, England.

Please enclose a cheque or postal order to the value of the cover price and allow the following for postage and packing:
UK: 80p for the first book and 20p for each additional book ordered up to a maximum charge of £2.00
BFPO: 80p for the first book and 20p for each additional book
OVERSEAS & EIRE: £1.50 for the first book, £1.00 for the second book and 30p for each subsequent book.

Name ....

Address ....

....

....